WHERE THE LIGHT IS BRIGHTER

C. C. Griffin

&

Thomas G. Fiffer

Published by Christmas Lake Press 2023

www.christmaslakecreative.com

ISBN 978-1-960865-14-4

Interior layout by Daiana Marchesi

Dedication

In honor of those who receive care and those who give care in homes, wherever those homes may be.

To my grandmothers: Claire, a dedicated nurse, who was excellent at playing cards, and Sadie, a seamstress who enjoyed a good party.
— C. C. Griffin

To all who stand up in the presence of the aged. — Thomas G. Fiffer

Acknowledgments

It takes a team to make a book. I would like to recognize Nicole Hower for cover design, Daiana Marchesi for interior layout, and Parker Gordon for copyediting. Your creativity, care, and attention to detail have made this book brighter. And a special thank you to my co-author, C. C., for trusting me with your story and allowing me to accompany you on this journey.

— Thomas G. Fiffer

Thank you to...

The founders of Christmas Lake Creative—Tom Fiffer for your collaboration and guidance of this project, and Julia Bobkoff for supporting the vision of this book.

Nicole Hower, Parker Gordon, and Jennifer Blankfein.

My colleagues in class at the Westport Writers' Workshop, and specifically Ina Chadwick.

The writing community in Ridgefield, CT, including Adele Annesi and Chris Belden, creators of the Ridgefield Writers Conference.

Blaine Langberg, Author of *Journey of a JuBu*—thank you for sharing your writing journey.

Erica Meier—your creativity has influenced this project.

Vin Penry and Rose Pryor—thank you for your encouragement and for not letting me quit in my early years as a nurse practitioner in the long-term care setting.

Jeanette Galvez-Piscioniere—for your perseverance and finding the positive.

My fellow nurses, physicians, and staff of subacute and long-term care facilities—thank you for your professionalism and compassion that continued despite the challenges of the pandemic.

My friends and family, who have provided much needed support along the way.

My husband Christopher, and my children, for their patience as they listened to years of my stories.

And finally, my parents.

— C. C. Griffin

Author's Note

While there are proper names in these stories, all stories are fictional. Any resemblance to actual persons, living or dead, or actual events, is purely coincidental. Today's date is unknown, the month is a season seen out the window, the year is strange to hear, and age is the spirit coming alive with a song.

Contents

Prologue

I pull my father's Rolex out from underneath the cuff of my sleeve. *Three thirty in the afternoon.* Feels later, but this watch has been keeping time since before I can remember and keeping me on time since I got it from Mom on my 18th birthday. They don't call it an Oyster Perpetual for nothing.

I look up at the house, sunlight slanting over the gabled roof. Three bedrooms. Flat, half-acre lot. Good bones, good location. Ornate molding with chipped paint. *This place will sell as soon as it hits the market.* But the junk luggers sure have their work cut out for them before the realtor can show the house. Sixty years of hoarder's gold that needs to be tossed.

Hard to believe she is gone, Mom. Always bustling, even as she dealt with the pain of age, offering a hot cup of tea every five minutes, even when I already had one in front of me, but she didn't forget how she felt about her clutter.

Half an hour should be more than enough time to take one last look around and see if there's *anything* here worth keeping. After that, I have to catch my flight back home.

Between Mom's funeral and work, it's been some year. *I need to get away. Just another two weeks.* I'll feel better once we all get on the big plane and cross the Pacific—the beach, the hotel, Christmas with the wife and kids in Bora Bora. *What could be better?*

The door opens with a familiar creak. *I won't be needing the old house key after this.* Inside, the rooms are stuffed with furniture, but the house feels oddly empty. *Nothing worth saving down here.* It's all going to

Goodwill. But Mom made me promise to go through the whole house, and I always keep my word.

Upstairs, I stand in the doorway to my bedroom, bare now except for the old dresser with a knob missing on the top drawer. Above it on the wall is the triangular outline of where my Yankees pennant used to be. I run my finger along the door frame, tracing the faded ink notches Mom marked as I grew—the thickest lines for when I hit four, five, and finally six feet.

International banking has taken me all around the world, shown me the best life has to offer, but in this place, it's different—the joy of a few scribbles on the wall overshadows the biggest deal I ever closed. Mom's bedroom seems smaller than I remember, the bed frame taking up almost the whole space, and so does the tiny guest bedroom with its sloping ceiling and corner closet—the only guest who ever slept there was the dog.

At the end of the hallway, the attic door is slightly ajar. I peer up the steep stairway covered with old carpeting then down at my white button-down and pressed khakis. *The uniform of success Mom taught me to wear.* Up those stairs was the place where, as a child, I would get lost for hours, always finding some new old thing. Now it's a sentimental time warp, filled with memories and dust... *but I promised.*

Walking up towards the pitched eaves, it's nothing but boxes, more boxes, and bags, overstuffed and overflowing. Dad's leather sitting chair, covered with plastic—for nearly forty years—is piled with blankets next to an old broken card table. *Why the hell she held onto all of this, I will never understand.*

The light from the late afternoon sun floods through the front dormer. As I bow my head not to bump into the rafters, a glittering, green-red sparkle catches my eye. On top of large crates crammed into the far corner, I spy our old tabletop Christmas tree with a few bits of paint left on the bulbs. I suppress the urge to plug it in, though I'm sure it still works. Mom would only buy decorations that would last a lifetime—and beyond.

And there's the ragged-edged cardboard star sticking out of a box labeled "Christmas" in faded red marker. *How old was I when I made that thing?* My letters are large and it's hard to make out where the scribbled JOE B. begins and ends, but there's Mom's note on the back, in ink, still clear—Kindergarten '69.

With a flash of child's delight, I find myself searching through the box for more. Uncovering one decoration after another, I cough, brushing off the dust, as the reel of my early years starts to roll: the dark eyes of a scruffy-faced St. Patrick's Day leprechaun; the delicate, rose-painted teacups of Mother's Day; and that oversized, orange ceramic pumpkin, stuffed with ancient bags of Halloween candy. Each one of these old friends had a place on the mantel for a day, a week, or a season, always showing up for their holidays—the timekeepers of celebration.

With age, Mom slowed and there was a shakiness as she lugged around her boxes of ornaments, centerpieces, and elaborate displays, but despite the struggle, her eyes twinkled, and her smile stayed wide. I knew better than to interfere. Arthritis wasn't going to weigh her down; she had the lighthearted energy of a young girl as she decorated for each holiday.

My shirt is wrinkled, my pants coated with dust. Mom never kept it simple, and now, it all blurs together, into one year-long clutter-fest. *Come on, Joe, this is how houses end up like this—full of sentimental crap.* I know Mom would want me to save every last trinket, but it's all got to go.

I glance at my watch. *Time to leave.* Then I notice Mom's old Coach travel bag, the indestructible one I got her on Fifth Avenue in New York City. It's propped between two wooden crates, along the far wall. A sheaf of papers sticks out over the edge. *Just move on* my better judgment tells me. But I feel a duty to check it out. *"The whole house, Joe..."* OK, Mom. I have a few more minutes before I'm late for my plane.

Holding the slightly crumpled pages in my hand, I recognize Mom's unmistakable handwriting flowing over the loose, yellowed pages, her cursive letters perfectly wrought. Suddenly, the attic disappears and I'm in her kitchen with the dandelion wallpaper, hearing the stories she used to tell... sometimes with laughter, other times with a distant expression of sadness. I sit down on the cracked wood floor—filled with the same splinters I pulled from my skin decades ago—and keep reading.

"Joe," her glasses often fogged from the heat of the oven and she'd take them off, wipe them on her apron, then get right back to dinner, "that old Irish man I've told you about surprised me today—he smiled. Yellow stubs for teeth. Must have been the coffee." Bustling around, she'd talk as she cooked. "Well, did you hand in your homework on time? There is no good reason for homework to be late."

She was like a bloodhound when it came to school, and I'd try to distract her by asking about her day at work, to get her to share more stories from the "home," which is how she affectionately referred to the old folks place where she worked. As she leaned against a cabinet, fiddling with her wedding ring, the furrow of her brow would soften, and as she described the residents, she'd say that when she got older, she certainly was not going to be like that one, but maybe she would be like this one.

The pot of sauce bubbling over on the stove would bring a halt to story time.

"Again," she would sigh and roll her eyes, "burnt-bottom sauce—my specialty."

Frustrated she could never finish her stories, she often said that one day she'd write it all down. But clearly, she'd been doing it all along, leaving a legacy I knew nothing about. Opening my eyes wide, I wipe the film off the face of my watch... and realize I've missed my plane.

Up here, time seems to stand still.

I text a few words to my assistant, ones she's seen countless times before: "Rebook tomorrow am." I start to organize Mom's fading pages, but the sun is gone now, and I pull the old rattling chain to light the naked bulb, hoping it doesn't break. A yellow glow fills the room, and I settle in on a journey to places both familiar and unknown.

Editor's Note

My mom, Patricia Ann Bachman, worked for decades at River's Edge Manor, a long-term care facility, in Poughkeepsie, NY. She was hired in the early 1980s to do clerical work and served in a variety of positions, then continued to volunteer there after she retired, almost to the very end. She always said that she could never imagine life without work—wonder where I got that—but I now know, after reading her stories, that her work went beyond the halls of River's Edge.

Mom was obsessed with holidays and organized her stories around the way she experienced time and the way the residents marked it at River's Edge—through a year of timeless celebrations.

Looking back, Mom, towards the end of her own journey, ended up being a little bit like all her characters—and a lot like one in particular.

Welcome to River's Edge

Edith Sharp

'm not where I'm supposed to be. Cold on my shoulders, fingers numb, I manage to pull the edges of my hat and scarf tight around my neck.

The empty driver's seat next to me... He was never one to sit still. "William?"

From outside the car, I hear his calm voice call, "I'm getting your wheeler."

I only need it for the curbs. My ski pole was better than this clunky thing. I'll have to tell him no getting rid of the old stuff with this "big cleanout" of his. And the house should be locked up—tight. The front door has to be pulled and the handle jiggled to lock it properly since the wood has warped. Time bends things. It can't be avoided. Now, did I leave the outside lights on?

William opens the car door. "Mom."

"Yes, dear?"

"It's time to head inside."

I shiver, looking into my son's gentle eyes. His hair is peppered. *When did that happen?* Rubbing my hands together, I can't feel any warmth. "I think we should go back, check the locks and the lights."

"Mom, it's time."

Time? It's never time to come to this never place.

And there it is, up on the hill... I heard it was fancy. Hmmph. *This is it?* Poorly trimmed bushes trailing beneath the dirt-smudged windows, the drab building rising one floor after another, ice dams on the gutters, and the stone at the corner—it's crumbling! And things get stolen here, that's what she says. My neighbor, my friend... what's her name? *Come on, Edith, the one with the car.* I can't believe I've forgotten her name after all these years. It'll come back to me. I just need to sit in my recliner. At home. That's where all my memories are, where everything makes sense.

But here I am. I pull my scarf tighter and squint at the fogged-up windows. *Will one of them be... mine?*

"William," I say, then forget what I wanted to tell him. I pat down the soft wool of my coat to give the thoughts time to return, if they choose to return.

Oh, well. William's car is warm and comfortable. I don't mind staying put. Besides, he was the one who insisted we go out in the cold on a day like this. So, I indulged him. *My handsome boy.* At least it's only temporary. *A week, maybe two.*

"Mom," he says, unfolding the wheeler, "I'm not rushing you." He blows on his hands, rubbing them. "It's a big day. Moving is never easy."

"Visiting," I correct him. *My beautiful boy.* "Moving shouldn't be allowed, particularly at this age." *Just leave me in my house. I'm fine there.* "Now where are your hat and gloves?"

"No gloves needed back in sunny California." He leans closer. "Mom, just think about it. Blue sky, sun on your face. No more of this awful cold. I keep telling you, we would love to have you live out there with us. Kate's mom and you. We can find a way to get you both the extra TLC you need."

California! Over my dead body. I fix my scarf. "I can't leave your father. He's here, in Poughkeepsie."

"Mom! It's been fifty years. I'm sure Dad would be happy to see you making life easier. I think it's what he would have wanted."

"Fifty years and it seems like yesterday. I visit him every week, you know. My friend drives me, in that little red car of hers. The flowers always need water, and his stone always looks better with the holiday decorations. And he did so enjoy a nice Christmas wreath."

I close my eyes and let out a long breath. "He was my greatest love," I smile at William, "until you, of course—my beautiful surprise. He used to say, 'we're never ready for change, but change is always ready for us.' And he never steered me wrong. So," I turn towards the half-open car door and put one foot on the frozen ground, "would you be a dear and open the door a little wider and give me your hand? And for heaven's sake button your coat. I don't want you to catch cold."

William carefully opens the door and brings my wheeler closer. It's a wide one with a bench seat—good for storage, the salesman said. But what would I need to store? Everything has its place—at home.

I insisted we park in a regular spot, not a special one close to the entrance. These places have people who are sick, not just old. The ones who really need help.

"Will you look at that!" I shake my head and point to a large dent along the side of the red car next to ours. "This other car, it's been hit, scratched up. It probably was, that one, you know, my friend?" Irritated, I rub my forehead, as if that will bring back her name. "She drives me everywhere and gets frustrated about going back to the grocery store when we forget something, which is every time. Starts yelling at herself and me about keeping a list—and bad drivers."

"Mom."

"Her complaining is so unladylike. I told her she is not allowed to visit me here unless she takes a cab."

"Agnes." William moves his hand closer to help. "Accident Agnes. How does that woman still have her license?"

"Yes, yes, Agnes!" I laugh. "She's the lost woman who doesn't know she's lost. Agnes said when the car goes, she goes. And after her last mix-up, I don't have to worry about her visiting anytime soon." I smile. "Besides, I won't be here long, right? Better if no one comes. Better to see my friends back home. I'll just keep to myself." I lean closer. "Anyway, this is a place no one really even *wants* to visit."

William looks away.

"Agnes can call me, just as she does now. She doesn't hear that well, but she still calls. Three rings at night, every night. She never forgets... and she never forgets to remind me that she never liked Cosmo."

"Mom," William sighs, but not the sigh when he's frustrated with me. "Agnes *put up* with Cosmo. I know you thought that dog was smart, but she used to call me in California about his obnoxious barking. And yet, she was the one who visited you every day after the little furball died."

I pat down my soft, cashmere scarf. Cosmo's fur, so comfortable on my lap. He's in a better place now. The place we all go... eventually. William's hand is safe, his grip reassuring. He helps me out of the car, taking a moment to steady my legs behind my wheeler in this slippery parking lot with its patches of snow, maybe ice. We should have waited until spring.

Steady, Edith, steady. All it takes is one good fall. I hold the handles tighter, avoiding any hint of shine with each slow step. With William at my side, we make it to the dry sidewalk leading to the door. Breathing out with relief, I realize how much I was holding in. The air crisp, the sun bright, my legs reliable, I walk towards the glass entrance. Cosmo always walked with his head held high, ears flopping in the breeze, and if I'm going in here, it will be on my own two feet. Feeling the stiffness that keeps getting worse, I straighten my shoulders and look ahead. I'll check out this room. *But I still have my house key.*

Entering through the automatic double doors I notice William relax a bit.

"Don't tell me it's nice here. I'll judge that for myself."

The ceiling seems awfully high, and I spot a sitting area with greenery and—ugh!—wheelchairs, and old people, some hunched and leaning to the side! They sit like stones, markers for what they once were. Only they're living.

Other than this depressing crowd, the lobby reminds me of my years working at Town Hall—the same ornate white trim and scalloped molding. Suddenly I remember the retirement party they gave me at... oh, that grand restaurant along the river. What was it called? We had the second-floor balcony all to ourselves. So thoughtful.

But here, the air is stuffy, and I cough after my first few breaths. I look back at the others in their chairs... I'm sure they didn't walk in.

"Looks like there's a line at the receptionist's desk," William says.

"I'm in no rush."

Along the far wall, a well-dressed woman—practically a kid by my standards—with stiffly sprayed hair sits behind a wide desk holding a clipboard and attending to an elderly gentleman and his attentive companion. And behind them, a mailman with a large pile of letters. These people—they wouldn't even know if they received mail. Moving my stiff shoulders back, I stand a little straighter.

"When the line dies down, Mom, we can check in. I'm going to get more of your things from the car." He zippers his jacket to his chin. "Over there, near those windows, looks like a nice place to sit."

Potted plants. That's what I call these people half-asleep in their chairs. Next to the large windows are some real plants and it seems like a safe place, away from the others. With the lock on my handles clicked into place, I shuffle over and sit down on my bench, but my nose is cold with the draft.

Tissues, do I have any? I search my pockets, but my eyes catch a flash of blue going by. A person in uniform, who I assume must be a staff member, pushes a wheelchair with a body caving inward. *Dear God.* A pit in my stomach, seeing the edges of his thin bones outlined under all that loose skin. Deep-set eyes reflect the blue of the scarf knotted neatly around his neck, and the cuffs of his sleeves are rolled back evenly over thin, discolored hands. At least he's managing to stay well dressed.

I look away towards the hall, but not before glimpsing his eyes, startling and alive.

The corridor is lined with pictures, and suddenly a woman, a cripple with white curled hair and some sort of badge on her blouse, shines a flashlight on a famous work—the night sky, with blue swirls and stars. I know that painting. It's by the artist who cut off his own ear. But it's her hunched posture, like a modern sculpture, head bent forward almost to her shoulders, that causes me to stare.

Is this what happens to people here? *Other people. Not me.*

"One week," I mutter, but no one is listening.

Catching a glimpse of myself in a mirror above the plants, I'm not surprised I look a bit frazzled. I straighten the front of my tweed coat. With my cashmere scarf tied around my neck, my mother's cheekbones are still holding up. I smooth my white hair so it neatly falls just below my chin. My stylist did a good job with this last cut, but then again, my hair has always held its shape, and my white with a few silver streaks has never needed to be dyed. But I do look pale this time of year. I could use a little sun.

So many here just sitting. Waiting? For what? Others milling around, going no particular place. I was never comfortable with loiterers. I stayed away from that part of downtown.

Shaky, my nerves frayed, a little dizzy, I breathe. *Where is William?*

A pleasant voice from behind me pulls me back.

"Excuse mae..."

Finally, someone normal. I turn. A woman in a yellow raincoat with a matching yellow rain hat over her nicely done curls, clutching a folded umbrella and red plaid pocketbook, taps her feet, shuffling the wheels of her chair forward. With a friendly brogue, she says, "Excuse mae! Can ya tell mae when dur bus is comin'?" She pushes a curl back behind her ear. "I need to git on dur bus, and I tink tis comin' soon."

"What bus?"

"Dur airport bus. Well, I'm goen' ta Ireland today!"

"Really! I'd love to go myself, but traveling has been tough," I turn my head towards my wheeler. "Harder to get around."

Her brow furrows, eyes serious. "Er you da bus driver wit' my ticket?"

My heart sinks. She's clearly not all here, and she's not going anywhere. And is that... oatmeal dribble on her shirt? *No one should have dribbles.* Doesn't anyone take care of people here? I turn away, straightening the collar of my white button-down underneath my coat.

My purse? Where is my purse? Panic shivers through me. *Stolen! I know it.* My friend was right. My life will be stolen here. The key to my house is in that purse. It's always with my coat. And now... it's gone!

My eyes dart to the glass doors for William, but no one is coming.

How will I unlock my front door when I go home? My chest beats faster. I'm sure someone has it. I scan the room, looking for the red of my purse on the blanketed laps of the ones in their chairs. Trembling, I try to stand, but I need an extra hand. This floor... it's uneven.

"William!" I yell. He'll let me in with his key and then I'll have it copied. Again, louder, "William!!!"

The ache in my shoulder and neck is sharp as I try to wave my arm at the receptionist, but she's on the phone. So I shout, "A thief! A thief!"

"Bless you," says a craggy old man hunched in a chair.

It's hopeless! I'm getting out of here. Pushing off from my bench, thankful that my wobbly legs are working, I tighten my fingers on the wheeler's rubber grips, and walk straight out the doors.

Oooooh. Cold on my face. The glass doors slide closed behind me and there are cars all around. I can't remember William's. So warm just a few minutes ago. I'm lost. Frozen. *How will I get home?*

Wait... someone's walking, moving forward through the sea of cars. Green... could that be... William's jacket?

"Mom! What are you doing out here?"

"William." Finally, I can breathe. "Thank goodness I found you."

Fingers cold, I don't want to tell him they steal. "I... Just take me home, please."

"How long have you been out here?"

My nose is running. *How long?* Searching through the unsettling feeling of time. "Well, must be... an hour by now."

He sighs and steam fills the air between us. "I haven't been gone more than ten minutes," he puffs. "But minutes," his tone softens, "can feel like a long time." He adjusts my bags on his shoulders, puts out his hand, and I see the red of my purse... and my red notebook.

"I found these on the front seat."

Hearing the rattle of my keychain, my heart finally quiets. I slide the purse and notebook into my coat. How could I have left them in the car? Must be my nerves—this place.

"Mom, let's go back inside where it's warm."

Loosening the grip on my handles, I turn my wheeler and plop down on my seat, next to a stone bench. "No, William. I would like to go home."

Suddenly my sweet son is sharp with me. "This is what I mean. This is why I can't let you be by yourself."

His green eyes are wide with worry. He just needs to be reminded. "I've always been fine on my own. When your father died... I went right to work at Town Hall."

A bird lands on the branch of a tree above, far away from down here.

"Twenty-eight years I worked there. And when I was Town Clerk..."

"Mom, that was a long time ago. You're 98 years old. Amazing for your age, but... have you forgotten why you're here?"

I glare at him. "Everyone thinks I'm so forgetful. And I'd certainly like to forget this day. But I know exactly where I am, and I don't wish to be here."

"Mom..."

His tone is softer, and I see my opportunity. "You know, William, it's almost New Year's. We should talk about this place *next* year."

"It's either here or move to California with us." His face is set, his tone firm.

My mouth drops. "I don't *know* anyone in California."

Raising his eyebrows, "You know *us*."

I shake my head. "Too far away."

"Then that's it. Let's go in." He starts walking.

"William, wait! Things will happen to me here. I'll end up like... like *them*. I can't go back in. I *won't* go back in."

His eyes suddenly narrow. "Mom, it's not like me to say this, but if you won't come to California and you refuse to go inside... I... I may have to ask the receptionist to have someone—maybe there's... security—to walk you in." He fixes me with a stare. "Because the next time you set fire to the kitchen, the firemen might not come in time!"

Security??? We'll see about that. "I'll take security into my own hands." Crossing my arms, I let out a humph.

"This is what I mean, Mom."

I glance at the grooves of his furrowed brow... I appreciate his worry. But it's his tone. "Don't talk to me like I'm a child, William." I begin wagging my finger, "I never needed *security* to help me in my life." *To help me, to help me.*

Shaking his head, he stares up at the sky. "Then what am I supposed to do when you act like this?" He looks down, rubbing his forehead. Quietly, I hear him saying, "How do I protect the strongest person I know? The firemen have known you by name for a while now. And I'll be too far away if you fall." Moving his boot in the slush, he glances up at me. "I need help to help you, but nothing seems right. This is..."

I feel a soreness in the back of my throat. Swallowing, I realize I must have yelled. *How unlike me.* I steady my legs and then my voice. "This is... I just burned the toast, that's all." *Lord knows I need help, but not this kind. Not this.* I cover my face with my hands.

My son's arms close around me. Warm wet rolling down my cheek. I've never been one to cry, but tears like these cleanse the heart.

His voice, with a quiver, "Only you, Mother..."

A ray of sunlight hits his face. Are his eyes glossy? Agnes's words run through my mind. "Old faucets get leaky."

Managing a smile, William wipes his face with the back of his hand. "Leaky, indeed."

Pulling a tissue from my sleeve, I dab my eyes. *I can survive just about anything... even a stay here, if that's what he needs.* "Well, your list of reasons makes sense, for you, anyway. I've never wanted to be a worry." Clearing my throat, "You see William, if you live long enough, you get to experience everything. Even *this*..."

"Mom," he says, sitting down on the bench next to my wheeler, "speaking of good old Agnes... remember when we were packing up the house, she barged right in? Knocking on the front door after she's inside, talking too loud in that Brooklyn accent. She said that if she did ever come to one of these places, she'd *insist* on a private room. Insist, as if insisting—not paying—would make it happen."

"Agnes is a gossip. She would knock on everyone's door, be in everyone's room and everyone's business. *I'm* the private one. Did you bring the rock she gave me? The one with the writing on it?" He nods.

"I want you to know, I'm grateful," I swallow, "that you're taking care of your mother. Now it's cold out here." I shiver. "And... and this is just for a short time."

Resolved to deal with life the way I always have, I find my legs and stand.

William wipes his eyes and looks up at me. "Looks like you are ready."

Holding the handles of my wheeler, I straighten my coat. "I'll never be ready," I mutter under my breath. Then I look ahead. "But yes, dear, let's go in."

Lightness returns to his voice as we walk, together, to the doors. "Just like you taught me when Dad died. We do what we have to do. Let's get checked in and take a look at *your* private room." *My sweet boy.* "Did you see that table of decorations in the lobby? I swear they got that center display from your attic."

My attic! Now that's the most wonderful place, filled with all good things. I sigh, going through the contents of each box in my head. "You won't be throwing any of my decorations away, will you? You might use them, you know. You can't buy the well-made ones anymore. It's all cheap, disposable... and I'll be home by Valentine's Day, if not before, in time to put chubby Cupid up on the mantel."

"But, Mom, the house is..." William shifts back and forth on his legs, the same way he did when he was uncomfortable as a child. "I mean, I can't store all that stuff."

"Sorry dear, I need it all."

The air inside is warm and thick, with the smell of... bleach. *What on earth are they covering up?* The line at the receptionist's desk has dwindled, and I shake my head, knowing we'll be next.

"Mom, look at that group of trees around the fireplace, all those lights," William points. "They do a good job with this stuff."

Indeed, decorated trees surround a stone fireplace in the far corner of the entrance, and wreaths with blue, white, red, and gold shine from the mantel. A center table sports an oversized silver and gold "Happy 2018" display—horns, hats, giant wine glasses—a New Year's celebration in the making. Fringe hangs off everything at the table.

"You know how I feel about fringe. Leaves a dreadful mess on the floor, falling off everything. Someone could teach these people a thing or two."

"You sure could."

Exhausted I sit on my wheeler, but I admit the decorations do brighten this horrible day. And then I see it. Hanging off the edge of the table—a small, chipped, wooden sign carved with the words, "Welcome to Our Home." I turn to William and point out the sign. "*Their* home."

William looks towards the desk. "The line is almost gone at the receptionist."

Did he not hear me? I straighten the collar of my shirt. William's own white collar is showing from underneath his coat. I taught my son early that a white button-down is a good choice to wear in any situation.

"Well, it certainly will *never* be *my* home," I mutter.

We walk past two ladies parked close together, each with her head down and tilted in the same direction. I'm sure they're asleep, but how uncomfortable! And their thrift-shop clothes. A gold cane rests across the lap of one. She's wearing a bright floral dress and looks like a wilting bouquet stuffed into her chair. The other is decked out in a leopard print shirt and her thick, red-framed glasses sparkle with a diamond-studded (certainly not real) chain. They teeter on the tip of her nose, and her red curls glisten in the sun from the windows. It's clear she's made an effort, but that bright red hair is a little much. I point her out to William. "Quite the dye job." I sense their eyes aren't fully closed, so I glance away. They seem oblivious. I'm sure they didn't hear me.

Pushing my wheeler forward, I notice the gentleman ahead of us in line wearing, of all things, a tropical short-sleeved shirt. *It's winter, for Pete's sake!* That's a sign this guy needs help... and those dents on his wheelchair!

The receptionist says to him, "No appointment today, Mr. Romano. You know I'll call you if someone comes."

Romano. We had an Italian family down the street. He was a stonemason, and always so polite. Rolling away, Romano's wheels wobble as he passes in front of me. He reaches for the handrail, pulling himself forward, and I see the arm pads on his chair are ripped. *I can't believe no one has given him a new chair!*

He catches my stare. "Hey, doll."

How dare he... I quickly turn my head away.

"Next," the receptionist says.

I nod and look up, noticing her perfectly sprayed blonde bun and a sophisticated silk scarf wrapped around her neck. Liberty of London if I'm not mistaken. And she's well turned out in a powder blue sweater set. I feel comfortable with people who know how to dress.

"How can I help you?" she asks.

Clearing my throat, "Hello, yes, I'm here about a room."

"Yessss..." she draws out the s, implying there is more to the story.

"I mean, I'm... moving in today." I breathe, surprised at how calmly I am able to state the plan. William's plan. "Just for a little while." She bats her eyes at William, then looks back at me.

"You must be Edith."

She must have known I was coming. "Yes, Edith Sharp."

She looks down at something. "Well, Mrs. Sharp, welcome to River's Edge." She moves the clipboard closer towards me. "Please sign here." The top of the list in bold reads "**Residents**" with all sorts of messy scribbles below.

I sense her watching me to make sure I sign. But my pen sticks—*Do I start at the top of the E or the bottom*? "You know, at Town Hall, the signing in and out was done under my watch." I wrinkle my nose at her. "Why do you need my signature?"

She glances at William. "It's a big building," she smiles, showing off a row of clearly whitened teeth, "six floors. I'm not losing anyone."

I squint at her, *"Losing* anyone?" I glare at my son.

As if she's found something that was lost, she says breezily, "I forgot to change the day!" Flipping the numbers on a small stand next to the clipboard, she chortles, "December 30th. One more day to New Year's Eve!"

"Holidays should be celebrated at home," I grumble. "Fine, I'll sign." Circling for a moment, I'm relieved when I find the first loop and it all flows from there.

Edith K. Sharp. 12/30. My penmanship has always been called elegant, but like me, it's getting old. Or is it getting younger? The shaky letters are like a child's spooky script.

The receptionist raises her eyebrows at William. "You'll fill in the year for Mother?"

Indignant, I shake my head. "What is your name, young lady?"

"Beverly." She pulls her cardigan back to reveal her badge. "But everyone here calls me Bev."

"Bev," I say, frowning, "I know perfectly well what year it is. It's just my arthritis."

Behind me, the tapping of a formal stride. As I turn, a bright white coat, dark bushy hair, and matching eyebrows approaches the desk and hands a folder to Bev, who offers a friendly smile. "Yes, thank you, Ms. Bryon. And the new hire is here early for your meeting."

"Send her in." Bushy hair nods briefly in my direction. The breeze from her coat brushes past me, and she zips away, high heels clattering down the corridor.

Bev smooths her hair around her ears and gives William a look. "*That* is our Director of Nursing, Ruthann Bryon." Then, lowering her voice, "Much better than the last one we had. Efficient, keeps this place running like clockwork." Louder, she continues, "So, Mrs. Sharp, your new address is 104 Oak." She points to another long corridor, not the one bushy hair took. "Off Chestnut Street."

"Street? You have streets here? With names?"

"Yes. Each resident has an address." She reties her silk scarf. "We try to make it feel like home."

"This will *never*..." I start to say, but William's hand is on my shoulder.

"William," Bev says as if she's known my son for years, "will you and Mom be attending the New Year's Day luncheon?"

"Yes," he answers. "Put us both down for it." He smiles at me—the same winning smile from all his childhood pictures that makes everything OK.

Smoothing her already smooth hair, Bev glances up at William. "Looking forward to seeing *you* around."

"He's taken," I scowl, "and if you're from Poughkeepsie, young lady, I probably signed your birth certificate."

William walks next to me as I push my wheeler forward down the long yellow-gray hall. *It's good that he's here.* I'd walk anywhere with him, even down this cluttered corridor, carts piled high with poorly folded linens and a metal frame contraption with giant hooks (*what on earth could that be for?*). Branches of green and dark nuts on the walls change to autumn leaves as we turn the corner, and... I nearly crash into an abandoned chair! *They need those firemen who were always coming to my house to remind them to keep these hallways clear!*

My legs tire. *It could be the walking. Or maybe... there's nothing good ahead.* I slow to a standstill and take a moment, peering into the rooms. Are these residents sick or just sleeping? Some doors are open, some closed, all have names and numbers. And the doors—to my horror— different decorations: shamrocks, top hats, pumpkins, and... Valentine's hearts—what an awful mess! I'd straighten it out but suddenly I can't remember what season we are in right now. My breath catches. *Come on, Edith.* I look for a window to check the weather and notice the sleeve of my wool coat. Ahh, it must be winter—*These, what do they call them, senior moments...*

"Mom, it's OK to stop and rest," says William.

"No rest for the weary, dear. I'll keep going."

The next two doors across from each other match—wrapped in gold paper pictures of champagne bottles and clinking glasses with fringe along the edges. Now it comes back to me. New Year's Eve. Celebrating the year ahead. *Who wants to do that here?*

William stops in front of the next door with my name in bold black letters. We're finally here, but it all feels out of place. I glance across "the street"—as the receptionist called it—over at the open door across the hall from mine. I can't believe how bad off some of them are here. *How awful.*

And so close. Just lying there. Pale, all skin and bones, not moving, no color. Just a crimson baseball cap over his face. *He can't be dead—they wouldn't leave him here like that.* But you can't call that living. I shiver and turn away.

William pushes the door to my room open and we step in. The sterile smell of a hospital hits my nose. My eyes take in the empty white walls, a table, dresser, cheap nightstand with a phone, plastic shelf with nothing, and a small bed with a thin, baby blue blanket. I'm already cold.

At home, I'm warm in my queen-size bed, with the sturdy wooden frame William Sr. built for us when we were first married. The curved finial, so smooth under my hand. My husband knew his way around a woodshop. But lately, I've been sleeping on the couch downstairs, under an extra thick quilt. One of these days I'm going to get up those darn steps again.

The walls here are blank. How will I get to bed without my routine? My pictures! My husband in the Navy, our wedding, the faded, yellowed snapshot of Mom and Dad with me and my sisters at an outing to the pond. I spend a moment with each one before bed. But without them... *there's no one here to say good night to.* Shuddering, I pull my coat closer.

A wave of worry twists my stomach. "I don't think this is the right place," I say to William.

"Mom..." he looks at me and I know that face—so composed. The one his father used whenever we faced a crisis. "We haven't even brought your stuff in yet."

He's trying to do the right thing. *But for who? Him, or me?*

William slides the bags off his shoulders and opens a door next to the closet. "Look," he beams, "the bathroom has the wrap-around handrails I wanted to install at the house. And here it is, your same old pink tile halfway up the wall. And it's private, with a slip-proof shower!"

I shake my head. "Water better be hot. Nothing worse than a cold shower on old bones." I roll my wheeler over to the window, lock the wheels, and turn the bench, my tired body relieved to sit.

"See Mom, you've already found the corner spot. I'll go get your Victrola from the car and you can listen to your favorites."

"Don't bother." I glance across the hall. "People are sick here. It doesn't seem like much of a place for music."

At least the floor seems clean, but my eyesight isn't what it used to be. "Would you believe how dark it is in here? I think we need my Tiffany lamp."

"I told you, Mom, it hardly gives off any light with the stained glass. And it could get broken."

"A Tiffany lamp makes any room—even this one. Please fetch it for me—now."

William leaves, and, alone in the empty space, the walls feel close together. I sit still, not moving a muscle, pretending I'm young again, pretending I'm not here. It's hard not to feel old. *Dear God, why am I here? Why am I still here?*

Out the window, far in the distance, the sun reflects off the river whose curves I've watched flow between the hills from my kitchen window at home. The sturdy tree with branches reminds me of the oak in my backyard where the cardinal visits. I wonder if he'll find me.

Weary, I close my eyes for a moment. With a start, I wake to all sorts of strange people talking to me as if they know me. A man with a blue uniform and a baseball hat covering a mess of curls appears in my doorway wearing a badge.

"Halloo! Maintenance. Gotta put up your clock. How are you today, Edith?"

Before I can say "Mrs. Sharp," he's on a ladder, hanging a huge clock on the wall.

"I don't know why I bother setting the time on these things," he says, looking at his watch. "They break every other week. Besides they just make everyone anxious. People seem a lot happier when time stops."

I sigh. *An amateur philosopher.*

Just as he leaves, another one, a woman with long blonde hair, bounces in. Squealing in a high-pitched voice, she tacks calendars and schedules to my wall, a big smile broadening her garish red lips. "Meals, activities, Lunch Lido Deck 12, bingo, Vista Lounge music, 5 o'clock, lights out at your choice."

My heart thumps. *Have I missed something already?* A pink gift bag appears on the table in front of me with "Welcome to River's Edge" printed in green curved ornate lettering. Inside the bag—pen, pad, ChapStick, and some type of large-print newsletter called *The Gazette*, which I toss in the tiny wastebasket. How disappointing. Then I take out what looks like two coupons. "Coupons?" I ask the blonde. "For *what?*"

With a flip of her hair, she says, "Your welcome packet from our shops downstairs. A free salon cut at Shear Madness and a free bag of sours from Keepers' Mart!"

Have my hair cut here? Never.

Welcome, welcome, welcome. Welcome to what? It's honestly too much.

Thank God William is back. And he's brought my lamp—a golden iris Victorian from Tiffany. Suddenly the room is brighter.

"Did I hear coupons? Mom loves those." My son's voice—enthusiastic. "She gets her hair done every two weeks."

"Correct." He knows my schedule for a good wash and trim. "But not here. With *my* stylist, in her shop downtown. She knows my length. Agnes takes me."

William turns to the blonde. "Mom just needs a little time. Nice to meet you, I'm her son, William."

She smiles a little too long at him. "I'm Kim, from recreation."

A clank at the door. The flirty blonde walks out and a young nurse in purple uniform who seems to be all business wheels over a wire basket on a pole with a screen next to where I'm sitting.

"All right, Edith, let's get your vitals." She nods at William and me. "I'm Eve." Head down, she presses buttons on the screen. Her nails are red and badly chipped. Clearly, she does them herself. But why when the salon charges so little?

I never liked that blood pressure cuff, too tight against my arm. And I hate the plastic taste of the thermometer. She listens to my heart. She's still smiling, so I must be OK. Picking up a clipboard, she turns to William, and after some chit-chat, addresses me in an official tone: "Directives, heart stops, resuscitation."

My teeth clench. "I'm not dying here!" I shout. "I'm going to be like Mother, 102. She just kept going, out there with her flowers in her gardening clothes: summer skirt, cotton sweater, cloche hat with a red silk ribbon. Dropped dead holding the watering can. The lilies, the white ones, were her favorite."

Exhausted, I turn to the window—a ray of sun shines on a branch and I search for my cardinal. The tops of the tree branches sway with the breeze. My heavy lids droop...

I hear William say to the nurse, "At 98, she's napping more, but other times she can be impulsive."

Opening my eyes wide, I sit up straighter. "I've got more energy in my little pinky than most people have in their whole bodies."

They keep talking to each other and I grumble, "Impulsive..." But now they're saying something about my valuables. Moving my two rings back and forth on my finger, as I've always done. *They haven't been tight in a while.* My engagement ring with the small stone slides off, more easily than expected. "William," I turn to him, "take this one back to the house for safekeeping."

William starts to say something, but he knows better than to give me a hard time.

The stretchy white plastic bracelet feels bulky as the nurse rolls it onto my wrist. This one's all business. A door key hangs from it. "This is your ID bracelet, with your room key. There are others," she points to different colored ones in her basket, "but those are not for you." She leans closer, "They're for the ones who want to leave."

Of course, they want to leave. I want to leave. Who would want to stay? Thankfully, I won't be here long.

"Now Edith, your son William is your main contact. Do you need help showering, dressing? Hearing aids, glasses, dentures? Friends and family—do you want them involved in your care?'

"William is my only family, and all my friends are gone, except one, who should be housebound. I prefer to spend time by myself." My hands start to shake. *What time is it?* Five minutes past three says the big clock on my wall. *Did I eat?*

"All right then, what do you like to do by yourself?"

"Well, I'm busy all day... I... I..." I can't think of a thing. "There's getting ready, yes, laundry, I walk outside to get the mail, and dinner, what do you call it, doing things all day... well, and sometimes I can't even get it all done. Why are you asking me? I'm busy. I don't have time to just sit and talk like this."

"OK, just a few more questions. Meals are in the main dining room with the other residents, or you can have a tray served to your room. Assistance with eating?"

"I'll eat in here. And I'm not an infant. I can feed myself."

William raises his eyebrows. "Mom—your clothes are getting looser." He whispers to the nurse, but I can hear him, "She insists she's fine, but I think she forgets to eat."

"And you forget my hearing is just fine. Do you want me to be fat? He wants me to be fat." I smile at the nurse. "I've never been fat in my life. And if I don't eat, it's because I'm not hungry." Now it's my turn to whisper a bit too loudly. "Forget to eat. How ridiculous."

William busies himself taking my framed pictures out of a bag, and I breathe easier as he places them on the plastic shelf across from the bed: Cosmo wagging his tail, William Jr. with his father and their big catch—the bass that day tasted so fresh—my dear parents with all seven of us sisters. But my eyes stop at the big picture of our blue cape with the white picket fence. William Sr. had it framed and gave it to me when we first got the house. I want to open the white door, walk back in, and sit in my recliner, but it's just a picture in a frame now—until I get back.

William spreads my green and white quilt crisply on the bed the way I taught him.

The nurse looks at him. "She must be hungry. I'll call down for her lunch tray."

"She is hungry," I say, "and she's sitting right here."

An annoyed look crosses her face, and she turns to me with a forced smile, then whispers something to William about it being the "best time." *Best time for what?*

Turning in my direction, she chirps, "And I need to give you this." She unhooks a cord from the wall with a red button on the end and ties the cord around the side rail of the bed. "Just press this buzzer if you need assistance. Did you meet Raffee?"

"I don't know. But I know I don't need assistance."

I touch my bracelet with the new key. "William, you've found me a lovely room, but I'm worried about the house. Please make sure my driveway gets plowed."

"Thank you for taking care of Mom, Eve."

So that's her name. I'll have to write it down.

"I can tell she's in good hands," he continues. "And Eve, call me if Mom needs anything at all. I'll be back tomorrow."

My face drops as I look at William. *Tomorrow.* "William..."

"Mom..."

"I'm sure this is just a wrinkle—as Mother used to say. We'll smooth this out in the morning."

"I'll call you tonight. The phone is right there on your bedside table."

"You have my number? You haven't *forgotten* it?"

He smiles. "Eve gave it to me, and I wrote it down, just like you taught me. Listen tonight for the phone to ring."

He shifts back and forth on his feet. I can see I need to be strong for my boy, just as I've always been. "I'll be fine, dear. You can go now."

He keeps looking down. "Goodbye, Mom."

"Goodbye, dear."

"Don't forget to eat your lunch!" he chirps.

I open my arms, and his warm hug never seems long enough.

"Bye, Mom. See you tomorrow."

I put my hand over his and do my best to hide my tears.

Along the hillsides of the valley, rays of orange and red spread across the sky, landing on the oak tree outside my window. I hope I'll be able to see the river when it blooms. I suppose they'll have to trim the branches. And on that long bough, is that a tree swing? Who on earth could that be for?

My stomach feels unsettled, more than usual, and then I remember, it's this time every evening when I walk after dinner, but I haven't eaten yet. Or have I? And where will I walk here? The loop along the brook on my street is the perfect distance to soothe my digestion. But here there's no brook, no street—just hallways with tree names all cluttered with carts and chairs and dirty dinner trays and meals people have forgotten to eat. I've got to get outside—bundle up and get some evening air. I may be old and frail, but I refuse to be a shut-in.

I know well enough to use the bathroom before my walk, and to go through my routine: purse, house key so I don't get locked out, hat, scarf... what am I forgetting? *Whatever it is, it can't be that important.* I get behind my wheeler and start to head out. Suddenly, I hear noises—loud voices in the hallway. Alarms buzzing. "ALERT, WANDER ALERT, WANDER..." My heart skitters. *What's happening? Have I done something wrong?*

A deep rumbling voice yells, "OUT!"

Shaky, I grip the handles of my wheeler. *Is this a fire drill, like we used to have at Town Hall? Or a fire?* I look down the hallway, sniffing for smoke.

Then the alarm stops. "WANDERER FOUND." The yelling quiets. I start to relax, but my stiff fingers are clutched on my wheeler, and it takes a minute for them to loosen. *Now, where was I going?*

As if nothing has happened, a young man in a blue uniform with a hair net pushes a tall, stainless-steel cart past the open door of my room. Oh dear, I forgot to close it.

Clearing my throat to get his attention, I ask, "What's all the fuss about?"

He turns but doesn't stop moving. "The usual," he chuckles. "Someone hightailed it outta here. You know, it's sundown." He smiles broadly, with a mouth full of crooked teeth. "Don't you worry. Dinner trays will be comin'." And he keeps rolling past.

Dinner. I take my walk *after* dinner. But dinner is coming. This place has me all confused. I wheel back through my door to my spot by the window and sit on my bench. Maybe I'll feel better, clearer after I eat.

Outside, the oak's bare branches are still, the swing empty. The last light is leaving the sky. The most peaceful time at my house. But I'm... here.

A deep voice booms in the hallway, "Helloooo," as if hello were a song. Someone is in my room! I startle, almost falling back.

"Dunht," he rumbles, shaking his head, "Dunht, dunht." A tall, young man with a wide, bright smile and dark curls wearing a bright green uniform is standing in front of me holding a pitcher of ice water that looks as if it's about to spill. Moving to a beat, he sets the pitcher down on my bedside table and stares out the window, singing louder than full volume on my Victrola. "Dunht... dunht, dunht." He adjusts an earpiece in his ear then turns to me. "You know this old song?"

But he turns away before I can answer and looks at himself in the mirror. Fixing a curl so it falls over the top of his headband, he continues to check himself out. "Nah, probably not your thing..."

Nodding his head to the beat, his voice higher, "Aquarius... A-quar-eeee-usss!" His hands and fingers playing a trumpet that can't be seen.

I shake my finger at him. "Shush, now. You're going to disturb that very sick man across the hall." *Just lying there with that mane of white bushy hair under his crimson cap.* "There is no singing where people are..." but he keeps belting out his song, "where people are... dying!"

"Who's dying?"

I point across the hall.

"Him? He's doin' pretty good today. You know, he was a transplant surgeon. A famous one. Doc Mansfield." Putting cups next to the water pitcher, he looks me straight in the eye. "You know singin' helps everyone, right?"

"How on earth can it help him?"

His tone quiets. "Doc's not supposed to respond much, but I know what he needs. I know how to take care of him. And when I sing, I get a little smile, and sometimes even a little hand tappin' when I'm really in the groove."

"Maybe the tapping means he wants you to go away."

"Maybe," he laughs, "but if I ever end up like *him*, I want someone like *me* bringin' in their song."

I shrug.

"A little music is better than a cup of pills any day." Fixing his headband, he continues, "Is that a record player over there, one of those old ones? I love vinyl—got me a big collection."

"That's a Victrola. From well before your time. You know, *all* three times my friend Agnes broke her hip, they played classical music in the hospital—the same Mozart pieces, over and over. Did you know Thomas Edison invented the phonograph?"

He fusses with some boxes on my desk, then picks up my red notebook.

"Are you listening to me, young man? And don't touch that, you're being rude."

"Actually, I'm quite helpful." He starts flipping through my notebook. A—Agnes, B..." He pages all the way to the end. "What do you keep in here besides phone numbers—all your secrets?"

"Put that down! Now!"

He looks at me, his eyes dark saucers surrounded by white. "So, who's Agnes, your sister?"

"I had six sisters, but they're all gone now. Agnes is my neighbor, the old woman who doesn't know she's lost!"

He finally puts my notebook down and picks up the painted rock Agnes gave me from my shelf.

"She calls me, Agnes, every night. Three rings after dinner. That's how I know she's OK. Oh dear, does she have my number here?"

"What?" He takes the earpiece out of his ear, "What are you talking about?"

"My phone number."

Moving the phone on the bedside table so that it is within reach, he laughs, "It's right here on your phone."

"I keep all my numbers in that red book *you* moved. Please bring it back so I can write my number down." He hands me my notebook. "And who are you?"

A broad smile comes over his face and he sits further back on my desk. "I'm Raphael Williams." Pulling his badge on a lanyard towards me, he adds, "But Momma is the only one who calls me Ra-pha-el." He sways to the beat of his snapping finger. "Everyone here calls me Raffee." And with that, he's singing again, "Dunht... dunht, dunht."

"No sitting on the furniture."

"Damn, you're takin' my jam away." Snapping his fingers, picking up a beat, "Ms... what do people call *you?*"

"Mrs. Sharp. Mrs. Edith Sharp. And jam is for toast." I reach over and smooth the wrinkle on the edge of my bed. "This is *my* room. And you can go now."

"All right, I'm outta here!" He hops off the desk, quickly saying, "I'm your nurse's aide if you need anything," and in the blink of an eye he's out the door.

"A helper that needs help," I mutter. *Just what I need.* My gaze falls on my picture of my mother. She got old, too. I helped wrap her legs, swollen with sores. Still, she kept tending her flowers. But this is a place without... flowers.

More voices in the hallway, a blue plastic tray brought to my bedside table, roast beef sandwich, but I asked for ham, with Swiss, on rye, and brown mustard. I pick a little at the coleslaw, but it's room temperature. I won't ever have an appetite for this type of food.

My shoulders and neck remind me, it's been the longest day. I never wanted this day to begin... and now it just won't end. Startled! My phone rings from the table across the room. Getting dark outside... must be Agnes. I count the rings... another. I'm just too tired to get up so quickly. And one more... three. My heart calms; Agnes has found me.

Quiet for a moment. Then the phone starts to ring again. I know this one needs to be answered, and I'm able to get my hand on the receiver in time. It's the sweet voice of my son. "Mom, you sound exhausted. How was your day?"

Feeling better just hearing his voice, and sitting, I try to remember what I tried to forget... *this day*. "Well, it's been very busy... all the faces, the food. They want me to eat three meals a day. And I'd rather spend my time doing other things. At my age, time is getting shorter, not longer."

"Mom, we've talked about this—good nutrition, for your bones."

"A sandwich I didn't order... oh, and chicken soup, which I only have when I'm sick. And I'm *not* sick."

Raffee, the helper who needs help, pops his head in, smiling as he takes the tray and closing my door as he leaves.

William asks, "What should I do with all that tea in the kitchen?"

"Don't clean out my box of special tea bags. Those tea bags made you feel better every time you were sick as a child."

"Mom, they're not the same teabags."

"Well, I never threw them away."

"Or anything else."

I'm grateful that I'm still able to laugh as I share this with William. "And before you ask, I'm putting my red purse with my house key in the top drawer next to my bed, the one that locks. And I keep this bracelet for the door here around my wrist..." I roll it off and put it on my bedside table.

The oak tree glows in the moonlight outside my window. William's tone changes. "I'm glad you are getting the key straightened out. Now, I have something to tell you."

I hold the phone closer to my ear, to make sure I hear what doesn't sound good...

"Something has come up at work that can't wait until after the holiday."

This tone.

"I'm sorry, but I have to head back to California earlier than expected. The only flight I could get leaves early tomorrow morning."

"Oh." My heart sinks.

"You know the firm, Mom. If there was any way I *could* be there, I would."

My boy with his big job. "But you'll be back?"

"I know we had our lunch date... but this deal might tie me up for a few weeks. I'll come as soon as I can. And I'll keep calling you."

Closing my eyes, I hold my forehead in my hand. "Of course, dear. I understand. I'm fine. Maybe Agnes will take me home when I leave here."

I hear the smile in his voice, "If she's not lost already." He promises to call tomorrow. "I love you, too."

He can't come? Did I really hear him say that? I know he works very hard...

My door flies open. Hands full of towels, water, extra toothpaste. That young man again, with the headband and those earphones.

"No more people barging into this room." I cover my face with my hand and feel myself fly off the handle. "Are you one of the people who thinks I'm going to die here? Is that why you keep coming in, to make sure I'm not dead?"

Raffee's smile fades.

"This is a place where there should be lots of time alone. And I can't get away from all of you." My heart pounds with anger. "Now, what did William just tell me?"

Raffee carefully arranges the toiletries on the closest spot... my desk.

"Get out."

Sitting in my desk chair, looking back at me calmly, he says, "Ms. Edith..."

"GET OUT!" Tightness across my back with each breath, "YOU don't need to be here. And I don't need to be here."

"I hear you, Ms. Edith. Life is not easy." An expression of sincerity older than his years crosses his face. "Whether you're in here or out there, yellin' don't make it any better. At least that's what my momma says."

He's right about the yelling. I wouldn't yell at home or in the grocery store. It's this place, making me crazy. Swallowing, I clear my voice, "I wish to be alone."

"OK," He shrugs his shoulders, and quickly stands. Before he walks out, he turns and looks at me, "But, Ms. Edith," he says quietly, as if I never raised my voice, "we're going to take care of you... you just tell us how."

He leaves the door ajar.

I've used my last ounce of energy to sit on the bed. Suddenly I feel all of my 98 years. Too tired to get up again, I say goodnight to everyone in my family, as I've done every night—each picture starting with William Sr., then my parents, then all of my sisters. I pull my quilt to my shoulders to warm the chill. The door partially open, I peer across the hall. There's a small lamp next to his bed, he's just lying there, motionless. A white lily stands tall.

Not dead, just sleeping. Not permanent, just temporary.

New Year's Eve

Edith Sharp

Morning sun. Goodness—how did my bedroom get so bright? Did I forget to draw the curtains? Wait... this is my quilt, but this is not my bed! What are my pictures doing on that shelf? White walls, a Formica nightstand? This is not my bedroom. Oh dear, is this a hospital? *Did I fall?* My heart skips a beat.

A face I don't know bursts into the room with a tray resting on her shoulder.

The smell of syrup and coffee hits my nose. *Where am I?* The face adjusts the table so it slides in front of me and lifts the warming cover off the plate. Dry eggs and undercooked toast, soggy pancakes, some sort of cereal, orange slices clearly from a can. Breakfast in bed. I mutter, "Am I sick?"

In a rushed response, "Well, you're gettin' regular food, it's not all mushed. Some people get their whole meal—just like pudding. Down in the kitchen, that stuff plops when it's scooped out of the blender. But you're probably OK."

Probably OK? "Where am I?"

"Why, you're havin' breakfast, right here at River's Edge."

So it happened. William said he was going to do this, but I didn't believe he ever would bring me to a place like... this. *My beautiful boy.* Suddenly, I can't breathe. Taking in air is like pushing through a heavy weight. I look at my pictures lined up on my shelf, knowing that's where I belong. *Enjoy the breakfast, Edith, this is only temporary. You're going home soon.*

The woman who brought the tray points to the wall next to the mirror. "Everything you need to know is on this whiteboard: Today is December 31st. The New Year's party starts at 4:00 pm. Your Nurse is Eve, your Aide is Raffee. Eat up now while breakfast is still warm. Need help opening anything?"

"No, I'm fine." I don't want to tell her how unappealing the food looks. I'd rather keep it all closed. It seems I've lost my appetite. Outside, the frozen grass on the hill reflects the sun.

As she walks out, I think again about leaving. On my own two feet. Did I get my walk last night? I'm honestly not sure. It's probably cold, but I have my warm coat and my cashmere scarf. I glance around the room for my wheeler, which is folded against the wall, and my purse, since I know things get stolen here.

At home, a big breakfast is my favorite meal—eggs over easy, crispy sausage, toast that's actually toasted, and apricot preserves (not jam or jelly)—I can count on eating well. My father always said you can't start the day hungry. But this...

The safest thing here is the coffee, and I take a sip. Lukewarm! And needs more creamer. I look again at the disappointing tray. The eggs aren't that dry, the oranges are those little mandarins, and the toast appears to be whole wheat. And I didn't have to make any of it and burn myself trying.

My knuckles are too stiff to peel open the milk carton. Besides, it's skim milk, not whole. I take one spoonful of the dry golden cereal flakes, but without milk it sticks in my throat. The fork is easier to manage, and I try to wash the cereal down with the eggs, which I'm now certain are powdered. Not even worth doctoring up with those useless salt and pepper packets I can never tear open. But the pancakes—with syrup already on them—are surprisingly warm. I dig in.

After breakfast, a blur of different faces, some helping me dress, others asking questions but not wanting to stay and talk. The nurse with the dreadful nails stays with a cup of pills that looks like too many.

"I recognize those hands from yesterday," I say. "A salon manicure costs almost nothing, and it never chips like that."

She gives me a look. "I'm always working here, washing my hands every minute, it seems. Not even superglue would keep my nails from breaking. But after work, I'm treating myself to a mani-pedi before I head into the City, you know, for New Year's Eve."

"Ah, New Year's." I close my eyes and can still see the red velvet on the backs of the chairs, the chandeliers glittering, the men in their tuxes and women in their cocktail dresses swaying to the rhythm of the swing band. "That picture on the shelf is of my husband and me dancing... We danced many a ballroom on this night. And my nails were always done. On our first New Year's, at the Bardavon, I taught my husband to foxtrot. A proper ballroom, that's where to be on a night like this. Do you know the Bardavon?"

"Never heard of it. Please take your pills. It's a busy floor."

Memories of my silk A-line dress, my little black Halstons, and dancing. The band had a clarinet, a saxophone, trombones, and a trumpet player whose cheeks always looked as if they were about to burst. "The steps were back, back, slide together close; back, back, slide together close. The tempo was slow, slow, quick, quick..." The delight of remembering.

"Do you need help picking up your drink?" She moves the cup of pills closer and the swirl of my dance fades. A heaviness settles over my body. When did all my memories become pictures on a shelf? The new year may be here, but I like the old ones better. There are certain joys that should never be lost. Head down, I run my fingers over the soft cotton of my embroidered quilt.

"End of an era," I mutter. "End of many eras." A cloud covers the sunlight.

"Your pills, Mrs. Sharp." A dimple forms above her cheek. "Will it help you if we count them together?"

"Just leave them here, and I'll take them when I'm ready."

"Of course you will. But let's do it now, while I'm here. There's sugar, blood pressure, tremors, stomach, thyroid, bones, memory, and then your vitamins. Eleven pills. Is that right?"

"Ten," I correct her. "I don't need the memory pill. I had quite a to-do with Dr. Smith over that. I've been seeing him for thirty-five years and I've never missed an appointment. And there were several times I showed up and *he* wasn't there. I just get upset when people keep thinking I'm losing my memory and giving me those awful tests with all those silly questions. Today's date, what month is it, the year I was born, and, worst of all, how old I am. Keep that up, and I might need a pill just to calm down. I don't need to be reminded. And I'm *not* losing my memory. I just need to write down names, like any old person. And I'm *too* old for there to be anything really wrong."

"Your pills."

So impatient. Always in a hurry. I glance at her. If she only knew—and I hope she never does—what it feels like to have it all taken away. I stare at our house in the frame: William Sr. handed that picture in that frame to me, and I can still see his ear-to-ear smile and the twinkle in his eye. "We got the house, *ma chérie*." It was the house I loved. Expensive, but with the GI bill we could just afford it, and he promised to rebuild it from the inside out. And he did. And there was plenty of room for a family...

What's left of her red nail polish—party red, much too garish for me—catches the light coming in through the window. I hope she has the kind of fun that leaves good memories... Finally, I take my pills, doing the best I can. The big white chalky one takes the longest to go down.

Suddenly, I remember I have a date. "Do you know when my son William is coming? I believe there's a luncheon today. I'll need time to get ready."

"The luncheon is tomorrow—on New Year's Day. But," she offers a sympathetic smile, "your son called and had a long chat with the nurse on duty last night. He feels terrible, but unfortunately, he's unable to come because of his work." I stiffen. "He *said* he told you."

Told me?

Brokenhearted, remembering what I forgot, I rub my forehead and swallow a few times to push the lump back down. My chest feels like it's going to burst, and there's no room for breath.

The branches of the oak outside my window are bare.

She drones on. "I should also mention that your son was worried last night when he was told you were yelling at the staff." She glances at the picture of my house on the shelf. "I see this often. They call it adjustment disorder. A big change in a short time. A different environment from what you're used to. The sooner you start thinking of this as your home, the better off you'll be."

Putting my hand over my eyes, "I do *not* have a disorder. This room is like Hong Kong Harbor or the Berlin runway during the airlift. It certainly is not a *rest* home. And it's never going to be *my* home. Do you understand?"

"Early evening, after sundown, that's the time. Something about it. Everyone's on the move, disoriented and moody."

The witching hour. That's what my mother used to call it.

"It happens all the time when you're forgetful."

"Forgetful? I remember it all—very clearly." I wag my finger. "And I remember how I'm treated. Maybe I should report you for being so rude. And no one knocks—everyone just barges right in." I pause to catch my breath. "And did you say '*moody*?'" My voice is trembling. "You all act as if I'm supposed to be happy about all this. Well, I'm not."

She refills my cup with water so I can take the last two pills. "I'll tell everyone to please knock before entering. But you also need to get yourself adjusted. I can send a social worker..."

Still swallowing, I shake my head vigorously. With the pills gone, she throws my paper cup in the garbage. She is almost out the door when she turns around. "I almost forgot. Are you going to the party? To ring in the new year?"

"I'll be in my room, thank you."

She leaves, not fully closing my door. I call out, "Would you please close my..." but she's long gone. I'm so tired. Finally, a moment of rest. I just want to hide under the soft glow of my Tiffany lamp. Every time I look at it, I marvel at Mr. Tiffany's design. It's no wonder his full name was Louis Comfort Tiffany. He certainly understood what people need.

Bang! My door flies open. "Where's Sadie? Where's mae famlea? Did they leev mae here?" Yellow rain hat and matching coat, clutching her plaid pocketbook, the one from the lobby who's lost her marbles barrels her chair into my room. Her cheeks are flushed, her eyes intense. Something's very wrong. My heart races.

"Help!" I yell but don't know who I expect to come. "A lost woman is in my room!"

She rolls closer, madness in her face, with her tight curled hair and clumped up pink rouge. I have to get up and get her out of here, but my wheeler is over against the wall. Moving towards my desk, her fast fingers touching my boxes. What if she opens them?!?

Her eyes dart around. "Do ya know Sadie?"

I stare at her. "I don't know who or what you're talking about. You need to leave."

As her eyes lock onto mine, her mouth forms a wicked grin. "Sadie, you go very well, now and again."

All gibberish.

She keeps moving, touching my tissue box, fussing with the water pitcher, rearranging the cups, and now my bracelet with my key is in reach. "Not my key!"

On the wall, the whiteboard... Aide—Raffee.

"Raffeeeee, help!" I didn't realize how loud I could scream.

Her hand moves over my bracelet.

I gasp, swinging my legs over the side of the bed. "Stop!"

She springs from her chair—standing on wobbly legs—and grabs a few sugar packets off my tray, sliding some of them in her pocket.

"You! Sit down!"

She bends down stiffly and stuffs more sugar packets in her socks, then plops heavily back into her chair.

"Stealing sugar and anything else you can find," I yell. "Out."

"Sadie, why did ya leave me?" She reaches over and puts her hands on either side of my face, staring wildly into my eyes. Her palms are moist, and I can smell stale food on her breath.

I pull away, waving my hand in the air. "DON'T TOUCH ME! GET AWAY! GET OUT! GET OUT OF MY ROOM! Raffeeeee! Willllllliiaaam! Hellllllpp!"

She stares at me blankly.

"And I'm *not* Sadie."

At the door, there's coughing and throat clearing, then knocking, loud knocking, on my door that's already open. Thank goodness, help has come.

Another cough. "You are most *certainly* not Sadie. She loved Nellie."

In rolls the one from the lobby with the floral dress, stuffed in her chair, golden cane across her lap, tubing under her nose. What a sight! Glancing at me, she wheels the rest of the way through the door. "Now, Sadie had this room done up properly. Embroidered curtains, a quilt she stitched herself—before the arthritis stopped her—you know she once made a wedding gown for the cousin of Sophia Loren."

Am I supposed to be impressed? "I don't care who she stitched what for. She's not here, and I am. And I want you all out. Now."

Floral Dress points to the sugar thief in the wheelchair. "Poor Nellie. She doesn't realize Sadie's passed. We've been telling her she took a trip—

back to Italy." The one called Nellie shifts in her chair and looks at me with a lopsided smile.

Holding up her golden cane, Floral Dress continues, "Now what was all that yellin'?"

"Well, isn't it obvious... Yellow Raincoat, what's her name... Nellie, just barged right in, touching everything—even grabbing me! She nearly stole my key!"

Rolling closer to my wheeler, she looks me up and down. "You're not Sadie, that's for damn sure. Sadie always knew how to have a good time." Then with a raise of her eyebrows, she somehow acknowledges I've passed her test. "But you're all right."

As if I need her approval. Glancing over at Nellie the sugar thief, I grab my key bracelet and slip it over my wrist. "You think this is all OK?"

Clearing her raspy throat, she laughs, sounding like Louis Armstrong. "Of course Nellie steals. She's packing for her trip." Taking a few cookies out of a bag in her lap, she gives one to Nellie, who starts chewing. "Actually, it's the 'heimers that steals, steals everything right out from under you." Floral Dress lowers her chin, then takes a cookie herself. It's gone in one bite.

Nellie coughs.

Floral Dress accentuates her own chewing, "Come on, Nellie, chin down, chew, swallow." Nellie tries again, and this time a piece of the vanilla cookie falls to the floor.

Another knock. Another chair rolls in. Short red curls and thick, red-framed glasses—didn't I see her the lobby, too? She looks around and sniffs. "This room!" She throws her hands up. "There's nothing on the walls, and there's... nothing on the door. Sadie had the best decorations!" Suddenly, she pushes her glasses up on top of her head and wipes her eyes. "Even when she was sick, even when she was *dying*, she kept up appearances, and kept the party going. And with her wooden spoon, she'd move all the sweets in front of Nellie." Red Frames sighs. "I thought," she sobs, "I thought Sadie would live forever."

I glance over at her ridiculous glasses and correct her. "No one lives forever."

Holding her tubing in her nose and breathing in, Floral Dress looks to an audience out the window, raising her hands. "One day it's Sadie. One day it's gonna be you. So we gotta live like there's no tomorrow. Cause the Good Lord is comin' for his children... we're all his lil' babies..." She sits up—to the extent possible—in her chair and struggles to lift her cane. Staring my way, "You gonna be prepared? Or you gonna miss it?"

Her brown eyes widen, holding mine. I inform the intruders, "Well, I've just arrived. But I'm only staying a short time, then I'm going *home*. And *my* decorations are in my attic—*at home*—where they belong."

Adjusting her glasses further down her nose, Red Frames shakes a bony, wrinkled finger at me. "I should have known you were going to be like this. No holiday spirit in here. What is it you say about empty doors without decorations, Stella? The people inside don't have a good soul."

My jaw drops and I feel my blood begin to boil. "You horrible woman! My soul, that's between me and the Good Lord." I sigh to Floral Dress. "People like her, who wear cheap plastic..."

Red Frames turns to Floral Dress. Holding her hand to her ear and turning it in my direction, "How's that? Did I hear you say cheap? Ouch... coming from someone who has no style. Just a closet over there full of the same boring white shirts. Stella, she needs Residents' Council to help her decorate—*and dress*." Turning towards me, she slides her garish frames farther up her nose. "*My* door has frills. Makes the whole neighborhood, don't you think?" She rolls closer to my pictures. "You were almost pretty when you were younger. And this shelf could look good if you switch a few things around." She picks up my house and starts rearranging all my framed photos.

This is too much. "That's it! HANDS OFF!" I shout, slamming my fist on the table so hard it hurts. Pain radiates up my arm. "ALL OF YOU, GET OUT!"

Three heads turn as one and stare at me.

Floral Dress Stella clears a glob of phlegm from her throat. "I must not have introduced us... *We're* the welcoming committee." She points at

Yellow Raincoat, whose name I've now forgotten, with her cane: "You've already met Nellie. I'm Stella, and this," she nods towards Red Frames, "is Roula."

"Well, you can welcome yourselves right out of here. All of you." I point at fast fingers Nellie in the raincoat. "Especially her. And make sure she doesn't have any of my things in those hideous socks."

"Roula," says Stella, "she needs to hear about the activities."

"Don't bother," I say. "I told you, I'm only here for a short time, so I won't be getting involved with you or your *activities*."

Stella clears her clogged throat again. By the sound of it, it's a miracle she's even breathing. Raising her head and adopting the tone of a southern preacher, she bellows, "Short time, long time, that's up to the Good Lord. Hale and hearty one day, headin' to heaven the next. But while we're here, He fills this life with dreams, parties, and songs, to get us into the spirit. You hear me?" A dazed expression comes over her face.

"You didn't hear *me*. Out!" I say.

Red Frames Roula turns, "Come on, Stella, I don't hear everything everyone says, but it's clear she doesn't want us here."

"You got that right," Stella says.

Finally, she seems to hear me. Then, lifting her golden cane, she looks me in the eye.

Oh dear, she doesn't have it right. She's not leaving.

"The first year takes some getting used to. It's all new. As head of Residents' Council, it's my job to welcome you. And once you know us, you won't want us to leave. Roula here works in Keepers' Mart, where you can get your necessaries, snacks, sympathy cards, magazines. We do the parties, the holiday decorations..." She leans a little closer. "But," she winks, "it's all about the *food*."

I gained a bit of weight after giving birth to William, but this one—those rolls... my Lord—what can they be eating here?

She closes her lids and takes a long, deep breath from her tubes. "Did you know at Christmas the angels come visit us?" Then, raising that golden cane of hers, she breaks out with "Fa la la la la" from "Deck the Halls."

This half-dead woman can barely breathe, but her notes fill the room—she sings like an opera star. Clearing her throat, gasping for a few breaths of air, she coughs out a question, "You'll be here at Christmas, won't you?"

She must be confused. I'm sure Christmas has already passed. And I certainly won't be here next Christmas. I look back at her. "One doesn't sing Christmas songs *after* Christmas."

"Fa la la la la," they all join in.

"Next Christmas," the one called Stella says, "you'll be singing with us."

"God willing, I'll be home."

Stella's smile widens. "So, what should we call you?"

"My name is Edith. Edith Sharp."

"Well, Edy," Stella says, "Tonight is New Year's Eve, and you're gonna party with us."

"It's Edith, not Edy, and not on your life. Also, party is a noun, not a verb. And I've asked you all to leave." My hands tremble with exhaustion and frustration. "The welcoming committee has overstayed its welcome. And you, with those glasses," I turn to Red Frames, forgetting her name, "my mother had a word for you."

"How's that?" Adjusting the frames around her neck, she quips, "You know these are designer. With real ersatz diamonds, so I know they're mine when they're stolen." She turns away in a huff, and gestures for Yellow Raincoat to follow her out the door.

Floral Dress gives me a disappointed shrug.

And with that, the three graces finally roll out.

Somehow, it's afternoon. I don't need that big clock to tell me that. I try to take a walk at this time, no matter how much everything hurts. That's how things get worked out. Stepping out of my room with my wheeler, passing door after door, steadier with each step, I know I'll be fine. Walking was how I survived after William Sr. passed so young. And walking is how I'll pass my time here, until I go back home. Making my way to the reception area, I notice the decorations on the center table of the atrium shining under the lights. Not so bad after all. The receptionist looks up over her glasses.

"Good afternoon, Mrs. Sharp. Where are you going?"

"For a walk." *That's all she needs to know.*

A quick smile, "Just sign here if you are headed out." She looks back down at her papers.

"That won't be necessary. I'm just going out for a stroll."

"I'm afraid everyone needs to sign in and out."

"Well, I'm not everyone." I move towards the doors.

Suddenly she shouts, "Excuse me!"

I ignore her. The air outside is cold, and I realize I've forgotten my coat. Too much effort to go back. I'll just take a short loop around the parking lot. I push my wheeler forward. *Oooh, that wind. And so many cars. Could William still be here?* Then I see it. A red car with a square trunk close to the ground that looks familiar. And there's a dent and a scratch along the side! Agnes has come to visit! She can take me home! In her warm car, which I can see is running. I plow through the slush, eager to see my friend.

Agnes must have come for New Year's, and I'll bet she brought the good champagne, not the fake stuff. We've always celebrated New Year's together, ever since William Sr. died. She goes to Gulliver's Wines to get the Veuve Clicquot, named after a French widow, only four sips with our chocolates—solid milk chocolate, not with the cream or the liqueurs that make me silly.

Knocking on her car window, my hands cold, she doesn't seem to hear me. No surprise. Those ears of hers. I knock harder. "Agnes!" I say her name loudly, a few times. The window rolls down.

A rounded nose, soft, saggy cheeks. Agnes can't sit still long enough to let an ounce of fat stay on her, and this one has extra around her several chins. My stomach drops. Speechless, I stare. It's not Agnes.

"Are you lost?" Not Agnes asks. "Should I call someone to help you?"

Cold on my face, my feet and fingers numb, the sea of cars making me dizzy. This is not my walk. Where are my landmarks... the red brick ranch house, the little bridge over the brook? What's happening? I'm lost!

Not Agnes starts to get out of her car. Then I see the glass doors of the entrance to the stone building—that place—and arms in a green uniform waving, dancing, yelling. "Ms. Edith, you're going in circles! The receptionist called me. You're gonna catch cold!" *I recognize that voice.*

My green angel seems to float across the parking lot, and, relieved, I take his arm. We carefully push my wheels through the slush. Reaching the sidewalk, I pull the edges of my shirt collar closer together. "You know," I say, taking a few deep breaths and loosening my grip on the handles, "I can walk blindfolded on the sidewalk along the brook. I know every crack."

"I'm not surprised to hear that, Ms. Edith. But it's real slippery out here."

I look down at the frozen ground. "I know how to walk when there's ice. Never step on the shine. But I'm sorry to go so slowly—you understand, don't you?"

"I do, but neither one of us has a coat." He shivers. "Let's get us both inside."

"You know... I think that lady stole Agnes's car."

"That old thing? Not worth stealing."

Inside, the building is warm. A break from the cold. Passing a few poor souls sitting in wheelchairs, we walk slowly, but not slowly enough, down the long hallway, approaching my room, my bed. Exhausted, my hip aches and I use my trick of stopping to admire one of the paintings on the wall. But unlike William, Raffee doesn't shift his feet. He seems to have all the time in the world for me.

Finally, I lay my tired bones down on this bed, to sleep.

"Sorry to wake you." A new face pops her head through the doorway.

"Is it tomorrow already?"

"No, but it's almost next year. And the residents' New Year's party is starting soon, at four o'clock. They have those little hot dogs and the mustard you can dip them in. I can help you get ready."

"I'm not going. That awful welcoming committee will be there. And I might miss my son's call."

"Well, you can't sit and wait for the phone to ring and miss the party."

"I most certainly can. I wish to be alone. Please close the door when you leave."

Another that doesn't close the door all the way. I'll close it later, can't risk a fall. When the legs are tired, the legs don't listen. You can never be too careful.

"Yoohoooo?" The raspy voice outside my door. That noisy group again? Now what are they saying?

With my door open a few inches, I'm able to see Floral Dress, Red Frames, and Yellow Raincoat. Floral Dress is wearing what looks like a dime store headdress. I wish I could remember their names, this welcoming committee.

"Come on, Roula," Floral Dress rasps, "maybe she's changed her mind."

Red Frames Roula rolls by and stops in front of the door. Taking those tacky glasses off her head, she hangs them from a silver chain around her neck with—are you kidding me—dangling gold letters that spell out "Happy New Year." In that New York accent of hers, she asks, "Changed her what?"

"Her mind!"

"A grump never changes its spots."

Grump? I've never been called that. But I've heard these places change people. I shake my head. *Not me.*

Floral Dress clears her throat, sounding like a race car driver revving the engine. "Roula, it's our job to be welcoming to *everyone*—even the grumps—something *you're* still working on."

There's that word, grump, again. Are they really talking about me?

Coughing, Floral Dress continues, "Fired from Shear Madness, on probation at Keepers' Mart, you and your opinions..."

Fluffing her red curls, "Well, Stella, my opinions happen to be facts."

Stella rolls her eyes and shakes her head.

"But me ticket is ta Ireland!" The one in the yellow raincoat wheels herself in and gets stuck in the doorway. "Ta Ireland!"

I clear my throat, hoping they'll leave. But it's no use trying to keep them out. "All right, come on in."

A golden cane flings my door fully open. "Is that you Edy? Calling for us? Now that's the spirit." Wearing a plumed-feather tiara and a long string of shiny, colored beads around her neck, Stella presses the tubing to her nose as she takes in a breath. "We're having a party! The Vista Lounge. And you're coming!"

"Well... I've done a lot of New Year's—probably more than any of you—and I'm done celebrating."

I can't tell if Stella is laughing or coughing, her rolls bouncing in her chair. "Honey, we're *never* done celebrating. And who can believe this is gonna be 2018?"

Roula nods, the glitzy letters shaking on her chain. "Eighteen? I remember being 18. I was a looker."

With that dyed red hair, all that makeup, leopard print shirt two sizes too tight, more like what rhymes with looker.

"It's time for resolutions," Stella says. "Mine is to lose all this weight. I'm getting up and walking. Roula, what's yours?"

"I'm going to write a letter to that Director of Nursing, Ruthann whatshername. I don't care if she doesn't want to hear from me again. How do they expect us to live with only two colors of red for hair dye in the salon?"

Yellow Raincoat chimes in, "Claire de Lune..."

Roula smooths her hair. "No Nellie. Not lune... loony. It's crazy how we have to live without."

I fix the collar of my button-down. "Well, we all have to make do."

"True words, Edy, true words," Stella smiles. "What's your resolution?"

"Resolutions are for dreamers. My William always said, there are those who make resolutions and those who get things done."

Stella huffs, "To each their own." Through her chuckles, she struggles to breathe. "Can't afford... to miss... a holiday. But you can't go looking like that."

"Looking like what?" I glance in the mirror to make sure nothing's happened to me. Classic beauty, I've always been told. "Well, if I look like an old lady, it's because I *am* one."

"Old?" says Stella. "You just need to get festive! Roula's right, you need frills." Rolling next to my rocker, she takes a string of beads off her neck...

Those aren't for me, are they? I move away, but she places them around my neck and starts to fuss with them. "You gotta learn how to let people take care of you." Before I know it, she's topped my head with a plumed-feather tiara!

"Now you look like a princess!" Roula says approvingly. "You just needed some style." Repositioning her frames, she squints. "Everyone—the princess of River's Edge!"

I slowly reach up to touch what's on my head. William Sr. used to call me his princess. If he could only see me now.

Stella adjusts the red, gold, and green beads around her neck. Smiling, she looks at me. "Relax, Edy, enjoy what you can. You're in a home and *we* like to have a good time. The new year is coming." She raises an imaginary glass. "Here's to happy years ahead. Tonight we've got our health and each other. God gave us an invitation, and we can't be late to the party!"

I glance back in the mirror. Who is this woman I see staring back at myself? Wearing beads and a ridiculous tiara? And then it comes to me... *The princess of River's Edge.* That's who she is. I've never been alone on New Year's.

Look at that. Festive Edith. Princess Edith. One more New Year's... Well, it certainly will be new.

Valentine's Day

Bruno Romano

Tick tick tick tick...

Ahhh, the hum of a classic ride. Rolling out of the elevator, down the wide-open hallway, my destination is in sight—that pretty receptionist with the honey-colored hair up in a bun. She'll know if my appointment is today. Now... her name? Starts with B. Barbara?

My elbow's talkin' to me, achin' like hell, but I'm not one to be late. Besides, you never know the crowd that's hanging around down there— might be a lovely lady or two.

With one hand, I reach for the rail along the wall and pull my chair forward. *Who says this baby's too old to rumble?* Gaining speed, I reach further back on the rims with both hands—cool metal against my stiff fingers—and shifting the hips forward, I give a hard push down on my well-worn wheels. Whoosh! I can still feel fun! The wind brushes my face, passing door after door. Have to straighten my hair when I get there. Feeling the shake of my front wheels hitting maximum speed, a smile moves across my dry lips as I roll... like a bat outta hell.

Rims spinning through my palms, "Ouch!" I yell.

A shot of pain burns my hand. Pulling my fingers off the metal, the front wheels suddenly swerve and turn. I'm stopped, and the wall is too close to my face.

Checking my glove near the spot where my hand hurts, I see it. "A hole!" The black leather is worn, my skin red, split open underneath. *Another damn blister!*

But these are top-of-the-line driving gloves, with full leather padding! Can't get 'em like this anymore: fingerless, breathable top mesh. They'll have to be patched.

I can fix this. Shifting my grip, using the outside of my palm where the leather is thickest, I push down, not quite as hard, against the wheels until they start moving. *That's it.* My ride rolls forward, slowly at first, then picks up speed.

Dizzy, I shut my eyes for a second.

"Shit!" What did I hit?

I look up.

Ahhh, just where I wanted to be, the reception desk. And there she is. Beautiful Beeeee... Baaaa... maybe Becky? Ahhh, who cares what her name is. "Hey baby, is my appointment today?"

"Bruno." Lady B. rolls her eyes and mutters, "That dilapidated chair." Shaking her golden tower of hair, she raises her nicely shaped eyebrows, "Watch the speed. I'm talking with Edith. *You'll* have to wait."

She smiles briefly as she turns away and addresses a striking woman with straight white hair to her chin and a starched white collar sitting on her walker's bench seat. Hands folded on her lap... hmm, have I seen this one before? From the way she sits, I can tell she's got class.

Her name? Did I hear it right? Starts with an E? Well, she's nice looking. I strain to hear their conversation.

"Now that handsome son of yours, Edith," my B. with the beautiful bun says, "I'm not surprised he sent you such beautiful roses. The Valentine's social is at two, an hour from now, so you can leave the flowers here. I'll have someone help you bring them to your room after the party."

Standing, admiring her giant bouquet of red, pink, and white, she smiles. I hear her say, "They *are* lovely flowers. I taught my son well."

Rolling my eyes, I groan. "Hmmph, a bouquet." Only useful for funerals or apologizing to Vera—God rest her soul—for another screwup. Looking towards the floor, I squint from the glare off those damn glossy tiles. Searching my shirt for my Ray-Bans, I notice the top few buttons are open. Where the hell are my shades? I look down. *Jesus, Bruno. They're on the chain around your neck*. Sliding them on, my eyes relax. *That's better.*

White Hair pushes the handles of her bench seat, turns, and walks right past me. She's still got good legs.

"Hey, lady, do I know you?" I lift the cap off my head to pat down the curls—what's left in the back.

She stops and turns. I know that kind of smile—got it all the time back in the day. She thinks I'm good-looking. And she's right. I nod back. It's my hair—I haven't really lost that much. "Hey, doll. Do we know each other?"

She ignores me and continues down the hallway. Her loss. I glance back at the receptionist looking down at papers on her desk and clear the crap out of my throat. "Hey, sweetie. I have your name on the tip of my tongue." I rub my forehead and put my cap back on my head.

"Bruno," she scolds me, "I don't have time. It's busy today with all the holiday deliveries, so we have to do this quickly." She raises her eyebrows.

We both start with "B... e..." She waits for me to join her.

Together, "Beeeeeeee..." My mind blank. Finding her eyes, I search for direction. Shaking my head, frustrated, I mumble, "Betty?"

Her tone flat, smile gone, speaking curtly, "Come on, Bruno, who was your favorite old girlfriend? The one with the blonde curls softer than a puppy's ear."

Ah, those curls. I close my eyes, remembering. So soft, and sweet smelling. And that unforgettable perfume. "Beverly." I let out a sigh.

"Yes, I'm Beverly. Bev for short."

I notice her hair, all stiff and sprayed, and shake my head. "Well, you're not *my* Beverly, but you're all right. You know, I had a *lot* of girlfriends. Can't remember their names now—just the pretty faces. I did a *lot* of traveling as a salesman—and what happened in the hotel, stayed in the hotel. But *Beverly*." I sit back in my chair and breathe deeply. *Nothing like her scent.* "She was German, and the perfume, it was German too. Starts with a B... Beiersdorf." I surprise myself. *How the hell did I remember that?* I shift in my seat. "My wife, Vera. She knew about Bev. You couldn't get anything past Vera. That woman kept me honest. And she always forgave me."

Bev glances up from her paperwork and frowns with her thin lips, "We've made it to the honest part..."

I clear my throat, "Yeah... well, sort of." Looking away, I see others slowly rolling, but not moving to any particular place. "Now, what am I doing down here?"

She sighs, "Bruno, I *actually* needed to get in touch with *you* today. Just so happens that you *do* have an appointment. The salesman for your new scooter is coming. In fact, he might already be here, waiting in the sitting area near the Lido Lounge. I was going to call you, but then, I heard the tick, tick, tick of your chair, and, sure enough, here you are, just like clockwork."

"Honey, I'm always on time. Never too early, never too late. Mark of a good salesman." But I don't need what *he's* selling. No new chair for me. I know just how to get this salesman outta here real fast. "Where'd you say the idiot was?"

She points down the hallway on the other side of the doors. I roll off, pushing down on my wheels harder than usual, and my chair reaches a steady clip. This guy's looking for a quick sale, easy money, thinks he can pull one over on us old folks. But old timers know all the old tricks, and the new ones, too. I'll send him packing.

Around the corner, past some potted plants, I get jammed up in a parking lot of wheelchairs. It's mostly old ladies sitting in their rollers, with a few young men like me. Stopping for a moment, I glance around at the crowd and take my cap off to pat down my curls—again. Young at heart, anyway.

Through the big picture window overlooking the courtyard (must be fifty feet of glass), the sun shines on the ice-covered garden, and I can make out the river in the distance.

Now... where's that salesman? I squeeze through the crowd to get closer to the window. "Excuse me, ladies." I smile, confidently maneuvering my front wheels, getting close but never bumping their frames.

My arms ache, but I'm not worried. I can turn on a dime with this jalopy and feel when my brakes catch. I hear that snap, then spin my right wheel forward. Works every time. But damn, I need to rest. I'm starting to get dizzy again. Settling my elbows deep in my well-worn armrests, the grooves of the old padding fit like a glove. No sir, no new wheels for me.

In the distance, an ancient couple sits chair to chair, under a red heart shot through with Cupid's arrow tacked up on the wall. But he's leaning away from her. This guy's got a lot to learn at his advanced age. I mean, a little facial droop won't kill your game—but his eyes are closed! No sleeping on a date! I could give him a few pointers with the ladies—it's all about attention. *Look alive, buddy.*

Pushing my Ray-Bans back up my nose, I glance down at my light cotton, short-sleeve, palm-leaf Panama Jack shirt and smooth out the wrinkles. I remember when Vera gave me this beauty—still looks good— practically new. I wipe a few crumbles that tumble off... hmmm... so that's what I had for breakfast.

Glancing back at the couple, I sigh—now she's holding his hand. *You don't know how good you have it... until it's gone.*

I've still got a good smile and a strong heart—three coronaries and still kicking. Vera was with me for the first two. That woman stayed with me through everything. I sure got lucky. I didn't deserve a faithful wife. She's in a better place now. I miss her, the way she fussed over me. But she would have hated it here. Nothing to do but sit still.

Suddenly I feel really dizzy. My vision dark. *Shake it off, Bruno. You're fine. Wait for it to pass. It always does.*

Where am I? Is that music I hear? I glance across the side of the hallway where four ladies in chairs are lined up along the window, each resting with their heads tilted the same way. Four peas in a pod! One is stuffed into a wheelchair three sizes too small, and she's coughing, gulping air from the tube in her nose. I feel a little lightheaded, could use some oxygen myself. She looks up, "Yoohoooo."

Does she know me? I turn and offer my best smile, but she's looking past me. What's a guy gotta do to get noticed?

Next to her is a woman in a seat with handles, straight white hair to her chin. Looks familiar. Nice looking broad. Have I seen her somewhere before? Sitting on a bench seat with hands folded, real classy, she whispers something to the heavy breather in the chair.

I roll towards them, picking up speed, letting my eyes close, feeling the breeze. But when I open my lids, yikes! An oversized chair. *Stop, Bruno!* "Oh shit, we're gonna hit!" Metal clangs. I lurch forward. My neck jerks, as I slam into a man with white spiked hair and a crooked black eyepatch, my footrest wedged under his outstretched leg, which is strapped to some kind of metal brace. What a mess!

I'm sure I've seen this guy around before. I've got a name for him: Scruffy the Fisherman. There's ink on his upper arms—a thick ringed cross on one and a six-pointed Star of David on the other. *Make up your mind, tire kicker!* Shaky, I'm barely able to take a deep breath.

I size him up... a pirate who doesn't know how to steer his ship. With a sneer, I let out, "Ahoy, Cap'n!"

He eyes me back with the eye that still works. Squinting, he grumbles, "What are ya, limey? Crashin' into me like that. Three sheets to the wind?"

Grrrr. Using all my strength, I try to reverse, but I'm good and stuck. To hell with it. I'm not gonna be pushed around by this guy. "You," I say, "were in *my* way.'"

His shoulders stiffen. "Oh Yeah? This here is my spot." He waves his hands in the air. "My spot for livin', my spot for dyin'."

Sitting up straighter, I shoot back, "Well, I'm not dead yet!" I start to untangle the chairs, but then he reverses, finally separating our frames. He turns his chair and blocks me with his battering ram of a leg. A roadblock, cutting off my only path through the crowd—where's my tire iron when I need it?

Never mind. I still have my fists, and I still got a little of the ole boy in me. I'm about to pop him one, but then I notice an attractive woman. Sitting on the bench seat of her wheeler along the window, straight white hair to her chin, white buttoned shirt, hands folded, a classy dame. Her gaze catches mine. I glance at Scruffy, then back at her. Christ, I can't hit him, not in front of a lady. *But this guy deserves to be whacked. Damn.* Looking at white hair, I quietly say, "Excuse me."

His teeth are crumbled, and a new name comes to me as I catch a whiff of his breath: Captain Stinkbreath. This guy needs a few shots of that spray in the little yellow bottle. Comes in handy with the ladies. What's it called? Ba... Baa... Bianca!

Captain Stinkbreath slowly turns his wheels, finally moving his tollgate of a leg so my chair can pass by.

I'll give it to him, pretty clever use of a bum leg.

I adjust my cap and turn my chair, wheeling back away from the crowd. The tick, tick, tick of my wheels louder... the sound of another dent. What the hell, I'm dizzy again. Doesn't usually happen so soon. And sweaty. I gotta pull over. I scan the corridor, the chestnut wallpaper. Where is that tree with the white bark... the birch, where I live? My chair moves in circles, my head spinning. My room, I need my bed. Blankness comes over me—I close my eyes. Pain creeps through my stomach, then the damn gurgling.

I'm supposed to be somewhere, trying to remember. *Maybe an appointment? About a car? A motorcycle?*

Dammit, my sons wanted me to look at that fancy scooter today, talk to that idiot salesman. My sons, sixty-something-year-old kids who believe this place is safer for me than home but think it's a good idea for me to race around in a motorized chair. How's that for logic? Is that what I put them through college for? And salesmen—do I know about salesmen. It takes one to know one, and I know how to make this guy wish he'd never set foot in this place.

Finding the energy that comes with needing to kick someone out of the house, I push my wheels towards the crowd. And there he is, in the far corner, so easy to spot. A young man with an eager face, and a yellow lanyard with a badge hanging from his neck. Impossible to miss. Sticks out like a sore thumb, proudly standing next to a large red scooter, selling what I don't need, a foreign-made gas guzzler.

Hand out, fake smile on his face, Mr. Hopeful says, "Hello, Mr. Romano, great to see you again. I see you're dressed for the tropics in the middle of winter, just like last month. Remember me? It's Philip from American Motor and Seating."

"Oh, I don't recall being introduced. Do you have a card?"

He reaches into his pockets, "Should have a card on me. I'll get you one before I leave."

I shake my head! He's off to a great start. "A good salesman *always* has a card." I take my sunglasses off, resting them on my chest. "What's your name, Sonny?"

He steps closer. "I'm Philip from American Motor and Seating, the mobility enhancement company. Mind if I take a seat?" He plunks himself down in a chair and pulls it closer, making himself comfortable. Too comfortable.

"Philip, right." I wave my hand in the air. "Yes, yes, I know American. Now weren't they... just American Motor, if I remember correctly? I was in advertising, you know. I had the American Motor account."

"Yes, you mentioned that the last time I was here."

Last time he was here? I've never seen this joker. But it's an old salesman's trick—*"Didn't we meet at the conference in Denver?"* I've used it myself, with great success.

"American Motor was the old company—way before my time—just motorbikes back then. Now it's expanded into various utility vehicles, and of course, one of our biggest lines, mobility enhancement machines." He points to the red beast over by the wall.

"Forty-two zero one," I say.

"Excuse me?"

"That was American's account number." I smile. "And they had the Ariel Red Hunter bike. Dunlop wheels, kick start. Beautiful machine."

"Yes, the Ariel Red! That was one of our best-selling bikes—years and years ago. There's a framed picture on the wall in the conference room. Say, you've got some memory, Mr. Romano."

"Call me, Bruno. Do you ride?"

"Me? No. I drive a minivan. Two kids under five and a third on the way."

I sit back. "Well, I don't trust anyone who doesn't use his own product." I point to the scooter. "I bet you sold my sons a story that my life will be better with that hot rod."

He clears his throat. "Well... this, uh, mobility enhancement machine *will* improve your quality of life."

I point my finger in the air. "Listen kid, don't bullshit me. We can speak honestly, right? One salesman to the next?" I put my hand on his pointy shoulder.

"Right, Mr. Romano, I mean Bruno."

"Good. So stop calling that wheelchair on steroids a 'mobility enhancement machine.' It's a fucking scooter."

"Yes, it is." He smiles weakly. "It's a scooter."

"A *fucking* scooter."

"Yes, that's right. A fucking scooter."

Now we're talking. He knows enough to know the customer is always right. I've got him on the ropes and it's only a matter of time until I get him out the door.

Motioning for him to come a little closer, I speak softly, "Listen, Filbert."

"It's... it's Philip."

I put my mouth right up to his ear, where I spot a dab of dried shaving cream. "Now, Phil, I'm gonna tell you something, salesman to salesman." I'm so close I can smell his shampoo, some herbal shit no self-respecting man would use. And now for my zinger. "Snowstorm's coming today. At least six inches. Bad for driving." I look him squarely in the eyes. "Trust me; I feel it in my bones. Age has its advantages, you know. I could be a weatherman."

He steps back, and before he can say anything, I deliver the knockout punch. "I bet you've got three or four more appointments to get in today, ones where you can actually make some money, so you don't want to be wasting your time with me."

He nods like a little puppy dog. "Well, I... I guess I'll have to keep this meeting short then. Your sons wanted you to learn about what a mobility enhancement, I mean, scooter can do for you. There's just enough time for you to take it for a test drive."

I fix my cap and stare into his beady eyes, "Test drive? Sounds like a sales pitch to me, pal. I'm not buying it."

"Mr.... I mean, Bruno, this is a top-of-the-line mobility... or rather, fully electric, power-enhanced scooter with a candy apple red frame, twenty-inch black leather Captain's chair, four alloy wheels for tight turns, front and rear suspension, speeds of up to eleven miles per hour..."

I look past him. "You know, I think the snow is coming down already," he starts to shift on his feet, "and reading me the specs you've memorized for a fucking scooter I don't need is a pretty lame sales pitch."

"Bruno, this scooter is the Hummer of its class."

I look at him blankly, "Hummer? Do you know what a Hummer is?" I close my eyes, the way I used to when I sat behind the wheel of my Mustang and the latest pretty girl put her head in my lap.

"Sorry, Land Rover. The Land Rover of its class."

"Rovers are shit. They spend half the year in the shop."

"OK, well what if I told you, it's the Mustang of mobility... of motorized scooters?"

"Mustang? Now *that* was a car. *My* Mustang was Rangoon red with a black interior: super V-8 engine, three-speed manual transmission, zero to sixty in just over eight seconds. The sound of that car made my engine race," I snort. "And the ladies couldn't get enough of it." I reach for my wallet. "Did I ever show you the picture of my car?"

"I believe you did."

Suddenly my lids are heavy and I'm yawning. Feeling a blast of warm air blowing from a vent in the hallway, I shift my front wheels closer to the heat.

"You seem tired, Bruno."

"Just resting the lids."

The dizziness rolls around in my head, another yawn, my brow starts to sweat, my eyes close...

Where am I? I feel my cap tilted, almost touching my nose, and I push it back as I swallow a few times, clearing my throat of the crap that fills it after a nap.

I glance around... the big glass window... Where are all the people that go nowhere in their chairs? With no traffic to jam me up, I roll close to the window that brings the outside in... and rest my head against the cool glass, squinting at the afternoon sun reflecting off the ice-covered garden. I find my Ray-Bans, dangling on my chest. Eyes soothed, arms resting on my padding, it's good to have the place to myself, but something doesn't feel right in my stomach—there's something I think I should be remembering...

Down the hallway, I spot the receptionist, her honey-colored hair up in a bun, working behind her desk with bouquets of flowers in front of her. *Is today a holiday? Shit, did someone die?*

Rolling towards her, I smile wide. "Hey, honey, lookin' fine today. That's a lovely set." She raises her eyebrows, giving me a look. "I mean your sweaters." She shakes her head. "Now didn't I come down here for something?"

"Bruno, Bruno, Bruno. The salesman was here, but he left in a rush. Something about a snowstorm coming. And he came over here to tell me that you fell asleep. But," she points to the corner, "he left that gorgeous scooter if you want to try it. From what I've seen, it's top of the line." And there it is—shiny red paint, tall captain's chair, thick alloy wheels—but I don't remember talking to any salesman. The receptionist beams at me. "And I know a handsome guy like you would appreciate a first-class ride."

Handsome guy. She's right about that. "Oh, yeah? He was here?" I feel something in my shirt pocket, and take it out, holding it as far away as possible and close to the light from the window. It's a business card: American Motor and Seating, Mobility Specialists, Philip Stowe, Sales Associate.

"Not much of a card. So he came here? Must have missed him." I rub my forehead, trying to clear the fog.

"Speaking of missing, Bruno, you're missing the Valentine's Day party. Do you hear the music?"

Valentine's Day? Well, that explains the flowers.

She continues, "It's happening in the Lido Lounge." Pointing down the hallway with open double doors, she gestures...

I run a finger through my curls and look up at her. "Hey, Be... Baa... baby, we've known each other, right, for a long time? Will you be my Valentine?"

"Come on Bruno. You know I have to stay here at the desk." She pushes her outer sweater aside, revealing a name tag.

I squint. "You know I can't read that. My eyes don't work so well anymore."

Together, we start again, "Beeeeee..."

"Remember, blonde curly hair, German perfume?"

"Beverly, yes Beee-verrr-ley. She was a looker. And you're not so bad yourself."

Rolling her eyes, she purses her lips.

Crap, I know that look. *What did I do?*

I hear footsteps from behind, and Beverly looks over me at a woman walking, pushing the handles of a bench seat, straight white hair to her chin. I always remember a pretty face, but I can't place this one.

"Oh, Edith," the receptionist says with a friendly smile. "The Valentine's party just started. Are you going?"

That straight white hair... Vera's hair turned white when she got older, but it was all curls.

"Oh dear, Bev, am I late? I just needed to get my pocketbook. You know I don't like to leave it in the room. Now, where is the social, dear?"

"The Lido Lounge, head straight through the double doors. And this is Bruno—he was just headed there. Bruno, this is Edith."

I fix my cap, "Hello, Edith." *Edith, Edith, Edith.* For her, I can make it to the party.

"And Bruno," she tilts that bronzed bun on top of her head towards my new lady friend, "Edith needs help carrying these flowers back to her room after the social." From behind her desk, she sighs as she looks at the bouquet. "Such beautiful roses."

Roses. Like the ones they use in those memory boxes in the hallway to mark the ones who aren't here anymore. I sit up in my chair. *No time to think about that now. I got a girl and I gotta keep going.* "She'll be all set with me. I've got room in my chair for those blooms." I look at White Hair—silk scarf, white collared shirt. "Sweetheart, I don't want to forget your name."

"I'm not your sweetheart, but my name is Edith. Edith Sharp."

"Edith." *Edith, Edith, Edith.* "That's a pretty name for a pretty lady." *I don't want to tell her I won't remember it a minute from now.* I roll next to her as she walks, pushing her handles towards the doors of the lounge, and I try to square my shoulders.

Inside the lounge, there's old-time music—loud enough to hear—and people who seem to know me. Not a bad way to start. "Twilight time..." A sea of hearts hangs from the ceiling, and there's that cute rec therapy lady, the one who's always smiling, her big print nametag, "Kim," saving me the trouble of remembering. With long blonde hair flowing down from her head, Kim points to the table of snacks along the wall. In that sweet sing-song voice of hers, "We've got trays of cookies, cakes, red punch—and ice cream coming later! You know, the color red helps keep you awake, and it's good for the mind. So enjoy! Love is everywhere!"

I find an empty table in the corner with plenty of room for the two of us, me and... what the hell was her name? The table is covered with crap. Who needs all this stuff? Tissue-paper roses, a metal heart that looks like it's gonna fall over, vases full of twigs with a few red berries on them. One rose, that's all you need for V-day. And your date's goddamn name.

I'd walk up to Vera holding a rose behind my back. She knew what was in my hand, but she always acted surprised. And the rose didn't really matter. It was me she wanted. I'm all a woman needs for Valentine's Day. Me—and a big box of Fannie Mae chocolates.

We settle in at the table, and I dig into the bowl of red M&Ms—the real ones with the letters on them. My sons may be a pain in my ass, but they put me in a classy joint. Leaning towards my date, I say, "Hey, I got something to show you," nodding my head as I add, "Edith." She looks at me strangely, and then I feel the chocolate dribbling down my chin. I wipe it off with a red napkin.

I search in my shirt pocket and pull out my old Lord Buxton wallet, frayed with time, but the plastic sleeves still show off my photos. Showing her my shirtless picture, leaning on the door of my 1965 Mustang, down at the beach. "Me and my baby."

"What a lovely shade of orange."

"Orange? She was red. Full-body red. Rangoon red—they only made that color for two years."

"Well, it looks orange to me. Now my friend Agnes's car, it's *red*." She studies the snapshot. "What beach is that in the background?"

"Jones Beach," I grumble. *Who cares where it was.*

"I know Jones Beach, know it well. I used to go there with William— my son—and William Sr., his father. We would pack breakfast, lunch, and dinner, spend the whole day. So many memories. I have a picture on my shelf. Or maybe it's at home." She clears her throat.

Shaking my head, "Well, do you like the car?"

She unfolds her napkin and puts it on her lap. "The decorations on the table are lovely, but you should see my house on Valentine's Day."

Did she even notice my ride? Or my physique? What's wrong with her? Maybe she's one that forgets.

"That red hammered heart centerpiece reminds me of one I have at home. Sturdy, the ones that last..." She glances at me. "Like your car, a classic."

So, she did notice. And my smile returns. I wish her name hadn't wandered away.

She continues, "Now my decorations are all in my attic. For when I go back. My attic is the most wonderful place..."

"E... E... E... Edith." *There it is. Thank God, her name comes to me.* "Edith, would you like some cookies, Edith?"

She fusses with the collar of her white shirt, "No thank you, Bruno. I'm not much for sweets."

"Ok, hon, I'll get you something else."

Rolling over to the snacks, my chair lurches forward as I reach for a plate. Feeling the wheels slipping... *steady the frame, Bruno...* just need to use my routine. Right-hand wheel, reach for the lock. Left-hand wheel, lock. Wheels stopped, I put the plate on my lap. Now what did she say? Lots of cookies? No, no, not much for sweets. I remembered! But damn, what's her name?

I grab a plate of fruit and another plate of cookies just in case. All the bases covered. And now that love song is playing. I start humming, "Cupid..." Unlocking the wheels, right, then left, I roll back to the table. Now there are three more ladies! And I thought this was a date!

One is wearing a floral dress, breathing as if she's just run a marathon. Another's got some cockeyed, red-framed glasses matching her dyed red curls, and the last one is bundled up in a yellow raincoat. "Where's the storm?" I want to ask her, but you never know about the people here, and I think better of it.

My date, with the straight white hair, is the best looking of the lot. "These are for her," I say, hoping one of the other ladies will mention her name.

Grabbing the plate, the big in the floral dress says, "Just put the cookies down in the center, young man. We'll share."

"Stella," says the gal with the crooked red shades, "Pass me the fruit. It doesn't have to be just for Edith."

Ahh, Edith!

Edith moves her fingers through her hair. "Oh, thank you, Bruno!"

Nodding my head in her direction, I repeat, "Edith."

She continues, "Now, see those chains of heart cutouts—in fabric—along the wall. At least it's not just cheap paper."

The hefty one waves a big cookie in her hand. "Edy," she coughs, "that's why you need to come to Residents' Council, then you can tell Ruthann Bryon how to fancy up this place."

Suddenly I hear singing. Some kind of island music. The sound is coming from a young man in green, swaying to the beat. He slaps red bowls on the table and starts dumping scoops of vanilla ice cream. My date hardly gets any. So I call out, "Hey, hey, over here, this lovely lady needs more ice cream." But he's not paying attention to us, just moving to his own rhythm. And then he's gone.

"Oh no, that's not necessary," she says.

"No," I bark back, "she *needs* another scoop."

The loud one in the floral dress raises her golden cane in the air and belts out, "Yoohooo, Raffee!"

The guy in green runs back over. "Stella, put the cane down."

She puts the cane on her football field of a lap. "Ice cream here." Smiling, she takes a deep breath from her nose tube and winks, looking over. "Works every time."

The guy in green slaps another scoop into the bowl. "Anything for Ms. Edith." But Edith isn't interested, so Floral Dress grabs it and sucks it down, licking the spoon with every mouthful.

Someone brings a TV to the center of the room, and I make sure my gal can see from where she is sitting. They're showing "Ozzie and Harriet." I settle in, and my reel plays its story.

Leaning back, I put my elbows on my padded armrests and take a long breath. "We know each other, right?"

She gives me a scowl. "Yes, we're acquainted."

"So, I can tell you this. This show reminds me of Vera. That woman was too good for me."

"Your wife?"

"Mmm hmm."

She turns towards me. "Reminds me of William Sr., my husband. An angel, gone too soon." She sighs.

"All I did was disappoint that woman."

"Life is full of disappointments. It never turns out the way we think, especially when it comes to love. I was so angry with William Sr. for dying. Of course, he didn't do it on purpose. And I put flowers on his grave every week for fifty years. Can we get my flowers now?"

A woman in charge. Just like Vera. "Of course." I wait for her to stand. "Ladies first!" Then I pull out from the table and start rolling behind her. It feels like a long way back, but my arms find strength, and I manage to keep pace. *This one can walk!* Suddenly my front wheels turn towards the wall. Pushing down hard on the right, I'm able to straighten out, but it takes all I have, and I need to rest. She keeps moving. But I've got a trick.

I grab the rail along the wall, then give a push, then tap my feet on the floor to pick up speed. *Nothing like a woman to keep you young.*

The receptionist has a bouquet of red, pink, and white roses at the front of the desk. "Bruno, Edith's bouquet may be too big for you to carry."

Edith. I'd forgotten again. I scoff at the receptionist and turn towards my lovely. "Edith, let me take those for you." Rolling closer to the desk, I ease into my routine—right, lock, left, lock. Looking up at the receptionist, I smile. "Hand 'em over."

With my chair steady, I balance the bouquet across my lap, then unlock—right wheel, then left.

The hallway ahead is long, and my front wheels spin towards the wall again, my elbows aching from pushing on the handrail. But I'm just able to keep moving. "My sons want to take away my chair. Get me one with a motor."

"Really. And who could blame them," she says. "That tick, tick, tick, is dreadful."

I frown. "There's nothing wrong with this chair." I slow down. "You know, I never expected I'd be in a chair, but here I am, and this is the chair to have. You just need a routine, to steady it, you know, when you need to carry something." Stopping, I show her. "First, you find the right wheel, then push down on the lock, then you find the left wheel, and lock. With a classic chair like this, I can carry whatever I want." I glance at her wheeler. "But you don't need to know any of this, walking around like you do."

"My son William chose this wheeler for me. It's top of the line. He spares no expense."

I follow her down a hallway lined with wallpaper featuring tall trees and those little nut things the squirrels are always chewing. She stops in front of Room 104. The nameplate says Edith Sharp. *Edith, Edith, Edith.* I try to gaze into her eyes, but she is fiddling with the key around her wrist.

"My room is up a few floors." I double-check her nameplate and proudly say, "Edith, if you want to take the elevator..."

She opens her door. "Oh no, I have to wait for my call. My son, William, I have to thank him for the flowers. I'll take those now." She smiles. "Your name again, so I can thank you properly."

Giving her the bouquet, "Bruno."

"Thank you, Bruno."

She shuffles, keeping close to her wheeler and clutching the vase, then sets it down on the desk near her door.

I lean forward, but she smiles again, partially closing the door.

No goodnight kiss. It's all right. I'm too bushed for a roll in the hay anyway. I push forward a few feet past her doorway to rest. My arms and legs are exhausted. It's been years since I've been on a date. I hear her phone ring.

"Beautiful roses. Thank you, William. I met a nice gentleman. Oh, his name is Br... Br... Bruno, yes, that's it, Bruno. Looks like Mr. Florida in his tropical shirt, but he helped me bring the flowers to my room."

I smile. Never mind Mr. Florida. She called me a gentleman. I look down the hallway—seems longer than usual. I'm sure I have a meeting tomorrow. With someone? I haven't met with anyone recently. I'll have to go down and check with the pretty receptionist. *What the hell is her name?* My boys keep talking about what I need. But what do they know? Pushing down on the handrail, pain shoots from inside my arms, and my wheels hit the wall. "Shit." Lids heavy... dizzy feeling circling in my head... a few beads of sweat on my brow... trying to keep... eyes... open.

A crick in my neck and wet in the corner of my mouth. A staff person walks over. "Falling asleep again, Bruno? You've been snoozing for a while. Let me help you straighten your wheels so you can get to your room."

"No, I don't need help, just resting the lids."

"Are you feeling OK?"

"Can't take a nap around here without everyone thinking you're dying!"

"OK, Bruno. You took a long nap in your chair. Take a minute, then I'll be back."

The dizziness starts to ease, and I take a deep breath. My neck is kinked, and I'm thirsty. *How long have I been out? Maybe this was more than just a nap.* Blinking, I'm able to peer ahead down the hallway and get on my way.

I have just enough strength to push down on my wheels and glide forward. And there it is, the tick, tick, tick of my steady ride. *This chair still works. I still work.* Maybe not as well as I used to, but... Shit! Shit! "SHIT!" I hit the wall in front of me. For Christ sake! Front wheels to the side. I try backing up a few times, but my hands aren't working—they're stinging and numb. I can't push down. Stuck! Staring at the wall, I yell, "To hell with this!"

Broken down, with no one to throw a fist at, I wait. Stranded.

A lady walks out of a doorway and over towards me. "Now back up one wheel at a time. Just go slower. Right wheel back, then lock. Left wheel back, and lock. Then unlock and go."

She sounds like she knows what she's talking about. I wonder where she learned that. Slowly I back the wheels. Right, then left, and straighten out. Sometimes the people around here can be helpful. "Thank you."

"No, thank *you*. I had a lovely time at the party. And if it hadn't been for you, my flowers would still be at the reception desk."

I look back at her. Straight white hair to her chin. Good looking. Seems familiar. "Hey lady, do we know each other?"

St Patrick's Day

Sullivan O'Neill

Bedsheets a mess. Blanket by my ankles, just out of reach. I twist this way. I turn that way. But there's no comfort—or warmth—to be found. My head doesn't turn so easy, so most of the time, the grimy rose-colored curtain, pulled tight from tip to toe, is all I see. I want the sun, but I want the dark more. I want that pill that helps me sleep. Where's the damn cord with the ringer at the end? Arrrhhh, they never come anyway. But I don't want to lose my life preserver. If I can just... arrrhhhh... got it... my SOS, securely in hand. No man dies at sea if he knows his ship and keeps his lines tight. Wasn't that an old Irish proverb? If it isn't, it should be—with my name carved next to it: Sullivan O'Neill. We Irish know a thing or two.

I still feel that cold breeze, only it's not comin' off the water but right through the wall, thin as paper. I wiggle into the dip in the mattress under my back and slide my pillow over my head. I reach for my blanket... but the pain in my shoulder! Rest. I need... rest.

Slumber's comin', but what's that noise? Damn Cortez with his coughing! It's a miracle his lungs are still inside his chest. My belly churns, telling me I need my pills. The little red ones, they're my best friends, never let me down. I squint through my good eye as a bit of sun from under the shade lights up the chipped paint of the cinder block, the part below the finished drywall. That's where the damn draft is coming from—no insulation in there for sure.

In the dark corner, where the two walls meet, crumpled tissues, a plastic fork, and my pee cups scattered along the floor. Add a few long necks and it'd look just like the cave I used to call home. I almost feel safe here, doing time in my house of pain. Almost. *Deep breath, O'Neill, deep breath.* My body feels heavy, joints on fire, back's got knives in it, something stiff on my leg. Acid burns in my stomach. They said they cut the lump out, but I'm sure it's still there, somewhere. Doctor said something about the years I'm not supposed to have. Not much to live for here, except for my lovely pills.

More coughing, and that high-pitched whistling—can't stand it—and then the gasp for air. Enough! Enough of his hacking on the other side of the curtain. Wish he'd go to the other side for good. Grabbing my cup of water, pain shoots through my shoulder as I throw it. "Shut up!" Water splashes on the floor and wet drips down the drape.

Another cough. Sounds like he's retching. That's it! If he needs help, he's on his own. *He's not my brother, and I'm not his keeper.*

There he goes, ringing his call bell... and the noise of his infernal routine begins. The beeping of the alarm, his SOS. The waiting. The coughing. The wheezing. The bang of the door opening against the wall. The soft footsteps on his side of the room, with her rubber-soled shoes. The "Oh, you poor thing," and the "Here, let me help you." With me this nurse is all business, never wants to hear about my pain, or how my meds cut out an hour before the next pill comes. Always sharp with me, like a nun with her ruler, ready to strike. But sweet with him, like a mother hen fussing over her favorite chick. "Let's put on your mask, Mr. Cortez. It's going to make you feel much better."

The mask. Just smother him with it.

"I need my pills!" I yell.

She doesn't answer.

"You're not deaf. I know you heard me."

Nothing.

"Ahhh, to hell with you."

Tinkering noises and the whoosh of the machine, the spray blowing. Rubber footsteps leaving, door closing, coughing quieting. Finally... peace.

But I'm in too much pain to sleep. I shift the patch over my dead eye. *How can they just leave me here?* Months in this bed, cracking up, aching pain everywhere but nowhere, wanting to stay hidden. Brushing the bits of breakfast toast off my T-shirt, I glance at the ink on the loose skin of my upper arms. I remember the fellow who gave me my tats—those light green, almost yellow eyes. A master artist—saw right through me—such a kind-hearted gaze, been searching for it ever since. I stumbled in dead drunk and woke up with my thick-ringed cross on one side, my six-pointed Star of David on the other. I'll need 'em both when I meet St. Peter.

Ah, youth lost in alleyways, spent in bars where liquor burned my throat. Nights enjoying the comfort of a woman—when I could afford her. But my best times were out on the water—alone—nothing but me, sea, and sky. I glance further down my forearm. Through the wrinkles, I can see Betty's big cartoon face, black hair, round body, eyes winking, ready with the life preserver, answering the prayer of the SOS. She's the one who will never leave me. The two of us will ride the waves—into the storm together—just me and my girl.

Age doesn't leave a man with much. A broken body. A sour stomach. Some fading pictures on my skin. But that master artist, surely dead by now, gave me somethin' besides my ink: my little black case with my sweet music maker.

Somewhere between my ragged teeth and my sore gums, my tongue discovers a bit of bacon, the flavor still good. Shame to waste it, so I spit it out and put it on my bedside table, just in case.

One day soon, the eyes, or in my case, eye, won't open. It's the way of all flesh. But when death, my welcomed friend, finds me, I'll know where I am. The sand under my toes will finally make 'em warm, and the sun reflecting off the water will be so much brighter than this dark dungeon, because I'll be walking again, pain free, on my beach.

Arrrh, this neck. Where's my pillow? Acid churns in the back of my gullet. I start to close my eyes, think about what it'll feel like when I go, but what's that shaft of light streaming under the shade? It's so bright, I have to squint. Behind the patch my dead eye squints too, even though it went dark all those years ago. Sunk in my bed, I shift my weight—why can't I sit all the way up? I know I'm not the man I used to be, but this is too much.

I can barely see out through the strip of window where the light's coming in. But I can see the sky! So bright and blue it doesn't seem real. And those clouds—crisp, white puffs, what do you call 'em—a sign of clear sailing ahead. And there, farther in the distance, patches of ice and snow down the valley, and a glint of the river. Feels like it was last week, bait between my teeth, boat on the water, captain of my own ship. *Where the hell are these good thoughts comin' from… maybe some extra pill they're giving?* The best fishing was when the full moon dipped lower at sunrise. All alone, the sea like glass, I'd wait, soaking in the quiet, then open the little black case and take out my harmonica. Ahhh, the sweet sounds of my Saoirse.

Where is she? Is she here? Where's my black case? Did someone…? They move things around here. I'm sure they took it, just like my apartment. Always some reason it's all taken away. But that, that box… there she is, behind the damn lamp. Now I can breathe.

And there's my baby picture. That little fellow had no idea of the rough seas ahead—if only I could have warned him. And my baseball with the pinstripes—a souvenir from the only game my dad ever took me to. And the picture of my boat moored at the dock where this river meets the sea. The sandy shore of my beach, with the warm breeze, waiting for me.

God, everything hurts! My back and my leg, my shoulder, just from straining to look out the window. They never give me enough of those damn pills to take all the pain away. "Get me some weed!"

Ahhh, there's my door hitting the wall... maybe it's time for more of those little round crackerjacks that make everything OK. Footsteps closer, but not ones I recognize. Shuffling feet, and voices—females—a group of them! Not the clanging noise of that housekeeper I have to keep from cleaning near my bed, or the thud of the maintenance boots barging in to fix the shades. Residents!

I'm used to growling at all my unwelcome visitors, but I soften my tone and ask, "Who's here?"

An older woman's voice. "This isn't the store."

Another. "No, it's not the right hallway."

The first one again. "This is definitely not Keepers' Mart. I think someone lives here."

Now a third one chimes in. "Errr we're goin' ta Ireland. Mae family's missin' at home."

I know that voice. She's missing more than a few marbles. If they're lookin' for the store, they're definitely lost. I clear my throat, "Hello, over here, other side of the curtain." Damn Cortez's machine. I can barely hear the ladies.

"Oh, thank goodness! We are looking for the store—Keepers' Mart? Do you know where the store is? Stella, what's that noise?"

Joints aching, back spasming, I try to reach the curtain, and I'm just able to grab the edge and slide it back a bit to see what the wind has blown my way.

"Arrrh!" Light comes pouring in from Cortez's window and I slap my hand over my seeing eye. Blinking, I notice not three but four friendly visitors. Damsels in need of a safe harbor... what a day for an Irishman! "Ahoy!"

White Hair pushes her bench seat in and gives me the once over, then turns to beckon the others. Rolling in behind her is the bat in the yellow raincoat, and another with fire-red hair she surely wasn't born with and sparkly red spectacles. The last one is sucking in air from a portable tank and has huge flowers on her dress.

"Just look at the trash on this side of the room," says White Hair, her brow furrowed. "A disgraceful mess! Roula we are in the wrong place."

The one in the flowered dress bellows and splutters, coughing, "Edith, yoohoo, back this way. I told you this is the wrong floor. But you insisted on leading the way. What's gotten into you today? Don't bother these gentlemen."

Gentlemen. Ha! If only white-hair Edith knew. Cortez hunched in his bed, mask hissing, that ratty blue scarf 'round his neck like a noose. And me, in my sweaty sheets, unshowered, unshaven. I stare at Cortez to see if he heard, and his eyes, wide as saucers, suddenly meet mine.

He blinks first. I turn to greet my visitors. "Nice people like you don't usually come 'round this neighborhood," I say, slipping into my Irish accent. "You're on the wrong side of the tracks." I snicker at my own joke. "But don't mind Cortez, here. He won't be around to bother us much longer. You know..." I fake a horrible hacking cough.

"Oh, dear. Another rose on the wall..." says Edith, fussing with her white hair.

I sit up straighter, as strong men do.

She shakes her head. "I have my wits about me enough to know we all have to die somewhere, from something," then looking at the floor around his bed, "but this way? In squalor?"

"Damn housekeeper," I shout, noticing the cups, crumpled napkins, and papers strewn around my bed, "the one with the limp. She never comes to clean."

Fixing her collar, Edith says, "Now how *did* we get here? I've always been good at directions, and I told them to follow me, and well... this is *not* the route to the store. It's via Route 9 back at home—well, Agnes drives—but... I'm not there. I'm all mixed up. But I've always known where to go. I navigate by landmarks, but it's hard to find them here. It just looks different. The hallways... there are too many doors. Someone told me to always decorate my door. Oh dear. I was feeling so good today." She looks down at the floor.

Now the redhead, pushing her red specs up into her nest of curled hair, turns to me, "What a colorful accent you have! Are you from Ireland? Our friend Nellie's from Ireland. Maybe you're related?"

"The batty one? Nahhh, but she could be related to me brother. Both of 'em loons." I smile. "Now ladies, it's been so long since I've had real company. My name is Sullivan O'Neill, and my Irish comes out in the presence of angels. Remind me of your names again?"

Edith points to the redhead. "This is Roula," then to the one in the yellow raincoat, "and Nellie," then to the one in the flowered dress, "and Stella."

"Would ya' like to set down?" Turning to try to get out of bed, only one leg moves, and I flinch as pain grips my hip. "Damn immobilizer!"

"Immobilizer?" Edith stares at me.

"Grrr." I rub the scruff on my face. "I'd offer you all seats, but my leg is anchored and my extra chair—stolen. I'd need that damn lift to hoist me out of bed."

"We don't need no seats," Stella huffs. "We come prepared with our chairs. Edy even has a bench."

Nellie rolls her wheelchair up close to my breakfast. "His eye, ders a patch," she says to no one. "Take that patch off!"

"And his hair? Standing up straight as an arrow! How do you get your hair to stand up like that?" Roula asks. "Is it mousse or gel? Do you tell the stylist cornstalk or beanstalk? And is shocking white your natural color?"

"The ladies have always loved me curls." Suddenly, Nellie stands, wobbles, and reaches for the sugar on my tray. "That one's going to fall!"

"And that she is," Stella laughs, "but that don't stop her from goin' for the sugar."

"Nellie, leave his sugar alone!" Roula barks. Nellie jerks back her fingers and lands in her chair.

"Ehhh, take 'em. I drink my coffee black... with a shot of whiskey." Cortez's eyes are closed, but I know him, he'll try to get their attention soon. It's only a matter of time. "Help me pull that curtain closed."

Now Edith is agitated. She gives me a stare like the nuns who slapped me with their rulers. "This room is a *mess*. Someone needs to do the dishes. And just look at those trays, piled with half-eaten sandwiches. I'm surprised you don't have vermin in here."

"I've never been one to turn away a good sandwich. But a few months back, the kitchen started messing up my order, sending me ham and Swiss on rye instead of corned beef. So..."

"That's *my* sandwich!" She shakes her bony finger just an inch from my face.

"Well, if it's for the taking..."

"It is most certainly *not* for the taking. But the taking doesn't surprise me. You look like one of those vagrants. And," she sniffs, "you need a shave and a good hot shower. I made my son shower every day, and I always kept a clean home."

I wave my hand in the air, "This ain't my home, now that's for sure."

Edith looks at me all odd, her eyes a pale blue, maybe green. Then, in a quieter voice, "No, I suppose it isn't."

I stare back. She's probably old enough to be my mum, but I feel older. "The water is my home with my companion, Saoirse." I reach towards my bedside table and I'm just able to grab my black case, rubbing my fingers over the etching. "Hand-carved, the image looks different each time, gold paint can only be seen in the light." I wait until she shows me her baby blues again. "I'll die here. That's the plan, but me harmonica needs to be taken care of. She's a part of history."

Edith perks up, "Did you ever see the wall of history at the Poughkeepsie Town Hall? I created that when I worked there."

My harmonica heavy in my hand, "She don't belong on no wall, my Saoirse. She needs someone to play her." I blow through the holes, vibrations cool against my lips, as always. After I stop, the harmony lingers. "Do *you* have a companion?"

"Well, William Sr., God rest his soul, is always with me."

I try to keep their names straight. Roula redhead, Nellie screw loose, Stella stuffed into that chair, and Edith with the white hair. Four ladies—in my room—maybe my luck is changing.

Edith slides the corner of the curtain forward, and I close it at last. No more Cortez. Now I can entertain my guests. Spin a good yarn, just like me dad. The ole man… never gave me a word of praise, only the back of his hand. My stomach churns the way it did all those years ago. I shut my eyes, trying to stop remembering.

Out on the water together, a long neck bottle in my ole man's hand. I was learning to do the lines. But I couldn't hold the weight of the thick, twisted fibers. Burning, slipping through my fingers, and suddenly—overboard! The sting of knuckles across my face. His hand pushing my back. The splash, the cold, as I'm over the sides and into the water with the lines.

"Swim, Sully!"

Arms and legs thrashing, gasping for air, body heavy, sinking, going down. Pushing my head above the surface, mouth full of ocean salt. Yelling for help, but only gurgling. Heart racing. The side of the boat—too high—drifting away… blackness of water all around. Kicking, fighting, losing my strength. Needing the breath… pushing for air. Flailing. Finally, a flash of red floating towards me. The old, round, cracked life preserver tumbling over the waves.

"That'll teach you."

A vise grips my chest. I can't breathe, as if it's happening right now. My lungs feel full of water, even though I'm on dry land.

Cortez's muffled voice comes through the curtain. "O'Neee, you bueno? Agua?" he asks.

"No!" I scream. "No agua! No agua!" Slowing my breath, I shake the ole man out of my head. I look at the ladies, rub my forehead. And then it comes to me, what'll make me feel better. We O'Neills know how to tell a tale.

"It's yarn-spinning time," I say, coughing through my fear, "and I don't mean knitting. Listen," I lean back, "did I ever tell you about my accident? Had a fall, I think it was not long ago, then the leg. But no one here listens about the pills."

"Don't get me started on the pills," Roula cackles. "You're either waiting forever, or they're telling you you've already had them."

Stella pats the folds of her dress. "That's what pockets are for."

"They just want to hoist me out of this bed. Won't give me no whiskey neither, only on holidays. I have an order, they say. And even then, only a nip."

Nellie chimes in. "Nip of it."

I scratch the scruff on my chin. "But there's something here, come closer, look out this window." My good eye blinks, and its blind partner does the same. "Do you see it? The light off the water. A perfect day for catching fish."

"Every Irishman has a fish story," says Stella, her head bobbing up and down as she shifts in her chair. I ignore her.

"I was in a storm once, the waves comin' right up over the sides ready to drown me. A storm that makes a man start talking to you-know-who upstairs." I point upwards. "But I kept my eyes on the horizon. And I worked to stay afloat all night. A man of the sea knows how to balance the weights, empty the buckets, hold fast to the lines." The ladies' eyes widen. "Anyone got a toothpick?" I run my tongue along my crumbling teeth. "The ole man, the one thing he taught me: a good story should be told with a bottle in one hand, a toothpick in the other. Did I ever tell you about my boat?" Just like at the bar, the ladies need a reason to stay, to hear the good part.

I point towards the window with my crooked finger. "You gotta keep your eyes on the horizon. No sailor who knows his boat should ever die at sea. Once I knew I was in the clear, I looked up—at the blackness above and all around—and I took out my harmonica, still safe and dry in her box. Alone is the best way to hear Saoirse's music. Alone and knowing she'll never leave me. The next morning, I woke up to the sunlight sparkling off the waves." Smiling, I rest my hands across my belly.

"Your boat?" asks Edith, pointing to the picture on the dresser.

"Aye, there she is," I tilt my head towards the Kodachrome, "anchored on my beach."

"I know that type. My son William had one, took it out as a boy on the river all the time, coming home with buckets of crabs. What did he call it? A dinghy!"

"She ain't no dinghy! Did your son ever catch a sixty-pound striped bass?" I clear my throat. This woman is irritating. "Now, weren't you asking about how to get somewhere?"

"Oh, yes, I'm all set to go home, I still have my key." She tugs on a bracelet around her arm. "William knows I'll be going home soon. But, as he says, I'm here for... right now."

Nellie picks up an empty cup. "Err, right now, mae cookies are done, but the tay, wait for the color to be ready, and te honey. Good with candy, too."

"Nellie," says Edith, "now I remember where we were headed, to the store with the candies."

"Mmmm hmmm." Stella crosses her arms and shakes her head.

"Pearl gets the soft caramels for me, and I share them with you. You *always* want more caramels. You have a sugar problem. But I suppose we all need one good piece of candy to celebrate the holiday. Maybe a green mint."

The holiday. Which one? And then I feel the joy shooting through me, like that first sip of whiskey at the bar. I smile. The one day a year my ship comes in. The holiday for the Irish.

"And today is St. Patrick's Day," she says, straightening down her helmet of white hair. "My mother was Irish—a Brennan—and I have a big leprechaun, almost full-sized, in my attic at home. Looks a little like you with that scruffy beard!"

This one's insufferable. I breathe in and let the breath out slowly. I can't be angry. Not today. *Paddy's Day!* The bright sun, light dancing off the water, the visitors, the lightness in my belly. Now it all makes sense. My day has found me. And later if I'm lucky, some Irish coffee—with a kick.

"Well, now that we all know where we are going," Edith pushes up on the handles of her bench seat, "we'll have to hurry to the store. Pearl closes at noon."

I used to go to the store, pick up a pack of toothpicks, can of Orange Crush, get the latest scoop from the nurses on who's causin' trouble, but now, just getting up to go to the john... with this bum leg, it's all too much. "Ahoy, ladies. The store is in the basement. Take the elevator down until you can't go down no more."

Edith pushes her bench seat, and one by one they roll out the door just the way they rolled in.

I peer out at my shaft of bright sun landing on the river. The freedom of the water. The only place that felt like home. All my crap jobs, all my crap bosses—they could hire me, or fire me, but out there—screw everyone, I'm the captain.

Footsteps down the hallway, coming closer to the door, sounds like a fancy shoe. And something else... scurrying. Could it be that miserable excuse for a dog?

"Hello! Mr. O'Neill. Hello! Mr. Cortez! It's Jen, your favorite social worker! Happy St. Paddy's Day! I'm sure you heard me coming. I should know better than to wear heels with these long corridors. But that's what I get dressing up for the holiday!"

Jen's a looker. The whoosh of the curtain sliding across the rod sends a slight breeze across my forehead along with the smell of her sweet perfume. I see her glowing round face, and, on her pretty head, a sparkling green top hat with four-leaf clovers over her shiny brown locks. What a lovely lass! My eye opens wider. I'm suddenly alert.

"Mr. O'Neill," she smiles, "Isn't it a wonderful day? Look who's chipper with such a big smile. Must be my hat!" She shakes her head as the clovers dangle. "But," she waves her hand under her nose, "ooooh, you need a good shower and shave and we need to work on those teeth."

"What I need, lassie, is a drink."

She sighs. "Some things never change. Now, we have to talk about why you are refusing care and barking at the housekeeper when she tries to clean your side. I thought we had an agreement."

"I didn't agree to anything. Go talk to the hacker, then come back to me."

She turns and pulls the curtain closed—the one time I'm actually liking the light.

"Ohhh, Mr. Cortez," she says, "let me see those baby blues. So handsome with that scarf. Everyone says your eyes are like looking into the ocean."

He couldn't last a day out on the water.

The scurrying of feet, a few yips. That pooch of hers.

"Dexter! Here boy! Say hello to Mr. Cortez." I hear the mutt's collar clanging. "We're so lucky to have Dexter as our emotional support animal at River's Edge. He knows just where to go." Her voice higher now, like she's speaking to a baby, "You've jumped up and found a spot on his bed. Good boy! Dexter knows a good soul."

Stupid dog. My Henry Morgan was smart. A German Shepherd—the smartest. That night, after the bars closed, bad crowd with broken long necks pointin' my way, Henry Morgan risked his life trying to protect me. Growling and barking somethin' fierce, he wouldn't let those bums get close.

I glance at the pile of bacon on my tray—it won't take much to distract this cur.

Her voice even higher, "Now, Mr. Cortez..."

"Pleeeez, my name, Mau... ri... ci... o."

Unbelievable. He's flirting with her from under his mask.

"Such a beautiful name..."

Grrr. For such a horrible person.

"Now let's make you more comfortable," she continues. "I can help you with your mask, looks like the medicines are done. Don't tell anyone, I'm not supposed to help the nurse, but let's take that off so we can talk."

A few weak coughs, "Theenk you."

Those are his coughs for her. I know his real coughs.

"Well, Mauricio, it's nice to see you again. How *are* you today?"

"Bueno."

"Bueno my arse. He's gonna suffocate one of these days. But he brings out his best Spanish for the pretty ladies."

"So," her voice more serious now, "I'm here on business for both of you. Not to wreck the holiday spirit, but it's quarterly assessment time. We'll have our conversations, then I'll be back later for the St. Patrick's Day celebration—don't want to deprive you of the good stuff. But now let's check to see if you need help making decisions. Just a quick review."

"We'll have our conversations," I say, imitating the fake happy in her voice. Review the plan—for my dying... help with decisions—they're *my* decisions.

"OK, Mr. Cortez... *Mauricio,*" her voice all singsong, "on your demographics sheet, your birthday, September 9th. A Virgo, just like me! Sensitive, caring—we do things a little better than others."

"Ahem" flies out from the back of my throat.

She cackles. "And everything is filled out: religion: Catholic, emergency contact: Manuel Cortez."

"Si! Manny!"

"Yes, your handsome grandson."

"Mi nieto, he clean three months now."

Clean? Who is he kidding? That kid steals my extra chair for the visitors, smacks his gum, rattles on about twelve steps. The streets teach you all you need to know. I always had a job, a place of my own, twelve steps from the bar. Last call was 4:00 am.

"Now," she keeps at it, "words to remember. I'll ask you about them later. Here they are, sock, blue, bed. I can say them in Spanish if you want."

Coughing, and sputtering, "So-ock, Blu-ue, Be-e-ed."

"Excellent, excellent. Now, I'll ask you what those words were in just a few minutes. On to the wellness check. Are you able to do the things you enjoy?"

What a question. How can anyone enjoy anything in this place?

"I pa-aint."

"Yes, the nurses tell me you insist on making the journey to the art room every day, but that you've been more tired recently. Is it harder for you to get out of bed?"

More coughing, "Si, si... the li-i-i-ift."

"Right. You need the lift now, and then a driver to roll you to the basement. With all that, how do you feel you are doing?"

"I pa-a-a-int."

He pa-a-a-ints. To hell with this guy. Thinks he's Picasso. The li-i-ift, the cha-a-air, the gra-a-ave. *Once you start, there's no going back.* I'd be out on my boat, if I could just get this damn leg working.

"Mauricio," she blabbers on, "I've noticed the hallways have a few more paintings hanging since you've moved in. Your Starry Night looks so beautiful near the lobby."

"Paintings are dead art," I grumble. "But song, like I make with my Saoirse, hangs in the air forever."

Ignoring me, she keeps chattering, "And I saw another one of yours on the wall in the art room... somewhere in the Mediterranean perhaps, that glorious blue water seen through the small opening of a broken wooden door. That's some painting. You are an inspiration."

"The do-or... to other side... mi, mi cuerpo... muy cansado... how you sa-ay, tired? I stay... for Manny."

Enough. I throw some bacon on the floor. Thump. Small feet scurry and the bottom of the drape rustles as the pooch with its mop of brown curls pokes its head up from underneath the folds to gobble the meat. I stare at the dog. Henry Morgan would have eaten it alive. This can't be a real dog, maybe some sort of half-breed?

"Dexter," she barks, "we are checking in with *one* at a time. Come back and sit with Mr. Cortez. We want to hear more about his painting."

I used to paint houses inside and out. I didn't get these strong arms from nothing... and his itty-bitty brush marks are what she talks about.

"I pa-aint for Manny."

"I remember your grandson from the family meeting, blue eyes same as yours. And so sweet. He wanted to make sure you had everything you might possibly need."

Damn family meetings, little Cormack, four years younger, trying to be in charge of me, his older brother. He didn't do such a great job when he poked my eye out with the scissors. An accident, he was just a child they said, but still... old enough to have known better.

Chirping like a bird, she says, "In all my years of working, I'd never been to a family meeting with children, grandchildren, and great-grandchildren."

"Mi familia. We are... how you say, ble-essed."

"Shaddup. The only thing blessed is an Irishman with a pint." I wonder if she heard me.

"Now, Mauricio, do you remember the three items I mentioned earlier?"

Nothing from Cortez. But I can think of three words: Leave. Me. Alone.

"Mr. Cortez, do you remember the words?"

His coughing starts again. "Agua, agua!"

I've got a full pitcher on my table, but he's on his own.

A loud clank. Hard plastic hits the floor. The rope line, a call bell, falling on the tile. I check: mine's still in hand. He's the one without his SOS.

"You dropped your call bell, Mr. Cortez. Here you go. I don't want you losing it. Sometimes these clips get loose. I'll attach this to your *bed*."

Hmmph... a hint... his lucky day.

"Now, the words. How about something you wear on your feet to keep warm?"

"Como se?... Sssock."

"Good! Now how about the other two words? A color? I'm not supposed to give you a hint, but the color of your eyes?"

"Blue."

"And the last one, what are you lying on right now?"

"La cama."

"In English?"

He lets out a huge, spit-filled cough. "Be-e-e-ddd."

"Excellent cognition. Let's move on to the paperwork. We're going to review your code status. Should something happen, your heart stops, or you stop breathing, we need to confirm your wishes, see if anything's changed since you first moved in."

Wishes... I wish to be out on the water, riding the waves.

"If your heart stops, Mr. Cortez, or you stop breathing, do you still want us to revive you, with the chest pumps, the tubes, and machines? Or do you *not* want resuscitation?"

Another gob of phlegm comes up. It's a miracle he can speak. "If I... you no-no come take care of me? You leave me to... die?"

"Of course we'll take care of you, Mr. Cortez. We want to bring the *type* and *level* of care *you* want. We can do everything to save you... or, if your heart has stopped and you haven't been breathing for a while, we can respect the time of passing and not intervene. It's called 'Do Not Resuscitate.'"

"Spaniards do *not* give up. Restusticate! Restusticate!"

"OK, no change. I'm going to check this box: Full code."

Spaniards shmaniards. He thinks he's gonna live forever. I'm not giving up either. But I'm done here. I'm goin' fishing. I'm falling asleep in this bed—don't wake me up ribs broken, barely breathin' and peein' and eatin' through tubes, worse off than I was before. If I'm on my beach, and I'll know because the light will be brighter, I'll be seeing with both eyes, and if they pull me back with their rib-crackin' and heart zappin'... there'll be hell to pay.

"OK O'Neill, your turn, I'm going to open your curtain. Are you, ahem, decent?" The hooks on my drape begin to rattle, waiting. "Dexter, over here now."

I feel the wind from the curtain as she brushes it aside, and I squint from the light. Such a comely lass, but that ridiculous hat with four-leaf clovers hides her pretty face. No real Irish girl would wear such a thing.

Quickly, all business now, "O'Neill, you know the routine for the quarterly rounds. A few words to remember and then the questions. Any concerns?"

"Well, I do have a little itch..." I point towards my shoulders.

"O'Neill," she shakes her head, the shamrocks on her hat wiggling, "why are you still in your pajamas? By this time in the morning, the staff has everyone dressed."

"I am dressed."

"You," she says, "are in a johnny coat. Looks like you've been in it for a while. In fact, I heard, the last time you agreed to get out of this bed was a month ago, Valentine's Day. They had you cleaned up, not quite shaved, but for you... well, Bev at reception said you almost looked happy wheeling around the lobby."

"I'd be happier if you'd scratch me back." But she ignores me. "And the reason I was out is because his whole damn family took over the room. All that talk... and all that prayin'. I had to get out. Besides," I narrow my eyes at her, "who says I don't *want* to get up? I'd be out and about if it weren't for this damn prison iron on my leg."

"Good, I'll tell the nurses you'd like to get cleaned up today. A shower, a clean shirt, and don't refuse the shave. Then I'll be back later tonight with your St. Patrick's Day treats. Some warm soda bread and your favorite—the Irish coffee."

"With a kick!"

"Only if you're clean and shaved when I come back tonight."

"For you and a pint, I'll shave."

"Always the same shenanigans, O'Neill. You know, if you had just asked for help to get around you probably wouldn't have fallen, and now you're stuck with that immobilizer on your leg. You're still refusing your follow-up orthopedic appointments and the medicine for your stomach," she wrinkles her cute little nose, "and those teeth."

"Toothpicks work fine."

"Impossible. That's what you are. Your brother always says you've been like this..."

I clear my throat and boom, "Over my dead body will that baby brother of mine make any decisions for me. He never knew the back of the ole man's hand."

With her head shaking and that stupid hat, is she stifling a laugh? "I don't see what's funny about it."

"We go round and round on this every time. If you won't cooperate, we could have the state appoint someone..."

"Ehhhhh!" I wave my hand in the air. "The state never cared much for me. Don't know why they'd start now."

"Listen, if you want your nip of whiskey, you'll get cleaned up and we'll get through these questions. I have things to do to prepare for tonight. Now, quick check of the demographic sheet. And look at that... your birth date, November, a Scorpio, fearless, but hard to handle that sting. And religion, still *undecided?*"

"I was raised Catholic, but whiskey's my religion. Who needs Jesus Christ when you've got Jack Daniels, Jim Beam, and Jameson?"

"Moving right along, words to remember: sock, blue, bed. Repeat them back to me?"

"Always the same words. How 'bout you take your damn blue sock and shove it where the sun don't shine."

"Aaaaand, are you able to do the things you enjoy?"

"Do you enjoy pissin' in a plastic pan?"

"If you'd take the lift to get out of bed, go to physical therapy, and listen to your doctors, you might be able to get back to using a walker."

"Blarney!" I scream. "I'm not being hoisted up with those chains."

"I think we can skip whether you're happy with your roommate..."

I nod my head in his direction. "Grrr."

"Last on the list. Code status."

"You can forget about those damn tubes. After a life like mine, I want a good death. Do everything to make me comfortable at last. And if someone pulls me off of my beach..." Her eyes are beautiful, brown, the color of whiskey. "Well, you know..."

"OK, no changes to your paperwork since last time. Do not resuscitate, check."

"Restusticate! Restusticate!" Cortez shouts from the other side of the curtain.

"Not you, Mr. Cortez," she says. "Him."

"Just leave me on me beach."

"No funeral, check."

"Not payin' for other people to drink."

"Cremation, check. But we need your signature. And what will be done with your ashes?"

"X marks the spot. You're going to scatter 'em at sea, aren't ya?"

"Now you know I can't do that myself. But I can put in your request."

"Well, at least that's something. The old inkmaster's words have stayed with me, just as permanent as his tattoos. And I know he's right. He told me, you will live your life by the way you see your end."

Her eyes wide, she tilts her head. "I'll be back later with your Paddy's Day treats." She turns, and the whoosh of curtain blows a breeze across my face.

I must have been sleepin', because she's back now, rolling her cart in. My face is smooth. They used the electric this time, not one of those cheap women's razors. My shirt feels stiff, and I can smell the starch.

Cortez coughs and says, "Come, come... siiiit."

"Are you coughing again? I'll ask the nurse for your mask."

"No, no. Eees OK."

"Would you like coffee or a vanilla flavored shake?" she asks. "The vanilla shake is green but not mint-flavored."

"Greeeeeeen."

"That's the spirit, Mr. Cortez," she says. "We're all Irish today."

"All Irish my arse."

She continues, "And here's a nice big piece of soda bread. Be sure to break it into little bits. And small sips of the thick shake—can't have thick shake in the lungs. If you cough while you're eating... Now, let me just pop in and give O'Neill his drink."

I close my eyes and breathe deep. The curtain parts. There she is. Her face glows even at night.

"Mr. O'Neill! A clean shave and a spiffy shirt. I hardly recognize you."

She grabs a large mug piled high with melting cream and a huge piece of bread. "Sometimes, O'Neill, wishes really do come true. The nurse said your doctor gave the order: Irish coffee, with a kick of Jack."

"How about *two* kicks?"

"Don't push your Irish luck."

Ahhh, the sweet smell of the cream mixed with coffee and the hint of whiskey. I dive in and feel the tingling on my tongue, the burning in my throat, the warmth in my belly. Memories of the bars, freedom.

"I've never seen a grin that big from you," she smiles back. "Would you like me to open your shade? You can still catch the sunset."

Right now, she could say anything. It used to take a pint or two, but now a nip of Jack makes all the difference. I nod. I let her fix my broken shade, adjusting it a little higher. The last bit of sun, deep orange, some yellow, evening sky.

"Enjoy," she says. "Do you want the curtain between you and Cortez closed now?"

I nod my head and bite into the bread. "You're leavin' already?"

"I'm just going to talk with Mr. Cortez for a minute." She slides over to him, closing the curtain.

I swallow my emotions the way I always have—with my drink. My best friend. And my sweet Betty, faded, but still right here on my arm. The kick swirls in my head, a few crumbs left of my bread.

Down the hatch with the rest of it.

I hear singing before I realize it's me, "Irish eyes a'smilin'."

Then, from the other side of the curtain, "Mauricio, it's always great talking to you, but I have to go. Take little sips of that thick shake, and try not to swallow the wrong way. Enjoy. Goodnight!"

I raise my empty glass, "My angel."

Suddenly Cortez starts coughing, a gasping I haven't heard before.

Licking the cream off my lip. So sweet. I think about my boat, the spray all around as the water gets choppy. My head spinning, a good spin. Ahhh, Paddy's Day. Everything is as it should be. Except for the damn hacking.

He'll probably start his usual routine: fumbling for his bell, a call to the nurse, the machine with the whirring. Happens every time.

But he just keeps sucking in, like a vacuum with something stuck in it that can't draw any air. Why on earth doesn't he call? They can put his mask on, and I can enjoy my buzz. Or he can wheeze to death. I don't suppose I'd miss him, or that whole damn family—takin' over my room, stealin' my guest chair, to hell with them all.

Now he's heaving, the vacuum tryin' to clear the clog.

And then I hear something clank against the floor.

His call bell. I know that feeling too well, a loose rope, an SOS out of reach. I look down, where the curtain meets the floor, but don't see anything. I feel around in my sheets for mine, search between my covers. Where is it? Maybe I dropped it, too? Finally, I find the line and haul my life preserver in tight to my hand. Dizziness swirls in my head, and I close my eyes to keep my ship steady.

Maybe he'll live, maybe he'll die. It's in God's hands, above my pay grade.

I pull the covers up to my neck to rest.

But I can't sleep.

I look at my arm, Betty staring up at me with those cartoon eyes, sharing her life preserver... Betty and I, riding the waves together.

He's dying.

I'm dizzy.

What if he gets there before me?

"Ehhh," I mumble, "It would finally be quiet in here."

But what if he gets to my beach, takes my spot, and I go to that other place? The place without light. That's in God's hands too.

It's quieter now. His lungs are tired. No air. The blackness of the water in all directions, the sides of the boat moving farther away. Betty looking up at me, reaching to share her circle of safety, telling me to hold on.

No sound at all. Is this it? And then I hear his voice, except he can't be talking, because I know he's not breathing. But I still hear it. "Restusticate! Restusticate! Spaniards never give up!" The fear of the rope slipping out of my hands makes me tremble. *OK, Betty, I remember how it feels to lose the line. You don't need to remind me.* I grab my button and press it hard...

And then I wait for the routine to start. The beep of the alarm. The clip of the nurse's rubber-soled shoes, the mask, the hissing of the machine, and when they realize how far gone he is, the call for the ambulance... and then the heavy steps of the boots that will bring him to the hospital.

I hear them coming. But it feels slow. What's taking so long?

"Keep your eyes on the horizon, Mauricio. They're comin' to steady your ship."

The wheeze is soft. *Christ, he's barely breathing.* The last one went just like this, and the one before him, too.

"Help is on the way, my friend. But," I raise my voice to make sure he hears, "I'm warning you: if you get there before me... stay off *my* beach."

Finally, they burst into the room. Heavy boots. Tense voices. My curtain sways with the commotion.

No shipwreck tonight, partner. No Spanish galleon sinkin' into the sea. Not on St. Paddy's Day. Not on your life.

"May luck always be in favor of your wishes."

As they hover over him, I look on my nightstand and reach for my Saoirse, grasping her case. I open the black box. The metal of the harmonica, heavier than I remember. But damn, she feels good in my hand. The cold frame around my lips. Clearing my throat, I take in a deep breath, then let out the slow vibrations of sadness that soothe the soul. The sweetness of the gallows song fills the room, as Danny Boy brings us home.

Mother's Day

Terri Riley, Nellie's daughter

Almost a year and I still can't get used to it. As I walk up to the sliding glass doors of River's Edge, I hear a shrill yell coming from a window high above. Unmistakably Mom—probably her purse, can't find it. I'm sure that's all it is.

Once inside, I stare at Bev, the receptionist, with her stiffly sprayed bun, smug over her sign-in list. She'd never make it in my fourth-grade classroom where you can't call security every time someone gets out of line.

I scribble my name along with the time in: 12:00 noon. Back when Sundays were normal, Mom used to serve lunch. Then I made it—or packed it up—and brought it. Then she moved in with me. Now I have to sign in. With Bev. To this place.

"Excuse me, Terri." Her voice matches her lacquered hair.

Turning my shoulder away, I figure she'll get the message. I pick up my flowers, my balloons, my bags, and step towards the elevator, hoping to get to Mom's room in time for lunch. I need to get there before she starts her pattern of following the others to her usual spot in the dining room. I've learned not to interrupt her routine, since she threw her purse at me a few weeks ago. The buckle nearly grazed my eyebrow.

"Terri."

Ugh. The way she says my name. I look back at Bev. Her overly professional tone hits a nerve of rebellion buried deep under my follow-the-rules, fourth-grade teaching career.

"Will you be going to the Mother's Day tea with Mom?" Her head twitches to the side. "It's at 2:00 pm outside on the veranda."

Trying to balance balloons, vase, bags, and pocketbook, I watch the elevator doors close. *Damn.* I can't take the stairs, and the last time I took the service elevator I almost gagged, wedged between the garbage and the laundry. *Take a breath, Terri.* I resign myself to being late and lumber back to Bev's command center.

"See these bags?" I point. "Party supplies, family pictures, organic honey, Mom's china teacups. You know how she is. It's easier for her to celebrate in her room. And if the elevator will cooperate, maybe I'll get there before she wanders down for lunch."

"You've probably missed her already."

Was that a snicker? This woman has no idea I have a ramp zigzagging across my front lawn, a path of handrails from my living room to the guest bathroom, and a major guilt complex because I can enjoy a shower without worrying. Bringing Mom here was the hardest decision of my life, and I'm still second guessing myself. And with people like Bev, how could Mom be happy here?

Bev smiles with that patronizing look of hers. "The tea party is not until 2:00 pm, so you'll still make that. It's *outside*. And on a gorgeous day like today, Nellie might enjoy some air."

What does she know about what Nellie might enjoy? Aside from the hairspray, she looks like she could be my age, but that bun and the buttoned-up shirt make her seem like someone on a 1950s TV show. *Relax Terri. She's just a receptionist.* But with people like her, I wonder if this is the right place for Mom. I try to smile politely, but outside isn't going to work today. "The sun. We Rileys burn easily. Safer to stay inside."

"Well, your choice. Just make sure you are not bringing in any *outside* appliances in those bags. Our policy is that anything that gets plugged in needs to be checked by maintenance. Don't want to blow a fuse!" she grins.

I'm an inch away from blowing mine.

Last time she had a fit when I brought in Mom's hair dryer. I decide I've had enough. "Well," I say in the voice I use to scold my fourth graders for misbehaving with the substitute, "if you had *actual* hot water, *real* hot water, not *lukewarm*, to use for tea, I wouldn't have to go out and buy an electric tea kettle that can speed boil." I rap my finger on her desk, just like when I need to quiet my classroom. I know from experience I should stop here, but I can't. "And if you need to know what I have in these bags, I've brought my mother's Royal Doulton, so she can enjoy a cup of Barry's tea, made with hot, *hot* water, that's needed to let the bag steep in the bone china for at least five minutes until it's caramel color, after which you add a spoonful of honey for sweetness." I take a gulp of air. "*That* is *our* family tradition. And I'll be celebrating Mother's Day with *my* mother *in her room*."

Bev smiles broadly, fakely I'm sure, and tilts her massive beehive to the side. Hands full, I stride towards the elevator and take a deep breath, letting out the frustration of dealing with people like her. How can this woman know my heart breaks seeing my mother this way? Seeing her slip slowly away. She didn't know the real Nellie. The real Nellie would have put her in her proper place with one look. I'd give all the tea in China to see that.

I make sure my pocketbook with Jen's card inside is on my shoulder. Jen's words to her grandma. I promised not to read it, so it would be special when it was shared. I pass a center table with a large cake made out of fresh flowers—assorted pink, red, white—spelling out "Happy Mother's Day." Finally, the elevator doors slide open, and I rush forward.

My heavy pocketbook—*God, I need to clean this thing out*—slides off my shoulder onto my arm, and the weight of the overstuffed bag feels like a bowling ball against my hip. I lose my grip on the balloons. *Shi... Shoot!* Those balloons weren't cheap. I catch a few, but most of the bouquet of assorted spring colors floats towards the high ceiling, settling in a corner, just out of reach. Today is *not* my day.

Bev shakes her head and picks up the phone. "Maintenance, to reception area. Again, maintenance needed at reception."

I'm not usually one to abandon a mess, but what can I do? I have to get to Mom. The elevator doors have now closed again, and I step over to an alcove, taking a moment. *Just. Breathe.* Holding what's left of the balloons, I put down the bag of party supplies, and my oversized pocketbook that I swear is filled with rocks. Everything feels lighter without that strap on my shoulder. I hear Mom's words, "no fuss," and I know she's right. But even with a master's in education, I'm just beginning to understand the brilliance of her simplicity. All she ever needed to celebrate was to sit for a "wee totty bit" with a good hot cup of "tay."

A plain woman, but she did love—and still deserves—nice things. As I put the bags of party supplies back on my arms, everything feels mysteriously lighter. *Come on, Terri, stop overburdening yourself.* The bouquet of real flowers along with the helium-filled ones is, I admit, a little much. But I've never forgotten that research study on memory I read in *Elle*: "Lively colors stimulate the mind and lavender scent is soothing." Maybe I should just focus on spending time with my mother.

The elevator button lights up, but I push it a few more times. Just to be sure. A poster on the wall decorated with roses reads: "The 56th annual River's Edge Mother's Day Tea—on the patio, 2:00 pm. All antique girls and their family, friends, acquaintances, and anyone interested are welcome to enjoy a spot of tea on Mother's Day." *Who on earth writes these things?*

I'm family, but I feel like an antique; the fresh faces in my fourth-grade class would certainly think so. But I'm not dyeing my hair yet—still chestnut brown with only a few strands of gray—not bad. My teeth are yellowed from all the coffee, but they seem to be getting better with those strips. I guess my shirt does puff out a bit, well, maybe more than a bit, from the inner tube around my waist. And to think this was my favorite—dark blue knit, three-quarter sleeves, scoop neckline. Ugh—time to take it to Goodwill. Time to ditch the spare tire. Time to hit the gym.

Ding! *Please let the elevator be empty.* I need a minute to myself before I see Mom. The doors open, and... there's a glint of blonde from the corner. Thank God it's the one person I actually like around here, flashing her big smile with gobs of red lipstick, her hand resting on an empty cart.

Stepping into the elevator, I glance down at her badge, "Jacqueline Rosario, Manager," but Grandma is what everyone here calls her, and I can't imagine calling her anything else.

"Terri, no rush," says Grandma. "Put your bags right here. Make sure you have everything with you. I won't let the doors close."

Lost in the comforting scent of her perfume, I can't help but let her wrap me in a hug, my face pressed into her enormous bosom. Since my Jen's been away at college, it's been so lonely—just me and the cat. Grandma's embrace is so warm, and it all seems so natural with her, despite her blonde-from-a-bottle hair. I could learn a thing or two from this woman who doesn't let the world judge her.

"So, honey, how *are* you?" she asks, and from the way she says it, I can tell she really wants to know. And I really want to tell her. "My oficina is abierto," she continues. "Talk to me."

"I went at it with Bev," I say, rolling my eyes. What does *that* tell you?"

"Eh, maybe she had it coming, maybe she didn't. But you, you're a walking fiesta."

Glamorous hair, overdone eyes, her light brown skin amazingly smooth... not what you think of when you picture a therapist, but this woman understands people. I'd book a session with her any day.

The doors close and the elevator starts lumbering upward. It's always a local, and it's going to take forever to get to 4.

Slumping against the wall I say, "I don't know where to begin."

She smiles. "I was thinking about you the other day. My granddaughter started looking at colleges. And she was talking about schools in Colorado. I told her not to go so far, cause Grandma will never see her nieta, right? It's got to be so hard for you, no? Now, which school is your daughter at?"

"Jen is a junior—already—out at U. C. Boulder."

"Boulder. I remember you telling me how beautiful the mountains are out there. How does she like it?"

The elevator doors open on 2. We wait. No one is there. Finally, the doors close again.

"She loves it. Studying education, of all things. Misses home though, and her grandma, of course. They've always been close. And now, half the time, Mom doesn't recognize her voice. Jen had to stop..." I almost choke up, "calling her—it was too upsetting." I gaze at the bad grout job along the tile floor, which could use a good mopping. "Look at this filthy floor. Mom always kept our floor at home sparkling. Floors you can eat off of—she took pride in that." I look up and find my "good morning class" smile, focusing my eyes on Grandma's garish red lips. "You know how it is. Anyway, I haven't seen you in a few weeks. Have you been back to Mexico to see *your* family?"

"No, honey. Just taking weekends off, but Mother's Day is always busy here, what with the tea party and all. So here I am. You're going, right? All Nellie's friends will be there. I call them the pandilla."

"Ha. Her gang..." I raise my hand to my forehead, "Mom used to have friends over all the time, catching up on gossip, sharing stories from the old country, or just old lady quiet time. Birthdays, christenings, funerals... 'a cup of tea for all.'" I sigh, heaving up the past. "But not anymore..."

Grandma's heavily lined eyes moisten.

"Here," I swallow, "she can barely manage a cup of tea in her room... if she doesn't send it flying at me. I can't trust her with these porcelain cups—only plastic, which makes the tea taste terrible. Oh, I'm sure she'd love a party, but I can't have her smashing everything—my world is already in pieces. So, no, we're not going. But as you can see, I'm bringing the party to Mom."

The button for 3 lights up and the elevator slows, then jerks upward, then back down again.

"Listen, Terri. You can't control everything. I know this is not your first time hearing this, but your mother's dementia—there's no magic pill. There will be good days and bad days, some better than others. I know it's not what you imagined this time with her would be like, but you have to meet your mother where she is, enjoy what you can, when you can. All we have are the moments."

"But she gets overstimulated so easily. What if she has one of her outbursts—in front of everyone?"

"But what if she doesn't? And so what if she does? You can't let her withdraw completely into herself. And you know she'll have fun at the party."

I hang my head.

"Terri! There's no judgment here; no one is failing a class—no mistakes. It's all about finding... a moment—if it will come, if you let it come—taking a breath, drinking a cup of tea for all... a way to find the joy."

I shake my head. "Joy. I think I've forgotten what that feels like."

Grandma pushes her bangs back, revealing black roots under the blonde. Then she winks at me and pulls out the red hold button to stop the car between floors. "All right, Terri, we can finish our talk here. If I try to bring you to my real office, we'll be interrupted every step of the way."

I sigh, "I know I'm not your only client, and Mom's not the only one here who gives the staff a hard time." I shake my head, somewhere between laughing and crying.

"Oh, honey."

"She smiles at me, then screams at me. She tells me to turn on the news, then calls security cause she thinks I'm a criminal. It's crazy making."

Grandma nods. "I hear what you're saying, but who are you keeping her in her room for? Her? Or you? She's your mother, and today is her day. Let her enjoy it."

"I... I... I've got her shoebox of old pictures, her special tea and honey, even her bone china, which I'm praying she won't break and I... I think it's best if we... just have our own party, Mom and me."

"Well," she throws up her hands, "you gotta do what you gotta do. But you are both welcome to come to the party if you change your mind." She winks.

"Thanks. So, how was she this week?"

"She loves painting the horses with the rec group in the art room. There's got to be five or six lined up along the wall." Grandma looks down, and then steady into my eyes, her voice softer. "But there is something I wanted to talk to you about. She's always said she wanted to go to Ireland—that's not new—but now she's trying to actually *leave* a little more often. Her exit-seeking behaviors are getting worse. She's clever, that Nellie. We know her safety bracelet triggers the wander alarm, but somehow, she gets into parts of the building where she can still open the doors."

"I know this is a serious problem, and I shouldn't laugh, but at least Mom hasn't lost her adventurous spirit. What else does she have left?"

Grandma pushes the red button to release it. Then, ding! the lighted numbers change to 3. The doors open, and three women are waiting to get on.

"Yoohoo, Grandma!" says one in a floral dress. Next to her is another with bright red hair and matching red frames, and another with a bench seat walker and elegant white hair to her chin. All three are waving at Grandma. "We are going to the tea party!" wheezes the one in the wheelchair. "Got room?"

"Stella, Roula, Edith. The three musketeers! You are early for the party," Grandma points to the balloons, "and we're full up here. You'll have to wait for the next one." The elevator door closes and we begin moving upwards until Grandma pulls out the hold button once more.

"On a good day, she won't stop until she gets someone to sit in her room and eat a cookie that she's baking right there on her dresser. That went on for two weeks after the cooking program with recreation. But that we can handle. It's when she manages to shuffle her way out of the building... Lord knows how far she would walk! Down towards the river, or, God forbid, into the city."

"Did you know she moved from Ireland when she was eighteen? No money, no formal education, but she learned how to play the piano—used her bartending tips to pay for the lessons. Legend has it she was a spitfire, bright red hair, used to get in trouble as a teenager for sneaking out to bet on the horses."

"She's a free spirit, that Nellie." Grandma's deep brown eyes twinkle. "But safety first. That's the rule. If this keeps up, we will have to talk about sending her to another facility... a locked unit."

Locked unit? I grimace. "Well, I need to keep her here. It's twenty minutes from my house, and I'm still always late. If the facility is farther away... anyway, she knows everyone here. We'll just have to make it work." I let the balloons hit the ceiling of the elevator.

Grandma sighs and shifts her weight from one foot to the other.

"Well," she cracks a smile, "Nellie has a home here. There's Edith with the straight white hair, one of the three musketeers. A bit of a busybody. She's started keeping an extra eye on Nellie and even reported to the nurse when she saw her on the swing outside her window." Grandma shakes her head. "She's also doing better with her weight, not losing any more, and last week—when she let us get her on the scale—we saw she'd gained a little."

"Well, I don't know what she's eating because each week, she seems to be eating less of her lunch. And the article I just read about brain health says to limit sugar."

"With your busy schedule, I don't know how you find time to read all that stuff!"

Banging on the outside of the elevator doors.

"All right, all right," says Grandma. She pushes the hold button in, then hits 4, and I feel the pull of the elevator as it resumes its path. "How old are those kids you teach? Fourth grade, is it?"

"Yes. A handful, but I love them."

The doors open. I grab my balloons and bags off the cart.

"We'll keep talking, Terri," says Grandma. "Most important thing you can do is to keep the dialogue open." Once again, I relax into the strength of her arms.

"Always an adventure... wish me luck."

Pushing her cart, her long blonde curls fall around her wide shoulders, "Happy Mother's Day, honey."

"And to you, too." Loaded down once again with all my party trappings, I make my way to Mom's room.

Opening the door, I guide the balloons in, looking for a place to lighten my load, but a tray full of food occupies the only table. Her padded chair is facing the window, but the blinds are drawn, and—I gasp—the top of her recently curled white hair is peeking out over the back. *Why isn't she at lunch in the dining room? I need time to settle in and set up!* Cautious with my greetings, never knowing if an energetic hello or a quiet nod is best, I let the clunk of the honey jar and boxes speak. Her sneakers respond with a shuffle in my direction, and I see her furrowed brow and the downward folds below her eyes and cheeks as she peers out from the side of the chair.

"Hello, Mom."

"What er we doin' here?"

"Mom, it's Mother's Day."

Her brow remains tense. "Er we safe?"

"Of course, we're here together, in your room. And I brought the tea party to you."

"What er we doin' here?" She looks back at me blankly.

"Well, when I was a little girl, you used to make me tea, the way it tastes the best, Barry's tea, in the bone china." I put the jar of honey in front of her, hoping she'll remember. *How can someone forget everything they love?* "A little honey with that."

"Well, tat's a lot," she says. Her brow relaxes. The thick plastic bracelet with a small square encircles her wrist. For safety, of course, but it still throws me. I take her hand. Fingers gnarled, knuckles swollen. And so cold.

"Happy Mother's Day!"

She pulls her hand away.

I pick up a card on her bedside table. A piece of paper folded into fours with a stamp of a rose on the outside. Inside, it reads, "Best Mother's Day Wishes! from Residents' Council" in block letters. They probably all get one of these cards, even the men.

I glance back at Mom. Lumps bulge in her socks and edges of white packets stick out from the tops. More lumps hide under her bra. Sugar packets are piled up on her bedside table. *Where are the sugar police? Probably busy with other criminals.*

So much to do. Mom's special day needs to be special. Tie the balloons on the back of her desk chair. Arrange the flowers in the vase. Place them between the pictures on the shelf. And there's Mom's photo of baby Jen playing in the sandbox, another of her and Dad, so young, pushing me in the stroller. I catch a glimpse of myself in the mirror. *That's Mom's jawline, all right.* But my color is off. I could use some lipstick, maybe some blush, but she starts for the sugar...

Tilting her wedding photo on the shelf towards the front, I say, "Look at this beautiful lady. One of my favorite pictures of you."

"Err, my mother was not a nice lady."

"I remember when Grandma lived with us when she was older. I used to sit and watch you brush her long grey hair."

She rips open a small sugar packet from the meal tray that's still almost full and pours it into her mouth.

"Mom! Eat your real food."

She glares at me.

I step closer, "I know what's under your socks."

She scowls. "I got nothin' to hide."

"You never liked sugar before, only honey for your tea." Pulling out the teacups with the delicate hand-painted design, I set two on the bedside table, then use the bathroom tap to fill the electric kettle and plug it into the outlet. The light flickers for a second, but it works. *No harm, Bev.*

"Who's Birrtday?"

"No birthday. Mother's Day. It's *your* day. Now, how about a few more bites of that grilled cheese?"

"Finish yer lunch, Terri."

Taking a closer look, I guess I wouldn't want her soggy sandwich either.

Stepping over to the window, I throw open the blinds. "They're getting ready for the tea party outside. There must be ten tables out there, all covered with red and pink flowers. And drinks and snacks. Do you want to go?"

She grips the handles of her chair tighter, then turns her head quickly as if she's lost something.

"Mom, what is it?" I say.

"You knew, ehh? You didn't tell. You took everything. You broke me heart."

"Mom, you're safe here. You have everything you need."

"Where is it?" she yells. "Mae purse! You stole mae purse!"

Where's her red plaid clutch? It's not in its usual spot on her dresser, under the sign I wrote in black sharpie "Keep Mom's purse here." That's the problem with this place. Too many faces, and they don't take the time.

"Mom," I say, in my calmest teaching voice, "I'm sure it's here. I already have my own purse." But I don't. I rifle through the bags and boxes. No purse. Just fear. Like the dream I have of all my students laughing at me because I'm naked in the classroom. *Where could it be?* I would have felt it fall off—it practically knocked me over downstairs. My credit cards, my money, my phone, and the card from Jen... two purses lost. *What a day. What a Mother's Day.*

Mom has the same fear in her eyes that I know I have in mine.

"I'm sure your purse is here, Mom. And mine too..." Opening the drawers of the dressers, searching under the bed, I shift gears. "But if it's not, I'm happy to buy you a new pocketbook. A fresh, clean one, maybe soft tan leather?"

She glares at me, "You have it. Yer mother would know."

Noticing a bit of red in the corner of the closet, I point, "I think it might be in there." *They can't do this to her, move her purse like this.* I'm going to let Grandma know.

"Don't look in tere," she says.

"Mom, I think it's in the closet."

"No!" her voice louder now. "I'm gonna call. I'm gonna call te cops!" She reaches for the phone.

I speak slowly, knowing it's pointless to reason with her. "I've got an idea, Mom. Hold off on calling for a moment. I'll be right back."

She holds the phone up, fingers over the buttons. She knows how to press 911. "Yer gonna leave mae, Terri, Terri?"

Quickly, I step outside the room, looking, hoping, needing a nurse. But I only see a woman with messy curls wrapped in a bandana who looks like last night's party lasted too long slowly mopping the floor. The housekeeper's metal cart stands in the hallway, hung with brooms, dusters, spray bottles, trash bags, and paper towels.

"Excuse me, do you know where my mother's nurse is? She's about to call the cops, and piano players have fast fingers."

"Huh?" From the neighbor's door she removes a hand-written "Knock Before Entering" sign. "Who wouldn't knock?" she mutters.

"I need help! She could play 'Flight of the Bumblebee' with one hand. 911 is nothing for her."

"Flight of the bees? Oh, that Mami," she says, in a thick Puerto Rican accent, tossing her head and putting her mop down. "So sweet. She calls *me* darrhhling. I go get a nurse."

I shake my head. She's darrhhling, but even on a good day, I'm chopped liver. Watching the housekeeper shuffle away with a slight limp, I stand outside the door of my mother's room, not wanting to agitate her, hoping my pocketbook is somewhere downstairs, near Bev. *It's got to be.*

On Mom's door the nameplate reads "Eleanor Mae Riley" in black letters, and someone has written "Nellie" below in practically illegible script. I peek back in the room, and see her rocking in her chair, my box of teacups still on her bed.

Suddenly blonde hair flutters down the hallway, followed by a dash of red lipstick. Grandma! I want to tell her someone took my sign down that read not to move Mom's purse. And no sugar packets—only healthy food. Grandma approaches, an aide behind her, and I'm both horrified and relieved to see the small cup she's carrying. The serenity pill. Mom was never one to even take Tylenol. But she'll be calmer. And hopefully nicer. With luck, she'll stay awake just long enough to enjoy some tea.

Grandma catches me eyeing the cup. "You know the drill, Terri. I try to soothe her by talking a little first, and if that doesn't work, we give her the two o'clock pill—a little early. Give us a few minutes."

I go down to the window at the end of the hallway. I hate the pill, but I know she'll be... peaceful. Maybe I should take one, too. I steady myself against the handrail. Maybe if I had come a little earlier, or read her Jen's card, but I can't even do that because I want to scream, "I don't know where my goddamn purse is!" *Calm down, Terri. Calm down. A panic attack won't help anyone find your purse. Remember what you learned in therapy...*

And I start to ground myself, standing in the hallway of this place. There are people here taking care of Mom. Maybe not exactly the way I would, but making sure she's comfortable in a way I couldn't sustain. She has a room. She has a routine. Down the hall, the rhythmic movement of the housekeeper's mop, back and forth, and the familiar sharp scent of Pine-Sol like Mom used in our home growing up. I relax my clenched jaw and rub my stiff neck.

Mom's door—when did it close—opens a crack. I walk back over and listen in. I hear the aide's voice, "Nellie, you will be dressed to travel, with your raincoat and your purse. Well, this bag is heavy. What's... ah, there must be 30 packets of sugar in here. So *that's* where it's all been disappearing to. I'm going to take these out, and I'll just leave two packets for you."

Mom yells—the same yell I heard when I arrived, the same yell she used during my short-lived "rebellious stage."

"Oh no you won't! Don't you touch mae purse!"

I go back to the window, wanting to scream about losing my own purse, about losing my mother to this damn disease.

Moments later, the aide wheels Mom out of the room in her chair, with her plaid purse, yellow raincoat, and brow still wrinkled but face more relaxed. If only someone could find my purse and calm me down like that. "Cleaned out all those sugar packets, plus a sock, a bra, just left two sugars in the purse for her tea."

"Thank you. Mom looks good."

"Ta hell with yer!" Mom barks.

Ouch. That's a gut punch on Mother's Day, but maybe I can salvage something, a moment, to make this day special for Mom. I go into her room and gather up her cups, the Barry's tea, and the honey into a bag. I'll bring it all to the party. If she's awake enough for the tea, I'll make sure it's a perfect cup.

Mom looks blankly at the aide, then a smile crosses her face. "Take me to the bus. The bus to Ireland."

The aide rolls Mom's chair over to me. "You can drive."

I shoulder my Barry's bag and wheel Mom down the hallway towards the elevator. We wait, the back of her neat white curls leaned to the side in her chair, resting. On the wall next to the Mother's Day tea poster, is the list of names in a box with a single rose: "We remember." *Time is short. Where's the damn elevator?*

Downstairs now I wheel Mom over to reception, where—sure enough—my purse sits in the center of Bev's desk! She glares at me, as if I carelessly lost a child at the playground.

Tilting that solid steel bun of hers, she says, "I see Mom's sleeping. I'm sure she will wake up when she feels the warm air outside. It's just what she needs."

Enough with the air. They seem to think it's the answer to everything. But my purse is found, and I'm too exhausted from Mom's outburst to argue. "I suppose you're right."

She pushes my purse and the clipboard at me. "Special sign out for the tea party."

"Bev, how long have you been doing this?"

"Too long," she sighs, "but let's see, five years already... and my sixth Mother's Day after Mom passed."

"Passed?" My face drops. "Oh gosh, Bev, I'm sorry, this can't be an easy day for you." I push my purse up my arm and rebalance my party bag.

"No. It's not. But at least we shared her last Mother's Day here— together. They had us all in the Lido Lounge. Did you know I'm the one who encouraged the administration here to host the tea party outside?" Clasping her hands, she looks at Mom and smiles. "When my mom was going through this, I found she was always calmer with a little fresh air."

My shoulders soften and I nod.

She continues. "I hated this place at first. I had Mom in three different facilities and almost left this one, too. I knew exactly what she needed, and I wanted everything to be perfect, because that's what she deserved."

I take in Bev's perfect hair, perfect silk scarf color-coordinated with the swirls of mauve in her sweater (must be cashmere), her perfect eyebrows and lipstick blotted without a smudge. "You always seem so together." Her face lights up, and suddenly, I see a real person, a pretty woman in her fifties hidden under the stuffy uniform of a lady who has to look like she's in charge.

"Seeming is believing, right?" She laughs.

"Fake it 'til you make it." We share a knowing smile.

"You know," she leans closer, and I catch a whiff of coffee and sweet perfume. "I thought I was doing Mom a favor, chasing down the exact right place, but I was driving her crazy. She just needed to get settled. It wasn't until I overheard a resident with a few thin wisps of hair complaining to an older friend about—of all things—her lack of bangs that I had my epiphany. The friend said, 'So your hair isn't perfect. Was it ever perfect before? In 94 years, I've never had a perfect cut. Not once.' Perfection is a myth and it only caused me to lose precious time with my mother. Time is all we have, and," she takes a deep breath, "it's gone before we know it." Her voice softens. "You know who helped me figure it out, Terri?" She leans even closer, like a child sharing a secret, "Grandma. She gave me the straight talk. And a hug that could melt the North Pole."

We both laugh. Mom stirs in her chair, then seems to doze off. Better than all that anger, but I hope she'll wake so we can have our moment outside.

"Anyway, I applied for this position after my mom passed. Did you know Nellie sits right here during the day sometimes? Her fingers move to a rhythm, tapping my desk as if she's on the keyboard. Sometimes she draws a crowd for her imaginary concert." Bev straightens her scarf. "I know I sounded like a scold about the kettle, Terri, but I had a few near misses with Mom and hot water."

"I understand." Looking down at the floor, it all makes sense now. "Thank you."

Signing Mom out, I note the time, 1:45 pm. Bev slides a blue and white pamphlet towards me. "This group helped me a lot. They meet downtown at the library on Tuesday nights."

The by now familiar pamphlet reads, "In it together, supporting the loved ones of those with dementia." Maybe it's something I should think about. I slide it into my bag.

Bev's eyes soften, but her voice is clear. "I'll press the buzzer," she says, "so the alarm won't get set off."

As we approach the patio, the warmth of the sun hits my face, the smell of flowers intoxicating. Classic piano music warbles through the speakers. My bags feel lighter. The world feels lighter. *I needed this.* There must be a dozen tables laden with cookies and crumb cake surrounding centerpieces of carnations and a delicate porcelain painted teapot. A teacup and teddy bear grace each place setting. We're early, but the tables are already packed with residents and visitors. *Where will we sit?* Things never run late at River's Edge.

In the ten months that Mom has lived here, I've learned to steer clear of groups, especially women wearing pink, and ones who appear a little too sweet. Pink blush, pink lipstick, pink hair bows, and pearls are a sure sign of terror on wheels; a clique with no interest in entertaining a stranger, especially one with her head tilted to the side and a faded red plaid purse sticky with sugar. One casual comment about how nice these ladies look constitutes an open invitation for critiques of your appearance. My good mood fading, I start to wonder if we should have stayed in.

A table next to a row of lilacs offers a splendid view of the river, and I spot a space where I might be able to squeeze Mom's chair. Most of this group of three seems to be resting, except one, whose eyes are in everyone's business. This woman is familiar, with tubing around her nose and a large green floral dress. The two others have their heads down, no movement. The sun probably put them to sleep. I smile quickly then glance away, thinking perhaps Mom would enjoy a group that is livelier.

But options are limited. The woman with the green dress is waving her hands for us to come closer. *Ugh.* I've seen this type before and know they can go from friendly to feral in a heartbeat. I give her a half-wave, the way my students raise their hands when they don't know the answer.

She starts to cough, struggles a little, then manages one deep, loud gurgle, followed by a long breath. With a victorious grin, she says, "Just a tickle," and wipes her mouth with her flowered sleeve.

Pretending I see someone we know, I start to wheel away.

"Yoohoo." Another cough. "Back this way!"

I don't want Mom to get sick, but if it's not a cough, it's a sniffle, or a rash—with all of them—and at this point, it's either a table of ferocious dolled up pink piranhas or this germ-spreader. The token men's table is out of the question. There's one dressed in a short-sleeve tropical shirt dozing off like a Florida sunbird, sitting next to a scruffy-looking guy with arms full of tattoos. Across the table is a circle of caps with old men underneath—a blue US Navy, covering a few tufts of white hair over brown eyes and a steady gaze, and a crimson H '56 over bushy eyebrows and skin and bones that remain bent despite the reclined chair. Navy has a pink shake in front of him, and, as he leans forward to sip from the straw, tattoo arms growls, "Easy, now. No drowning in your drink, Sherman. That's my job."

I look away, glad I don't own a baseball cap—and praying never to end up like that. But at least they're outside.

Now Floral Dress is yelling, "Nellie sits with *us*. We always have extra sugar." Then she taps the downcast head next to her, and a woman with red curls and thick, red-framed glasses teetering at the tip of her nose perks up. She, in turn, taps the head next to her, a helmet of white hair over gold hoop earrings and a crisply starched white shirt. They are all awake. And I realize, it's the three musketeers from the elevator. Maybe this is our spot.

"Mom," I whisper, rolling her chair closer to their table. "Are these your friends?"

Mom stirs. Floral Dress clears her raspy throat and interrupts my moment, "You're family? You don't come around much."

Well-practiced in stifling an appropriately horrified reaction and masking an exasperated tone—another skill I've learned teaching fourth grade—I respond, "I'm her daughter," continuing with a nice-to-meet-you nod, "I'm Terri."

"Ooooh," wrinkling her tubed nose with obvious disapproval, "you're *Terri.*"

"We've heard about *you*," the others chime in. Suddenly all eyes are on me. Some friends. Maybe the pink piranhas would have been better.

Red Hair adjusts her frames upward. "You must be the teacher," she says, in a sharp New York accent. "The nurses talk about you. You know I was a teacher—a good one, very organized. Now I'm straightening this place out. Sometimes her sugar is gone. Is that why you came?"

I fake a smile. "Happy Mother's Day." It takes her a second. *Did she hear me?*

"Of course," she fidgets with her frames again. "You came for the party. That's the only reason family ever comes."

"And I have lunch with Mom, every Sunday," I add, as if this woman's approval matters. "She needs healthy food, good nutrition to stay well." I frown at the pile of sugar packets in front of her on the table.

Nearly choking on a huge cookie, Floral Dress picks a few crumbs from her lap and stuffs them in her mouth. "Oh Sundays. We're busy on Sundays. That's *movie day* for us. That's why we've never seen you." She finishes chewing. "I'm Stella, head of Residents' Council."

Just like in class, my memory tool for names snaps into place. *Repeat the name three times.* "Stella, nice to meet you, Stella." Stella with the floral dress.

Stella points to the woman across from her with straight white hair to her chin and says, "That there is Edith, and I've been trying to get her to join the Council ever since she got here."

Edith shakes her head without a hair losing its place. She snaps back, "Not for me."

"Edith, nice to meet you, Edith." Edith with the straight white hair.

Her tone pleasant now, Edith addresses me. "Did you know my stylist comes in to do my hair? And my son sent a beautiful vase of white lilies this morning. He calls almost every night."

"Sounds like a wonderful young man."

"Well," she smiles, "Wonderful yes, but not so young anymore."

Red Glasses shakes her head. "*My* two daughters live too far way to visit, but they sent me this necklace," she crows, holding up a maroon pebbled pendant.

Stella points at the jewels and glances at me. "That's Roula," she says, then turning to Roula, "and she needs to move her chair over, so Nellie has her spot."

Holding her pendant in the center of her chest, Roula pushes her thick red glasses up on her nose and shrugs. She stares at me. "*Nellie* has to learn how to park that chair." Then, focusing on me, "Now what was your name again? I don't hear well."

Even with all the makeup and dyed curls, there is a familiar quality, particular, reminding me of my Aunt Mary who always had my favorite candy in a drawer when I visited. Slower and louder, I speak with my face in her direction in case she is reading lips. "Roula, nice to meet you, Roula." Roula with the red hair and matching glasses. "My name is Terri. I am Nellie's daughter."

She rolls her eyes. "You don't have to talk so loudly. And your hair could use some color, maybe a few highlights."

"Don't listen to Roula," Stella rasps, "she was fired not too long ago from our hair salon, Shear Madness. Reorganized some of the hair dye—a couple of customers got the wrong shade, and oooh let me tell you..."

Roula glares at her, then back at me. "As I was saying... I'll show you how to steer a chair, so Nellie doesn't get bumped around. Back up slowly and straighten the tires. Line them up in the direction you want to go, and *don't* let the wheels turn."

Stella clears her throat and lifts a golden cane into the air. "Get this young lady a chair."

I'm about to tell her I can find one myself when she flags down a staff member pushing a cart piled with plates of cookies,

"Yoohoo!" she shouts. "Need a chair and extra cookies." She turns back to us, her face animated. "As a waitress, I would always give a few extra. Sweets keep people comin' back."

With Stella's cane down, I relax and focus on Mom, opening a napkin on her lap and scooping fresh berries onto her plate. A chair appears behind me, and a platter piled high with chocolate chip cookies is dropped in front of me. It's nice to be waited on for a change. Maybe I can actually enjoy this. I put my Barry's party bag under the table but keep my purse on my shoulder. *Don't want to lose it again.*

Stella smiles, "Edith, give Nellie a chocolate chip, those are her favorite."

Edith uses a spoon to push a small plate of cookies in front of Mom. She perks up, grabs one, and starts nibbling. *So much for healthy food today.*

Stella scarfs down cookie after cookie off the plate, coughing between each bite.

"Stella, if you keep eating like this," Roula scowls, "you're not going to make it back through the doorway one of these days."

Taking a napkin, Stella delicately dabs the corners of her mouth and glares at Roula saying, "You could use a few more to sweeten that attitude." Then she clears her throat and leans in my direction. "People around here, they can be cuckoo. I know what that's like."

I smile politely but keep quiet and edge away a bit in case she coughs or decides to throw that cane.

And she coughs. A raspy cough that propels spittle from her mouth. Gathering herself she says, "I don't know how long ago it was, but I was cuckoo once. I would wake up, in different rooms, with doctors, nurses. I had drains coming out of my head, and words coming out of my mouth. Didn't know what I was saying." She looks at me and then at Mom. "Now the room I keep waking up in is here. By the way, Nellie likes to have a drink with her cookies."

I don't need this one to tell me what to do, but at least she cares. I hold the straw in the glass of water in front of Mom, and she takes a few sips.

Roula raises her eyebrows over her red frames. "Before our conversation was interrupted by this one," looking in my direction, "we were sharing personal stories about Mother's Day. Edith, what were you saying about *your* mother? Keys? Where?"

"Mother?" Edith answers, seeming confused. "Oh yes, when Mother would visit my house, you know way back when William Sr. was alive and William Jr. was so young, she would visit on the holidays. She was a very clever woman. You know how I am about keys. Well, she taught me not to lose them." Holding her wrist up with a key dangling from a bracelet, she continues, "Mother would put her house keys in the refrigerator, right on top of the leftovers so she wouldn't forget to take them home. 'You'll never forget the leftovers,' she'd say."

I paste a smile on my face. All the wisdom of the ages comes down to where you leave your keys.

With the bright sun reflecting off her red hair, and sparks of light flying off her diamond-studded glasses, Roula shakes her head. "Well, my mother was even *more* clever. She knew how to travel and would hide the important stuff in her brasier." *Another country heard from.*

Then I remember. Mom used to smuggle stuff the exact same way. I glance over at her and whisper, "I know someone like that." The beginning of a smile creases Mom's mouth.

In the background, a Mozart piece comes on—a piece Mom used to play. Her eyes are glazed with a distant expression, but her fingers start in a rhythm on the ivories only heard by her. Enjoying the smell of the lilacs from the large bush behind Stella, I take a deep breath, savoring the moment.

Roula leans towards Stella. "Now, Stella, I bet *your* mother had secrets..."

Stella's face goes suddenly intense, smile gone, lips pinched, eyes squinting. Flailing her cane, she shouts, "Judging by me, she must have been a big woman. And she was filled full of secrets, all right. But I never got to learn any of them. She left her biggest secret right here, back when River's Edge was an orphanage." She struggles to catch her breath. The cane drops to her lap. "Me."

Silence.

"So, while you all had your mommas changing your diapers every morning and putting you down to sleep at night, mine wasn't there, not for one single moment." She starts rocking, and her breathing slows. Softer now, "The only one... there for us... is the good Lord. We start... as His children, His babies, and we end... as His babies, too. And the baby, the baby is comin'. You all gotta remember that."

I look at Mom, half-asleep from her pill. Thank God she's still here. Thank God she's always been here. I can't even imagine.

Edith touches the edge of her hair. "Oh dear, Stella. I had no idea. Mother gave me so much. Her quiet grace stays with me to this day."

Then Stella yells, "We need music! Not this piano... I need to hear Etta. Etttaaaaa!"

Roula looks towards the staff, always hard to find. "Stella needs her music!"

Stella huffs at me, "Terri, turn up my tank." Then she points behind her chair in the direction of the tubing. "Now!"

Wow, this place can get crazy fast.

Mom is still nibbling on cookies, oblivious to what passes for excitement here. I walk slowly over to the tank, where I see a large knob next to a meter that's pointing to 2. But I'm hesitant to touch anything. Where's the staff?

"Go on. Turn it up to 5. It won't kill you—or me." A few tight coughs and she holds the tubing closer to her nose, her dark eyes intense.

I hesitate, searching for a nurse.

"Did you turn it up? I don't feel the air! I need that oxygen to breathe!"

I glance around at each table.

"What are you waiting for, woman? No one gonna come."

I turn the knob up to the line marked 5.

Stella moves the tubing closer to her nose, inhaling deeply a few times, then smiles and exhales. "That's better!" I sigh right along with her. Her face is now relaxed, with folds of skin dropping down from her cheekbones like dough. her chin resting comfortably on her collar.

The tempo of the music changes, as the soft sound of the piano is replaced by a deep soulful voice resonating through the room. "At last..." Swaying, Stella joins in, her voice powerful and clear. "My love..."

As she rocks from side to side, the flowers on her dress move back and forth, as if they're alive and dancing in a light spring breeze. Each of these ladies, even Mom, sways with the smoky vocals, the rhythm and the blues. They've all landed here and getting here is no easy journey. But they all seem to have found a moment to enjoy.

With the sparkle of the sun off the river, the perfume of the lilacs, the green lawn, and a table full of cookies, Mom is calm. Maybe there's more to a little fresh air than I thought. As the final note is held, and the violins wind down, the teapot is filled.

Now the ladies bombard me. "Terri, can you get me an extra tea bag? Some more cream, Terri? Be a dear and turn *down* my tank, don't want to waste the air"—*as if I'm all their daughters*—"Push my chair in further. Terri, I need an extra napkin." And Mom, asking me for a cup of tea when there's one right in front of her. I'm working hard. They're all headed to a hundred and even harder to take care of than the little ones. Another cookie is put in front of Mom by her neighbor, and I'm too busy pouring tea to give her strawberries instead.

Stella, gulping her tea, looks at me. "You know, when Nellie first came here I didn't know she could walk. But she sure can when she gets outside, walking over the roots to get to that swing. When she decides to get up and go, we got to keep up with her."

"Well," Edith fixes her collar, "When you stop walking, it's all downhill from there. I've always had a good sense of direction."

Shaking her red hair, Roula adds, "I've got two new hips and the surgeon says my scars are beautiful. And that man over there in the crimson cap, he's the surgeon that saved my husband... gave him a new liver and another four years."

"Well, he ain't savin' anyone now," Stella rasps, "and your hips ain't workin', pretty or not. It's Nellie keeps us rollin'. Anyone for more tea? Terri's pouring."

Too busy to explain that Nellie can't walk safely, I signal to the staff for a fresh pot before Stella can raise her cane again. A staff member brings a new pot, but she puts it in the middle of the table where no one can reach it. I guess it's up to me to pour. Shifting my pocketbook strap, I lean in and extend my arm. But my shoulder goes stiff. I've been carrying too much all day. Shuffling my feet to maintain my balance, I'm just able to reach the teapot, but—gah—my bag slides down my arm, crashing onto the table like a bowling ball, knocking over the teapot and toppling the flowers. *Disaster.* All the cups are sideways and dark liquid seeps slowly across the formerly white tablecloth. *Why did I listen to Bev and Grandma! Why didn't we just stay in Mom's room! I knew this was a bad idea.*

"I'm so sorry. This purse... too much stuff..." I grab some napkins and dab the table, but tea is already dripping off one side. Mom scowls.

Frantically, I turn the cups back over and put the few dry cookies, now in pieces, back on the tray, but the spout of the teapot has cracked off and the flowers are drenched. *Terri and the terrible, horrible, no good, very bad day!*

The ladies just stare at me. The frowns on their faces make me want to disappear.

"Well, shit," says Roula.

Edith shoots her a look. "There's no reason to compound this mess with that foul mouth of yours."

Roula shoots back. "Why the fuck not?"

Stella waves her cane in the air, "Yoohoo!"

Swears, swipes, and cane are all flying. A staff member in green scrubs with dark curls and a big smile appears. "No biggie. Happens all the time."

I'm saved.

He's swaying to music, bouncing to his own beat, with those wireless headphones in his ears. He points to my purse and signals me to take it off the table. Picking up the ends of the tablecloth, he folds it all into a sack.

Edith addresses him. "Raffee, won't you stay and sit with us?" She turns to me. "He always stays and chats with me in *my* room."

"Sorry, Ms. Edith, no time to chat. Boss is around. You know the drill."

Sitting around the bare, chipped tabletop, Mom picks at the napkin in her hand. I mumble, "Well, at least this doesn't happen every day."

Roula fusses with her red frames. "It did in my home. That drunk, my father, was always knocking things over, breaking dishes, throwing pots and pans. All the other kids looked down on me, on us. I swore I'd never marry a man like him… and sure enough I ended up with one. I knew he'd break my heart, but I married him anyway." She cackles, diamond-studded frames glinting in the light.

"No matter how much we love them, we can't fix them," I mumble.

"But in my *classroom*," Roula adds, "I was someone the students looked up to. I stood out for the right reasons. You know, I was teacher of the year."

"Well dear," Edith starts, "I was always an A student, but I got my life lessons from my mother. When *I* was young, she taught me the importance of always being well turned out and insisted that I make my bed in the morning and take time to smooth the wrinkles. She even inspected. The day I stop getting dressed and making my bed is the day I won't be able to do it anymore. So I just keep at it."

Mom. Surrounded by friends and staff who can give her what she needs when she needs it. It's not just me and her. It's me and her and this whole community. Roula's sure been through it, but she keeps herself together. And this Edith character—she's the good kind of nosy, looking out for Mom when she wanders outside. And Stella, with that cane of hers, could get the Pope's attention while he's conducting mass. River's Edge is home for Mom. And I'm going to treat her and her friends to something special.

"Yoohoo! I need hot water and a fresh tablecloth," I wave my hand in the air and yell to one of the attendants. The one Edith called Raffee rolls up with a cart covered with thermoses and whisks new linen onto the table. "Make sure that's hot, hot water," I say.

"You sure? Don't want to go burnin' anyone's tongue."

"I'm sure," I say, in my teacher's authority voice. "The water has to be piping hot, so after the tea steeps for five minutes, it's the perfect temperature for sipping."

"Well then, sounds like you got a plan. And I'm not gonna get between you ladies and your tea. This thermos here, it's the hottest one. I know because I just filled it. You take it. But no spillin'."

With the new white linen down, I bring out my party bag from under the table with the Royal Doulton and box of Barry's tea. "Ladies, you're going to experience a Riley family tradition—a proper afternoon tea. I'm going to pour the water—without spilling—but you have to wait at least five minutes, until the tea is a rich amber color. Then, you add just the right amount of cream until it turns caramel." I clunk the large jar of honey down in the middle of the table.

"Tat's a lot," says Mom.

As I place a cup in front of each woman, I notice gold specks in the bone china's painted floral design that I've never seen before. A vase of flowers, double the size of the one that fell, appears on the table, along with multiple plates of gourmet cookies and fresh fruit. Raffee is a whirling dervish. The table is perfect. It's as if the tea never spilled.

Stella smiles, then grabs a giant brownie from the plate. "The best stuff always comes out at the end of the party. And... it always helps when I treat the staff to pizza. I ordered out last night—courtesy of Residents' Council." She coughs. "I scratch their back, they scratch mine."

I know exactly what she means. We all need a little help. At work, I bring extra fruit for lunch to give to the maintenance man, and he waters the plants in my classroom every Friday. With my face burning from the sun, I reach under the table into my pocketbook and pull out my sunblock. The ladies clamor for it, all asking at once, and I dab a little bit on their cheeks. It blends with Roula's overdone rouge. Edith's skin is like porcelain. And Stella must moisturize often—hers is as soft as a baby's. Mom turns her head from side to side, and I can barely get a drop on.

"Is this sunblock from Florida?" Roula asks. "It smells like my apartment there."

"Walk te beach with me, Terri," says Mom. "Look at te ocean. So blue!"

I turn to Roula. "Mom, God bless her, thinks the river is the ocean. Don't tell her otherwise. She used to rent in Pompano, right on the beach."

"Well, I was in Naples. I was head of the St. Vincent DePaul Thrift Shop volunteers. Good workers, but they never stayed long."

Surprised they didn't mutiny, I want to add, but my cynicism is fading.

The fragrance of the lilacs soothes me and I start to relax at last. Despite everything, there is something to be enjoyed. And by the looks of the ladies, they seem to agree.

In the bright sun, Mom is sweating, and I try to help her take off her raincoat, but she's not interested. She's kept it on ever since she's been at River's Edge. She'd even sleep in it if they'd let her. I, on the other hand, am about to strip in front of these ladies—at least metaphorically. I've got nothing to hide, nothing to lose! So, I decide to bare it all.

"You know, Nellie was traveling on her own just a few years ago." I start rolling up my sleeves, but I'm still hot. I shed the knit blouse, which is too tight anyway. I'm now down to my cotton tee, which I only wear in my house, and I can finally feel my body start cooling. "She was living in her own place, hosting on Sundays, taking long walks. Strong woman. And let me tell you something else. When I was pregnant with Jen, I was right out of high school. Abortion wasn't an option and college was about to slip away..."

Mom fidgets with her napkin. "Te baby." I place the napkin on her lap before she dips it into her tea.

The honesty feels good. "Mom stepped in, even though my pregnancy broke her heart. We weren't a traditional family, but she never let on. Always proud. She took care of my daughter, Jen—and me—a grandmother and a mother at the same time. Now I'm supposed to be taking care of her, but having her home was," I choke back my tears, "just too much. Even so, I can't get used to not having her there, at home, with me. I know I should be enjoying the time we have together here, but sometimes..." I swallow.

It's Stella who says, "Honey, can't you see *she* brought you here?"

"She didn't bring me, I brought her."

Stella smiles. "Terri, maybe this is Nellie's way of taking care of you."

The tears start flowing. Now I know how I ended up in this place. I repeat Stella's words, "She brought you here..." Sniffling, I try to change the subject. Anything to stop these tears. "Jen is a beautiful kid. In college already, in Colorado. And oh, I almost forgot!! Her letter. I have to read Jen's Mother's Day letter to Mom."

Rifling through my purse I panic for a moment. *Relax, Terri. You got this.* But I can't seem to find it! I wipe my eyes, and there it is. Under the Kleenex and hand sanitizer, I feel the edges of the envelope. Card in hand, I look at the ladies.

But before I can speak, Edith chimes in, "My William sends the loveliest cards, never misses a holiday." She fixes her collar for what must be the fiftieth time. "Good mothers raise good sons."

"And daughters." Stella taps me gently with her cane.

I wonder what these women would say about how I scrambled through the early years with Jen. And what a mess I look like now. But I move past it all, and my full teaching voice comes out. "Can you all hear me? Jen says her card is meant to be read out loud, so I think she would want her words to be shared with all of you. She's a talented writer, and she's becoming a teacher."

"Just like her mother," Stella smiles. They all lean closer.

"Mom, this card is from Jen," I say, speaking slowly, "Jen, in Colorado. Our Jen."

Her eyes find mine for a moment. I swear they light up, but maybe I'm imagining it.

"Mom... words for you..."

Dear Grandma,

Happy Mother's Day. The mountains in Boulder would take your breath away. I try to get out hiking as often as I can, and I think of you and all of our walks we took along the river when I was younger. You've been walking me around since I was a baby in the stroller. Makes everything better, like you always said. That, and a hot cup of tea. My studies are hard, but it looks like I'm going to make it and be a teacher like Mom after all. Maybe even fourth grade!

I'm taking a class about learning and memory. For the kids, they say when information is put to music it unlocks long-term memory and stays protected. It made me think that maybe whatever disease it is that has made you forget, there might still be a place that music can reach. This was one of my favorite nursery rhymes that you and Mom would sing: The old Irish one... I think it was one of your favorites too.

Toora, loora, loora,

Toora, loora, li...

I'd give the world if you could sing that song to me this day...

I love you, Jen

Watching Mom rocking gently, I continue the lullaby, and her lips slowly form the words, "Toora, loora, loora..."

The ladies join in, "Toora, loora, li..."

The tea is now a rich color, and I pour the cream into each cup and stir, as we all sing.

"OK, ladies, time to sip."

They nod their heads, enjoying.

I sit back in my chair, and stir my cup, Mom's cheeks pink. I fix a white curl over her ear, the way she fixed mine when I was a girl. "How did we get here, Mom?"

"Have some tay?"

The cup already in front of her is full. "Mom, you have some right here."

She takes a sip, her face peaceful. She looks at me and says, "Darrhhling, need a little honay wit tat."

Fourth of July

Edith Sharp

Be well. That feels like a tall order for today. One day you feel full of energy, the next like a deflated balloon or a light bulb flickering on its way to burning out. I really hope nothing's wrong. At least the river looks the same, cutting its pathway through the hills. Out my window, the summer leaves flutter in the wind. I miss my kitchen. Morning coffee in the bright breakfast nook, with Cosmo's soft fur warming my feet, and my cardinal, always perched on his branch. And sometimes staying in my robe until noon. Now breakfast in my room means waiting for someone to bring a tray or walking to the dining room for crisper toast and warmer coffee. But these legs... they don't seem to be following where I want them to go.

Maybe it's my age, or maybe it's this place with the same old routine, making me feel out of sorts. I'm never this tired—no umph. I check the photos of William Sr. and me dancing at the Bardavon, the picket fence he used to touch up each summer with fresh white paint around our sturdy cape. A time when life made sense.

Suddenly I startle as Nurse Hurry (that's what I call her) barges in with her cup full of pills, each one a different color and size. I guess I didn't take them after all.

"Jumpy today."

"I'm fine." I'm not going to tell her I think something's wrong—Lord knows what extra pills she'll try to give me. I just open my hand to count. This one needs to be reminded that I studied bookkeeping and I've always been excellent with numbers.

But she's not smiling, and those chipped nails need to be trimmed.

"Everyone needs their pills on time Edith, not just you. Let's move this along."

Apparently, I'm counting too slowly, but you can't be too careful here. "You've given me eleven pills, and I only take ten."

She shrugs. I put the yellow pill—supposedly for memory—back in the cup and hand it to her, then swallow the rest, one by one, saving the white oval for my osteoporosis for last. "Satisfied?"

She puts the cup with the yellow pill down on my tray and walks out of the room. I toss the cup in the trash. *My name is Edith. My son is William. I remember what I need to remember. I'm doing just fine.*

On the whiteboard next to my closet is today's date: June 25th, Nurse: Eve, Aide: Raffee—thank God for Raffee! He actually helps, doesn't rush me. That Nurse Hurry doesn't even have time for anything, not even her own nails.

"Ms. Edith?" Raffee bounces in from the hallway, dark curls almost touching the tops of his ears. *What's that he's holding in his hand? My rock?*

"I found this over in Nellie's room."

"Stolen again."

"Who'd want to steal a rock?"

"Read it."

He reads, holding it close to his face, "'The ornament of a house is the friends who decorate it.' Is this from your friend Emerson?"

"Yes. And I believe he would have been my friend if we'd lived in the same century."

"Woulda been? Of course you'd have been besties, you both like painted rocks."

After setting my gift in just the right place, Raffee helps me get my foot into the stiff leather of my sturdy Mary Janes. Maybe my legs will be steadier now. I certainly hope so.

"But I do have to tell you one more thing, and it's important." Raffee is fidgeting, hands flexing, back and forth in the chair. "Goodness, Raffee, how long have I been talking? Agnes insists she'll keep ringing my phone until she becomes the lost woman..."

"who doesn't know she's lost," he says, finishing my sentence with me.

"Oh, I guess I've told you that before."

He bounces towards the door. "See you later, Ms. Edith. Be well!"

Be well. Come on Edith. Push yourself. Walking always makes you feel better. Get out the door. Go get your breakfast. Pushing my wheeler, I rest at each door, only to admire the decorations of course, and I quietly catch my breath. Grinning pumpkins, dancing Santas, cornucopias... last I checked it's summer, and this motley display is enough to confuse even the clearest mind. I peek in an open door and look through the window. Bright sun, trees in full bloom. Summer, indeed. Roula's door, which I pass next, is the only one I can rely on always to be in season, and sure enough, she's put up a large red, white, and blue striped top hat. Independence Day—July already. Where does the time go? I hate when the social worker comes in and asks me what year it is. But I've perfected my answer—one I'll never have to change as long as I live—it's the year I haven't died yet.

"Knock, knock." I rap on Roula's door, but there's no answer. That lazy bum tells everyone how hard she works at Keepers' Mart, but five'll get you ten she's in there sleeping. And on a gorgeous day like today... why, it took all I had just to get dressed, and I'd much prefer to have stayed in bed, in my pajamas. But I could hear Mother; she always sent my sisters and me out to play, no matter the weather. "Make the effort to get outdoors every day, and you'll never be a shut-in." Still, I don't suppose one lazy day a month would hurt at my age. I'll have to tell Stella to put my idea on the Residents' Council agenda—one leisurely morning a month when everyone wears housecoats and robes to a late breakfast. Just like the pajama days they used to have at William Jr.'s school.

And another thing that Council can address—cleaning up the neighborhood. Enforce the rule of seasonal decorations only and get rid of those dreadful summer Santas. If it's confusing for me, imagine the ones who are going gaga. They won't know what day, month, year, or season it is. I must give credit to Roula. Red, white, and blue for the Fourth of July. Stars and stripes forever!

As Town Registrar for Poughkeepsie, I took the minutes at meetings. My hands cramped trying to keep up. And when Independence Day came around, I spent hours making sure all the plans were in place. A live oompah band that played music during the fireworks, miniature flashlights and little stick flags for all the children. Oh, how little William loved to wave his flag.

My, this hallway a mess—laundry carts, one of those awful lifts they use to get the invalids out of bed. And the usual array of residents sleeping in their chairs. I suppose it's a whole lot easier to travel that way, but once you're in, you never get out. I'd rather shuffle even with these stiff old joints. But why on earth would the dining room be this far away? I hear the noise... tick, tick, tick... I slow down. And here's Mr. Florida, in that ratty old excuse for chair, just in time for our morning routine.

Stopping and turning towards me as he gets close, off come the sunglasses.

"Hey doll, you seem familiar. Do we know each other?" His tropical shirt is unbuttoned halfway to his navel. "We should go someplace expensive together. When you're feeling good like this..."

"Button your shirt, Bruno," I surprise myself, remembering his name. *Just keep walking, Edith.* He'll keep me here for an hour if I let him. I am glad that he feels good. I wish I felt good today.

"Where are you going, doll? I thought we had a date."

"Bruno. It's Edith. And I'm not your doll." I straighten my collar. "I'm on my way to breakfast. Have a lovely day." Tick, tick, tick, and he rolls away.

Exhausted, I finally spot the open doors to the dining room. My table, by the corner, next to the large window, seems so far away. But I'm fine. I'll get there. Pausing every other step, I reach my chair. The trees, all green now, are so pretty. Now I can sit for a while and get my strength back. I just need to eat.

"Edith? Would you like more coffee?" A staff member holds a pot ready to pour.

My name brings me back from the trees. *How long have I been sitting here?* Fixing my collar and my earrings, I stare down at my cup, half empty. I don't remember having a sip. Maybe the cup was never full. I push it away.

No thank you, dear.

"Well?"

I thought I said no thank you. Now I want to say maybe it's not my cup... but it's right in front of me, the taste of coffee in my mouth. Out the window, I see the rolling hills below. The sun is shining through the wisps of clouds. *What month is it? July? August? Oh dear, did I miss the fireworks?*

"Coffee?" she says, with an edge.

I stare back, then glance down at the maroon-colored plastic mug. *I'm fine, dear.*

She looks at me, shrugs, and walks away.

And there's Uncle Sam's hat hanging on the far wall, along with stars and stripes streamers dangling from the ceiling. All that would be down if we'd already had the fireworks. So, I haven't missed them. And I don't need that memory pill after all.

The staff member refills the emptied sugar packet holders on the table that I'm sure were pilfered by Nellie. On my plate, there's a small stack of syrup-soaked pancakes, and I take a bite, but I'm not hungry. I don't know what's wrong with me today. With my hand that seems to shake more than it used to, I put down my fork. Taking my last sip of cool coffee, I wipe my mouth with my napkin and slowly move my chair. I'm able to grab the handle of my wheeler to stand. As I shuffle out of the dining room, my legs feel like I'm wading through the syrup I just had on my pancakes, along with the usual ache in my shoulders and knees. But there's a new pain now, in my lower back, a cramp, maybe a burning. These things happen, I just need to walk. I'm sure I'll be fine once I get to my room and lie down.

Taking a tissue out of my pocket to wipe my nose, something crumbles in my hand—a shortbread cookie with a purplish hue. *How on earth?* Then it comes to me. These were served by Roula in her room. I must have been out late again last night, or was it the night before? At my age I should know nothing good ever comes from staying up too late. But with Stella and the gang, after dinner is when the fun begins. Thank God for that blessed, all too short, rush of energy before bed. Still, tonight, I'll go to bed early. I don't care if Roula and Stella are playing Cash, Sinatra, or Streisand. I'll be in bed, even if I can't sleep.

One foot in front of the other, I settle into my rhythm, pushing on the handlebars as I start the walk back to my room. Whatever fog was making me confused this morning seems to have lifted. Staff are picking up the breakfast trays and bringing fresh towels, and I smell the soap for the morning baths. Just fifty yards more to my door and I can take a lovely afternoon nap.

Is that? It can't be. There are no babies here. And that woman's much too old... but she's singing. Rockabye baby, in the treetops... to her baby, wrapped in a blanket, the way I used to wrap William Jr....

And in that room, over there, another baby, and stuffed animals... where am I? Did I make a wrong turn? This is a nursing home, not a nursery.

Oh dear, I'm so confused.

Is that... William Jr.'s room? It looks so much like it, with sun pouring in through the windows and that comfortable rocking chair.

But where's his crib, the white one with his soft yellow blanket and his Winnie the Pooh mobile hanging from the ceiling?

Suddenly, my legs are pushed out from under me. "Gahhh!" I'm toppled onto all fours! Dirty tile an inch from my face!

What... just... happened?

My hands sting, my knees throb, I can barely breathe.

This is... dreadful! The worst of all things... a fall.

Take stock, Edith. See what's what. Dear God, I hope nothing's broken. If it is, I don't want to know. I'm frozen, afraid to move. My bones... like Swiss cheese the doctor always said... if it's my hip, I'm done.

Just stay still, Edith. Take your time.

Slowly, I turn my head to the side, as much as my stiff neck will allow. And there's my wheeler, sideways, in the middle of the hall. Do I dare crawl towards it? My oh my, this is a terrible day. I can't believe this has happened to me.

Before "Help" can escape my mouth, a yellow raincoat in a chair wheels over, and there's Nellie peering down at me. "Mae horse tis' a bet, goin' home." The one time I need her to make sense, and she's speaking gibberish. But now I realize what's happened—and it's all her fault.

"Nellie!" I exclaim. "You bumped me! You knocked me over. I know it was you! You need to watch where you're going!"

"Yes, mum! Rocks get skinned on knees, but the girls were little, run too fast."

"You're dangerous. I could be... dear God... really hurt. You shouldn't be allowed in these hallways by yourself. I'm going to call..."

"No!" Clutching her red plaid purse, brow furrowed, "I'll be late... ta bus to Ireland."

"You're not going anywhere. You're a menace." There. It had to be said. Shaking, I don't dare get up yet, but I can still shout. "I could have broken something, Nellie!"

Dear God, did I break something? No sharp pain. No bones sticking out. I roll back onto my bottom and cautiously sit myself up. No hip pain. That's a good sign. I look at my legs. Somehow, I'm still in one piece.

"Ta country bus, over and back, green horses, riding the hills, to swing in the air..."

"Nellie Riley," I scold her. And I'm about to add, "There is *no* bus to Ireland," but I stop myself. My pride is injured but my bones aren't broken. No sense in breaking her heart.

Nellie stares at me, her mouth slack.

She needs to know her place. "The next time you wander outside to sit on that swing, I'm going to call the cops. That's not the swing you grew up with in Ireland. You're in a home. River's Edge. You need to remember that. And you need to be careful where you drive!"

Nellie shakes her head, "Tat's a lot." She wheels away.

Need to get... off of this cold, hard floor. But I don't dare do it without help. "Nurse!" I shout. "Raffee!" But the words come out quietly, more like a gurgle. A nurse whose name I can never remember comes over. "Oh dear, Edith. Let me help you up. Are you in pain?"

"I... don't think so. I might have scraped my hand. And my knees ache, but... please just help me up—carefully." The nurse stands my wheeler up, locks the seat in place, and then I wait for her to wrap her arms around my midsection.

Small, but strong, my savior raises me with one swift movement, and I'm back sitting on my bench seat. Nellie, who didn't go very far, watches from her chair.

"Edith, I want to be sure you're OK," says my nurse. "Let me see those hands and knees."

Struggling to straighten the collar of my shirt, hands trembling, I notice her badge. "I'm fine, Nora, just a little, well, more than a little shaken up." I glance over at Nellie. "I'm wobbly, a bit dizzy, and I hurt in all the expected places, but," I manage a laugh, "none the worse for wear after 98 years."

She smiles. "You're going to have bruises."

"Yes, and they too shall pass." I wipe my hands together. "'You can't keep Edith Sharp down,' that's what William Sr. would say, after I wrote another one of my nastygrams to the editor of the *Poughkeepsie Journal*. And boy, do I need to hear it now."

Nurse Nora smiles. "I'd love to have read some of your letters."

Nellie, fidgeting in her wheelchair, now wheels away as quickly as she appeared. At that speed, she could knock down another pedestrian. Nora looks back at me and says, "Stay right here, Edith, let me get my stethoscope. I just need to check your heart and your breathing. Then I'll catch up with Nellie."

All I want to do is get into my room and into my bed. "Thank you, but there's no need for an exam." Then, wagging my finger towards Nellie, "At that speed, she should be fined, or... or lose her license."

"Take it easy, Edith. We all have our moments."

We certainly do.

Standing up, I seem to be fine. Or am I? The fog seems to be rolling in again, and something doesn't feel quite right. Rest is certainly in order. But I have to keep moving to get to my room. Taking a few timid steps. I'm fine as long as I can walk. "I can still do the old lady shuffle," I say to no one. But I can't bring myself to smile. This one was too close for comfort. I'll have to tell William Jr. about it when he calls. No, on second thought I won't. He'll just worry.

Finally, I reach the sitting area, already winded and only halfway to my room. The alcove is packed with those who sit. Not me. I'm just resting. I find a spot to park my wheeler and take a breather. Truth is, I could sit for the rest of the day. *Five minutes, Edith. Just five minutes.* My eyes aimlessly browse the walls. On the whiteboard: Memory and Movement, Current Events, Morning Movie: *West Side Story*.

"Tonight, Tonight" is playing on the big screen TV, such a lovely duet, those young voices. And there's Nellie, rolling through the crowd, as if nothing happened, forcing others to move out of her way. I should get up and say something, but I have no energy. Maybe I had too much coffee at breakfast. Or maybe not enough. I need some time to settle myself.

A familiar voice says, "Hey doll, I think we know each other. How about a little soft shoe?" That man, with his sunglasses and tropical shirt and that tattered wheelchair. I'm in no mood to tango. He's such a pest. And today of all days. I ignore him, but he won't give up.

"Hey, dollface!"

"It's morning, Boris. Too early to dance." He gives me a strange look. *Oh dear, that's not his name. But it starts with a B.* I don't mention that all I want to do with my legs right now is rest them on top of my bed. The sun shines down on the blanket of green leaves out the large window, reflecting off his mirrored sunglasses.

"You could use a good foxtrot."

"What a lovely summer day," I say, hoping to distract him. Glancing back, I'm forced to squint. "Must you always wear those mirrors over your eyes—there's so much glare."

Taking his glasses off, he rests them on his belly. I never noticed his striking features. There's a light in his eyes today, and his color looks unusually good. Has he been tanning outside? Or maybe they're giving him the anti-aging pill. I could use one of those today.

"Perfect day for a drive," he says, sounding chipper. "Want to join me?" He makes a vroom-vroom noise.

"Bruno," (his name finally comes to me) "enough of that." I rub my forehead. I don't want to discuss my fall. But I can't help myself. And he won't remember anyway. "You should know I've had a frightening fall. Nellie, in the raincoat over there, knocked me flat. Nothing's broken, but a nurse had to help me up. I need to sit and compose myself, and then I'm going straight to my room."

"All right, then. I'll sit with you. Beats standing up." He laughs at his own joke and fiddles with his brakes. "Just look at the dancing in this movie. How their feet glide. How they leap—and fly. We should do that—together. You and me. Come on. Let's dance until we drop." He looks into my eyes with the smile of a teenage boy and puts his hand on top of mine. "Dollface..."

He's never reached out and touched me before. I try, but I can't pull my hand from his grip. He's surprisingly strong.

"Hands to yourself!" I shout. I search for a nurse, and glance over at the residents watching the movie, but no one seems to notice. No one ever notices anything here. He leans forward and brings his mouth down, trying to kiss my hand. This crosses the line. With no one to help, I'm running out of options.

"Rude!" I yell. "Stop."

He startles. I manage to pull my hand back. Still too shaky to get up and walk to my room, I shift to the other side of my bench seat—to get an inch or two farther from him and fold my hands together properly on my lap. Then I give it to him. "Try that again and I'll slap you."

Sheepishly, he looks away and starts pulling at the frayed edges of his armrests.

Thank God for *West Side Story*. The music, the dancing... the actors so alive. Suddenly William Sr. is spinning me on the dance floor, so handsome in his tailored suit. He's standing, as he always does, chest out, shoulders back, head high, a few steps ahead of me, holding out his strong hand, waiting for the beat to start.

But William Sr. is gone. Moving my toes back and forth inside my Mary Janes, I glance back over at Bruno, who's now watching the show. Oh dear, he's seen me look at him.

"A little soft shoe?"

Utterly incorrigible. Nothing to do but ignore him. Nellie in that yellow coat, wheels close to the TV, standing up, and fidgeting with the buttons, right in the middle of... suddenly *West Side Story* disappears and we're watching one of those awful talk shows where people tell their embarrassing secrets and scream at each other. Nellie, wobbling on her feet, seems like she's about to topple. That would be poetic justice, but I can't bring myself to wish ill on anyone. Somebody had better grab her before she goes down.

Mustering my strength, I yell for help, but the shouting match on the talk show drowns me out. A flash of green and there's Raffee, thank goodness, smiling brightly, bouncing in and over to Nellie, catching her just before she falls. He holds her upright and guides her back into her chair, but she stands again, legs shaking, and they take a few steps together. Raffee smiles, turning it into a gentle dance. Ginger Rogers and Fred Astaire. He balances her. She plops down in her wheelchair, and he changes the channel back to the movie. Then he pulls up a chair next to Nellie and sits. With the touch of a button, Raffee the miracle worker returns the whole room to the world of dancing and song. Finally, a moment of peace.

Now Bruno wheels over—again. "Check out the new brakes on my chair." He leans closer, and I can smell his coffee breath. *Go away.* I don't have the patience for him and his bragging. "I can turn on a dime, and these babies catch every time." He pushes his cap further back on his head and one of his eyes closes. He must be winking at me. "Hey, thassa rhyme. Diiiiime…"

The word stretches out as he says it. I hear the snap of his brakes unlocking, then—"Riiiightttt, sssppiiiin… wheeeee… diiiizzzzy…"

His mouth is drooping. He doesn't seem right. Face slack, his other eye closing. He struggles to look back at me, his head bobbling, lower lip twisted down. *Dear Lord.* My heart fills with fear.

Staring blankly at me, he tries to open his eyes, but they just quiver, and the corner of his mouth hangs open.

"Bruno! It's Edith. Stay with me. I'm calling for help. Raffeeeeee!!!!"

But it may be too late. I've seen this before. Just before William Sr. died, he looked exactly the same way.

Raffee rushes over. I shout, "Something is wrong… Bruno needs help!" Raffee says Bruno's name a few times, but Bruno just keeps blinking his eyes. No one is home.

"I'm bringing Bruno to his nurse." Raffee whisks Bruno away. The tick, tick, tick of his chair trails off as they head down the corridor.

The day I lost William Sr., we had just come back from Jones Beach, and in the midst of bringing things in from the car, he dropped down on the sofa. His tan face went pale, his bright eyes darkened. And I remember that awful feeling, watching him struggle trying to speak, to breathe, clutching his chest. Then he passed out. The ambulance came, but it was too late.

Poor Bruno…

He helped me with my flowers. He's a kind man. It is terrible how he chases women. I'm sure he's done it his whole life. But now, now something has happened to him, and… I'm worried. This I'll have to tell William Jr. later when we speak.

What a day! First, Nellie nearly kills me. Then Bruno. They say bad things come in threes. I need to get back to my room… before anything else happens. This old body is done for the day. My, the hallway is long, seems longer than usual. But the only way is to walk this off… to keep moving, just as I always have. Agnes would say just keep going until you can't. *Just a few more steps.* Back in my rhythm now, one foot then the other, and I'm at my door at last.

Getting into bed, a weight lifts off my body. Just as I'm sinking into sleep, Nurse Hurry rushes in, asking if I'm in pain after my fall. What terrible timing. All I want to do is rest. She bombards me with questions. Pain medicine, vitals, something about a period of observation after a fall, this, that, the other. It's all too much. Rest is all I need. And where was she when Bruno needed her?

I raise my hand, signaling no to all of it. "I'm fine. Please leave."

In truth, I'm not fine. The pain is worse than I let on, but I'll manage. The last thing I need is a fuss. I've actually had worse falls in my room, one where it took me 15 minutes to crawl to the bed. But besides my stiffness, there's this new pain in my back, along my side. I rub, maybe it's my kidney? I'd better stay hydrated. Don't want to get one of those infections that makes you tinkle all the time—or worse, almost kills you. I take a sip of water from the cup on my bedside table. At last I can rest.

I hear coughing, and suddenly Stella is next to my bed. I must have left my door open. "You're napping Edith, and you *never* let yourself nap during the day. It's almost three o'clock."

I rub the sleep out of my eyes. *Why was I napping?* Then I remember. "Didn't you hear what happened? Nellie bumped me, with that chair of hers, racing around trying to 'catch the bus.' Knocked me flat on the floor! I'm lucky I didn't break anything. She could have turned me into a cripple."

Stella coughs and clears her throat, "Nellie's got a one-track mind."

"Well, that doesn't excuse her carelessness. Maybe she's too dangerous to be here. And I hurt." I rub my aching side.

"Edy, I got this." She pulls a pill bottle out of the folds of her dress and offers me a small white capsule. "When pain keeps me up and I'm tossin' around in my bed, I can't wait for no lazy nurse. These little beauties bring on a nice, calm starry night. Know what I mean?" She hands me a pill. "One for you, one for me." She swallows hers dry.

I do know what she means. The waiting makes the pain worse. Against my better judgment, I take her pill with a sip of water, hoping it will kick in quickly. The sun glints through my window. "I love warm summer days. Bringing William Jr. to swim at the river."

Stella smiles. "Fourth of July's comin'. We got a pretty good view of the fireworks from my room—or Roula's. One of us will have the party. It's in a week or two."

"When I worked at Town Hall, we made sure we had the *best* fireworks display for fifty miles. We always stayed for the Grand Finale."

Stella shakes her head. "You hear about Bruno?"

"Mr. Florida, with the sunglasses and tropical shirt? Did I hear? I saw it happen. How is the poor man doing?"

"They sayin' it was a stroke."

The picture of Bruno's twisted face returns to my mind. "Right before, he grabbed my hand and wouldn't let go. It shocked me. He's never touched me before... just talked a good game. But this time... he held on."

Stella shifts in her chair and leans towards me. "Sometimes, when that happens, they tryin' to tell you something. But I hope he was just gettin' frisky."

"Frisky, I'll say. He didn't use his words. You *ask* before you take a lady's hand. *That's* the proper way to do it."

Stella's face serious, she breathes deeply through her tubing. "Grabbin' your hand could have been his way of saying..."

"Oh, dear..." I fidget with my collar. "Does anyone know if he's all right?"

The sound of doors closing in the hallway grows closer and closer, one after another.

"Damn," Stella sighs.

Nora, her face somber, strides into the room, speaking quickly. "Doors have to close."

Stella says, "I didn't hear no fire alarm."

"No alarms for this one," she snaps.

Stella looks at me, then at Nora, "Bruno?"

Nora is still for a moment. This can't be good. She stares back at Stella.

Stella waves her cane. "We should be allowed to know who's sick or dying around here." Nora takes the cane and rests it on Stella's lap. Stella continues, "We have a right to know who's in the bag. That ain't just a dead body. It's a person. And these people are our friends, our family. You can't just close the door on death."

"I'll open the doors in a few minutes, once the gurney passes." Nora walks out briskly into the hallway, pulling the door closed behind her. But Stella thrusts out her cane, stopping it from shutting, and with a strength I didn't know she had, pushes the door back open so we can peer out. For a moment, all is silent, then men in black walk by on either side, rolling a waist-high metal cot with a black, zippered bag on top.

I shudder. "He... seemed so... strong today. I mean... brighter than usual, even wanted to dance."

Stella says, "Oh, I'm not surprised," she shakes her head, jowls jiggling. "It's like that sometimes. For years they fade, they fizzle, their light grows fainter. Then they flame. The extra energy needed to go."

"I'll... I'll miss him," I say, casting a misty eye on the pictures of William Sr. on my shelf. "Time confuses me," I say softly. The breeze from the window warms my face, and my back pain is finally easing. Next to my wedding photo is Agnes's rock. Agnes... she's the only one of my friends left. The last one standing.

"You know what we have to do now," Stella rumbles. "Put his name on the tribute wall, add it to the monthly memorial service. The whole routine. I'll have them get drinks and the good cookies," Stella yawns, "from the bakery. All this talk is making me tired, or maybe the pill..."

How do I carry this weight I know all too well? How do we put all the sadness back where it belongs? So much loss. So much we'll never understand. Like the good doctor across the hall. A lifetime of giving, and what does he have left?

Are those the party beads from New Year's draped over my tiara? Roula told me I'm the princess of River's Edge, but at this age, I know what I am: I'm the queen of... funerals. And no funeral is complete without a good sendoff. When the end comes for a friend, it's essential to have a party. I'll have the ladies in my room tonight.

But this room is a mess. *How did this happen?* My wastebasket is overflowing, my food tray still here, and I have to get up and make my bed. I'm so tired... and thirsty. I'm sure a glass of cold water will help me shake this fatigue. I turn to Stella, but she's fallen asleep, breathing loudly, snoring. She'll be no help.

I ring my call bell. With effort, I'm able to reach my Deerfield Beach bag with the palm tree on the front. Agnes bought it, but she didn't want to keep it. Souvenirs are too much clutter, she always says. I dust off Humperdinck, Elvis, and Sinatra... those blue eyes, so young. Finally, a staff member comes in and I ask her to fill my pitcher with ice water. "I'm having a gathering in my room tonight." She takes my pitcher and heads into the hall, then brings back two—filled high with ice! "Be a dear and set up my Victrola."

She puts the boxy old record player up on the desk. "Don't forget to invite me later."

A bag of the caramels and the mints that Pearl sells is waiting on my shelf to be opened. Good thing I went down to the store recently—I'll need to find a place to put those out. Mother had the most elegant silver candy dish, and she always placed it right in front of a giant vase of fresh flowers. I suppose I can rinse out this bowl with the canned pears from lunch I refuse to eat. As for flowers, the baby's breath from William's Mother's Day bouquet is still serviceable. I just need to freshen the water. Then the room will feel like I can have company. So much to do. I take a moment to rest on my bed and look out the window. This time of year was our favorite, William Sr. and I. He called it the "extended twilight of summer." Out my window the oak tree stands under the distant pink clouds of sunset amidst the familiar chortle of birds saying goodnight. More tired than usual, my eyelids droop then slowly close...

Mother would be horrified. The gang's all here, and I'm still in bed. And my room—it isn't ready. Holding my forehead in my hand, I try to calm myself... *Let it go, Edith. Let the party start. Where's my wheeler?* One doesn't entertain from one's bed. I sit up quickly—ouch—there's a sharp pain in my side. Breathing through it, I slowly put my feet on the floor, then move towards my wheeler cautiously. Something is not quite right... I just need to sit. Nellie makes a beeline for my Victrola and opens the top.

"Nellie! Hands off! You've done enough damage today!" My sharp tone surprises me. But it works. She folds those hands of hers back on her lap. Sometimes I think this place would be safer if she really did go to Ireland. But she does have that lovely daughter... the young woman with the tea.

Stella has brought plates of miniature chocolates. She rolls my bedside table to the middle of the room and sets out the delicacies. "These are from this week's French class. They have real *cordial liqueur* inside."

"Leave it to the French," I say, smiling. "Chocolate *and* alcohol. They know how to live."

Stella nods her head, "They know how to *indulge*."

My energy picks up. I put out some paper napkins and my pitchers of water with a few small dixie cups under the warm glow of my Tiffany lamp. It's party time. "And for those who aren't 'drinking' tonight," I point to my bag of candies from Keepers' Mart "we have some good old-fashioned caramels and mints."

Roula, with extra red lipstick smeared around her lips, brings in a lap-full of glass goblets and sweeps my paper cups off the table. "I know good glassware when I see it. And I found these in the latest shipment at the store. Pearl is lucky to have me volunteering there now. I'm straightening that place out. You know, after I retired from managing my sixth graders, I managed a thrift store five times the size of Keepers' Mart—St. Vincent DePaul's."

Stella and I both roll our eyes. We both know Pearl is the one managing Roula, and straightening her out, since she keeps trying to rearrange everything down there—-and in my room, too. Suddenly my appetite returns, for the first time all day. Stella's spiked chocolates go down easy, making me feel warm inside. It's so easy to have another. And another. After half a dozen, I lose count.

Roula parks herself next to the Victrola—as if the party is at her place. The album cover of the record she is about to play is water-stained but oooh, that picture of Humperdinck with those smoky eyes of his. The record spins as his voice serenades, "Lonely..." Although it's hard to hear when Stella joins on the loud notes, the words come back to me, along with memories of William Sr. at the Bardavon.

Oh dear, I'm feeling a little tipsy. *How many of those chocolates did I have?* I've always been sensitive to liquor. But maybe just one more. *To heck with it. This is a party.* I take two.

The ache in my knees and hips is quiet, and I barely notice the pain in my side as I sit on the seat of my wheeler. Everyone seems to be enjoying the chocolates, the music, the soft light. Maybe I just worry too much. Through the window, the moonlight reflecting off the river is gorgeous. It's a full moon, bringing nighttime light to the river valley. I can't remember the last time I felt this... happy. Humperdinck's voice swirls through the room.

Stella says, "I must say, Edith, you throw a good party. I didn't think you had it in you."

I shake my head. "And you thought I was a grump. Remember? Well, I entertained quite a bit in my day. With my grandmother's china, crystal from William's aunt, and always linen napkins. We even had someone to help with the dishes."

Pouring the water in the goblets, Roula pushes up her red glasses. "It's the drinking glasses *I* brought that make the party." *Just let it go, Edith. Everyone is having fun.*

Stella takes a deep breath and rolls her eyes. "I must say, Roula, this is one of *our* better parties." She points out the window. "Look at that moon!" Clearing her throat as she sings a few notes, Stella continues, "Ladies, we are the queens of the castle! The chocolates, the music, the view..." Holding her glass up, she toasts, "To friends!" Sadness crosses her face. "And to Bruno!"

"Bru-no, Bru-no, Bru-no."

"Ahh Bruno," I sigh, with Nellie repeating in the background. "Maybe up there he'll get a brand new chair!"

"Nah, he'll be drivin' that fancy car of his!" Stella laughs.

The water tastes good, washing down the sweetness in my mouth. My head is light, and the pain from my fall is all but forgotten.

Even Nellie smiles, chewing on her caramel. Sugar is all it takes to please that one. Pulling at the bracelet on her wrist, the one with the white buckle, she hits her hand against the table. Stella rolls over. "Now Nellie, let me help with that."

Pulling a small pair of scissors from a pocket of her dress, Stella snips Nellie's bracelet in two. "Freedom!" she shouts.

I pick up my water glass. "To Ireland!" We all drink another water toast.

"Now, Roula," I say, "Humperdinck is nice, but how about, well... you know, old blue eyes?"

Roula frowns. "If Frank had known me, I would have been his favorite. We just didn't get our time together."

Stella throws her hands up. I can't help but laugh. Roula's expression is dead serious.

Sinatra's dashing smile and baby blues practically pop off the album cover. Roula changes the record, and the strong beat of "Luck Be a Lady" gets my heart thumping. This energy... it must be from those spiked chocolates. How many did I have? My feet dance as I sit on my bench seat.

Nellie's eyes open wider, and she starts to sway, repeating, "t'luck, t'luck, t'luck."

As the drums beat with the booming finale, Sinatra's voice croons, and memories flood through my head of William Sr. dancing, his arms on my waist, spinning me around the room. And with that moon, this seems like a night that will never get dark. The chocolates are long gone now, and Sinatra's voice is silky smooth. The sugary liqueur floats through my body. "And now, the end..." I feel a swell as his words echo in my mind. Stella sways with her golden cane across her lap in that chair that can barely hold her, Roula's red frames are teetering at the tip of her nose, and Nellie tilts her head from side to side, in sync with the rhythm. All happy. All so alive.

Frank's voice is perfectly pitched, as always. Moving to the melody in my seat, I begin to feel woozy. A breeze moves past me, and over the music, I hear someone say, "Do you want to dance?" A familiar voice... William? Glancing around the room, it's only my friends enjoying the rhythm. William is in Poughkeepsie under his headstone... but I swear I heard him. I rub my forehead. And I would like to dance. Do I dare? With the taste of liquor on my tongue, I marvel at the reflection of four ladies—Stella, Roula, Nellie, and myself—in the window. As I tap my shoe on the floor, the tempo of the song picks up.

A hand stretches out towards mine, and I see the silhouette of a man in the window glass. William Sr. I'm sure of it.

As the strength of Sinatra's voice reaches a crescendo the walls expand and suddenly, there's plenty of room for dancing here at the Bardavon. My husband, so handsome in his best suit, is just two feet away, his eyes gazing into mine. We're doing the foxtrot—slow, slow, quick, quick. I take a step towards him and reach for his hand...

Bright light. Where am I?

I try to lift my head, but it weighs a thousand pounds. And I feel so... tired. All my zip is gone. And this pain, not just one kind but every kind, everywhere—sharp, dull, nagging, aching, crippling, miserable. Turning my head ever so slightly to the side, I'm just able to peer out the window. Ahh, there's an oak tree I recognize... with a swing hanging from the large branch. I look around quickly... what's on that shelf? Sparkle, necklace, teddy bear, shamrock glass, teacup... those are my things! And there are my pictures of William Sr., our wedding, William Jr. missing his teeth, my house. All still here, thank goodness. For a moment, I thought...

But what's this tubing, blowing air in my nose? And the crinkle of plastic on my backside? Cotton in my mouth. I ache—everywhere. And my white collared shirts are hanging in my closet while I'm wearing a crumpled gown, thin worn fabric with a loose collar... a hospital gown. Dear God! What happened?

On my desk, a bouquet of yellow, pink, lavender, and red flowers. They're beautiful, but... this is no holiday arrangement. No, flowers like this can only mean one thing. Something's happened to me. Something... awful.

I pull up my coverlet, but it's stuck over my leg on one side. There's something underneath and a warmth on my outer thigh. Could it be Cosmo resting next to me? When I try to pet him, I can't feel his fur. I turn for water, and my lower leg seizes up. Pulling back the coverlet... there's a giant black frame holding my left leg! And a large towel wrapped in a ball, where I feel the warmth. No Cosmo. I must have... broken something.

A nurse breezes in. "Edith! Look who's awake!" *Why is she so cheerful?* There's nothing happy about this, nothing at all. As she tightens that awful cuff around my arm, I see her fingernails need to be cut. I know those nails, the nurse who hurries.

"What's happened to me?" I ask.

Her face tenses, "How do you feel, Edith?"

"Dreadful," I say. "Pain everywhere. What on earth has happened? And why haven't you gotten those chipped nails taken care of?"

"Edith, I'm not surprised you're a little fuzzy. You were transferred back to River's Edge last evening from MidHudson."

My face falls.

She continues. "You were there for ten days."

"Ten... days?"

She sticks a thermometer in my mouth. "From the hospital report, you had a pretty bad infection in the urine. You blacked out and fell, fracturing your knee and hip." She pauses. "And..."

"And?" I can tell she has bad news.

"What did the doctors tell you?'

I shake my head. *Nothing. I don't remember anything.*

"Well, there were... complications with your surgery."

"Complications? Surgery?"

"Well, yes, to repair the fractures. They almost lost you, Edith. Your heart stopped during the procedure. But they were able to restart it again. We're glad you made it back." Taking the thermometer out, she says, "97.8, just right. I know it's a lot to take in. Your son knows. We've spoken to him. Let me get your pills." And with that, she rushes out the door.

"I hope there's one for pain!" I yell after her.

A lot to take in. I don't know where to start. There's a lump on my forehead, tubes under my nose, a black contraption paralyzing my leg. And I'm wearing briefs and a hospital gown. I've had... surgery. I think my last surgery was for my tonsils as a young girl. And there were... complications. My heart... but my temperature's normal. And my heart is still beating.

Only my son would send such beautiful blooms. She said she spoke to him. I feel like I saw him, his green eyes, his peppered hair, so distinguished, just like his father. Was he at... the hospital? Oh, I just can't remember. Maybe it's better that way.

Suddenly the nurse is back, standing next to me with a cup in her hand and a glass of water. I didn't hear her come in. My tongue dry, I motion for a sip.

But she shakes her head no. "Edith, you have lots of new pills, and... because of your heart failure, doctors' orders to limit the fluids."

"Now you listen. How am I supposed to swallow all these pills without any water?

"You can have a little."

"Oh thank goodness. Can we start with the ones that will make me feel better?"

She smiles. "Each pill will help you in its own way. And you're going to get them all down with just one cup."

Now some of it starts to come back to me. "I was dancing. With my husband."

"Edith." Her brown eyes are calm now, looking at me. "You've been through a trauma. You're going to need time to recover."

"Time. Well, that's really all there is here, isn't it? Until there isn't anymore." I stare at the broad green leaves of the oak.

"You're actually very lucky. Aside from your broken bones, only bruises on your face."

As I blink at the morning sun, a memory flashes. "I... I *saw* the surgery."

"No, Edith, you weren't *watching* the surgery. You were *having* the surgery, and the anesthesia would have knocked you out the entire time."

"I'm telling you I saw it," I say, surprising myself with my anger. "There were doctors and nurses in the room, moving quickly, speaking loudly. I remember looking down at myself, feeling warm and comfortable, with no pain. And I was going somewhere. There was a tunnel..."

She gives me a strange look. "You were hallucinating. It happens sometimes with the really strong pain meds. Your recovery is going to be slow. No weight on that left leg for at least a month..."

"A month? What about my walking. I walk every day. That's how I..."

"Let's take one day, one step," she smiles, "at a time. The doctors have to see how you do before you can get on your feet again. They may need to do more surgery. I was told the pin in your hip is loose."

"I have a pin in my hip?"

"Yes, and it's shifted out of position. It can happen. But if it can't be fixed... they're not sure..."

"Don't say it. I won't entertain the thought."

"They said your bones are like Swiss cheese."

I stare at her. Then at my wheeler in the corner folded against the wall. "Walking... is what I *do*."

The magnitude of what's happened to me hits. I put my hand over the frame on my leg, and try to move it, but it's too heavy. A fall, broken bones, surgery, heart failure? I feel like throwing up. "I think I'm going to be sick." She hands me a paper bag and I put it over my face, then breathe in and out a few times.

"We can add another pill for nausea," she says.

I want to ask about side effects, but I don't have the strength. "Why not," I say, looking at the pile of multicolored capsules and tablets in front of me. "What's one more?"

Even with one small cup of water, I manage to take them all. The coolness is soothing, as I feel the liquid travel down my throat. I could drink a gallon but... *doctors' orders.*

"Your flowers are beautiful." Nurse Hurry rubs her hand through her dark hair and smiles. "That son of yours. I heard he flew in and stayed with you at the hospital until you were out of the woods."

So, this is out of the woods? I wonder what's it like in the woods. Then it comes to me. William's hand. William Sr.—I was reaching for my husband's hand... and then William Jr., my son, was holding my hand when I opened my eyes after the... surgery. "My Williams," I mutter, "they've always taken such good care of me."

"Edith," says Nurse Hurry, with a gentle smile, "let me know if you are ever uncomfortable, so *I* can take care of you."

Kindness, I didn't know she had it in her.

The breakfast tray is brought to my bedside table and the coffee is cool. I take a few bites of buttered toast. The powdered eggs make my stomach churn, and I put my napkin over the plate.

A mild dizziness swirls around my head. I stare out the window at the oak tree. The swing moves back and forth, but there's no wind. *How can that be?*

Focus, Edith. In the distance, the river. Now there's movement around the tree trunk. Are those... children running and playing around the tree? Their clothes are dirty, and they're smiling, climbing on the limbs, the way my sisters and I used to climb on the elm in our yard. I open my eyes wider. *Yes, Edith, you're awake. This isn't a dream.* I see them. They are there. I let myself watch, enjoying their playtime, on the swing, just as I would with William, Jr. playing outside under our tree for hours. The pain ebbs, my eyelids droop, sleep.

Opening my eyes, I see the sun out the window high in the sky. *Where has the day gone?*

"Edy, Yoohoo, Edy!" I know that raspy, out-of-breath voice. "It's so good to have you back. We missed you. We didn't know what happened, couldn't get information. You know how it is..."

Rolling in, panting as she wheels forward, Stella parks next to my bed, her face full of tears. "We were all so worried! We didn't know what was happening at the hospital. They wouldn't tell us, and we were thinking the worst... a... a rose on the wall. But you're *here*! And you don't look so good. Your face!"

I touch my cheeks, "My face?" Stella picks up a mirror from my desk and hands it to me. Dear Lord! I don't recognize myself. Black and blue across my forehead, and a big lump right in the middle. And my hair! It's long and flattened to my head! I glance back at Stella who raises her eyebrows.

"I told you so."

Suddenly I remember Nellie bumping me in the hallway. That awful menace! Anger bursts in my throat. "Nellie! She *bumped* me and I was on my hands and knees and... my fall is all her fault!"

Stella clears her throat, "No Edith—-you fell in your room. You threw the best party we've ever had. Sinatra was crooning on your Victrola. There was moonlight, and we were toasting Bruno with Roula's crystal. And those chocolates with the liqueur I brought—you had a whole bowl. I guess you love them as much as I do, and they sure sneak up on you. We were having a grand time. Roula and Nellie were here, and you were smilin', groovin' in your wheeler, happy as a Southern girl butterin' her biscuit. You stood up, looking strong, then reached for something, like you were taking someone's hand, and then..." Stella shakes her head back and forth, "Whooo, that ambulance showed up right quick."

I rub the lump on my forehead. "I'm... not remembering so well. But yes, the dancing, William's hand... I thought he would catch me... but I... fell."

Stella takes a deep breath. "You did. Now let's fix you up."

"You mean with one of your special pills? I could sure use one for this awful pain."

Stella roots around in the folds of her dress but comes up with only a couple of cookies. "Damn, I'm fresh out. They bring me those relaxers, tell me I'm too stiff to move around without them. But they'd need to give me double or more for those little things to help." She takes my bracelet with the key off the rock on my shelf and slides it onto my wrist. "Nellie and I visited your room every day."

"She... she didn't take anything, did she?"

"No, I'd find her just sitting there, waiting. But there is something I have to tell you. When you fell, Nellie tried to get up out of her chair to help you. And... well, she broke that fancy lamp of yours."

I gasp. "Tiffany. Irreplaceable."

"It's a lamp, Edy. We were worried about *you* being broken—or worse—and whether the doctors could put you back together."

Taking the brush off of my bedside table, Stella runs a few gentle strokes through my hair. Leaning in, she asks, "So, what happened at the hospital?"

"Well... I barely know myself. I'm just finding out. A pin, Swiss cheese, heart failure, and now, you won't believe this, they're saying no walking, maybe for a long time..." I pull my sheet up to cover the metal frame around my leg so I don't have to see it. "But you know me, I'll be up in a week or two. I just have to get this darn contraption off."

"Oh Edy, I'm sorry. You must feel..."

"Like shit." I surprise myself and my friend with the curse word.

Stella leans closer to me. "Talkin' like that, they must be givin' you the good stuff."

I laugh, but not too hard since I hurt everywhere. "No extra pills. I want to keep my head clear. But I do feel a little strange. The children," I say, pointing to the window, "I like watching them play."

Stella rubs her head. "Oh really, what do you see?"

"I see children, running and playing on the swing. Their clothes are tattered. Maybe they're playing hide and seek."

Stella fixes her dress and adjusts her cane across her chair. "Either you're getting *too much* of the good stuff... or maybe you're seein' my little friends out there."

"Friends? You *know* those children?"

Stella hums gently and starts to sway in her chair. "Those little ones have been here longer than I have. They'll always be here. And when the veil is thin, when we're close to leaving, they come to help us."

"Close to leaving?" I ask. "Am I close to... leaving?"

Taking her cane off her lap, its gold surface shining in the sunlight, she taps it on the ground. "Edy, I'm gonna tell you somethin', somethin' you wouldn't have believed until now. Those doctors and nurses, they don't know everything. There are some mysteries they can't explain. I've stood right up, all three hundred and plenty pounds of me, and walked out of this chair, legs workin', breathin' easy, no tubes, no nothin'. And I done it two times already."

My mouth drops. "What? You? Walk? Two times? How is that possible? Don't you always say it takes all the nurses in this place to get you into bed?"

"Not when I'm set free. The first time, I was paddling in a boat. It was a small boat, but I was paddling, strong, like I've always been. And I could breathe—no tubes. I was crossing the river. And I knew if I got to the other side, I wasn't coming back. But I wasn't ready. Your business has to be done here before you go there. Because once you cross over..."

I turn to Stella and lean closer. "That freedom, I... I felt it, too. Do you know that I *saw* part of my surgery? I heard the voices of the doctors and nurses moving around the table. I was floating, and I felt so warm, no pain, not a single ache. And... there was a tunnel out of the room. I started down it, and the light, it was so bright, just grand. Someone was there with me, but it wasn't William Sr. It was my friend who was lost. She told me I couldn't stay. I had to go back. It hurt, falling into my body on that hard, cold table. The beeping, the pain, tightness in my chest." I take a deep breath, remembering the complications. "You know... they said I had heart problems during my surgery."

"Well, you're still here, ain't you?"

There's my shelf, the pictures, the ornaments. All still here, like me. But what will happen to them, to all this, when I'm gone?

Her raspy voice clears through a cough. "We never know when that call will come to take us home. I found myself at the edge of the river twice, and each time I fall back into this beat-up ole body of mine, it's heavier, more puffed up, like a boiled sausage. My breathin' gets harder, and I feel like I'm drowning, that is if I'm not gonna burst. But my spirit, Edy, my spirit is lighter, my eyes more able to see the truth. That's why we gotta enjoy life, find the sweetness, celebrate every holiday—even the ones named after those saints we never heard of. We gotta live for today and not tomorrow, cause for us," she looks right at me, "tomorrow might never come."

I sigh. "Well, I don't know about tomorrow, but today is not a good day. And I doubt tomorrow will be better. I didn't expect... well, it's not the dying, it's just that... dying should be at home."

She ignores me. "The second time I was on that boat, paddling across that river, they were all around me, the children, or whatever you want to call them. They were playing, and I was ready to join their game. But the Good Lord keeps sending me back. I don't understand it. But ours is not to reason why." Tapping her cane on the floor, Stella breaks out into a few notes of that Etta song she sings sometimes. Holding the tubing to her nose she breathes in deeply. "Edy, if the walls of this building, could tell their stories... you know, it's always been a home, but not like this. Most people 'round here don't know this, but a lifetime ago, before this property was abandoned, it was an orphanage, run by the state."

Confused, I look at her. I thought I knew all the local history. But I never wanted to know much about this place. The place on the hill.

She fixes me with her eyes. "I got moved all around. But for a few years, I was one of those children, those orphans, running through these halls. And that big tree was small. We didn't get to play much, but when we did, I was in charge of the games." She laughs. "Just like now."

I smile.

"You've always had a little girl, right here, in your room, in the corner, standing next to your closet." She points. "You know who I mean."

I gaze around my room. "I don't see her, only the little ones *outside*."

"Oh, those are her friends. And she's here. Braids, with a red plaid dress. Lulu likes you."

A flash of red crosses my vision. But it can't be real. None of them can be. But I'm so confused. I rub my eyes. "I don't believe in ghosts. And neither should you."

"Who said anything about ghosts? These children are alive, they're just livin' on the other side of the veil."

"If they're alive, then what am I?" Grabbing my sheet, I feel the wrinkles. Those are real. I close my eyes and let my head fall back on the pillow.

Stella starts to shift her wheels. "Edy, you rest now. It's the Fourth of July, you know, and there's a party this afternoon."

For just a moment, a flash of joy moves through the pain. A holiday to look forward to... and holidays are my friends. "Oh, I didn't miss it? Will there be fireworks like the ones we used to have?" I try to sit up, but my body reminds me of everything I've just been through. "I don't know if I have anything left. I might... have to skip it." I pull my cover up to my chin and mutter, "I don't know if I can do this."

"You know, Edy, every time the Good Lord shows me that table He's set for us—that big feast up there, that chair that's just waitin'—the bigger the party I want to have down here." Stella bumps my bed as she turns her wheels, sending pain through my hip. "And there's gonna be a party tonight. Can't miss a holiday. I done told you that. And if you can't get out of bed, we'll just have to bring the Fourth of July to you."

She huffs out, leaving the door open. Across the street, there's the doctor, lying motionless in his bed, crimson "H" cap on his chest, and there's Raffee, bless his heart, playing music for him and putting the gloves on his hands to make him feel like he's in the operating room again. If I ever end up like that, at least Raffee will understand. He'll know how to take care of me.

A tray comes, but it's the wrong time for dinner. And anyway, I'm not hungry. I'm used to going and getting my food when I want it. Out my window the sun begins to fade. The birds are saying goodnight, which means it's time for my evening phone calls. I wait for Agnes's three rings, followed by William's rings that never stop. But will I be able to reach my phone? Or ever walk again? Anxious, my breath is tight. *How will I manage?*

The phone starts, but it's more than three rings. A pit in my stomach. The friend in the tunnel with me, it was... Agnes. And now she really is lost. I reach for the receiver, but my leg can't move under the weight of the brace. Taking a breath, I'm just able to pick up the phone. "Hello...?" William's voice! Everything makes sense when I'm talking to him. And now he's with me. "Yes, dear, I remember holding your hand, I understand no walking, for a while, doctors will see how I do." I repeat his words back to him.

William's voice changes, hesitant. "Mom, I have to tell you something... about Agnes..."

"It's all right, dear, I already know. A good friend, she'll be missed."

On my shelf is her rock of friendship. I see her face, smiling... the one who's lost but doesn't know. Tears form, and I look away, towards the bouquet of flowers, bright colors beautiful against the early evening sky. The phone in my hand, William's soothing voice. "Yes, dear, I'm still here. And you'll fly out soon. But I'm fine, really. You do your work... love you too." I rest my head and stare out at the oak tree. All is still.

Stella rolls back in huffing and puffing with two plates of red, white, and blue cake slices and a few of those little handheld American flags. They remind me of the ones William Jr. used to wave. Stella coughs. "Here's to celebrating good health. Enjoy!"

"I can't enjoy cake while I'm stuck in bed. I'll get fat. And eating while you're lying down is bad for your digestion. Don't you see the condition I'm in?"

"Come on, Edy, Roula will be here soon. She had a busy day, now that she's officially volunteering at Keepers' Mart. Don't be a grump. Being alive is reason enough to celebrate."

Maybe she's right. The sprinkles scatter all over the bedside table as she pushes a plate of cake towards me. For once, I don't mind the mess. "Give me a fork." She hands me a plastic fork and places an envelope in the middle of the messy table. The cake tastes sweet in my mouth.

"Here's a card. From us. You know that Pearl down there—been in charge of that place for over a hundred years. Well, she told Roula to buy one of those plain black and white cards with words about how bad we feel that you feel bad. But I said, 'there ain't no sunshine in that!' There's no windows in that store—that's the problem. I told Roula you needed a 'Welcome Home' card with bright colors to cheer you up. So, we found this one with the pretty red songbird."

I open the card, hand shaking. A branch with a cardinal, red feathers looking royal. Inside, I read:

We missed you, Edy.

The words, 'Merry Christmas' are crossed out, and underneath is written, 'Welcome Home!'

Love, Stella and Roula and Nellie

The cardinal, my William Sr. A welcome message from my red bird, but a re-used Christmas card? Well, I suppose it's the thought that counts. I look at the picture of my home with the picket fence on my shelf. I should be there now, out in my garden, pulling weeds, clipping white lilies to put in my crystal vase. But this leg… I can't move it at all. What did the nurse call this contraption? An immobilizer? Like the one that scruffy Irishman had when we wandered into his room. He said something about needing a lift, being hoisted out of his bed. My heart sinks, and… that feeling again… I can barely catch my breath. I'm trapped. An old lady in her bed. Too tired to straighten the wrinkles.

Out the window, the river, the rolling hills, the summer evening sky, and in the distance the sounds of a few fireworks from family parties, friends in the backyard. I'm able to breathe a little. Getting back home will take a bit of doing.

The oak tree… is it moving? I try to shift so I can see. It's the swing! Swaying back and forth on the branch. And there's something yellow. "Nellie!" I shout. Taking off her raincoat. Holding onto the ropes, she's rocking. *Oh dear, I hope she doesn't fall. Should I call the nurse?* I search for my buzzer, but it's out of reach. I can't save her. She's on her own with those wobbly legs… but at least she's able to enjoy her freedom.

I'd give anything to be able to walk a few steps right now, to walk through my front door, or even just out this one. Warm wet on my cheek. *Am I crying?*

Stella is humming "God Bless America," watching Nellie wobble on the swing, her own enormous body swaying in her chair. "Fireworks will be starting soon, like stars sparkling in the sky!" Stella keeps humming, "my home sweet home."

Home. The tears start coming again. "I want to go home."

Stella clears her throat. "Girl, we're *all* home, wherever we are. Don't you see? Look out the window. Look at the beauty God has created—for us. We're all in His house."

She keeps humming, and somehow, the pain seems easier. And just for a moment, in this place where I'm not supposed to be, I'm able to relax.

The oak holds steady as the swing moves. If William Sr. were here, he'd tell me all about the oak tree—just like his father told him—how it grows tall and strong in the forest and always finds the light. The setting sun glistens on the hills that roll down to the river.

"See that Nellie swinging over the grass," Stella says. "She's finally in those green hills of Ireland, where she belongs. She's home."

Labor Day

Pearl Haberstein

et to work, Pearl. That was mother's answer to everything. Even when you didn't feel 100 percent, she'd say—you'll feel better once you're up and at it. That woman... I remember when my brother found her, aged ninety-nine, slumped at the workbench in the back of our family store—with a smile on her face. *Who am I to kvetch?* She had a pen in her hand and the ledger open to the month's receipts. It was a good month. We all worked hard to make every month a good month at Haberstein's Hardware. How I miss those days. All the employees were like family—at least, most of them. Mother always gave them chocolates and cigarettes at Christmas, even when money was tight. And sometimes, I'd sneak a smoke with them out back. But never when my favorite nephew, Kenneth, was around. He looked up to me, and I saw great things in his future. Sundays we'd usually have a few of the staff over for dinner. They were always welcome. And they always brought something—bread, wine, or dessert. Of course, no one's left now, and Main Street is nothing but faceless chain stores. I'm older than mother was when she drew her last breath. Work'll do a body good, that's for sure.

And here I am, in *my* store—Keepers' Mart. The cornerstone of River's Edge. Still working. I know what all my customers need, and these folks need a lot. Those sniffles I had this morning, they're gone now. Probably allergies. Nothing more. Still, I worry, especially when seasons are changing. Sometimes I fear the worst. No one can run this store like me. *Ach, I'm fine.*

After the usual rush of residents coming for the newspaper and a candy, my hands ache under these darn plastic gloves. But it's a good ache— from handling merchandise, making change, punching the numbers on the register, honest labor. Settling into my chair, I feel weary. I've spent hours organizing these aisles. So much work to get things right. It takes talent to turn donations into profits... knowing which lamps, glassware, candy, and cards will actually sell. I can honestly say, I've done a tip-top job—with the help of only a few volunteers. Of course, I've outlived them too. And now that sniffle is back. And I'm oddly tired. No rest for the weary, though. *Shake it off, Pearl. You'll feel better when you're busy.* I sit up straighter in my chair just as my "assistant" rolls in.

"Pearrrrlieeeee..." The way she says my name makes me wince. She makes her entrance slowly, as if she has all day, those brazen red curls tightly coiffed.

I clear my throat, coughing up a little something. "Store hours are nine to noon, Roul-ar. But I shouldn't have to tell *you* that."

She snaps her gum—mother never let us chew when we worked—and looks towards me, puckering her lips. "It's Rou-*laa. Like oooh-la-la.*" Her thick coat of red lipstick emphasizes the movement of her mouth. "And I had to brush my teeth. You know they're all mine." And then, as if she's a movie star, she gently pats around her ears. "Do you like my curls? Just did 'em. Sorry I'm a little late."

I shake my head, fixing the surgical mask around my mouth. "A *little*? You left me alone for the busiest part of the day."

"Have to look *good* for sales."

How in the hell can she think she looks good? With sparkly frames on top of her head and another set hanging from her neck, she looks ridiculous. All she needs is one good magnifying glass. I point towards the back. "The lamps aren't going to dust themselves." She pretends not to hear me. "What's the point of having help if... ach, never mind."

She turns, nearly hitting the tightly packed shelves around the register with those thick angled back wheels of what she calls her "sporty" chair and rolls to the back of the store. I see those brassy red curls go from one aisle to another, futzing instead of dusting. At Haberstein's, futzing was a punishable offense.

She rounds a corner and goes out of view. She better not be rearranging the cards. So headstrong and hard to teach, this one, always with her own opinion. I tell you, I don't know if I have the patience for this Roulah-la. I'd fire her if I could, but it takes a long time to train a good volunteer— and given the numbers, how much time do I really have left? I'm already a hundred and two.

"Don't touch the cards," I yell. I'm about to roll back there myself when two patrons come in—staff in uniforms, a man flirting with a woman. I fix the mask again over my mouth and nose—at my age one can never be too careful—and pull the edges of my plastic gloves tighter as I listen to their gossip and lift my stiff neck just enough to snoop. The staff always talk too loud at this place, as if no one else is around.

The woman, in a pink uniform festooned with some sort of cartoon faces, whips her blonde ponytail, then smiles at the young man in all green with his dark curls. I know her.

She starts yammering. "Well, you think Ms. Edith is bad, I had to deal with Mr. Parker—who was in *some* mood this morning. I've been takin' care of him five days a week for years, and when he gets like that, I don't rush to answer every time he rings because half the time I go in his room, and he's already forgotten what he's ringing about."

With his dark curls, the young man I've only seen a few times before rubs his forehead. "Sad to say Ms. Edith is gettin' just like that. Ain't nothin' good enough for her since she can't walk no more."

Swinging her ponytail to the other side now, the pink one says, "One of these days, I'm gonna walk out of this place, while *I* can still walk. Stay here long enough, and you end up like these people. Stuck. Forever."

Shifting from one leg to the other, the man shakes his head. "Ain't nothin' I can do to keep Ms. Edith happy." He runs is hand over his curls. "And I know there are lots of other jobs I could be doin'."

Twirling her finger through her hair, the woman says, "These residents all think they're the only one. Jobs like these will take your soul, unless you realize you can't make none of them happy, no matter what you do."

I shudder.

The young man says, "You got that right. And when I stopped on 2 to get a cup of coffee, they were saying someone heard that administrator, who smiles like he's your friend, is talkin' like he's gonna cut some positions."

The woman shrugs. "He can do us a favor then and take the job. I'll take the unemployment. Might as well stay home and get a check."

"I think we're safe for now, though, cause from what they was sayin', sounds like Ruthann was goin' at it with him—he was talkin' about some corporate budget, needin' to fill beds so they have money to keep the lights on, but she was in his face, sayin' go ahead and tell corporate they are in the business of Health Care, capital H, capital C, and it's the staff that provides the care. No staff, no business."

My neck aches as I lean closer, trying to hear, but it's the same story every few years. This is a tough business.

The woman tosses her head. "Well, since I still have my job, I guess I should go do it." She steps in front of the man and approaches the register. Opening her hand, she reveals two Snickers bars. I'm about to give her the price, but she closes her fist, snatching the candy, and turns to her companion. I know exactly what she's going to say next. "Hey, Sugar Daddy, next one's on me."

He winks, grinning, "Sure thing."

Her ponytail bounces as she walks out the door.

Ughhh, she swindles a different sucker each time. Straightening my mask, and then my uniform, I say to the poor schmuck with the bill, "Next."

My knit hat falls forward—this damn neck—and I lift my eyes from my name tag. The P and the L of PEARL are fading, but at least "Keepers' Mart" is clear.

His smooth, unwrinkled hand places a pack of gum on the counter. The first premise of sales is eye contact, but I can't lift my neck far enough, so I glance at the tag clipped to his chest pocket—Raphael Williams. Now I remember, he's a talker. But it's slow right now, and I don't mind kibitzing with a customer at the register. It's good for business. "Are you working today, Raphael?"

"I sure am, Ms. Pearl." He rubs his hand across his forehead. "Man, am I working. I got Ms. Edith on that first floor. And she does nothin' but yellin' since she can't walk no more. 'Raffee, be a dear' is all I hear. She doesn't like what they're serving at breakfast, so I get her hot cereal. Then she's cold and needs an extra blanket. Then she's hot and wants the window open. She'll keep me there, moving her tray, emptying her wastebasket, fussin' with her shelf, and even if I do everything she says, sometimes she gets angry when I leave."

He glances around as if to check that no one is listening. Leaning closer, he says, "Ms. Pearl, she was never like this before. Always polite. Never so needy. Maybe it's the meds they're givin' her. I'm trying not to smoke on my break, but I tell you, I need something." He looks down at the gum and shakes his head. I nod.

This is the problem with kibitzing—someone else's earful becomes yours. I pick up the pack of gum and hold it towards him. "Chewing at work is not professional."

He gives me a strange look. "Well, I need somethin'. She's killin' me. She wants the water pitcher filled, but I'm told one extra glass a shift, doctors' orders. What am I supposed to do?" Shaking his head, "We are definitely not paid enough to do this job."

"Work is work, Raphael. It's what keeps us going. And Edith appreciates you, your caring, your patience, even though she's not showing it."

He smiles at me. "I'm sorry, Ms. Pearl. I didn't even ask about you. How's that stiff neck of yours?"

"Same as ever. But I manage." I turn to the door and spot the one with the floral dress, huffing and puffing as she rolls through. And there she goes, that Stella, straight to aisle two, for the candy—which she definitely doesn't need.

Craning my neck to glance back up at Raphael, I take the gum away from him. He startles as I reach into one of the jars on the counter. "Peppermints—my mother swore by them. They'll give you a kick. Twenty-five cents each, five for a dollar. And the Snickers for your *girlfriend*, a dollar each."

He looks longingly at the gum, which I've moved to the side, and hands me a crumpled bill.

I shine my hand-held, goose-neck lamp (special ordered) on the money. Good thing he's patient as my gnarled fingers move slower than my mind. It's a five. "This lamp," I say. "It came in last year, battery operated. So convenient. If only my neck would move the same way. I'm still trying to get more like it—there's a long waiting list." But I don't think he's listening. And I'm right. He keeps on kvetching.

"And you know, Ms. Edith, she asks all day about her phone, she's expecting a call, at night, but she don't want to hear..."

This kind of talk never ends by itself. I cut him off. "It's been twelve years since I first moved in here. You know, I'm a *resident...*"

That always grabs their attention. He gives me a sheepish glance. "You see this store, Raphael? It was a closet. Filled with cleaning supplies.

But I had a vision. I saw what people needed—a place to get a candy, a magnifier, or pill counter to make life easier, a tchotchke to brighten one's room, and, of course, cards. Did you know I'll be a hundred and two in November?" I smile. "And you can buy me a birthday card right here." I point to the area where the card stand sits in its own special nook. "That is unless *Roular* didn't rearrange them all."

He leans over, bringing his eyes level with mine. "Thank you," I say. "You know it's hard for me to look up." I stare right at him. "Life, Raphael. It's about figuring out what others need." He nods. "You're the kind who'll stick around in this business. Sure, you're young, you could leave at any moment. And Edith probably senses that too, but you have what Mother called the kindness, so I'm giving you my life lessons, proven out over a hundred years."

His eyes widen. I continue. "There's nothing easy about this business. There's no quick fix for life's pain. The system doesn't pay, and of course, budgets are necessary. But without business, there's no store, and no home for that matter. The lights need to stay on. But without care, there's no business. People in pain aren't pretty. But you have what it takes. You could run this business, this place."

"Me? I don't know nothin' about business."

"You're learning the business. And you already know all you need to know—you know how to care."

He quickly rubs his eyes, then whirls around. All I see is his broad back as he walks out the door. But he took my advice with the peppermints, so I know he'll be back.

Sitting back in my chair, I can just see the top of Roular's head move from the card nook to the lamp aisle. I'm concerned the red terror might be doing more harm than good, but my register duties keep me up front. I adjust the signs around the counter, moving the "No checks accepted" and "No bills over twenty" so they are easily seen. *Cosmo* and *Glamour* magazines are in front of the *River's Edge Gazette* and the *Poughkeepsie Journal.* I cringe.

My voice loud, "*Roular*... those frivolous magazines go on the rack!" I tidy up the newspapers, muttering, "*Roular*... sounds like a vagabond."

"Rou-lah," she rasps, "and those magazines are Stella's and Edith's favorites. And when I was the head of St. Vincent DePaul's thrift shop in Naples, we always sold out of *Cosmo* and *Glamour*."

I glare at her. "This is *not* Florida. I've learned a thing or two, you know. Numbers don't lie. Inventory is tight, and those magazines don't sell."

"Not if you hide them where they can't be seen." She tilts her curls. "And now they even talk about beauty at our age. Well, my age at least. You know, Pearl, you sound stuffy under that mask. Are you getting sick?"

Taking a few deep breaths through my nose to check, "No... if it's anything, I'm sure it's allergies." That's what I say to Roula, but I have a bad feeling. It always starts this way. I clear my throat, confirming there's nothing to clear. I put my hand to my forehead—a bit warm, but it's summer. I'm not going to let myself worry—yet.

I just don't have the energy to say it again. I've told her how many times? Those magazines never move off the shelf. As it is, this store barely breaks even after I pay to keep the lights on, and I won't let her make this place lose money. Haberstein's only had one losing year, and that was when our inventory in the stock room burned in a fire. Even then, we still found a way to sponsor the Boy Scouts' float for the Fourth of July parade, because the community needed us. For heaven's sake, they've talked about putting in vending machines here. People need to be told what candies they need. And who buys a sympathy card from a vending machine? The machine isn't going to ask who died.

Rolling my wheels back behind the register, I confirm that my calendar is flipped to the right month—August—with the field of sunflowers. We are somewhere around the tail end of it, I'm sure. Come fall, those nasty colds, and that most unwelcome guest, pneumonia, will be making their rounds. And I need to keep working. I take a deep breath—in and out—

from under my mask. These lungs, still strong, but my nose is a little full, my breath a little labored. *Get to work, Pearl.* Besides, my favorite holiday is coming up. Haberstein's was always open on Labor Day. People with their projects, always needing something. It was a great day to be open—balloons out front, patriotic bunting, and free popcorn. A Haberstein tradition.

I glance over at my "helper." Honestly, those plastic glasses match the red in her hair. It's over the top. They insist I have a volunteer here, but this one... if something happens to me... *Oy vey.* She'll be the one running this store—or running it into the ground. I can see them wheeling the vending machines in now. She rolls back over towards the cards. "Watch out for the glassware!" This one's a disaster waiting to happen. She'll ruin everything, the way the chain stores did in Peekskill.

In the aisle along the far wall, I see Stella hanging around the candies a little too long, and I yell out a reminder, "No sampling!"

With a lap full of chocolates, caramels, and lemon drops, she slowly rolls her extra-wide chair towards the register, her mouth clearly puckered around a "free" caramel. Taking a deep breath from that tubing around her nose, she clears her raspy throat a few times. "Pearl, as a waitress, I learned to take *care* of my guests, and they took *care* of me."

She thinks she's the president of this whole place, but she's just the head of the Residents' Council. And this is my store, where I'm the boss. I glare at her. "The candies always taste the same. Ready to pay?"

"They're better when they're free, but go ahead," she says, plopping a chocolate into her mouth. "Charge me for the samples. Now, what's eating you?" Her belly bounces as she chuckles.

I point to Roula. "The red one. She's *re*-arranging. I've found stuffed animals between the glassware, and she doesn't know a thing about sales. And why would she—spent her whole life in a classroom, and then she ran a *thrift shop*." I stop myself. *No complaining.* "I know I did you and the Residents' Council a favor, Stella, by taking her on as my assistant, but I have to decide if she's really going to stay. There's a lot to learn, and... I don't know if she listens. Things are done a certain way for a reason."

Stella smiles. "Good luck, Pearl. Teaching the teacher."

"You know, as a young girl, in our family store, I was considered the best teacher—fixing a faucet, repairing a screen, replacing a doorknob."

Stella turns towards the back, clears her throat again, and in a louder voice shouts, "Roula, what was it, forty years in the fifth grade?"

From the back, I hear "Sixth grade! Get it right!"

I can't stand these two yelling in my workplace. Can't they see the "Quiet, please" sign over the inside of the door? I shake my head. But oy, what did I expect? They are part of that first-floor crowd where the music plays all night.

Stella puts all the candies and the empty wrappers on the counter and hocks up more phlegm. "Listen, Pearl, I need your help. I need your recommendation on what to buy."

"Of course you do," I smile under my mask. "I'm always here for the customers."

"Well, I'm trying to get a little something for my friend, Edith, you know, the one who used to walk around standing up all straight and proud pushing that wheeler? Collared shirts and white hair all trimmed?"

I lean closer towards Stella, smelling the caramel on her breath. "Yes, I've seen her—a real lady. I gave her too much change once and she came all the way back to make it right."

Stella shakes her head. "That sounds like Edy. But she's not herself since the fall. She'll tell you everything's fine, but—it's an *angry* kind of fine. And I'm trying to find the right, something... chocolates, caramels, tootsies? She didn't use to like sweets, but now she seems to enjoy them."

"Mother always said, 'find the sweet in the sour.'"

"Must have been nice having such a smart mother. And where are those magazines? Edy likes the one with the name of her dog."

I purse my lips. "*Cosmo* magazine is nothing more than pictures of starving girls with lipstick. Edith is angry. From what I've heard, things are not easy for her right now, and they're not going to be for a while. I know how she feels—walking for her is like working for me. It's the one thing we can't give up. And I know *this* is what she needs." I push the jar filled with green apple-colored balls individually wrapped in cellophane and scoop out a handful. "Try one—on the house."

Stella unwraps one and as the candy hits her mouth, her lips and eyes both scrunch up. She looks like she's about to vomit.

I suppress a chuckle. "Sometimes you need to taste the sours, to get it out of your system."

Stella starts coughing and doesn't stop until the candy is out.

I tighten my mask, hoping to withstand the spray. Better to get this one with her hacking out the door. I let a few of the candies slide and charge her $2.00. It's all she can do to roll herself out.

With Stella finally gone, I wheel out from behind the counter to inspect Roula's work. Dust patrol is what the last volunteer with her French accent called it. The gold-trimmed porcelain dancing figurine lamps need to be cleaned carefully. No one should have to deal with a layer of dust dimming their light. Rummaging through the corner of my wheelchair, filled with tissues, blanket for my shoulders, my reacher, I pry my magnifying glass out from between the seat cushion and the frame. I pick up my gooseneck lamp in my other hand, and with the light *and* the magnification, my poor eyes can see that there is no dust. I may not like this Roula, but she's getting the job done. At least with the dust.

Through the open shelves, I see her waving the red, pink, and blue handheld fluff duster that she showed up with a few weeks ago, over the glassware. And... not again! There's a small stuffed bunny rabbit between the goblet cups. She must have won big at Bingo.

"Ahem. Stuffed animals go in the box."

Rubbing her lips together, her lipstick smears. "You have so many rules, Pearl. With the eyelashes and the pink hair bow, someone will love it. And it really stands out here."

"Yes, someone who *needs* it will. The cardboard box is in the closet." My neck cracks as I straighten it, and I wheel quickly to the nook in the back of the store, heading towards the most important items—the greeting cards. God knows what she's done.

I knew it! The four rows of cards have clearly been shifted. "Roulaaaahhr!" I am barely able to look up far enough to see the Sympathy section on the fourth row, and now the lower two tiers are full of——ugh—Happy Birthday, Get Well Soon, and Let's Be Thankful. Gah! With most of our patrons driving a chair, the lower two shelves are the only option that's within reach, and now the cards that are most important, the cards that express the deepest sympathy, have been replaced by those decorated with childlike drawings. This just won't do! "Roulaaahhr!"

I don't know where to start. I pull a card with a smiling sun and the outline of a sandcastle along the ocean on the outside. "Sunny days ahead." *Who would ever need that card here?* Horrified, I let the card and envelope drop to the floor.

"What is it, Pearl?" She looks at me, eyes wide through her sparkling spectacles. She has no idea what she's done. "You need me to pick that up for you?" She starts to lean forward.

I pull my reacher out from behind my cushion and swat her hand with the metal, swiftly picking up the card with the rubber ends. "The only thing I need you to do with the cards is undo what you did!"

"I arranged them all by color and size."

I don't know if I have the stamina for her.

Mustering all of my energy, I lay it on the line. Mother had a secret for raising eight children, a certain way of speaking with authority, and now it's time for me to use it. I take a breath for as long as it takes to run my fingers over each of the six points of the star around my neck to find my nicest yet firmest tone. "This store," I clear my throat again, "this store is the cornerstone of this home. The most important cards we sell here are sympathy cards." I take another breath. "Residents lose roommates, hallway mates, dinner mates." I feel my frustration rising as I watch her smack her gum. So unprofessional. "And God forbid something happens to one of the nurses or their family—there has to be a card with the right words. This is the land of condolences and memories, so those are the cards that need to be accessible, not the ones with rainbows and sunshine."

I've exhausted myself trying not to yell. With her bold red lip color, she looks back at me with contempt. Her smile shows off those teeth— "all mine" she's told me countless times. I'm sure that's why she thinks everyone can chew the tootsies.

"You could just fire me, you know."

She looks sad, but I think she may be faking.

"You know how I like the cards arranged. Fix it."

Loosening one of her tight crimson curls so it hangs down over her forehead, Roula snaps her gum. "I've done an excellent job with these cards. The display looks beautiful. And now you want me to..."

I stare daggers at her. "Do it before I change my mind."

She backs up sharply, turning her wheels, which catch the corner of the shelf displaying the expensive hand-painted lamps. I see it coming before it happens. The blue ceramic teeters, then crashes to the floor, shattering into pieces. Small bits scatter all over the tile. She turns and stares at me, mouth open, eyes helpless.

My chest tightens. "Oy vey, you're f..." I stop myself. I still remember how Mother handled me the time I broke a whole shelf of figurines while carelessly tossing a ball of twine up and down. I could tell she was not pleased, but she said quietly, "Shall we just call this an accident?" I look at Roula's sheepish face and shake my head. "Those sport chairs are dangerous and hard to maneuver. Accidents are bound to happen."

Rolling past me, looking straight ahead, ashamed and grateful, she says, "I'm... I'm... I'll call maintenance."

"Never mind. I'll do it."

Then she spins her thick knobby tires over the debris and continues out the door. As she wheels away, she calls out, "I guess you don't need me here anymore."

Did she just quit? She's got some chutzpah to roll right out of here like that without an apology. The aisle is a mess. Porcelain everywhere. I rub my forehead. The scattered pieces are too overwhelming. I knew it was only a matter of time. I'll just wait for the next volunteer who is inspired to try a third—or fourth—career in retail. I run my fingers over my necklace. I want to be angry. To get it out. My hands shake and my shoulders stiffen as I try to reach up and fix my hat. But my nose is stuffed, and I don't have the energy to be mad. I settle back in my chair, arms comfortable in the good old broad-width frame with elbow-height rests. It's the standard chair that lasts. *Just like me.*

Slowly, I push down on my wheels and roll over to the closet to get my scooper that attaches to my reacher. I'm tired, but this mess needs to be cleaned. *Get to work, Pearl.*

Then I hear, "You called, Pearl?" I sigh with relief.

Otto in his baseball hat covering his dark curls and his blue maintenance uniform is a sight for sore eyes. My arm strength isn't what it used to be, and I'm feeling so off today—my sugar must be low. Time for some candy.

Otto smiles, looking at the broken pieces. "Put your scooper away. I'm glad you kept your promise. Anyone over a hundred not only has the privilege but the *obligation* to call maintenance—for anything. Anything at all."

He takes out his broom and I watch his efficient sweeping as he starts on one side then moves to the other. I close my eyes for a moment.

"Pearl, I've seen this look on you before. Let me get you a candy." He puts down a quarter and hands me a sour apple.

"This is very sweet—or rather sour—of you." We both laugh. I open the wrapper and pop the ball into my mouth, but the flavor becomes too intense, making me smack my lips. I want to spit it out, but I'm used to it, and it's awfully good. I smile.

With the mess being cleaned up, I sit back in my chair. "You know, Otto, at Haberstein's, I started working at thirteen. The depression. Had to quit school in the eighth grade when we had to let most of the staff go. Stocked shelves, swept the floors." *Get to work, Pearl.*

He stops sweeping for a moment, listening.

"I wasn't allowed to work the register. That was Mother's job. For a couple of years, most people paid with notes. My mother would put the notes in a box, always looking the customer in the eye with a smile saying, 'When you can.' She knew they wanted nothing more than to pay. But she kept the window by the checkout desk open, and sometimes some of those notes would blow outside with the wind."

Otto puts his cap back on his head. "Pearl, that must have been a difficult time. Your mother sounds like an amazing woman. And you are living history."

I rub my knuckles, feeling the sugar from the sour work its way through my body. "Then the war came, and the store became a hub for gathering. My father ran the draft board. I was working from morning to night—we all were. There was so much demand, and many things were rationed. My nephew was a young teenager; he would help sweep the floors. I always gave him a candy at the end of the day, bought with my own wages, and we would sit together while he ate it. 'Awfully good' was the way he described the sours. Kenneth was fascinated with airplanes, and he wanted to learn how to fly them. Despite his strength, there was a gentleness about him, and he always seemed younger than his age, but I guess he was old enough to fight for our country." A warmth suddenly streams down from my eyes. "He didn't make it back."

Leaning on the broom, Otto sighs, "Pearl, you've been through so much. And with the stress of the store, you must be exhausted. Think about closing early today, so you can rest."

Rest. Hearing his words, I take a breath, finding the strength to finish my morning routine. *Get to work, Pearl.* I wipe my tears and blow my nose with the tissue from my sleeve. "You know, the body falls apart when you stop working."

Otto rubs his forehead. "Well, I guess that means *I'll* be healthy for a long time."

The floor clean, he bends down next to me and puts his hand on mine. "You are one of a kind, Pearl."

"Well, they're not making any more of me."

He laughs. "I'll get Roula back here tomorrow."

When I look up, he's gone.

And sure enough, the next morning, bright and early, I see that bright red hair rolling through the door. I'm feeling refreshed after a good night's sleep, and my sniffle is manageable, though it's not quite gone.

"Pearl, I... I need..." She looks at me, moving closer, with the same face she had when she broke the lamp.

"You need what?"

She continues, "to buy a card."

I straighten my name tag as I try to straighten my neck. "What *kind* of card, Roulaar?"

"Sympathy, of course," her head tilt acknowledging the importance of that sentiment above all the others.

Then she starts with that endless yammering that the card is for her neighbor, who lost her roommate, who's beside herself and can't get out of bed. Then she bats her eyes and asks, "Do I still get the employee discount?" *Unbelievable!* She's wearing her badge. and I realize this is her way of apologizing and asking if I'll take her back. She did make it in before the morning rush, so I let her refill the candy jars on the counter. Eventually, she finds her way to the back, that multicolored duster moving across the merchandise.

It's a slow morning, but August is the slowest time of the year for most retail—except camping supplies of course. The crowds here prefer to hang out on the veranda doing puzzles and listening to other residents kvetch about their late rides to their doctor's appointments, or their children who never call them or call too much, or their endless litany of aches and pains. They should get to be my age! But I don't mind the quiet down here. I've got no time to listen to complainers. There's that stuffiness in my nose again now, same as yesterday. This can't be happening. I *never* get sick before Labor Day.

Mother used to give us peppermints to clear the nose. I take one, but it fails to do the trick. This is just how that cold I had two years ago started. I know all too well how hard it is to shake sickness here, much less hold on through the deep rattling coughs of—God forbid—pneumonia.

A shipment of new donations arrives. *Get to work, Pearl.* Ordinarily I'd handle it, but I let Roula do one of my favorite jobs—unpacking the new items—while I supervise. She oohs and ahhs over a red and orange lamp with a fringed shade and puts it to the side. I suppose she wants the monstrosity for herself. She'll have to pay for it, but I don't have the energy to lecture.

Exhausted, I let her help me behind the counter. With each customer, she counts the candies, magazines, etc. to complete each sale. I just don't have the stamina—can't seem to get enough air. I take another peppermint and update my note, just like Mother used to do for our customers—twenty cents.

Roula fluffs her hair and starts kibitzing, and I'm stuck listening. "My husband was a drunk, a fall down on your face kind of drunk. But you'd never guess. For years, I pulled him out of bars at night. Then he went to work the next day, as if nothing had happened. He's the reason I went grey so young... but I've perfected my red over the years." She brings a hand up to her curls.

Dear God, I don't want to hear this yapping. Mother had a sign in the break room: "Leave your personal troubles at home. They'll be there when you get back." I cut her off. "We've all had our struggles." I check my forehead for fever again. Still warm, but maybe, just maybe, it's my cardigan.

"Yeah, but this guy, he'd get you, right there," she keeps babbling. She puts her hand over her heart. "A sweetheart underneath. One day, he turned yellow, got real sick, fast. The transplant gave him a few more years. When he was dying, he said the same thing he'd always say, 'You're the most beautiful woman I've ever seen. And I love your smile when you put your makeup on, everything done just right. But you don't have to do it for me. Do it for you.' And then he'd say, 'Find a way... to keep smiling...' she sniffles, "when I'm... gone.'" And here come the waterworks.

Her makeup smudges as the wet rolls from her eyes. I hand her a tissue.

"So now I keep doing the makeup, hair, nails, clothes..."

I cough and feel an ache in my side. *Please don't let this—Lord, just make it go away.* I need to rest, and all her talking is giving me this headache. I don't have a choice. I can't stay any longer, and I can't leave her here alone.

"I'm done for the day," I say. "Let's close up early." Of course, she doesn't mind.

It's too much for me to wheel myself, so I honor my obligation to Otto and call him for help getting me to my room. I stay in for lunch and dinner, hopeful I can knock out this cold before it gets hold of me.

The river valley out my window looks different each time I blink, and my eyelids grow heavy. Mother's wooden dresser stands on its clawed feet. On the top are my favorite pictures—the mahogany-framed news clipping of Peekskill honoring Haberstein's on its 75-year anniversary, a picture of me with the mayor, and one of Mother with the whole family, but everything is going in and out of focus. I blink and rub my eyes. Sleep overtakes me.

The next morning, coughing, aching, I can't get out of bed.

"You can rest easy, Pearl. Roula will keep the store open for you," the nurse says.

But I can't rest easy. The red one is a disaster waiting to happen. But I have no strength. I reluctantly put down my head.

The staff keep waking me up, coming to check my temperature and make me swallow spoonfuls of licorice-flavored cough syrup. They mean well, but they're annoying. I try to bat them away with my hands. I'm hearing whisperings of 'hospital' if I don't get better. I vowed never to go there again with those bright lights, loud noises, and cold beds. I'd rather just go.

Get to work, Pearl. Tomorrow.

I wake. What day is it? It's dark outside. There's sweat along my forehead, a burning in my lungs, and thick congestion in my chest whistles with each cough. I see a white coat (this can't be good) and a nurse standing next to my bed. Voices fade in and out, asking if I want to go to MidHudson ER.

"Treat me here," I say. "If you can't fix it, so be it."

A mask blowing cool, moist air is placed on my face and I'm finally able to breathe easier. Air pumping through plastic tubing dries the deep recesses of my nose, and nurses encourage me to swallow pills and spoonfuls of foul metallic-tasting liquids. What doesn't kill you makes you strong—I hope.

A warm towel washes my hands and face, and there's a soreness from a pan on my backside. Out my window there is sunlight, and I'm not sure how many days have passed. I sink deeper into the bed, clutching the covers, and my ribs, when I cough. I try to remind myself I always get better, it just takes time. *Get to work, Pearl. When you're ready.*

Now I feel the weight of a heavy doorknob in my hand. *Sir, the screw for the inside of this knob has been stripped. Go down to aisle three and pick a new knob. I'll tell you how to remove the screws. You'll also need a new latch plate. Aisle three.*

I know this is a dream, but there is something in my hand. I feel it, like I feel my head on this pillow. Opening my eyes in a haze, I am able to see the edges of a blue cap resting over a few dark curls. A familiar kind voice says, "Pearl, I made the call for maintenance this time. You need to get better."

I squeeze his warm, rough hand in mine.

"But it's OK to rest now," he continues. "I'm going to sit here on my lunch break. Don't feel like you need to talk."

It's my friend who fixes things. Coughing, I hold my sides. The plastic tubing blows air in my nose. I want to ask him about the store. Are the shelves stocked? It's good to have him here. I'm drifting off.

When I wake fully, he is gone.

Now my body's being rolled side to side, my limbs held so the lines connected to bags on poles aren't yanked from my arms. I'm spoon-fed a pudding of meatloaf, peas, and carrots. It's dreadful, but I'm too weak to make a fuss.

Another fit of coughing, and with all my effort I'm able to clear some of the congestion at last. My first normal breath. There's a rustling sound near my bed, and I open my eyes to see thick, red-framed glasses teetering on the edge of a powdered nose. Roula is rearranging things on my bedside table.

"Oy," I groan, "vey."

My eyes close, and I struggle to open them again. I feel my dry lips moving... whispering, "I have to tell you... the cardboard box... for the children." She needs to know about the box.

Opening my eyes, she is gone. But I feel a little stronger, able to sit up in bed, if only for a few minutes.

The picture of Mother and all five of her children has been moved off my dresser, onto my bedside table where I can see it up close. My eyes are fogged, but I spy a bag of yellow, green, orange, and red sugar-coated candies next to my knit hat, along with an envelope.

Searching for my magnifier in the covers, I find it under my pillow, and I'm able to switch my gooseneck light on and manage a deep breath. The black and white picture of my family looks brighter in the light, their smiles clearer. I've always believed that someday, we'll all be together, back in the store. But I don't want today to be that someday. Or tomorrow. I'm not ready to leave. Not yet. And Keepers' Mart isn't ready to lose me. I take another breath, a little less congested.

I rest, then gather strength to open the envelope with my name on the outside. The card is a print of the classic painting I love—swirls of light from the stars in the darkness. I'm just able to make out the handwriting inside.

Pearl—

Labor Day is tomorrow. Honoring the Haberstein's Hardware tradition, Keepers' Mart will be open, with balloons and free popcorn. Everyone is asking about you. Looking forward to having you back at work behind the register, when you can.

P.S. I ordered new cards with your favorite print—blank inside, so the right words can be written.

'Roula'

The different-colored sours glisten in the sunlight streaming through my window. I'll have one soon. Slowly I reach over to my hat and roll the wool between my fingers. Maybe Roula is starting to understand. A good business always puts people first. Maybe I can relax a little. At least for now. But only time will tell.

I notice the pile of blankets on my bed, but I still have a chill. With aches coursing through my bones and sharp pains between the coughs, I think of Mother. I remember her hands, like mine, bones clear through the pattern of folded skin. The store, the candies, Labor Day... *I'm tired, Mother. So tired.* But this time, I don't hear her saying, *get to work, Pearl.* Instead, she says, *the time comes when your work is done.* I know the time is near, but God willing, not yet. I promise I'll get back there... *when I can.*

Halloween

Edith Sharp

I t's taking all my strength being so angry at this place. But somehow, when nothing seems to change, it does. This time of year seems to come overnight, and it always takes me by surprise. Out the window, the empty swing sways back and forth, the brown leaves swirl. There must be a breeze, but my curtains are still, and the window is locked tight. The sky is overcast, the trees bare. I'm sure it's crisp out there, and I'd need a sweater... or with these cold hands, a jacket and gloves.

Ah, fall. My father, bless his memory, would predict it, as he endlessly adjusted his silk bow tie, squinting in the mirror, pushing and pulling to make each flap perfectly even and straight. I definitely inherited his fussiness, if not his ability to foresee each change of season... or to know exactly when it was his time to pass. He was peaceful, lying in his bed, still. But as William says, I'm worrying myself. I pull my top sheet to my chest. The heat is on, but it's cold in here. I've always been like Father, well dressed, fussy, looking for signs.

Is that a knock on my door? "Hello," I say, "is someone there?" Nothing. *Did I imagine it?* My mind doesn't usually play tricks on me... it's just... I have trouble remembering things sometimes. And I wish my back and leg didn't ache so. If this place had given me all my pills, then my bones wouldn't have been like Swiss cheese, but Nurse Hurry always gives me the wrong pills, not the ones I need.

Morning voices in the hallway, the staff, the wheels rolling, and it's all noisier than usual, even with my door closed. Just over the knob, along the wall, there are scrapes—some deeper than others—where the paint is chipped—left by the ones who lived here before. The scrapes continue along the wall. My father taught me to paint every five years; otherwise, your walls begin to show their age.

Knock, knock, knock—now I'm sure someone's here. "Helloooo?" But there's no response. *Is there something I'm supposed to do today? Somewhere I have to be?* My housecoat collar is loose and stained with coffee... when did I drink that? I should be wearing one of my crisp white button-downs, but my closet—half open—is out of reach. Did I have breakfast? The taste of... what... is in my mouth? Well, if I did eat, I'm sure the cereal was soggy. They always rush here—but nothing is ever on time.

Still no one. A knock on the door with no one there. At this time of year, that can't be a good omen. I wish my father had told me what his sign was, how he knew.

Ahhh, outside my door I hear that young man, the tall one with the curls, the only one who helps me, singing that "sunshine" song again. My shoulders relax. He always sits in my chair and keeps me company. Everyone else is always so busy. But why doesn't he come in?

My mind feels like jelly today. Time to take inventory. There's the photo of William Sr. and me dancing at the Bardavon. We were quite something back then. The get well card from my friends here with the royal cardinal is perched in front of the picture of our house on Sayles Street. How I miss our well-kept yard and white picket fence. William Sr. used to paint that fence every summer, and every time he'd make the same joke about Tom Sawyer. Oh dear, how did it go? After he passed, the paint faded, and finally, I hired a local boy to spruce it up again.

Well... that one with the red curls who thinks she's my decorator, she keeps putting that card there. I'm sure I told her to put it where it belongs, next to Agnes's rock not in front of it. And there's that hideous lamp she gave me to replace the one from Tiffany's that careless Nellie broke. Since my fall, it's been one disaster after another. That lamp was a wedding gift from my father's fraternity brother. Irreplaceable. Now I have this red and orange clunker with, can you believe it, fringe! I'd cut it off if I could.

My door finally swings open, and I startle as it thuds against the wall. Only Raffee opens it that way.

"I'll be right in, Ms. Edith. Have to get you out of bed for your appointment!"

My helpful friend sticks his head in with an extra-wide smile. Dear me, is he wearing a wig? What else could that puffy mess piled up on his head be? And... sunglasses? Raffee doesn't wear sunglasses. And... an appointment? Where would I be going? I'm not dressed. And... I... I... I am not getting out of this bed. Not unless I can stand up and walk. He should know that by now, with my leg and all. I look over at the far corner of my room, where my wheeler is waiting for me, folded next to that awful wheelchair.

"Time to rock and roll, Ms. Edith!" Raffee says, pulling the wheelchair over to my bed.

"Raffee? Is that you under there? I'm not going to sit in a wheeled chair! People get too comfortable in those things. They start rolling and that's it—they stay in them. Then they die in them, like, like Mr. Florida... what was his name?" I rub my forehead, "Bru-something. And he *liked* me..."

Raffee walks out, and then I hear a clank, right near my door. "Right on time," he says to someone.

"Ms. Edith!" Raffee steps back in and looks towards me with those mirrored lenses. He tilts his head, and that awful wig falls to the side. "I'm supposed to have you ready to go and in your wheelchair before 11:00. Ms. Hilda, from the salon downstairs, will be here to bring you to Shear Madness for a haircut."

I stare back at him, seeing my face reflected in his glasses. "I'm not going anywhere."

"But Ms. Edith, you have an appointment."

"That may be so, but I did not *make* an appointment, and I do *not* get my hair cut here. I've made that perfectly clear."

"Of course." He taps his head, fixing the wig. "So, can you guess my costume?

"Is that what that getup is?"

"Damn right. Don't you like my Miami disco?" He points his finger up towards the ceiling then down to the ground a few times, with a big grin. "It's Halloween!"

"Well, that's quite an ensemble." *Halloween. How could I have forgotten.* "You know, I used to love Halloween. Pumpkins everywhere—William Jr. loved to draw the faces, then carve them out with my mother's old kitchen knife. We put paper lanterns out on the walkway and lit them for the trick or treaters. I always had the best candy—full size, not those skimpy one-bite bars—and I let the children take more than one. And William Jr.'s costumes—hand-stitched every year, until he stopped going out his last year of high school."

"Ms. Edith. I would have loved to trick or treat at your house."

The last leaves are falling from the oak tree outside. Father used to sit in his wing chair next to the fireplace, smoking his pipe and telling tales. The smoke smelled like burning leaves.

"Raffee dear, can you sit for a minute? I have a treat for you, if you have time to listen." I know he's busy, but glancing at his watch, he sits down on the edge of my wheelchair and sighs.

"You know... my father... he had a favorite Halloween story... and, well, when I was young, after we went trick or treating in our neighborhood, we would sit with him, and he'd give us caramel apples, brought home from the general store. My sisters and I would gather around the fireplace—so much work to chew those apples, but they were worth every bite. Puffing his pipe, kids at his feet, he would start playing a song on our... oh, what was the name of that piano? You know, the one in all the concert halls, the finest piano made. I loved to watch the ivory keys move with the music, usually Bach, Mozart, maybe Haydn. Was it a Fenway?"

He laughs. "That's the baseball park in Boston."

"Oh, dear. How embarrassing. Then Father would tell us the Legend of Sleepy Hollow... Ichabod Crane and the Headless Horseman..." I shiver. In the distance out the window, I see more of the river now that the leaves have fallen.

"What's wrong, Ms. Edith? You look, like you've seen a ghost."

"This was the time of year my father passed."

He stops rocking back and forth in the wheelchair.

"You know, I was the oldest in my family. And my father... well, there were seven of us girls. We had a Packard Roadster—some people didn't even have cars back then. Light blue, and our car fit everyone for Sunday outings. And I was the one he taught how to drive. My father and I got along very well."

"That's how it is with you, Ms. Edith—always the favorite. Now listen, Ms. Hilda is waiting for you at the salon."

"Move that card on my shelf over a little, please, so I can see the picket fence in front of my yard. Come summer, it will need to be painted."

He bounces up from the wheelchair and pulls the framed picture of my cape to the front of the shelf. "That there's a beautiful house. I bet you did it up with decorations for every holiday. There's always one on the block, done up for Halloween the whole month of October."

I smile and take a deep breath. "Oh dear. It's October already? You know at Town Hall, I would remind everyone, as a courtesy of course, that quarterly real estate taxes were due November 1st, and to check on their vehicle registrations. Raffee, are you up to date?"

"Speaking of dates, Ms. Edith, let's get you down for your haircut. Ms. Hilda may be gettin' on in years, but she keeps a tight schedule."

"The shrubs in front of the house always collect the leaves, and the front gutter... goodness. It's time for the fall cleaning. And to have the furnace checked. Where's my red notebook? I'll have to call Smith for the gutters before he's booked. I'm sure his phone number is in there. You know how quickly a tree grows in your gutters? It happened to Agnes. I think it was a little maple."

Raffee coughs, "It's stuffy in here," and walks over to the window, opening it a crack. "Now about that appointment?"

"Be a dear and adjust my blanket. I'm always so cold."

He pulls my blanket up for me.

"Thank you, my friend. You know the rose bush on the south side of the house? It needs to be trimmed. I'm sure I could do it myself, if you would just take me home. But they're keeping me in this bed. I don't understand it. You could help, Raffee. You could bring me to my house... the hand pruners are in the shed."

"Ms. Edith, you know you don't have to worry about your house. Your son, that good boy, I'm sure he's taking care of everything. And the only place I need to bring you is down to see Ms. Hilda."

"But he's so far away. You have to do these things, Raffee. It's the practical things in life. Sometimes you don't *want* to do them. The roses are a little thorny, you know. But they come back strong the following year..." I sigh and mutter softly, "These things keep us going."

Raffee rests against the window ledge. "They most certainly do."

"Tell me again why you're all dressed up?"

"It's Halloween, Ms. Edith."

"Yes, yes, of course. I have to be there to give the trick or treaters their candy."

"Ms. Edith," he says in a firm voice, "it's time for your hair appointment. Nurse said something about this being a tough time of year for you and your son wanting you to have something to do, you know, something you want to get out of bed for."

"I'm not staying in bed because I have nothing to do. I'm just waiting until I can walk again. All I need is a massage to heal the muscles in my leg. But the 'experts' here don't seem to agree. They stopped coming to do that." Suddenly I have an idea. "Perhaps *you* could..."

"Now Ms. Edith! Only the therapists do those muscle therapies, and they say you're not ready to walk just yet. So, I'm here to get you into the lift and down to the hair salon by 11:00, 'cause I know how you hate to be late."

"How can I be late to an appointment I didn't make?"

Raffee appears relieved as the nurse pops her head in. "Raffee! You're running behind as usual. 105, 106, and 111 are all waiting. Can't spend all your time with one resident. I get complaints when patients are eating lunch in their PJs. One of these days you're gonna get written up and it won't be my fault."

He gives her a look.

"He's working in here," I say. "Can't you see that?"

Her black witch hat flops to the side as she leaves.

Raffee winks at me. "Nurse Hurry's gonna rush herself to the grave." He walks over to the whiteboard and updates today's date: October 31st, Halloween; Aide: Raffee; and Nurse: (in bold letters) **HURRY**. He looks at me. "That usually gets a smile, Ms. Edith."

I chuckle.

I much appreciate his perfect penmanship and large letters. He writes out the day's schedule: Hair at 11:00 am, Halloween Party 2:00 pm, Lido Lounge. "I know you don't like using the lift," he says, "but your son made this appointment for you."

I smile. "William." The edge of my hair is ragged, and the ends are frayed. But it will be so much work to get there. But my scalp itches, and William... *Maybe I should take the appointment. It has been a while.* "Yes, to the haircut."

"That's the ticket." He puts the pen back on the whiteboard. But then he slouches against the wall. "You know, you're lucky to have such a good son taking care of you. All I've ever done is give my mama grey hair."

"Oh?"

"She used to do this same kinda work. And when I was a kid, a little after three o'clock she'd get home, and how many times did she have to get right back in the car and drive down to the school with me so I could apologize to my teacher for whatever it was I'd done." Hands in his pockets, he looks down. "I couldn't do anything right."

"You know, I don't tell this to many people, but William, Jr. went through a stage. He was, well, let's just say he was impossible for the better part of a year. It takes time to grow up. And it's a mother's job to be patient."

"And he turned out so fine. Until I met you, I didn't know how many flowers a son could send his mama."

"So, what are you waiting for? Surprise your mother with some flowers for Halloween."

"Hmm. Flowers for Halloween. Wow. I never would have thought of that. I shouldn't be surprised, though. You've been teachin' this old man new tricks since day one." He looks in my mirror and fixes his wig. "Hey, you know there's a Halloween party in the Lido Lounge later. I'm hoping to win a prize for my costume. You goin'?"

"Not on your life. Parties frighten me when the leaves are falling. My father... it happened after a party, right at this time of year. No, I will not attend any parties today."

"Ms. Edith," Raffee takes off his wig, fluffs his own curls that need a trim, and lets out a long sigh, "I don't understand why old people worry about dyin' old. You've made it. Guys like me worry about dyin' young. If I make it to your age, I'll be hittin' as many parties as I can. Now let's get you ready for Ms. Hilda."

That means the lift, and I shudder. Raffee walks out, and then I hear a clang, a thud, and a creak as my door opens wider. A metal frame with tall arms and hooks slowly slides into my room. The curved metal swinging, the chains coming towards me. My stomach turns.

"Isn't there another way?"

From behind the machine, Raffee says, "I know that face Ms. Edith, you're getting yourself all worked up again."

My heart races. "Oh? You try getting hoisted!"

Raffee's voice, "I won't let you fall."

And I know he won't. But I'm still terrified. And he sees it.

"Ms. Edith, I'm the one everyone comes to for help with this lift. I use this thing probably ten times a day. I'm going to talk you through it. The swing's gonna lift you just a little off your bed, then we'll roll you to the wheelchair and lower you into the seat. Easy as pie."

The bar with the hooks on either side is lowered close. Cold metal against my sweaty hands. Raffee slips the sling behind and under me.

"Go slow. Remember I *ache*."

He grabs the long handle on the back of the lift and pushes down. "Up we go." Whoosh, whoosh. The sling pulls in tighter around my hips and back. My head tilts up, forward. I'm off the bed now, swaying in the air. Waves of nausea as I swing higher. I never did well with this kind of motion.

"Just hold on, Ms. Edith—and breathe!"

Swaying above the dresser, the branches of the tree seem closer. The swing outside empty but moving. I look for... Nellie. "Help! I'm falling out the window!"

"It's OK, Ms. Edith." Hearing his voice slows my breathing. "Just turning the lift, so you are over the wheelchair, then we'll lower you into the seat. You're almost there."

Waves of queasiness in my belly. I can barely open my eyes. In the mirror, hunched, pale, matted long hair, legs dangling. "That woman... in the mirror... needs... help."

"Stop lookin', Ms. Edith. I'll guide your legs into the chair."

Finally, I feel the security of the chair against my back. I'm sitting, exhausted. The chains are unhooked, and nurse Hurry rolls the lift out. But Raffee stays behind.

Tired, mouth dry, I rasp, "Would you be a dear and give me a sip of water."

He smiles and gives me a full cup. The coolness soothes my throat.

My feet are on the ground and the socks and Mary Janes that Raffee puts on them have never felt so good. "All right, Miss America! It's straight to the beauty parlor from here!"

"Well… I haven't shared this in a long time. I *was* Miss Poughkeepsie in 1939. They used to do that, at the summer fair on the green."

Raffee finishes with my shoes and pulls his wig back. "Ms. Edith, I am not surprised."

"Your mother would be proud of the way you do your job." Raffee stands a little straighter.

A high-pitched voice that could only come from a youngster crows, "Hellooo, is this 104? Looking for a lovely lady who needs her hair done."

Standing in the doorway is a girl—a teenager at best—with short, spiky hair in a haze of confusing color, flat on the sides, and pushed up on top like the back of a stegosaurus. *Why on earth would anyone do that to themselves?*

Raffee's face drops. "Where's Ms. Hilda?"

The girl's laugh lingers, "Ms. Hilda's out sick today. I'm Kaylee." She smiles in my direction, as if she knows me. "And you must be Edith Sharp!" Bending down next to my wheelchair, she examines me. "Long hair. I can fix that."

"Young lady, I don't need to be fixed. But *your* hair—I don't want to offend you, but, oh my goodness!"

"What, you don't like it?" Earrings go all the way up her ears, and something shiny pierces the tip of her nose. She tilts her head and smiles. "I could give you, like, the same cut, but I'm also good to go short with curls."

No smile from me. "I have a stylist. She keeps my hair chin length."

Her arm is covered with inky black swirls. "All that ink on your skin, terrible for a young woman. And your ears and your nose… why would you… damage yourself like this?"

"Ha!" When she smiles her dark purple lips open. "You sound just like my mother."

"Well, I'm old enough to be your great…"

She steps with her sneaker, thick-soled and purple-sparkled, doing a little dance, and interrupts me. "Would you believe, I haven't worn these since high school, which was, like, already three years ago? She glances over at Raffee, who's making the bed. "Go, disco!"

Raffee starts with his dance moves, and she joins in.

"You call that dancing?" I roll my eyes. "Now the foxtrot…"

She turns from Raffee and stops dancing. "So, Edith. The piercings and the ink are, like, freaking you out. I know. I get that a lot. But if you look here…" she points towards her elbow, "inside this bed of roses, that's my Bruce, all curled up."

Leaning closer, I examine the pattern of ink on her arm. "Is that a… dog?"

"I like to say he was purebred German Shepherd. But he was a mutt. It happened last year, hit by a car, and now… he sleeps on the roses."

"Roses mean something special here, too," I say. "And see that picture on the shelf? My Cosmo was a poodle. Pedigreed. From a breeder."

She walks over and takes a look, picking up the frame. "Handsome dog, your Cosmo."

"The smartest dog you'll ever meet."

"You'll have to tell me *all* about him." She places his picture back and comes towards me. "Let's bring you downstairs, and we can talk on the way. I like to know everything about my clients before I do their hair. Ready to go?"

"It's refreshing that you're curious. But I'm old. And I know how my hair needs to be cut. That's really all you need to know." I fix my collar and shift in my chair, trying to get comfortable. "Your name again? Is it Kay?"

"When I'm here it is."

Raffee walks over to the closet, grabs one of the thin blue blankets, and covers my legs—coarse cotton, the kind that stays stiff. "All right, Kay, Ms. Edith is in your hands. I'll tell you this, Ms. Edith will keep you workin', but she'll end up being your favorite."

Her hand gently rubs my stiff shoulders and moves through my hair. "Thanks, Disco-man, she already is."

Raffee moves across the hallway to the doctor's room, going through his usual routine. Bless his heart.

Whizzing by a blur of orange and yellow doors, I'm up a hill, then down, and the wind chills my legs through the thin cloth. This girl drives like a teenage boy who just got his license. Whooo, I'm dizzy. Someone did tell me there are hills here.

Next to the elevator, there's the memory box on the wall. Inside, a blue sky with the kind of clouds where angels sit. Somehow, the light from the window across the hall seems to shine from within. But the decorative rose is missing a bunch of petals. Below the words "We remember," are the names in black on curled strips of paper: "Penny Kolbe," "Albert Chambers," "Theresa Wilson," "Bruno Romano."

I take a quick breath, "Oh... Bruno..."

"Someone you knew?"

"Well, yes, I knew him, a real ladies' man. But every time we met was the first time for him. His memory, you know."

"That's why I don't know if I want a full-time job here," the girl sighs as the doors open and we roll into the elevator. "If I had to work here 24/7, I'd lose more than my memory; I'd lose my mind with all the loss." She presses the button. "So, how many years did you have your dog for?"

"Fifteen years of friendship. I swear that dog could smile. And we had our routine. Cosmo curled up on the sofa in the TV room, and me in my rocker. We would watch, let's see, countless hours of... that game where you say the question instead of the answer?"

"Jeopardy."

"Right, right... and Cosmo would look at me, more impatient than I was when I couldn't get it right."

My stomach drops as the elevator stops at our floor. She whooshes me out with the wind in my face, this time through the basement. Cutouts of goblins and ghouls line the walls. Not the ideal place for a hair salon. I pull my blanket up closer to my chest. "It's like a ghost town down here."

"Hopefully," she giggles "not because of my haircutting skills."

"Well, I don't believe in the supernatural, but there are some things, like premonitions, that we can't explain."

"Like, you wouldn't believe the stuff that I've seen. Elevator doors opening and closing. Things moved around on my table. Sounds coming from nowhere. And not just here. At home, in my school, everywhere. It's been like that for as long as I can remember. I'm used to it, and I know it's real. But my father told me I just had an active imagination."

"And you're so young, dear. When you've been close to dying like me, when you've left your body and come back to it, you've really seen it all."

My chair stops in the middle of a cold, dark hallway in front of a set of bright pink doors. Above them is a large painted scissors and a sparkly sign, "Shear Madness." The girl pushes a button on the wall and the doors swing open... to a pink palace.

The familiar smell of perfume and chemicals hits my nose. And there's a tune I recognize! I tap my hands together to "Bewitched, Bothered, and Bewildered." I would have come here sooner if I'd known this place was a real salon.

I'm going to get my hair cut!

The room is big—four bays with mirrors. On the walls, pictures roll by one after another. Broad black hats with clean edges, classic red lipstick, smoothed hair with a soft curl—poster-sized, some black and white—Ava Gardner, Judy Garland, Joan Crawford, and of course, Audrey Hepburn. When it comes to long-dead movie stars, my mind is clear. Things make sense down here. But upstairs, a new face every minute. How could anyone remember the names of all those staff?

Suddenly I'm parked in the bay at the end, with a large mirror in front of me ringed by bright lights. Long, white, matted hair surrounding angled bones, eyes lost in the shadows of a pale, withered face. *Do I know this woman? What have the years done to her?* I look away.

Sparkled-gold frames holding pencil-sketched silhouettes hang between mirrors and plaques, with one reading, "The fountain of youth is cluttered with lipstick, hair dye, and eye shadow." *If only it were that easy. You can't fix old age with a paint job.* On the counter below the mirror, another sign: "River's Edge Policy: No Tips. Just come again soon." *Maybe I should have come sooner.*

Clearing off the brushes, combs, and clips, Kay arranges her space. "It's hard to share a booth. I don't know how Hilda can deal with this mess." She sets out a painted rock and two pictures. An invitation for conversation.

"Your dog was handsome. I see German Shepherd... and maybe some poodle."

"My Brucie. He'll always be with me." She covers the counter with her own brushes and combs.

"Who's the handsome young man in the other picture? Your boyfriend?"

"Oh, that's Sasha."

"Sasha? A boy named Sasha? Well, you two make a nice-looking couple."

"We're not a couple exactly. He's just, like, my best friend." She cleans her scissors and takes out fresh towels. "Someone who just... well, we would, like, walk down to this stream, and in the spring the water would, like, rush over the rocks. We'd catch frogs, and lose track of time, under the trees. And all my problems would be far, far away." She moves the rock in front of the frames. "For my twenty-first birthday this year, he gave me a frog rock." The rock is painted with an outline of a round, green face, small ears, and large eyes. Her voice quieter, choked. "The best gift I got."

"The gift of a rock," I sigh. "I have one myself."

She wipes her eyes. "Really?"

"Make sure you keep it. Things get lost here." I clear my throat. "Now this Sasha sounds like a nice young man to marry, though you are a bit young."

She leans closer. "The problem is, as Sasha puts it, I'm, like, a girl who likes *girls*, and he's, like, a boy who likes *boys*." She tilts her head to the side, the purple in her hair bright under the lights. "We are both the same way like that. So, we, like, understand each other."

"Well, you would still make, *like*," I add to make her feel more comfortable, "a nice couple."

She smiles. I see her looking at me in the mirror. "So, Edith, how short?"

I feel my jawbone, sharp under the drape of thin skin. "Chin length, dear."

"It's Kay," she gently reminds me. Kay takes a section of my hair between her fingers. "Now... what if we add a *little* curl at the bottom?"

I want to instruct her exactly how my stylist does it, but she distracts me.

"The features on your face are quite symmetrical. Classic beauty."

"You're very kind, dear. My husband did say my eyes looked like Audrey Hepburn's."

"Yes, I see it!" she points to the picture of young Audrey on the wall. "And if we cut, like, just a little shorter and add, like, some curl, that will bring out those features even more. Do you want to try it?"

"Shorter? I'll look like an old lady."

"But I have short hair," she says, shaking her purple spikes at me.

"Or worse," I mutter, "an old lady trying to look young."

"Well, I can't make it longer. I'll even throw in a little makeup and nails. The Shear Madness special! On the house!" Before I can respond, she reaches for a smock. "Now, let's get you set up for your wash. You need this, so you don't get wet. Have you ever had your hair washed while sitting in a wheelchair?"

"No, I guess there's a first for everything."

"The sink comes to you." She walks away and returns with a tall rolling sink on a pole. "Ta-dah! It's got, like, a tilted basin, and I adjust the height until it's just right. Now with your type of hair, you know, like, old, I was taught that the structure changes and it has to be handled carefully. Only warm water, at low pressure, and I use baby shampoo. Keeps it soft. I'm going to start by putting a towel around your neck. I'll make sure it's warm."

She drapes and fastens the plastic smock over my shoulders, covering my lap and extending over my chair, and I have so much to tell her about my hair, but she's moving so fast...

"Ready for your wash, Edith? Then you can tell me about the cut."

A flurry of activity... warm water against my scalp, the feeling of wet hair. She takes a bottle, squirts liquid into her hand. Coolness on my head as she rubs it in. Her fingers are strong but soothing as she massages the top, back, and sides. A spray of warm water, then more pouring off.

"Ooh, sorry, did I get you in the face with the water?"

"A bit, but I don't mind. I'm not going to melt. It's just so lovely to have a good hair wash."

She smiles back. Now rubbing cool liquid into my hair, she works it through with her fingers. "Edith, you're gonna look gorgeous after this makeover. No one will recognize you at the party. You won't even recognize yourself!"

"Oh no, dear. No party for me this time of year."

"But Edith! You have to show off your look!" She pulls the conditioner through to the ends of my hair.

"Sorry. Not going."

"This time of year? It's Halloween. Who stays home on Halloween? You know when I was a little girl, one of my favorite memories I have is of my father. He'd get started in the morning and make, like, a really spooky scene in front of our house. Pumpkins next to ghosts dancing around a cauldron with a recording of "Ring around the Rosy" playing. All the trick-or-treaters loved it. It was one of the few things he did with a clear head, and he didn't drink most of that day. I've never been able to set it up the way he did. He died five years ago. They said it was his liver."

"I'm sorry to hear that." She dries my hair with a towel. "You were young to lose your father."

"Sixteen."

My mind travels backward. "You know, I was the same age when my father died. Now I'm old enough to be your grandmother, or great grandmother, or maybe even great, great... anyway, I remember, clear as a bell, the day he left us. It was right around this time of year when the trees have lost almost all of their leaves. The sky was overcast... ouch!" Pain starts in my left leg and hip.

"Edith, did I hurt you?"

"No, it's the pin in my hip. You know I had a fall over the summer. I almost died. The doctors say I'll never walk again. But what do they know? You don't get to my age without proving your doctors wrong. And I've outlived several of them. I'll be on my feet again, just you see. Now, would you be able to help me shift my leg?"

She bends down and shifts my Mary Jane in the chair's footing, relieving the pain.

"Ahh, thank you. Now what was I talking about?"

"Your father."

"Ah, yes. Sundays were our family day," I continue. "And Father told us that morning, about some unusual dreams of his over the past few months. There were six of us girls, and I am the oldest."

Combing my hair, she parts it down the center. "I'm the oldest too— of four."

"Not easy to be the oldest," I sigh. "That morning, he told us the oddest thing. He had a strong sense that this would be his last day with us, and he would be taking a journey, passing on. We didn't understand until he actually used the word. Dying! And we couldn't believe it. We were convinced he was wrong. But he insisted, until we were all crying, confused, and heartbroken. My youngest sister was clinging to the knee of his trousers. It was so strange and awful to hear. And it didn't seem real. Imagine a parent telling you this. Not a sick parent in the hospital. He looked well. He was healthy. But he'd always said, he would know when it was his time. We asked him if this had to happen. And... he said nothing could be done, just be ready for it. He told us he wanted to enjoy our last day as a family, and then, do you know what he did, despite all the crying? He insisted on going out—for a haircut!" My voice grows soft. "*Papa, how could you leave us even for a moment knowing we only had this day together?* Years later, when I lost my husband and went through the rituals, I understood. For my father, it was a practical matter. He wanted to be trimmed and shaved when he died."

"Edith, that's an unbelievable story."

"Unbelievable—but true! That's why this time of year is so bittersweet for me. The decorations make me happy, but I'm always wondering when my message will come."

She shakes her head, as if to dispel the gloom. Then, in a perky voice, she says, "I've never had anyone die in this chair, and I'm not about to start. So, sit back and let me make you look good. Not to... prepare you for anything, except the party if you decide to go." She lets out a nervous, rat-a-tat laugh.

"Oh, I suppose you can have at it." I glance at her hair. "Just no purple spike on my head, please."

Now she breaks into a belly laugh. "Edith, you're in good hands."

Scissors clicking, hair falling. *Oh dear, is she cutting too much?*

"Dear?" I ask softly.

"Yes..."

"If... if something should happen to me..." I clear my throat, "will you make sure my hair is done? When I go, I want to go in style."

The scissors stop. Her face falls.

Silent for a moment, she stares at me. "I'm probably not the best person..."

"Kay, I'm not asking you. I'm telling you. I need you to do this for me."

"I'm... I'm honored. If you'll have me, I'll do my best. But you're not going anywhere... I mean, anytime soon." She pauses. "Are you?"

"No, I don't believe so. I've had no premonitions… yet. I just hurt like the dickens. And when the trouble happened during my surgery, I felt no pain at all. So, every ache reminds me I'm alive."

Another nervous laugh. "That's a relief! Because they don't, like, teach you these things in beautician school."

"Thank you, dear. After his haircut, we went to church, then out for a drive in his roadster. It was unusually warm. Then we stopped by a neighbor's house, and they were having a party with lawn games, that one where you throw the ball. It was a lovely afternoon. And when we got home, Father said he felt tired. He went to his bedroom in the back of the house to lie down. And I remember him calling me in. I'd never seen him so pale." I close my eyes and swallow. "He told me… that… as the oldest, I would have… I would have the strength… to take care of the others. And I guess… I guess I did, because they're all gone now, and I'm still here."

"Holy shit, that's some story. No wonder you're worried about going to the Halloween party." She looks at me with kindness in her eyes. Then the hairdryer hums, and I feel warm air against my scalp.

"I'm thirsty, dear. I always talk too much when I get my hair done. Would you have a sip of water?"

"Of course, Edith. Wait here. And don't stop telling your stories."

I don't know how good this one is at cutting hair, but she's mastered the art of listening. I could stay here all afternoon. The girl holds a large glass of water with a straw in front of me. "Thank you ever so much… dear…"

"Kay."

"Kay." My head tilts slightly as I finish the water in one long sip.

"Wow!" she says. "You must be really thirsty!" Then her smile vanishes. "My father never drank water. He always had a can in his hand, and there were times when he'd even try to drink from the empty cans on the floor." She looks down. "He was… not a kind man. Right before he died, he also told me to take care of the others. That's about all he and your dad had in common."

In the mirror, a tear smudging the mascara under her eye. She wipes it away. "Must be all the chemicals in here, you know... making my eyes itch." She puts her warm hand on my shoulder. "We firstborns have to grow up fast. You can count on me, Edith, if anything should happen."

I touch her hand. The hairdryer hums again. "And my father, the last time I saw him—October 1935. He was lying there on his bed, like he was asleep. The curtain blowing in the wind. A smile on his face. Peaceful. But he was gone."

On the far wall of the salon, the sheer curtains flutter in the breeze. "It was my job as the oldest to tie his bow tie, Princeton orange and black, and fuss until I got it just right. I tied my son William's bow tie the same way on his wedding day. He waited too long to get married, and then he chose that awful Kate, who didn't want kids."

Thud. On the other side of the room, the salon doors open.

A cough, and then that raspy voice. "Yoohoo, trick or treat! I'm here for my Halloween makeover."

Kay looks up. "Stella, are you here already?"

"That's right, Kay! Is that Edy?" She struggles to get a breath. "Edy, you're out of bed! So good to see you up and about. I didn't know you were coming here."

Huffing and puffing through the tubing around her nose, she rolls into the booth next to us. "You should have... told me you had... an appointment. I would have come," she finally huffs, "earlier."

"Well, I didn't have... well, William... and you know I have a stylist... but this dear girl is wonderful. Do you know..."

"Kay," she smiles at me.

"Do I know Kay? She's gonna give me a Madness makeover! I brought everything down." Stella, in a bright orange, oversized shirt, opens a plastic bag that's on her lap, pulling out a pink boa, a large pink plumed-feather hat, and a sequined shawl. "I've always wanted to be a flamingo for Halloween." She takes a deep breath through her tubing. "Can't have a bad costume, not when you're ancient, right, Edy? I know Kay can do the job."

Kay points to the poster of Audrey Hepburn, which has a quote below her image: "Nothing is impossible."

"You know, William Sr. always used to say, 'the word itself says, I'm possible.'"

Kay smiles, quickly puts down the hairbrush, and tightens a few rollers around my ears. "You got that right. I'm twenty-one years old, with a bunch of grandmas for girlfriends, and I have better conversations here than when I hang out with friends my age!" Stella and I both laugh. Kay continues, "Now, Edith, we're ready to make the magic happen. Let me turn you around—away from the mirror—for the makeup. Then we'll add some color to your nails." She turns my chair and I'm looking at the posters of those who remain forever beautiful.

Suddenly... lipstick on my lips, a few brush strokes over my cheeks, sweet-smelling lotion on my hands, then she's painting my nails. Kay's hands move swiftly—an artist at work with her own unique style—the spiked purple hair, purple lips, purple sparkled sneakers—all perfectly coordinated, right down to the earrings that climb up her ears and accentuate that shiny band of metal in her nose. "Are you ready for me to turn your chair around, Edith? So you can see my masterpiece?"

I gasp. *Short white curls? Exquisite makeup? Burgundy nails? She looks almost... pretty again.* "Who is this woman"?

"Edy, your eyes shine with that short cut! You look like the one in that poster, over there. Just like her." Stella points towards Audrey Hepburn.

"Well I'll be. A little makeup goes a long way. Here's to Audrey."

Kay fixes the curls in the front of my face. "That's exactly what I was going for."

Turning my head from side to side, I see the edges are perfect, the curls fall just the right way, and my makeup is soft. My fingernails are colored like fine wine, with not a single chip. "William Sr. would approve!"

"Edy, we're gonna win for best looking at the Halloween party!"

"You're all convinced I should go to this party. I've made it clear I don't go out this time of year."

Breathing in deeply through her nose, Stella says, "What on earth are you worried about, Ms. Audrey Hepburn? You look like the bee's knees." Another cough. "There's no time of year that's bad for parties, so we're goin'. To the Lido Lounge. They have those mini hot dogs—mmmm, mmmm—but you got to get there early before they run out."

I start to shake my head, but Kay chimes in.

"Stella's right, Ms. Edith Sharp. I didn't just turn you into a movie star so you can stay in your room. You're going to that party."

"But my father..."

"Edy, I done heard that story about your father umpteen million times. And the thing is, he didn't worry about when the end was comin'. He lived his life every day, right up to the end. And when he found out it was his time, he got his hair cut and went to a party. And he would want you to do the same."

"Enough, everyone." I pull the blanket over my sore hip. The warmth is soothing. I sit up in my chair and straighten my collar, which shows nicely under my newly short, curled hair. And my face... it's glowing. I point to the poster of Audrey. "Well, she wouldn't miss a good party... so..."

Kay and Stella both shout, "Hooray!"

Stella struggles to throw the boa over her shoulder. Kay steps in and helps, then arranges the pink feathered hat on her head. "Now Edy, at the party, make sure you try the apple cider. It's served warm and tastes great with cookies. If only it was spiked."

I close my eyes for a moment. "My father maintained that apple cider was better with a touch of rum." I can see him now, in his chair, sipping a mug in front of the fire. "I suppose if I do get a sign, the way he did, nothing can be done. I can only be ready, looking my best. So let's go! And if it *is* my time, the spirits won't recognize me tonight!"

Thanksgiving

Edith Sharp

My door is shut—as it should be—but for some reason, that night, it was open a bit... and... I watched. The comings and the goings. His last night. Grateful the moaning quieted. Sleep came. He was peaceful at the end. One can only hope the good doctor is in a better place. A place where his hands and his brilliant mind work in harmony again. His room won't be the same. No matter who moves in there.

Was Winnie's last night like that? There was more than recognition... it was understanding in her eyes, the last time I saw her, at the facility, the place with the pines. They said she didn't know who I was, or anyone else for that matter. But I knew better. She knew I was there—I'm sure of it—and she heard my apology for my part in our dreadful decades-long rift. Mother promised her wedding ring to me, and as the oldest, by rights it was mine. But Winnie insisted it was hers, even tried to steal it. I offered her mother's diamond earrings, but she threw them at me. So ungrateful. On top of how difficult she always was, I couldn't speak with her after that. Her hand was trembling as I held it and told her how I wished things had been different, that sisters do fight, and that... I loved her. I know I saw something, a flash in her eyes. *You heard me, didn't you Winnie? You forgave me?*

But in a way, all of my sisters, even Winnie, were smarter than I. For one thing, they didn't hang around long enough to get this cold. Those damn thinners, they make you cold-blooded. My fingers feel like ice, and I rub my mittens together, but I can't find the warmth. Shivering, I gather the stiff collar of my winter jacket closer to my neck. Raffee says I'm not the only one he helps dress for winter in fall—coat, hat, gloves. It does make me feel I have someplace to go, although we never seem to get anywhere.

Is there something I should be doing today? It feels like it, but I can't think of what it is. I thought it would be the tiredness from doing that would eventually catch up with me... but it's the tiredness of not being able to do. Life here now is sitting and doing nothing, and that's what's doing me in... *nothing*.

Clank, clank, clank—the sound of the cleaning cart outside my door. They better not come in here. They better read my sign. I grab hold of the armrests of my chair. "Don't come in here. Leave me alone!" If it's one of those poorly trained cleaners, I'll scream. My floor is filthy under the mess of napkins, plastic cups, used tissues, Halloween candy wrappers, and sugar packets, but I'm going to wait it out until my housekeeper, who knows what to do, returns. Agnes warned me... about the stealing here. Thank goodness I sent my wedding ring home with William. She also said I'd lose things... well, that they would lose my things—but she didn't tell me I'd lose myself. No one can prepare you for that.

I brace for the intruder, wet dripping from my nose, with no privacy left to defend. Where's Cosmo when I need him? He would find that good strong bark when another dog walked by our house...

Uneven, shuffling footsteps. I take a quick breath of hope. Could it be? And knocking outside my door... in a familiar pattern. And then I hear, "Mommiii!" and recognize the loud voice. It's her! My door swings open, hitting the wall. Wrapped in her apron of brushes and painted with glossy lipstick under those dark curls.

"Oh! Oh. Thank goodness it's *you*."

She glows with a bronzed tan.

"You're," my tongue dry, "here." I can't seem to get words out. "You know... I can't trust... and my room needs... a good cleaning."

Standing in the doorway, she smiles, "Your Bella is back!" Head kerchief knotted in her hair... she told me the word for it in Spanish, but I've forgotten.

"To be stuck in this chair... this room... is terrible."

"Mommi, did I surprise yooou? Dios Mio!" She points at my open door. "'No Housekeeping,' 'Keep Door Closed.' Who is making all these signs?"

"The others don't listen and move my tissues... I'm so frustrated... with... with... this place. It would make any person crazy." Shaking my head, I glance down at the mess on the floor. "My house... was always neat as a pin."

"Well, you didn't let them clean. You wait all this time for me?" Bella stretches a pair of purple gloves over her brown hands with bright pink nails. Under her breath she says loud enough to hear, "El piso... que desastre!"

Even I can understand that. "I don't like it when people move my things. And... the other ones... they... they *steal*."

"Mommi. No one should take from you. But," she shrugs, "maybe it's good to get rid of some stuff in here. So much, how you say, *clutter*."

She steps closer to me, staring. Her smile fades. "You no look good, Mommi. You no eating?"

My breakfast tray is almost untouched on the side table. "I'm not interested."

"I go away for a feeeww weeks and this is what happen to you. Wearing a winter coat *inside*. You pale, skinny, nose running. Your beautiful straight hair—all short, kinky, like bird nest. What's wrong, Mommi? Feel sick?"

I look down then close my eyes, "I'm cold."

"You need a tissue." She kneels next to my wheeler, letting me pull a tissue out of the box. "Cooollddd... or something else?"

I want to tell her that they never leave my tissue box where I can reach it. I want to tell her I hate having to call someone when I need to wipe my nose. I want to tell her these people don't understand a thing about dignity. I want to tell her I'm waiting for my heart to get cold like the rest of me, and that will be it, but I'm too tired. Wiping my nose, I stuff the tissue in my coat pocket just in case, and say, "I'm fine."

"I no believe you. When I leave, your hair done all nice and your eyes so pretty. Telling stories about Halloween party. This is not the same Mommi, something is wrong."

She's right, but I don't know where to start... it's not just one thing... it's everything.

She takes an empty spray bottle from the cabinet on her cart and fills it part way with blue liquid, then does the same with another. "Next time I go, I leave instructions. Half-strength cleaning products, so your nose doesn't run, box of tissues on the table by your bed, garbage can close by so you can reach. But I leave last minute you know, no time to prepare." She drops one of the bottles, clanking as it hits the floor. Laughing as she picks it up, "Si Mommi, my body is here now, but my mind is still on the beautiful beaches of Puerto Rico. The sunshine, so warm. My soul aches when I'm not there. My home under the sun."

The sun. The sun doesn't visit this place.

Opening a cabinet in her cart, she takes out her cleaning rags. Looking up, she glances across the hallway and stops, her curls falling all around as she shakes her head. "He looked good before I left," she whispers.

I pull the cotton blanket across my lap. "His light was kept on at night, and he was propped up with pillows, kept comfortable as he... faded. There were people in his room—well one or two all night—and finally... a minister."

"En paz..."

"I wanted to walk over, to do something. But I could only watch." I rub my mittens together. "During the days, Raffee was so good about getting that Harvard hat on he loved so much—crimson brim over all that silver hair—and spoon-feeding him, helping him find his quiet place."

She takes out a new roll of paper towels from her cart and looks through her bucket of brooms. "These things always seem to happen around special days, holidays. I work here too many years. At least he was comfortable. That's all I want at the end." She smiles, but it's not a smile. Pushing a broom in front of her, she limps farther into my room, "Holidays can be so depressing." She stops and turns, "Mommi, is *that* what's wrong?"

Clearing my throat. "Wrong?"

"Holiday tomorrow. You feeling *sad?*"

"No, I just feel... what did you say? Holiday. Tomorrow?"

"Si, Thanksgiving. *American* Thanksgiving."

"Thanksgiving? Gracious, where does the time go? You know, I'm beginning to hate time. There's not enough of it, and then there's too much. And now Thanksgiving? I should be cooking, for... for family. But," my breath tightens, "there's no kitchen here... and no..."

"The party here, with the big meal, is *this* afternoon." Sweeping in the corner, she piles the candy wrappers, tissues, and crumpled notes. "This Thanksgiving, 2018, will be ten years since *my* mother passed. But my grandmother—tiny, like baby doll, and muy loco—she's still kicking!" She pushes the pile into her dustpan. "A month ago, when I had to leave, I go back to Puerto Rico to say goodbye. Her mind all confused, she no waking up much anymore. *But* she got better! Throwing pots and pans at the chicken she think are stealing her food, and I had to play piano in the living room before I left... only Beethoven calms her down."

I rub my forehead. "I'm sorry your grandmother has not been feeling well. What year did you say it is?"

"2018... Thanksgiving *2018!*"

To hear 2018 sounds like some time far in the future, but somehow it's now. "I was born in 1919. December 8th, 1919... not long after the great war and right in the middle of the terrible influenza epidemic. It's a miracle I survived, that's what my mother used to say."

"Strong Mommi."

"I'm afraid I'm not feeling very strong." My unmade bed is full of wrinkles, and I swallow the lump in my throat. "I can't do what I enjoy anymore... I'm always cold, and now I'm here on this holiday when I should be in my own house making stuffing. Would you be happy in my shoes?"

"You know, it's OK to be sad. Your Isabella knows too much sad feelings," she puts her hand on her chest, "in mi corazon. The place that I stay... I have to leave." She turns away from me, but not before I'm able to see an angry hand-shaped bruise on her upper arm and notice her discolored hand.

I've seen these marks before on her, and I know what they mean. We've discussed her situation, and she knows what she needs to do. But it's not simple. Our eyes meet. "You are a beautiful woman and you, all of us, deserve to be treated well. You're never going to change this man. A bad egg is a bad egg." She turns away and starts to clean her broom with a brush, but I'm sure she heard me.

"... so far behind. Boss lady is on me because I come back from Puerto Rico a few days later than I said. I have to catch up, get extra rooooms done. I work so hard, but there's always more work, and when I come back from vacations... like you, time is not my friend. Too many hours here, and never enough time to finish. They say they're gonna keep an eye on me now, make sure I get all my cleaning done, or... let me go."

I shiver.

"But who else will work tomorrow on Thanksgiving? And on every holiday?" She lets out a nervous laugh. "And sometimes I feel too tired— doctor say my heart—not working right anymore, some beats, then no beats, something about a murmur. He give me medicine to feel better. But like you, I don't take it."

"You have to take *care* of yourself." *For me, if not for you.*

Raising her eyebrows, she nods towards the small cup with a few of my pills on the bedside table. "Yours?"

"Yes. And now an extra. Because the way I put it, I'm not enjoying. I don't let anyone use the "D" word around me."

Taking a duster off her cart, she runs it over my shelf and motes of dust flutter in the air. Her chatter quieter, "It's sadness, makes you *sick*. And the Holidays... tooo hard." There are patches of grey where her hair is pulled back.

A sigh rumbles through my chest. "The thing about holidays is they keep coming, regardless of whether we feel like celebrating or not..." I pat the blanket on my lap, straightening the wrinkles. "There were times—when William Sr. first passed—that I cried as I decorated. But I kept the traditions, and a festive house, for my William Jr. The mantel above the fireplace was always..." I close my eyes, "the Cornucopias, candlesticks with real gold flecks—I know those are worth something—I think William has them now, that Kate of his better not give them away." I take a breath, keeping my voice strong. "And my eucalyptus garland woven through white pumpkins and the big baskets of pinecones and frosted berries I always had to dust off. Every week it seemed I was taking boxes down from the attic or lugging them up from the basement." I sigh. "The weight of a life. You carry it for so long, and then, you get here, and... you don't know how to put it down."

"No tears, Mommi..."

"At my age, you can't turn off the faucet. 'Tis the season of sadness..." Wiping my face with the tissue, "Just sit with me, Bella."

Handing me a tissue, surprisingly, she sits.

"It's so nice to have company. Otherwise, I feel like part of the furniture, just something to be moved and dusted. It's been so long since we've talked... now, what was it? Was it your apartment... something about them taking your down payment. Were you able to stay?"

She shakes her head. "I'm 'in between' now. I have a place, but it's not good for me to stay." She's still for a moment, then she starts working from the chair, picking up my unread *Gazettes* from the floor and neatly piling them on my dresser. She organizes my pens in a cup and collects loose paper clips in her hand. "In Puerto Rico, my heart was... how you say? Regular? Beat, beat, beat, like that. Doctors should give marimba to people with heart problems. Smoke a little. Or a lot. All better. No pills."

"You can't smoke a marimba. That's an instrument."

"No, Mommi. Not a marimba. *Mareeemba.* You know, weed."

"I don't approve."

"Well, I took care of business." A dark look crosses her eyes as she rubs her arm, grimacing. "But other things... not so easy to fix." Suddenly she is standing. "No more talk like this! I no good at sitting. I think too much, just like you, Mommi." Glancing back to the blank door across the hall, "Sadness all around."

Shoulders back, tossing her hair, "When I was little girl, my abuela would tell me... find el sol, it is out there somewhere. But sometimes in *this* place... hot like a sauna, and so stuffy. No light, no air."

"Well, I guess that's how it is, the air in here is, you know, *old.*"

"Let's see if we can find some sun for *youuuu.*" She starts sweeping furiously, knocking her broom into my boxes, stirring up dust, then moves to the window along the far wall.

"Let me help."

"You can put on our music. The song I like to clean to."

She wheels me over to the Victrola, and I sift through my records until I find the one I'm looking for. Orange and black. Bossa Nova. "I can never get enough of that girl from Ipanema."

As the music starts, she moves towards the window. "We have music, and now we need sun!" She pulls up the blinds and throws open the window.

"Please! I'm cold, and... my fingers feel like they're about to fall off."

She glances over, "I know, I know... only a crack." She brings the window partially down.

The blanket on my lap never seems thick enough.

"OK, Mommi, but you know I *can't* clean without opening the window, too much chemicals, even half strength make your nose run." She fixes her colorful kerchief and looks at me. "I tell you story to get your mind off things as I work. When I was in Puerto Rico, I had to bring a jacket to the beach in the morning. It was cold. How you say... steam would come off the rocks. But I would wait just a minute with el sol on my face, and then the outside of my jacket would warm, and then the inside, and then my hands and feet would get almost caliente—hot."

What I would do for warm fingers. I rub my hands inside my mittens.

She points towards my window. "See outside, this sky?"

"Too bright." I cover my eyes and squint at the light blue.

"This is one of those last days *before* the cold of winter comes, the season of sadness, but you and I, *we* have the sun." There's mischief in her smile. "When was the last time you felt the sun on your face?"

"I... I don't know. The sun doesn't seem to be able to find me here."

"Well, if the sun can't find you, let's go find the sun."

"In Puerto Rico? But you have so many rooms to clean here. And I'm afraid I'd be a slow traveler."

Wrinkling her nose, "No, sad Mommi, I take *you* outside. It's not quite Puerto Rico, but it's the same sun. There's nothing it doesn't warm, even the soul."

Suddenly, the wheels of my chair are moving, headed out of my room. All I can do is protect myself from the cold. Thank goodness for my coat and mittens. How did Raffee know I was going out today? Rolling past wheelchairs, walkers, linen carts, Bella drives through the halls, headed out to greet the sun. As we move towards the exit, I hear the receptionist, "Bella, is that Ms. Edith? Her son sent her flowers, and a package. You know he never misses a holiday. And he's such a handsome man."

He is indeed. And he married such a shrew.

"Your cleaning schedule, Bella!" shouts the receptionist. "Everyone's asking."

Bella slows my chair but doesn't stop. "I always get all my rooms done. I work through my break. Right now, sad Mommi need to get outside. And I need a cigarette." She tosses her head. "Fire me if you want."

Light floods through the panels of the glass front doors. A headache is sure to start any moment. Fearing the cold, I pull the threadbare blanket off my lap and up and over my head, bracing myself for the deep chill.

The wheels of my chair bump a few times. "Mommi, I'm going to park you in the sun, with these other ladies, your friends."

Under my blanket, protected from the wind, I open my eyes and peek out to the side. Brown leaves swirl in the air, under bare branches, but I taste and smell the freshness. It's been so long since I've been outside. And the cold that I was fearing... doesn't come. *How can that be?*

The air is crisp and thin and clean and...

"Yoohoo, Edy! Isn't this warm air delicious?"

The wheels stop, I recognize a raspy cough. Stella... I take the blanket off my head, squinting, feeling just a bit of cold on my nose. *How could I have forgotten the sun?* I pat the edges of my mussed up hair with my mitten, trying to fix myself. I must look like the dickens. And there's Roula, the pins in her red hair sparkling. These two are wearing sunglasses, sleeves of their sweaters rolled up, relaxing back in their chairs as if they're lounging on the beach. And for Pete's sake... no jackets!

Roula gently pats her face. "It only takes a minute in this weather, Edith, and your cheeks will get their color back. You just wait. Better than rouge." She flips her sunglasses to the top of her head. "I'll have to get you a pair like these. We just started carrying them at the store."

Now she's selling that crap to others. Someone needs to tell her that cheap is not a style.

I start to feel the sun on the top of my head.

Bella takes a pack of cigarettes out of her pocket. "I don't see the boss lady, so I'm good for a few minutes. Anyone want a smoke?"

Taking a deep breath from her oxygen, Stella pulls the tubing out of her nose and turns to Bella. "Light me up!"

Roula screams, "No smoking! You won't be able to breathe at all. And your singing voice. And oxygen is flammable. You could blow us all up!"

Stella glares back at her. "I been smokin' all my life, and I never set fire to nothin'." Stella holds her hand out towards Bella. "Turn off my tank and give me one of them ciggies."

Bella adjusts the tank, looks left and right, and hands Stella a cigarette. "You can't say you got these from me. Now they are from Puerto Rico. A little bitter, tastes like dirt, but good." She holds the open pack towards Roula who shakes her head no. Then she offers the pack to me.

"I really shouldn't."

"Says who?" Bella stares at me.

"Well, maybe just one."

As I inhale just a bit, I taste the paper and feel a slight burn in my throat. The smell brings me back to a lifetime ago... "I remember, I used to have two cigarettes a week—on Saturday nights when William Sr. and I would sit in the lounge at the Bardavon. I wore my little black A-line dress, and oh how that man filled out his Brooks Brothers suit. Their cocktails were to die for. Sweet, with a punch."

Bella takes a long drag. "Oh Mommi, you like *drink?*"

"Yes, they played salsa music and the drink was rum and cola. Cuba... something... Another life. I haven't thought of this in years."

"Cuba Libre!" shouts Bella.

"Yes, that's it! A Cuba libre." Remembering the sweetness.

Stella, nodding her head towards Bella, stubs her cigarette out on the arm of her chair and takes in a deep breath, coughing heavily as she slides the tubing back under her nose. "Edy, there will be drinks tonight at the Thanksgiving feast, one glass of wine each." She winks. "But I can get us more."

Roula chimes in. "And they decorate the Vista Lounge with shiny gold, red, orange, and green leaves coming down from the ceiling, always live music. Jazz last year. We'll all have a *go-od* time."

Thanksgiving. The holiday that starts and ends in my kitchen. Not here. Suddenly, I shiver.

"Edy," Stella says, "You cold?"

"A bit," I mutter. "The sun feels far away. Actually, everything feels far away. My house, my kitchen…"

Stella clears her throat. "Just be grateful you don't have to cook or do no work on Thanksgiving. When I was a waitress, we started at 6:00 am Wednesday morning and didn't stop until 2:00 am on Friday. Here, all you gotta do is show up." She looks at me. "And you gonna show up. None of this bein' afraid if you have fun here it means you're stayin'."

"It's just that… it's not the same if I can't smell the turkey cooking in my kitchen. And the stuffing, made from scratch with my mother's recipe."

Bella blows smoke into the air. "Mi abuelita… I don't know how to get her recipes… she no read or write. They all in her head. When she started feeling better, shuffled into that kitchen to cook. Stirring the pot for hours. Spice jars on her counter… a pinch of this and a handful of that… my favorite stuffing—well, Puerto Rican stuffing—with mofongo. You ladies ever tried to do mofongo?"

"William Sr. and I used to foxtrot."

"No, Mommi, not a dance." She throws her head, laughing. "Mofongo is fried green banana. You fry it, like potato, chop it up with some spices. I have to ask my abuelita what she uses to make it so good. Make her tell me and make a list. So you never try it?"

I frown. "Certainly not. William Sr. and I liked traditional Mexican food—tacos and such." Shaking my head, "Now make sure you write down your grandmother's recipe. One day, she'll be gone, and you won't be able to get it."

Bella snuffs her cigarette out under her sneaker. "Shit. I think I just saw boss lady Bryon at the door. I no want to get fired. Mommi, you warm enough to stay out here?"

Finally, feeling the tingling, soothing warmth from the heated blanket of the sun, I nod.

"I come back and get you after your room's clean."

As she strides towards the doors, I yell, "Please put clean hand towels in the bathroom... for the guests."

She waves with acknowledgment, and then—a pit in my stomach—I think, what guests?

Stella wheezes. "You know, we had the best stuffing at our restaurant. Vern was our cook—a good, honorable man. I never forget that recipe: he used bacon, gizzards, and sausage." Taking a labored breath, leaning towards us, "His secret was extra lard over all those dried up pieces of bread. Once the patrons left, we'd put that 'closed' sign on the door and it was all we could eat time. Vern always made sure there was plenty extra for us."

Roula prattles, "Best stuffing was my mother's, can't beat it. A whole can of crushed pineapple, the big one, a name brand type of pineapple, and Wonder Bread."

Stella coughs, "That's not stuffing, that sounds like canned fruitcake mush."

"I know the difference between stuffing and fruitcake."

Stella huffs, "Well, do you know what day it is? Did you ever deliver the Residents' Council Thanksgivin' invitations I gave you? You know the dinner is tonight, *before* the holiday, and people..." she jabs a finger at Roula, "they can't seem to remember dates around here."

Roula adjusts her frames. "You know I work."

Stella's voice deepens. "They need their invitations. Who is going to worry about them if we don't? You know I'm up half the night sometimes askin' the Good Lord to watch over each resident, and sometimes the next day, I find out I was worried about the wrong ones."

"You heard about the doctor," I say.

"Heard about it? I knew it was coming. The Good Lord is with us every step of the way. He feeds us when we're hungry. When we're thirsty, he gives us drink. And when we're finally ready, he comes calling. Squirt of Morpheus under the tongue—thank God for that comfort—and now he has eternal peace—his hands workin', his mind brilliant again."

Roula cackles. "When we die, we die. The body is done. No heaven. No hell. No Good Lord. Just sleep. A nice, long, sleep."

"Oh, Roula, you don't know from dyin'. You ain't died yet. I've done it twice. And now Edy knows, too." Stella can't stop smiling. "Right Edy? The road of life don't end, we just keep travelin' on."

Roula harrumphs. "That road is a dead end."

I've had enough. "Stop bickering."

Stella turns to Roula, "You're upset'n Edy. And she hasn't been herself recently."

"Madame President," Roula snickers. "She thinks she knows everything."

"Honestly, you two. My headache is starting again." I rub my forehead.

"Sorry, Edy," Stella says. "It's the holidays. You know, the stress."

"Well... yes... William was there, with that Kate, of course. And Agnes, well she's gone now. She would bring scalloped potatoes, which are just to die for. The turkey was on the table, it looked beautiful with my golden candles, my fine china with all the settings, Mother's crystal glasses I've been drinking from since I was a girl, my roasted turnips, but when they ate the stuffing... my mother's stuffing... their faces." Roula rolls towards me with a tissue. "Red pepper was the culprit... and maybe the butter was missing. I don't remember substituting, of course, Agnes was in the kitchen. Oh my, what a disaster. But I do miss cooking."

I dab the waterworks coming from my eyes. Maybe I just miss William and my dear friend Agnes.

"You ain't got no kitchen no more." Stella's voice is distant. "Some of us never did. But we got this place. And Thanksgiving dinner is cookin' here. I'm hungry."

Roula glares at her. "You're always hungry."

I can't say I have much of an appetite. I'm almost too warm, but the sun does feel delightful. I loosen the blanket over my lap. When Bella arrives, she's full of energy and moving quickly, telling us how many rooms she still has to clean. The sun has been pleasant but all this activity and those two going at it has made me tired, and my hip is acting up. "I'm ready to go inside."

I must have dozed off. Bella opens my door, and I can't believe it's the same room. Spotless! Floor clean, desk organized, not a wrinkle on my bed, and light pouring in through sparkling glass. And on my shelf... the mother of all bouquets. My William... he never lets me down. Overflowing from a huge crystal vase trimmed with a thick satin bow are the longest stemmed flowers I've ever seen—gold, maroon, and orange roses, mixed with yellow and burgundy mums, sunflowers, eucalyptus, surrounded with a forest of ferns. Lord knows how much it cost.

"That son of yours, Mommi. He outdone himself this time." She parks my chair next to my bed. "Now you have clean room, big flowers. Your Bella and your William give you beautiful *holiday*." She points to a brown paper package on my bedside table. "And more present for you!" Picking it up, she reads the return address, "William Sharp, Jr."

"He shouldn't have."

"But he did!"

She starts to hand me the package.

"Give me a moment." I settle myself and take off my mittens. So much to do when the holidays come. The wrapping is too strong for my numb, useless fingertips and I need Bella's strength. With one rip, she has it open and a luxurious cream-colored blanket with flecks of grey unfolds. Bella pulls the flimsy cotton off my lap and envelops me in velvety warmth.

"Cashmere." The softness between my fingers is like butter. My body, even my bad hip, relaxes under the soothing feeling.

"So beautiful, Mommi, the flowers, the blanket, you feel happy?"

"Well... of course I do. At least I know I should. William went all out, and it's not that I'm ungrateful... but..."

"You know, Mommi, free plate for employees tonight. Thanksgiving tradition at River's Edge. They can't fire me today! But I stop by to visit later. Is there anything you need?"

"That's very kind of you, but no. You work so hard, and you need your time off."

"Here's your card!" She reaches into the top of my bouquet and sets the card on my bedside table. Before I can thank her, she has disappeared out the door.

Using my magnifying glass, tilting the card towards the sun, I'm able to read. Written on the outside, in William's penmanship—we spent hours doing the push-pull pencil exercises when he was a boy—is the word, *Mother.*

Dear Mother,

I'm following your advice: if it's important, put it in writing.

And I know how much you love reading, re-reading, and eventually memorizing your letters. I wanted to write a real letter, not just a note, the way Dad did when he was overseas.

So here it is. I have a confession to make. You know clutter has always made me crazy. That mantel was always covered. And I never understood the fuss, as you called it, lugging the decorations up from the basement and down from the attic, and spending God knows how long decorating for every season, every holiday—until now. I never understood why you didn't make it easier on yourself, until I stood in our empty living room staring at a fireplace topped with bare white wood.

I miss our home. I know we both do.

It was hard to clean house.

Where was Good old Chubby Cupid holding the rusted heart? The orange bearded leprechaun? Uncle Sam holding the red, white, and blue pinwheels that somehow still spin? The one-toothed pumpkin with half the stem chipped off? It didn't feel like home without them. So right now I'm sitting in my living room looking at Mr. Thanksgiving Bird with the velvet top hat that you always said was hard to dust—and it is—and those mini-basket cornucopias on the brass platters. After a lifetime of throwing things away, I broke down and had them all shipped to California.

I bet you can't believe the clutter has found a way to my house! And you know how Kate doesn't like any of that stuff since she didn't grow up with it. But I've been working on her. You always said the decorations have a way of growing on you, and yours certainly got bigger year after year. Kate may not be ready to continue with the Sharp family tradition of taking over the mantel, but I'm hopeful she's starting to come around.

Well, will wonders never cease. But the mantel… there's no mantel here, no proper place for holiday decorations. They should have thought of that when they designed these rooms. At least I have my shelf for my pictures and these lovely flowers.

There's another thing I need to acknowledge. You always told me, you never wanted to be in a place like River's Edge—where the care is too slow and sometimes you don't want the care at all. And I heard you. I know you wanted to stay in the home you loved so much forever. I know how hard—how awful—it was for you to leave. No one wants to leave their own house and move into a place that is shared by so many. Independence runs deep in our family, which makes us probably not the easiest to take care of, in a good way of course.

I still feel bad about the way I barked at you in the parking lot when you moved in. I didn't mean to be harsh. But we tried every option. And getting Edith Sharp to get off the dime and do anything she doesn't want to do is harder than closing a multi-million dollar deal with people who don't speak your language. All I could think of was what if something happened to you at home when you were alone. I couldn't live with that, so I had to get you inside that door. And remember what happened this past summer. I almost lost you. Thank God help was there immediately when you had your fall... you weren't ready for change, but as Dad said, change was ready for us, and I had to be ready to help you through it. In a way, we both had to move to a new place. I'd like to think Dad was there with us, in me, guiding us along our path.

Speaking of Dad, you've always been my memory keeper. I was so young when he died, I learned who he was from you. All those pictures you framed, the scrapbooks you kept and made me look at, and the stories... always a story.

Although we are on opposite sides of the country, I know how lucky we are to continue to have each other in our lives. I'm grateful to have a mother who is the strongest person that I know. And I'm not sure if I say these words often enough.

Thank you.

Thank you for making the home I carry in my heart.

Tears pouring. I can't stop them. I fold the letter, not wanting a word to be lost. My boy is experiencing the joy I wanted to share. And now I'm the one who's grateful.

Drying my eyes, I read on.

I have our plane tickets all set for our visit in December. Home is home, so I'll bring the clutter. Sounds like the friends you've made there—that welcome everyone—will make sure there's no shortage of Christmas trees at River's Edge, and we'll find one to make ours. I'm bringing our dusty crooked star for the top.

Hope you enjoy the flowers. They almost didn't get there on time. The store was closing, and they told me they couldn't get them packed and shipped, but I did my best Edith Sharp imitation and said, "That just won't do." So they found a way. The blanket is from England—Kate found it and thought of you. We know it will keep you warm. I'm starting to get that coldness in my fingers that you talk about. Must be a Sharp family trademark.

We can't wait to celebrate Christmas with you.

Happy Thanksgiving!

Love William

Home will be here this year. He'll be bringing it. Home still has a place.

P.S. I know you say you're doing just fine as long as you still remember the words of the letters written to you. So keep reading...

And I read it again, and again, under the warmth of the cashmere.

My dinner arrives. A plate of food on a plastic tray. Dry turkey covered with congealed gravy next to some gray stuffing and wilted green beans. A tiny dot of cranberry. Maybe the aroma is similar, but nothing is homemade. I'm not hungry.

I used to walk along the brook on Thanksgiving after the meal was cooked and enjoyed, while my guests rested with their bellies full.

I used to stop and look up at the autumnal sky, mellow and magnificent with its burnt orange, deep red, and streaks of bright yellow.

I used to watch the sun set with its canopy of colors feeling the air on my face.

Now, I'm in here, alone, with the whole world outside my window, outside my reach. You never know when it's your last Thanksgiving. Maybe it's better that way.

"Hello, Mommi!" My door swings open and nearly hits the wall. Bella! Kerchief gone, her hair is down, falling all over, and she's wearing a jean jacket around her shoulders, as if she's going somewhere. "So, you didn't go down to the big feast? Instead you get this tiny, cold meal?"

"Please take this away."

"Mommi has to eat!"

"Please stop, Bella. I know you're trying to cheer me up. And William did his best—with flowers, a blanket, and a letter that warmed my heart. But I'm an old lady, alone, on a family holiday. And I'm sad. Sometimes you just have to sit in the sadness until it passes. Go be with your family and friends."

"Don't worry, it's only Thanksgiving *here* tonight. I'll celebrate with friends after my shift *tomorrow*." She fluffs her hair. "Now, let's get out of this room!"

I pull my blanket tighter.

"I'll set us up in the TV room and get you a nice Thanksgiving meal in the sitting area, right by the big window. You'll be able to see the sun go down. I think there's even a piano there."

"You don't have to do that for me."

"Keep that beautiful blanket on. We goin' for a ride!" She starts wheeling me down the hallway, and I know there's no sense in telling her otherwise.

Parked at a small table in the sitting area, I look out through the large windows onto the valley with the river in the distance and the last bit of the sunset. Bella approaches with a cart. On it are plates piled high, a foil-covered casserole dish, a few other small containers, and what looks like a flask. She fusses with the tray next to my chair and serves me a plate of turkey, turnips with broccoli, and a mountain of steaming mashed potatoes. "I make sure you have a nice plate. Eat like a queen." Then she winks. "The dinner is packed downstairs, loud jazz, no seats. Even worse than the usual crazy. But we have our own party right here."

"My head hurts just thinking about it."

She puts a small cornucopia next to my plate. "I stole this from the big table."

"You *do* know how to take care of business."

She makes a well in the middle of my mashed potatoes and fills it with hot, liquid gravy. "Save some for yourself, Bella, I don't want to take it all."

"No, Mommi, it's all for *you*."

"You know, when William, Jr. was a little boy, he would cover his plate with turkey, potatoes, and every side dish. I used to make a well for his gravy, too. But he would smother everything in a sea of brown and need a spoon to eat it. I always made extra for him." I lift up the fork and squint at the food on my plate. "He and Kate are eating restaurant gravy tonight. Restaurants never run out of gravy, I suppose."

With a full mouth, Bella mumbles, "Go ahead Mommi, such a nice plate, get it while it's hot."

"Before it's not," as I used to say to William.

"The only thing missing," she says between bites, "is Abuelita's mofongo. *This* stuffing is not the way *we* make in Puerto Rico. You no need gravy with mofongo."

I start with a mouthful of the safest thing, the cranberry. And they didn't wreck it. The gravy could use some salt, but the turkey isn't half bad.

Bella smiles. "Mommi, we're missing our drink!" Winking at me, "Tonight I'm a visitor, and visitors can bring—how you say—*treat?*" She holds the metal flask in the air. "Everything is better with rum from my island!" She pours the "dirty water,"—what William Sr. used to call it—into a small clear cup. "Only a little bit for you, no getting in trouble." Then, holding up her glass, "Cheers!"

The flavor touches my tongue. Deep molasses, tawny... ahhh. I take another sip. Slight burn going down.

"If you don't mind Bella, I'll have another."

"As long as you no walking, you can have as much as you want."

I smile as I toss back the second drink. "You know, I've had a good life." I feel a lightness in my head. "So much to look back on... so many good, kind people who love me. You know, my son William sent me the biggest bouquet of flowers, the loveliest letter, and the softest blanket... have you felt this?" I push a corner of the blanket towards her.

"Everyone here loves Mommi. They all talk about you. Raffee, Kim from rec, Otto the maintenance man. Even the nurses." She pats her belly. "Time for dessert!"

She opens a white box with orange and pink letters. Inside are two twisted donuts glazed with sugar. Steam curls in the air as she pours us cups of coffee. "My head a little dizzy too, so we have some java."

I nod.

She moves the box closer. "How you call these? Crullers. Sadie's favorite."

"Oh, Sadie? Where is she?"

"She... well, you live in Sadie's room."

"Did she move?"

"No, Mommi. She... moved on."

"Ahh. Stella and Roula used to talk about her. And Nellie is still looking for her."

"She was like you, well-loved."

"Did you spend last Thanksgiving with her?"

She lowers her head. "Yes, we were right here. Now have a bite of your cruller and a sip of your coffee. So delicious together."

Well, we never know these things, I might as well enjoy a bite of Sadie's favorite. I dig in. My appetite returns as the sweet glaze mixes with the warm coffee. Delicious. Sadie giving, even after she's gone.

"Let's have some music!" Bella puts down her plate and wobbles over to the old piano tucked away in the corner, walking as if she's had too much rum. She lifts the top. "I only know sad songs from those sad composers. But I thought you might like this one." I'm taken aback as the hands that clean my room dance over the keys with the notes of the Moonlight Sonata.

Suddenly, I'm sitting cross-legged in our front parlor where my father smoked his pipe and played Beethoven with all the girls around. I can see their young faces. Peaceful wetness winds its way down my cheeks.

Bella's curls fall over her shoulder, and she seems to play louder, the music more soulful, coming to its final crescendo.

I want to tell her...

But the song ends, she's already up and back to cleaning, this time our little Thanksgiving table.

"Sit for a minute, Bella."

"Yes, Mommi?"

I grab a last mouthful of cruller. "Bella, we don't always take time to say things, but this is something that can never be said enough."

Her almond eyes, tired with glimpses of age, are kind.

I wanted to make sure I tell you, and not just for today, "Thank you."

She looks up at me.

Hoping my face is not as wrinkled as my hands, I reach towards her. "Thank you for making a home for me here."

Leaning close to me, she places her bruised hand over mine, and I feel the warmth. Her breath smells of cigarettes and coffee, mixed with a touch of rum. "Thank you for letting me, Mommi. You make my heart beat good." Tilting her head, her smile bright with the sun-kissed glow of her island's beautiful beaches, she smiles. "Next year, I bring us a nice plate of homemade mofongo."

Christmas

Edith Sharp

'm still able to mix the sticky fruit and nuts—that's saying something. I set the loaf pan on the stove, ready to go in when the ham comes out. Mother's fruitcake. No one ate it then, and no one eats it now. But the smell of it baking—Christmas wouldn't be the same without it. Bing Crosby's "Silver Bells" booms from the Victrola and carries my tapping feet along the kitchen floor and into the dining room. Who's that elegant lady in the mirror? Red cashmere sweater, green wool pants, and the Christmas pin Father gave me, still sparkling after all these years. Through the archway in the living room this year's tall spruce twinkles by the window. William will be here soon to top it off with Grandma's silk spun star. A few thin strands of gold thread are fraying, but like the pin, the star hasn't lost its luster... a testament to things that last.

Basting the ham, I breathe in the aroma steaming from the open oven door—Smithfield, of course—and I enjoy a taste of the pineapple ring sweetness on top. Perfect. Now, when do I turn the oven down? Looking at the list in my red notebook: "Ham in oven at 11, turn down at 2, start green beans, cut veggies for platter, sweet potato casserole in when ham comes out."

Cosmo has been quiet for too long. He has that mischievous side, and with the ornaments low on the tree... I try calling his name, but the words don't come out.

A knocking sound. *Is that my door? Are William and that Kate already here? Agnes? Oh, dear, did I doze off? The ham... did I burn it? I don't hear any sirens. Last time, the fire department...*

I catch a glimpse of Cosmo's tail wagging behind the tree. He better not have an ornament. I hear a crunch and bend down stiffly to reach for him. It's my new centerpiece with the cinnamon-scented pinecones! "You rascal!" There's nothing worse than a poorly trained dog. And he just licks my hand when I scold him. I pull the mangled cones out of his mouth. Back to the kitchen, so much to do. Harder each year, but I'm not about to give up my favorite celebration.

A tap on my shoulder. My eyelids are like sandpaper, as I struggle to open them. *Agnes? William?* A small cup of red, green, yellow, and white is held out towards me. The four white walls close around, the peace of my dream is gone. "Take me back."

"Edith. You're mumbling. What are you saying?"

Irritated, I push the cup away. "I don't want any candy."

"Edith... Relax." Standing over me, nails chipped in need of a trim, she rattles the small plastic cup of what I now recognize as pills. "Wake up. You never sleep this late."

My hip aches and my feet are cold under the sheets. Only wrinkles at the end of my bed. No Cosmo. Heaviness settles in. "I was cooking. And the food smelled wonderful. I was happy. I was *home*."

"Something is going on with you. Lethargy and confusion can be symptoms of..." she stops and turns, taking the warming cover off the top of my plate that's sitting on my bedside table. "You didn't touch your toast, eggs or... the slice of ham. Maybe this is what you were dreaming of?"

"*That* is not Smithfield ham."

"It's time for your medications. But with the way you're acting, you could be getting sick. I'm going to take your vitals." She puts the cup of pills next to the breakfast tray. "I'm concerned you're becoming de-"

"Don't you dare tell me I'm delirious or any of those other words you say I am. I remember that I forget sometimes, but... but... I could smell the ham."

"I'm going to take your blood pressure. Then tell me all about it."

"Just because I was there in my house, cooking Christmas dinner, you think I'm sick? What is wrong with you people? You know I was fine before I came into this place." The only way to deal with her is to let her go through her motions since she never listens. "Here, go ahead," I extend my arm. She tightens the cuff, and her face relaxes as it loosens.

"Blood pressure normal. Heart rate is good. Any headache or nausea? Any coughing, or pain when you urinate?"

"None of the above. I told you, I'm fine. But my ham is burning..."

"Edith, snap out of it. You're at River's Edge."

"More like the edge of my patience. I'm in my house, making Christmas dinner. I'm going to stay there a little longer, and you'll just have to wait." I pull my quilt over my face.

Sharply now, "Edith, do you know where you are?"

"I know that you're annoying me. I know dreams are better than being awake. I know you have no sense of humor."

"Come on now, you also know the drill for acting confused. Now, just a few questions... what's your name, and the year? And pull that quilt down so I can see your face."

I poke my head out from under the quilt. "My face has 98 years of drooping. If you see something new, let me know. And of course I know who I am. Edith Ann Keeler Sharp. And my son is William. You're the one who's confused about my being confused."

She nods her head. "And... the date with the year?"

I look back at her and down at the wrinkled cover on the bed. "Well, it's certainly not the year I was born. And I wasn't born yesterday." Then, suddenly my head is clear. "You know it was just my birthday, and my son sent me the most beautiful cake made entirely of flowers. Ninety-nine flowers. For 99 years. So this year must be..."

"It's December 18th, 2018, and the Christmas party is today. There will be plenty of good food. The children's choir is coming to sing. I know you prefer to stay in bed, so I'm sorry you're going to miss out. We can have the meal brought to your room."

This one is impossible. Whose side is she on? A flash of irritation in my belly. First I'm delirious and now she thinks I'm a shut-in. "Well, I never..." Just beyond the metal frame of my wheelchair folded in the corner is my picture of William Sr. smiling at me from my shelf. "To be clear, I might not be able to walk, but I can still get out and do things. I'm *not* an... invalid." There I said it. I'll never be an invalid, no matter what happens.

She smiles. "Edith, if I didn't know you, I would say there was something wrong, but your feisty self seems to be back..."

"There is something wrong, but you won't find it with any of your tests. It's not my heart or my stomach, although I do feel it in both of those places." I sigh and look towards the window. "I've felt this way before, but not in a very long time. I must have been a teenager, maybe 13, when I was sent away to camp in the Catskills. Money was tight—it was the depression—but Father always came through for his girls. The camp was beautiful but the food was dreadful, and I felt so lonely... I wanted to be home."

Glancing up as she writes on her clipboard, she chuckles, "I'm trying to picture you as a teenager."

"Homesick, that's what I was. And that's when I started to get into my letter writing. My dear sisters—they each got a letter—and one for each of my parents." I rub my hands together and point at William Sr.'s picture. "Would you be a dear and hand me the picture of that handsome man at the end of the shelf. Yes, the one of my husband."

A wrinkled yellow edge of paper, thin as tissue, sticks out from the top corner. Carefully, I'm able to slide it out and unfold it gently, like opening a napkin. My eyes dampen. "William's letter..."

"Edith, it's a busy morning. I'll be back in a few minutes to give you your pills."

I tilt the paper towards the light of the window as I always do, using the sun as my helper. Squinting through my magnifier, I can just make out the words. I'm back in a place where life makes sense, where my dear William is speaking to me through the faded ink on the page.

December 24, 1944

My Dearest,

By the time you get this letter, it will be after Christmas... but as I'm writing this, I hope that you are near a beautiful tree, enjoying the warmth of the fire after having a delicious Christmas Eve dinner.

We are on these ▓▓▓▓▓▓▓ islands, someplace near ▓▓▓▓. When I look away from the ▓▓▓▓▓▓▓▓▓▓▓▓▓▓▓▓▓▓▓▓▓ base camp, I can see the rolling hills ▓▓▓▓▓▓▓▓▓▓▓. It's hot, muggy, and all the trees have wide, shiny leaves with little plums. It's easy to forget it's Christmas in a place like this.

I'm sure your mother, without a hair out of place or a wrinkle in her shirt, is keeping you busy turning your home into Holiday House, as I remember her calling it, with every corner decorated. All we have here is a wreath with a ribbon falling off in the mess hall. There's no way it's real, but at least it's green, with a few bells. Somehow it brings joy. Of course, they gave each of us a shot of cheap whiskey, which helped too.

I'd be lying if I told you I wasn't worried that this war isn't won yet. But my biggest fear is not being able to get back to the place and the people I love. When I return, l will bring you on a stroll down Main Street, get your favorite hot chocolate at Dillards with the extra cream and cinnamon, and then take you ice skating. I also have a question I've been wanting to ask you. And if you answer yes... I hope we'll spend many Christmases together, sitting by the fire. I'll even help with the decorations—if you let me... in our own Holiday House and every year I'll put the star on the tree.

Please tell your dear mother I thank her for sharing her secret of getting a crisp edge on my uniform collar. That's helped greatly with inspections.

It pains me to stop writing this letter.

I will write again soon.

Merry Christmas

Love,

William

My eyes wet with tears, the bright kind of tears, from the joy of hearing his words. I miss him so, but when his voice comes alive, I remember. I feel his presence, his love, our life unfolding together, and I feel like myself again.

Out my window, the branches of the oak have a dusting of snow. Fixing my housecoat, I smooth the wrinkles of my blanket. My stomach is calm, no longer upset.

Nurse Hurry rushes back in. "Well, that's a beautiful smile, and the color's back in your cheeks." She's rattling the cup of pills. "You always say you don't need all these pills. That crumpled paper seems to have done the trick."

"A letter I saved from my dear William Sr. He died many years ago. Too many years ago. And too young—his heart."

She nods, "You've told me." Shaking her head, she mumbles, "memories... stitches... keep us strong."

"What's that?"

She looks at me. "Have I told you about Sadie, who used to live in this room? She was such a lovely woman... with so many struggles, but she was always an inspiration."

"Seems like I hear that name often."

"She wore her heart on her sleeve. Just get her started, and she would go on and on with stories about "la famiglia," all her brothers and sisters and aunts and uncles and cousins, and pretty soon enough you'd be saying, "Madonna mia!" with her. She was a seamstress, and she used to say that *re*-membering was like stitching ourselves back together. A way for those we've lost to remain with us."

Her thick, white nursing shoes grip the floor in front of me, but her dreamy gaze goes out the window, and I can tell her mind is far from this place. She glances at me, "You feel better, don't you? That husband of yours is still helping you."

"He was never one to be forgotten."

Her chuckle is relaxed. "And that's the gift of re-membering. But we definitely don't take enough time to do it. We throw away the old dusty albums and hold onto the grudges instead."

"I'm too old now to remember who I'm supposed to be mad at, but don't give me any more reasons to keep my clutter. I have an attic full at home."

A knock on my open door and a head pops in, yammering a mile a minute. "Eve! Hurry up! 129 is yelling for a pain pill, 116 is nauseated, and 112 thinks her big toe is swollen, but to me they all look like little sausages." She disappears with her laundry list of problems.

Nurse Hurry's smile fades, and she picks up my cup of colored pills. "You know it takes all morning to get everyone ready by afternoon. Even when I hurry, I can't keep up. Let's get this job done so I can get my residents ready for the party." Pills in one hand a cup of water outstretched in the other, she stares at me.

I stare blankly back. "Now what are we doing?"

"Come on, Edith, our usual routine. You count every pill."

"My pills can wait. Tell me more about the Christmas party."

"It's the same every year. 2:00 pm, Lido Lounge, Children's Choir of Poughkeepsie. I'm not much for kids, but," she sighs and looks upward, "their little voices sound like angels."

"Maybe Stella mentioned this—she's either seeing angels or hearing them. I'd like to see for myself. I'll need to be dressed and hoisted into my wheelchair. There's no time to waste. Send Raffee, and why aren't you giving me my pills?"

"Here, count them."

I wave my hand in the air. "Never mind that now. I trust you."

She leans closer. "Just like that? Suddenly you'll take your pills?"

"Can't afford to miss the angels." The pills are bitter, and I wash them down with a few sips.

She raises an eyebrow. "It's only taken a year. I'm honored to have finally earned Edith Sharp's trust." And with that she is gone.

A glimpse of red out the window, and on the large branch of the oak, a white-breasted cardinal lands, tilting its head back and forth as if it can see me through my window. Against the snow, its deep crimson coat stands out like an ornament. The bird doesn't speak. But I know why he's come. "William, you never fail."

Bells jingle and Raffee appears in the doorway, his Santa hat cocked to the side, bobbing his head, arms embracing a bundle of green needles in a huge red pot—a miniature tree. I sigh. Two of my favorite things: Raffee and a Christmas tree. *Come on, Edith, pull yourself together. And remember what all these years have taught you. Old age may wear your body down—and it certainly has—but the spirit, the spirit is what keeps you young.*

"Morning, Ms. Edith. The Christmas party's this afternoon, and Bev asked me to bring this to your room." Reading the white postcard sticking out from a branch, "Just what I thought, it's from that son of yours. 'Dear Mother,'" he swallows as he starts reading, "'Merry Christmas. We'll be arriving on the 28th and staying at a nearby hotel to visit for a few days. Love, William and Kate.'"

My beautiful boy. He's coming. Rubbing my hands together with delight, I suddenly pause, thinking of that Kate.

Raffee walks the tree towards my desk. "I guess flowers are not enough, now he's sending whole trees." He shakes his head. "Any bigger and I couldn't carry it."

"It's just grand. Put it in the corner, next to my shelf." He puts it down stiffly, and I can smell it. A real pine.

Raffee's not his usual bright self. *Something's wrong. I know it. Where's his smile?* His bell flops to the side without a jingle. He's decorated, but no Christmas spirit. "Raffee, what's the matter?"

He stares at the ground and doesn't answer.

"I haven't seen you in a few days, have I?"

Taking off his Santa hat, he rubs his forehead. "Ms. Edith you don't miss a beat." Turning away, he starts picking needles up from the floor.

"Raffee, it's almost Christmas."

"Not feelin' it."

"The world expects old people like me not to be merry, but it's terrible to see you sad."

"I guess we all get like this, real sad, when... well, you know, after you broke your hip, you were either angry or asleep. I never saw *you* smile."

"We're not talking about me now."

He rubs his eyes. "It's my momma—she's in the hospital—a stroke."

"Oh, Raffee. Your dear mother... I'm so sorry. Strokes can be devastating. How is she doing?"

"Well, she's not moving much. And just mumbling a few words that are hard to understand."

Outside ice lines the edges of the window. "I'm afraid life doesn't get kinder with age."

"What was that, Ms. Edith?"

"What I meant to say is, I know this must be hard. Such awful things can happen to us, and everything can change in a moment. But your mother is strong, and she's a special lady, raising a special son. You always share so many wonderful stories about her."

His damp eyes brighten. "My momma has the most beautiful voice. You always know where she is in her apartment." He looks at me, and glances away. "I just," he swallows, "want to hear her sing again." He sits on my desktop, a chair that's only a chair when he is here.

"My dear Raffee, not one of the pills they give me for happiness or memory or pep let me forget the pain and hard times and only remember the good. Sadness is always ours to hold, and it can get... heavy." I sit up straighter. "But there is something that has the power to lighten a heavy heart." I try to find his eyes. "Even in the worst of circumstances, the smallest bit of joy can lift our spirits even while the tears are falling."

Tilting his head, he's looking at me as if I'm not making sense.

I clarify, "You see, there's always some sweet with the bitter. You came to work today and brought me a Christmas tree full of life. And it's a *real* tree. Breathe in and enjoy the scent."

He sniffs. "OK, maybe there's a littl' somethin' about bringin' Christmas trees—or flowers—that does some good for the one who carries them." He rubs his forehead. "But I'm so sad about my momma, I'm not bein' a good Santa. Here, Ms. Edith, you wear my hat."

"Thank you, dear, but I'd get dizzy if I shook my head. You're the only one who can jingle properly."

At first it's a laugh, then he covers his face with his hand, stifling the sobs. "And it's heavy... I feel like I'm buried under a million tons of sadness. I don't know what to do."

"You're so young. It takes a lifetime to figure that out. But I'll tell you my story. And if you've heard it before, which you probably have, you're going to hear it again. Fluff up my pillow, please, then sit yourself down in that chair so you can be comfortable while you're listening." Reluctantly, he sits. "Hard times are not easy. William Sr. died young, the pain was everywhere, and I still feel it to this day. William Jr. was a little boy, and my world, our world, was suddenly much different. What kept me going? It was the day-to-day tasks. Quite frankly, I couldn't get away from the routine; the practical stuff was all around. And as Mother always said, the first thing you can do, and must do, is make your bed. Smoothing the wrinkles somehow helped with the pain. You know I can't remember what day it is now, or what year, but I can remember her words perfectly." I pull my quilt tighter, flattening the wrinkles that I can reach, and direct Raffee to the bottom of bed. He walks over and fixes the quilt, straightening the edges. Then he moves along to organizing my bedside table.

"Thank you, dear. You'll find your celebration will be different this year... sometimes you just don't feel like doing."

Glancing up, his brown eyes wide with understanding, he grabs a stack of fresh, folded towels for my bathroom.

"Letting others do for you is not easy. But at times like this, you need. And no one will think less of you for taking help when it's offered." He's quiet. "You don't mind all my talking this morning, do you?"

"No, Ms. Edith. I'm just thinking about things." He starts to arrange my toiletries in a basin, jingling as he sways back and forth. It's good to hear his bells. "Now what were you sayin'?"

"I ask myself that all the time, but right now, I know exactly what I'm saying." *But I don't.* "It's... well, I believe... what *was* I saying?" The planter holding the tree is a deep red with candy cane swirl twisted like a vine along the top. "Celebrating. That's it. Why was I talking about celebrating at a time like this? Well, sit back down, and I'll tell you."

I wait until he stops what he's doing and sits.

"Celebrations aren't all about 'put your smile on.' If you live long enough, they start to look all different ways: happy, sad, light, heavy, joyous, bittersweet. I've probably celebrated over a thousand holidays, some at home with family and friends, some in hospitals or places like this, at the bedside of dear ones. I've been to christenings, graduations, and weddings as well as funerals, wakes, memorial services, and celebrations of life. We eat, we drink, we laugh, we cry. We come together during both the good times and the bad. And we tell stories. That's the way we remember. That's how life goes on." I glance out the window, then back at Raffee. "We're not born alone, we don't live alone, and if we're fortunate, we don't die alone. We see each other through. We gather for a reason, lighting birthday candles for our children or prayer candles for friends we've lost. But through it all, there's always one thing that keeps us going, one thing that renews us—whatever the situation, no matter how dismal, you'll always find it, shining like the star on top of the Christmas tree— hope." I let out a long breath. "There. Now I've said my piece."

Raffee shakes his head. "I'm tryin', Ms. Edith. I'm tryin' to find the hope. But Momma... the doctors are saying she'll never be the same."

"Sometimes the hope is simply for comfort or peace. You need to find the strength your mother has already given you. What did she do when times were difficult?"

He's silent for a minute. "Things were always difficult." Then the hint of a smile comes over his face. "And she is always singing. She says it helps the spirit stay strong."

"Then that's what you have to do. Sing to her. She'll hear you. She's there."

"Sing to her?"

"Music... someone once told me it's a better medicine than any pill. And that's the truth."

"Ms. Edith! That was me who said that!"

"Of course it was. No matter how low we're feeling it always revives us. That housekeeper, the one with the limp, she played Beethoven for me— on the old upright in the corner of the sitting area—on Thanksgiving, and it so lifted my spirits. You did the same for the doctor with the gloves and the music, and when you helped Nellie wobble up from her chair and start to dance."

His eyes widen.

"Your gift, Raffee, and it's a miracle since you're so young, is the time you spend with each of us. It brings out our spark, no matter where we are."

"I never thought of it that way."

"I'm not the same as when I walked in here. Things have happened, just like Agnes said they would. But you've been here for me. Been patient with me. I know I'm not easy, but you've lifted me up." I smile. "Young man, I may be down, but I'm not out. I can still go to parties—even as an old lady in a chair." I wag my finger at him. "Nothing, nothing is hopeless. Don't you ever give up."

He sits up a little straighter.

"A sip of water, please."

"You got it."

Throat soothed, I go on. "You're called to be a caretaker. But now you need to use all that energy and light you bring to us to take care of yourself."

"Damn, girl, you're on fire."

Glancing out my partially open door, I make sure no one is coming. I wave my hand, motioning him closer. "You see the likes of who I have to go to parties with here. One can't breathe, another thinks she's stylish with her tacky plastic frames, and the third one steals sugar and doesn't know where she is. But we share our celebrations together." I look over at the tree and notice there are lights already strung on it. "Raffee! Plug in the lights!" Suddenly I'm in a different room, one aglow with red, yellow, blue, and green twinkles. "Now it's Christmas."

Straightening his hat, he glances towards the corner. "You said it. The celebration *will* be different this year. But maybe Momma's room at the hospital could use a Christmas tree. I might just bring one over when I see her tonight."

"Now you're talking. You are a wonderful son. And I don't want to keep you here too long. We both have other places to be."

He nods and takes in a deep breath, savoring the piney scent. "Now let's get your routine goin', you need to be dressed and in your chair."

Finally, I see the flash of his smile.

"When I was walkin' in this morning, that Lido Lounge was decorated with a whole lotta trees and shiny ornaments. Somethin' special." He points to my closet. "What is Ms. Edith goin' to wear?"

"Red cashmere sweater, green wool pants, and on the sweater you'll find my Christmas pin. And go slow with that lift. I'll never get used to it."

"All the liftin' will be worth it, cause you got a celebration to go to."

"And you'll attend, won't you Raffee?"

There's a twinkle despite the sadness in his eyes. "I wouldn't miss it."

"I told you there's no spirit in her room. There's not one decoration on her door."

From outside my half-opened door, her voice has a way of piercing the ears. A glint of red plastic in the hallway. No matter how bright you make it, plastic will always look like plastic.

"And she thinks that rock on her shelf is an ornament. I don't think she's as with it as she lets on."

How rude. "I can hear you," I shout, but I'm drowned out by the sound of Stella's coughing.

Clearing her gravelly voice, after a fit long enough to make me wonder if the air will make it in, Stella spits, "Now Roula, even if she don't have decorations on her door, or in her room, doesn't mean she can't decorate. We just have to help her out."

These people... no one listens. I cover my eyes and sigh.

. All that turning and hoisting has made me hungry and exhausted. I lift the warming lid off the plate and set it on my bedside table, but even the smell of scrambled eggs and sausage is not quite right, so I take a taste of the oatmeal. My hand has decided to shake this morning, and I dribble oatmeal onto my cashmere sweater. There's nothing worse than oatmeal dribbles, and I quickly grab a napkin to wipe off as much as I can.

Even though I expected it, I still startle at the loud knock on the door, "Yoohooo, Edy!" A golden cane pushes the door in. Stella is decked out in a headpiece with gold foil stars and an enormous T-shirt with a snowman, a heaping pile of party beads strung around her neck. Tacky, but it's Christmas. Catching her breath, "Edy, the Angels are comin' today!" Her smile widens. "They're real angels from downtown."

Roula, pushing her glasses up farther on her nose, with another pair resting on top of her head, says flatly, "Hello, Edy." She rolls in the chair she calls "sporty." "I closed the store an hour early to get ready for the party." She winks. "Pearl, God rest her soul, would never approve."

Pearl certainly had her hands full with this one.

"Nice to see you both. Stella, you're quite festive. And Roula..." Holiday or not, the overly done red lips and rouge never change with her. I bite my tongue. "Have you seen my *real* Christmas tree?"

Stella sneezes a few times then works through her cough, "Am I smellin' pine in here?"

"It's from my son, William. It stands so lovely and tall, brightening up that corner. Raffee was kind enough to bring it to my room, but it was almost too big to carry. And did I tell you it's real?" I cast a glance at Roula.

Roula adjusts the oversized crystal-decorated frames on her face, "What type of Christmas tree is that? Only lights, no decorations? This is what you're happy about?"

This woman...

"Roula it's almost Christmas—you gotta start bein' nice. Only the Good Lord knows how many Christmases we have left. He could come for us tomorrow, and there ain't no misbehavin' like this in heaven. I'm sure we can help Edy with her decorations." Stella rolls over and manages to lift her arms and drape a few of her beaded necklaces over the tree.

Roula pushes her chair over, "I'll show you how to decorate. Give me the beads." Her crooked fingers rearrange the necklaces like gold and silver garlands. "Your tree just needed a little help, like you Edy." She untangles one of her many pairs of glasses, then another, then reaches up and drapes two of the chains over branches of the tree. "Not bad. I think there's hope for this little sapling."

Stella and I catch each other's glance and shake our heads. But with Roula's touch—the beaded garland and the hanging bows—I have to admit, it does look good.

Roula doesn't stop. Now the pictures on my shelf are being rearranged.

"I've told you not to touch my shelf."

"I've never understood why you keep a rock here."

Wishing I could hit her over the head with it, I throw my hands in the air. "Go ahead, pick it up."

"What?"

"I said go ahead and pick up the rock. Tell me what it says on the bottom."

She shifts her wheels to get closer and continues to rearrange a few of the frames before picking up the rock. Pushing yet another pair of glasses up her nose she reads the underside of the stone.

Dear Edith, Emerson's quote, changed a bit just for you: "the ornament of a house is the friends who decorate it." Love, Agnes

"You have a nice friend—this Agnes. She knows you can't decorate either."

"*Had.* She recently died." I look at the speckled marble of the rock and feel the memories.

"Oh, I'm sorry. I've lost more friends than I can remember." She rolls her wheels back over towards the tree, banging into my dresser along the way. "Your tree just needed a little love."

Bam! I startle. My door slams into the wall as a whirl of yellow blows in.

"'Er tay couldn't find, behind me house, hills, they were green. But tay were gon'in, home. Keep lookin'." Nellie in her raincoat rolls close, looking at me and then at my tray. Taking one of the sugar packets next to my coffee, she hides it in her shirt.

"Nellie," I say, "your hair looks lovely. Were you just at the beauty shop?"

Giving me a sidelong glance, she takes the other sugar packet from my tray and slips it in her sleeve.

Seems Nellie's not in a good mood. My water pitcher is in her reach...

Roula cackles, "With such a nice haircut, she looks like she might have gotten a few marbles back."

"That's enough, Roula," Stella waves her cane. "She can hear you, and you gonna get her all agitated."

More agitated than she already is? Fast fingers flick across my bedside table and start grabbing at my things.

"She's going to spill my water!" I shout. And she does.

"Now look what you've done!" Roula scolds.

I place a napkin over the puddle, and Nellie slips back into her sitting standing not-quite-falling routine.

"It's all right, Nellie," Stella tries to soothe her. "Come on over to this beautiful Christmas tree. It's got lights and beads. What else do you think it needs? Is that a candy cane in your sock?"

Nellie pulls the candy cane out of her sock and holds it close to her chest.

"Go on," Stella points to the tree, "put it on there."

Nellie stands up, hangs the candy cane from a branch, and remains standing, tottering over the tree.

"Now sit down," I tell her, "before you fall and take my tree with you."

She sinks down, then edges her chair forward, half standing, half sitting, up and down, up and down. "Nooo. Don' take me. I don' want to go."

"Come on, Nellie, don't be scared." Stella starts a throaty hum. Nellie, quiet for a moment, sits back further in her chair. Stella waves her hand, encouraging Nellie to join in, and Nellie does... singing every word. "Joy to the world, the Lord is come. Let Earth receive her King."

What a relief to watch Nellie clapping and singing with the beat of Stella's song. A moment of respite... for all of us. But as the song ends, and she starts tapping on her imaginary piano, fingers flying across my still wet bedside table.

I don't get a moment of peace with her. "Nellie Riley! Sit down before you hurt yourself!"

"No falls allowed on Christmas," Roula orders.

"Yer not ma mother!" Nellie wags her finger at me as she wobbles over her chair.

I take charge, yelling as loud as I can, "Raffee, we need you!" I extend my hand to Nellie... and she takes it. Squeezing gently, I think of how Raffee calms her when they sit together. "Now Nellie, you're right. I'm not your mother. But all of us here, we're your friends. You're safe here." Her warm hand relaxes in my palm. "And it's Christmas. My favorite holiday, ever since I was a young girl. Each one of the decorations on our family's tree had a story. Do you remember when you were young, the Christmas trees you had in Ireland?"

"'Er candles, sleep at the window and the door..." Nellie's explaining, and I try to understand, "tis' holly, er the candles on the door." She nods in agreement with herself.

Raffee arrives, breathless, his Santa hat tilted. "Ms. Edith, is everything OK? I heard you were callin' for me?"

"We did need you earlier, dear. Nellie was a bit out of sorts, but we've come to an understanding." He gives me a curious look. "Now we're ready to go to the party."

He smiles at me. "And you young ladies are lookin' fine!"

I touch the edge of my hair. "Well, I'm not sure about the short cut, but my pin still sparkles."

Stella points her cane at Raffee. "And we got to get to the party soon. We're not lettin' anyone else get the best seats, the best treats, or the last word on the decorations. This is our party, and we're gonna do it up right!"

With Raffee behind me, and my cashmere blanket on my lap, my wheels start to move, and I feel the welcomed return of anticipation. I want to hear the voices of the children. My hallway with the oak trees on the walls is bustling like a busy New York street. It feels good to be dressed for a party and ready, short hair and all, to be seen. "Leave my door open a bit in case William comes early."

We arrive at the double doors of the Lido Lounge and find them closed. Raffee turns the handle, but the door doesn't move. "Locked."

"Raffee! We spent the whole morning getting ready for this. Do something!"

Before he can knock, Stella raps her cane against the door. "Yoohoo! Open these doors!" She continues banging.

Finally, the door on the right opens a crack and that therapist with the long blonde hair, wearing a ridiculous elf costume with flashing snowflake earrings, peeks her head out. "What's all this noise?" She takes in the four of us and snickers at Raffee. "You brought them here too early."

"Merry Christmas to you, too, Kim," Raffee wrinkles his nose.

"Early," I say, "is to be on time."

Nellie shakes her finger at the elf. "Errr, not to stay, not a nice lady."

Catching her breath, Stella clears her raspy throat. "Ain't no such thing as too early in this place. They serve lunch here before breakfast. And as President of the River's Edge Residents' Council, and by virtue of my position on the statewide coalition of presidents of residents' councils, one of my many jobs is to oversee holiday festivities." Tapping her golden cane on the ground, her voice louder, "So, you're gonna open that door and me and my assistants are gonna roll in and start decorating."

"Assistant?" Roula whines, her Brooklyn accent suddenly stronger. "Who's the assistant?"

The elf rolls her eyes and snaps in her high-pitched voice, "Fine. Suit yourself. It's just me and the volunteers."

Roula wheels closer. "I supervised an army of volunteers at my thrift shop in Florida. I can teach them a thing or two."

The double doors swing open and... I'm amazed. We're rolling into the North Pole. No walls, just a forest of trees and hundreds of snowflakes falling from the ceiling. Volunteers are swarming around, hanging identical paper ornaments and fussing over the tables.

"Listen ladies," the elf says, "I have to leave to receive a delivery from the bakery—Stella's cookies. While I'm gone, you're welcome to help the volunteers with the final touches. But NO tinsel. I couldn't get that stuff untangled from the trees last year and I had to get all new ones. Almost broke the budget." She walks off briskly.

Stella and Roula roll around the room, inspecting the trees. If it weren't for this chair, I'd show them how to decorate properly. Roula keeps switching her glasses. Nellie follows, grabbing candy canes off the branches and stuffing them in her usual hiding places. "Whoo," Stella breathes heavily, "they done up these trees real nice. Just wait 'til they light 'em up at the party."

Roula frowns. "Eh, they don't have, what's the word I'm looking for? Pizazz. That's it. No pizazz." She is loud enough that a few of the volunteers turn her way. "What are you looking at?"

But she's right, although I'm not going to tell her that. They've done a passable job, but something's missing. I can't put my finger on it. I clear my throat, "The trees are beautiful. But they do have the same red and silver balls on each one. They look, well... like department store trees... you can't buy Christmas spirit. It comes from decorations lovingly collected over a lifetime. And... the tops are empty." I say to one of the volunteers, "Where are the stars?"

The volunteer shrugs.

"I guess you're trying. My son, William, will take care of this when he comes."

"It's not the stars," Roula shrieks. "It's tinsel. We need tinsel! And I've got some right here. Lots of it." She roots around in her chair and pulls out a plastic shopping bag. "That elf should know it's not Christmas without tinsel." She starts tossing silver strands onto the trees. "There, that's more like it." She hands a second bag to Nellie. "Come on, Nellie, make yourself useful."

Raffee, my driver, turns my chair and asks, "With all the empty tables, Ms. Edith, where do you want to be parked?"

Before I can answer, Stella chimes in, "*That* table over there. I'm not gonna get stuck in a wheelchair traffic jam and miss out on the napoleons."

"Stella," I look to the risers set up on the far side of the room, "I know you love your sweets. But we should be closer to the angels, so we can see them sing."

Roula taps her ears, "And *hear* them, too."

Nellie is munching on a candy cane, the plastic wrap still on it. Roula grabs it from her, "Get back to work." A few loose strands of tinsel hang over Roula's glasses. Nellie grabs the candy cane back and starts dropping tinsel on the floor.

Shifting uncomfortably in her chair, Stella sighs, "You're breakin' my heart over where to sit, but I guess we have to take angels over napoleons." She reluctantly rolls over and puts her cane on a table close to the risers. Roula and Nellie finish decking out the trees and join her. Raffee parks me with my friends, and at last I'm settled. From the bed to the lift to the chair to the hallway to the doors that were locked and finally to the table. What an undertaking! And I'm exhausted. It takes so much to do so little.

"Ms. Edith," Raffee says, "I got to hustle on out of here. Seems like everyone needs a lift to the party today."

I must have nodded off. Oh dear, did I miss the angels? Blinking, I hear Stella struggling to sing along with Mr. Andy Williams.

"It's... the... uh... mooost... wonderful..." but she's coughing more than usual and can't sing. Catching her breath, she looks at us, "Nothing... says Christmas like Andy."

The room is buzzing. A starched white cloth covers the table, but that's where the elegance ends. A plastic cup of hot chocolate sits in front of me, next to a plate of soggy chicken salad sandwich with a few cranberries and a sad sprig of parsley on top. I'd be embarrassed to serve finger food like this for Christmas. In the middle of the room, a dark wood fireplace stands on its own—on wheels—with a bright orange electric cord running all the way to the wall. That maintenance man with the cap is taping it down every few feet. A fireplace that plugs in... living this long, I get to see it all. Atop the mantel a silver menorah shares the light of the candles. The young social worker with the shiny brown hair strides in wearing a red holiday dress and cap. Taking an armful of green roping, she heads over to the fireplace on wheels and drapes it across the mantel. With a flourish, she pulls off her hat, removes a handful of scarlet ribbons, and drops them on top. A painting is set up on an easel—a snow scene of a stone building with ivy, warm light flooding in through the windows. Next to it, a cardboard box overflowing with stuffed animals. Now, where have I seen that before?

Stella clears her throat, "Yoohoo... Bev!"

"Follow me, gentlemen," Bev's loud words cut through the clatter. Next to her are two young men, one grinning in a flashy suit, the other with a salt and pepper beard wearing a dark blue uniform with gold cuffs and a gold badge near his shoulder. I wonder who they are and why they're here. Maybe they came to see the angels? With one man on each arm, Bev escorts them to a table in the front. Did she just bat her eyes at them?

Roula rubs her lips back and forth with bright red lipstick and fluffs the curls on her head. "So good looking! I hope *they* come over to say hello."

My attention is drawn to the man in the suit. "Stella, I think I know that man."

Stella rolls her eyes. "Of course you do. That's the mayor."

I do know the mayor. I worked at Town Hall. This man looks like the mayor I knew—same blue eyes and square jaw—but he's far too young. He still has all his hair, and it's slicked back with some sort of pomade. And that sneer. The mayor I knew always had a warm smile.

A sing-song stage voice booms through the room. It's the elf, and she's putting on a performance. "Hello, River's Edge, and Happy Holidays! We've made it to Christmas! And it's time to party!" She looks around. "I see we still have a few stragglers, so I'll give everyone another minute or two."

Raffee wheels in a resident with a patch over one eye and tattoos on his arm, and parks him at a table not far from ours. This man is unshaven and looks like a bum. Didn't someone help him dress? A dog comes over to him and starts begging. Why in God's name is he feeding it from the table? And where are the angels? Cosmo never got scraps unless he stole them.

The elf continues, "We all know 'It's the most wonderful time of the year!'" and breaks into song.

"She's no Andy Williams. And now that Ms. Bryon is watching," Stella coughs, "she's pretending to be a good elf!"

Scruffy one-eye shouts, "Where the hell are the angels? We came to hear the goddamn angels sing, not you!"

"Err, the angels?" Nellie yells, her fist in the air.

"Hush now, everyone. The elf has the floor," Stella booms.

I shift in my wheeled seat trying to find a comfortable spot for my hip. The angels better come soon, because I can't sit in this chair all day.

Arms spread wide, the elf draws out the last note of her song, "Yeaaarrrrr" and bows one too many times. She walks to the podium. "Welcome, everyone, to the 56th annual River's Edge Christmas party. Wait," she takes a piece of crumpled paper from her pocket, "I have everything written down right here. Better safe than sorry—don't want to forget anything important." Her flashing earrings nearly blind me as she nods up and down, reading stiffly. "For some of you, this may be the first time you're celebrating Christmas outside of your homes and away from your families. Here at River's Edge, we make Christmas special for you. Our generous volunteers have tirelessly given their time and effort to transform the Lido Lounge into a winter wonderland. Those of you who have enjoyed the holidays with us before, you know what's in store—the Poughkeepsie Children's Choir. And after you hear those little angels, you won't leave without knowing the effort to get here was worth it! Now I'm going to turn things over to our esteemed Director of Nursing, Ms. Ruthann Bryon."

White coat, crisp pants, not so much as a green pin or a red bow—where's *her* holiday spirit? And heels that click on the floor as she strides up purposefully. I don't know how this woman keeps her balance in those ridiculous shoes. And those bushy eyebrows, they need to be plucked.

"Thank you, Kim," she begins. "It's so nice to see so many of our residents up and about to join us for our annual holiday celebration. We encourage everyone at River's Edge to socialize and attend all of our wonderful, stimulating events here, and to spend as much time out of your rooms as possible. We know the holidays can be lonely, but studies have shown that human connection is the key to avoiding depression and enjoying a long and happy life. I'd also like to thank the sponsor for our decorations this year—Slip-Proof Shoes. Makers of all our fall-prevention footwear, including the lovely, fashionable socks you're all given on admission. Slip-Proof Shoes: keeping you upright with a spring in your step since 1954. So, Merry Christmas. I'm going to hand things over to our very own Mayor Watson, who has done such a remarkable job revitalizing our town. His administration has brought new ideas and fresh leadership but has never forgotten our seniors." As the man in the shiny suit walks up to the podium, she says, "Thank you, Mayor Watson, for joining us today, and for all you do for our community." There is a round of weak applause.

Smoothing his slick hair back with his fingers, the mayor flashes a toothy smile. "Wonderful to be here, Ruthann. Merry Christmas. Can everyone hear me? I know some of you have a little trouble. I have Lieutenant Joseph Santelli from the Poughkeepsie Fire Department here with me. Let's have a big round of applause for all our first responders. When you need them, they come quickly. They can be the difference between life and... um, um..."

The handsome fireman interrupts him. "It's an honor to care for all of you, and just remember, we're only a phone call away."

The room booms with clapping, and my stiff hands join in. The mayor waves down the applause. "Don't forget, while Lieutenant Santelli is out there responding to alarms, I'm putting out fires at Town Hall every day. And when I'm not doing that, I'm busy building a better tomorrow, a better future for all of us down the road. And speaking of roads, we've added twenty-seven new free parking spots on Main Street. Maybe you've seen them? It's part of my ten-year plan to make downtown a destination. Now, you can spend time shopping without worrying about getting a parking ticket. Time is our most valuable resource, time invested today to make tomorrow the way we want it to be."

"Tomorrow?" the man with the eye-patch shouts, "We could be dead tomorrow. We're lucky if we get through today!"

"Well, you're in good hands here. If anything goes wrong, there are plenty of people to take care of you. Now, in addition to parking, my ten-year plan..."

As the Mayor drones on, there's movement at the staff table. Nurse Hurry slides into a seat between Bev, who is shaking her stiffly sprayed bun and Grandma, who has her arms crossed in front of her. The housekeeper who works so hard and shared her Thanksgiving with me is stuffing her face with cookies.

Roula points, "See that young girl with all those piercings and the spiky hair at the staff table in the back?" She tut tuts. "The things young people do to themselves... attractive?"

I stare at Roula's rouged face. "And the things old people do to themselves," I mutter. And there's Raffee. What would we do without him. He keeps us all going, even when our get up and go has got up and went.

"And as for your property taxes..." the mayor continues.

The elf walks over to the Christmas tree and picks up the painting that is propped up along the base, then brings it to the podium. "Excuse me, Mr. Mayor? I'm sorry to interrupt. It sounds like you're doing so many wonderful things for our residents. But the children are coming soon, and there's a few more things to get to before they arrive. It's time for us to give you your gift." She holds the frame up. "It's River's Edge at Christmas, the same lounge we're in right now, with the doors open and the children's choir inside. One of our residents, Mr. Cortez, God rest his soul, captured the holiday spirit here through this lovely painting. It was the dear man's last wish to donate it to Town Hall."

The one-eyed man with the tattoos yells out, "Even from the grave, that damn Spaniard is trying to have the last word!"

"Thank you, Mr. O'Neill." The therapist continues, "Mr. Cortez will remain with us in our hearts, and many of his masterpieces are on our walls."

After another round of applause, the mayor accepts the painting. "Thank you so much. This is certainly, uh, one of a kind. There's a spot on the wall next to my portrait." He starts to head back to his seat, his shined loafers squeaking on the floor.

"Hold on, Mr. Mayor. We have something else for you and Lieutenant Santelli." The therapist picks up the cardboard box filled with stuffed animals and nods her head at Roula. "Roula has been kind enough to carry on our dear departed Pearl's Christmas charity tradition, God rest her soul. From the Keepers' Mart, Pearl collected donations of stuffed animals to help comfort the children impacted by fire."

The handsome fireman walks up and shakes the therapist's hand as he accepts the box, walks to Roula, and reaches down with his broad arms, doing his best to wrap her in a hug. Speechless, Roula stares back into his eyes.

Stella coughs, "Gotta another one of those, sugar?"

But his long arms are not quite able to wrap all the way around Stella.

As he walks off with the box, Stella waves her cane at the elf and shouts, "Now light the tree and bring out the angels. I'd stand up myself and do it, but you know, these legs ain't listenin' to me today."

The elf starts for the podium, but Raffee intercepts her. "Come on, Kim. These folks need the lights. No more speeches—we gotta get this show on the road. I feel the presence of angels, and I think I hear their noisy little feet. The choir's almost here." Before the elf can respond, Raffee jingles over to the tallest tree and grabs the end of a long electric cord. "I got this!" His smile is wide as he counts, "One, two, three!" In goes the plug, and like magic, all the trees are lit and the fireplace on wheels turns on. It's all so grand. And I'm so proud of Raffee for finding the spirit despite his struggles. I've loved Christmas ever since I was a little girl. And now it's here.

"Deck the halls with boughs of holly, fa la la la la..." Children singing! Christmas carols! The angels have come! I turn to see a parade of red and green, dotted with golden lights, marching to the front of the room.

Girls in red dresses and green scarves, boys in dark pants and bright red shirts, all holding Christmas lanterns. They line up on the risers, tall ones in the back, shorter ones in front. A concert. A Christmas concert. Arms open, the choir director conducts. Her dark curls fall to her shoulders, and her green, red, and black printed skirt flows below her gold blazer. She gestures for us to join in.

"Fa la la la la..." Everyone who can is singing, and before I realize it, I am too.

As the song ends, the director turns to us. "Ladies and gentlemen, the Children's Choir of Poughkeepsie. Aren't they wonderful?" My hands ache from clapping, and I clasp them together.

Looking at each little face, I study their features. Tiny noses, pink cheeks, and missing teeth in some of their smiles. There's one with dark hair over her shoulder and glasses, another with light hair and curls to the side, others whispering together, and a boy with a short cut over his ears, a wrinkled shirt, and hands stuffed in the pockets of his pants.

The choir director waves down the applause and speaks, projecting her voice across the room. "Thank you all so much for attending our Christmas concert, which has become an annual tradition at River's Edge. Our little angels have spent weeks rehearsing a beautiful medley of holiday favorites for you." Fanning out her gold blazer, she takes a seat in front of an electric keyboard and starts tapping, but there's no sound. Raffee runs over, grabs the cord, and plugs it in. She starts again, singing as she plays, and the children join her with "There's No Place Like Home for the Holidays."

The little angels move their arms from side to side with the beat. Home for the holidays. At home, William Sr. always had a bundle of dry logs in the carrier by the hearth. On cold winter nights, he'd light the fire and we'd sit together on the sofa, drinking our cocoa. Made with real melted Swiss chocolate. And on Christmas Eve, he'd put a little liquor in the mug.

Suddenly all the children turn their heads in unison towards a girl with strawberry blonde curls. Smiling, she steps forward and loudly sings, "Gee the traffic..." There's a bounce in her movements, and her ponytail swings from side to side as she moves with the tune. The choir joins right back in.

She's a doll. And that red plaid dress... I had one just like it when I was her age.

After a few more classic songs, the director stands and bows. "We're going to take a snack break and the children are going to give each of you a Christmas card and a jingle bell. They can also bring you a plate from the banquet table.

The children scatter, bells jingling. The strawberry blonde girl walks towards our table and drops cards and bells in front of Stella, Roula, Nellie, and me.

I give her an encouraging smile. "Hello, dear. My name is Edith. What's yours?"

She looks down at her feet and mumbles, "I'm supposed to ask you if you want a cookie."

"That's lovely, dear, but what is your name?"

She wipes her nose with her finger. "Angela."

"I enjoyed your singing, Angela."

Nellie starts to rattle her bell loudly. Stepping back, the girl stares.

"That's Nellie," I explain. "She loves music." I clear my throat. "You are just darling, and while you were singing, you were dancing beautifully. I love dancing."

The girl twirls her finger in her hair, looks around at the four of us in our chairs, and stares blankly back at me. "Do old people dance?"

"Of course." I lean towards her, "The problem is these chairs, they get in the way."

The gap between her two front teeth shows with her smile. "Why don't you just stand up?"

I fix the collar of my shirt. "Well, that would be a Christmas miracle. Now what is your name again? Old people forget things quickly."

"My name is An-ge-la," she says. "Like Angel, but with an extra A."

"Well, Angel with an extra A, I love your dress. I had one just like it, about a hundred years ago."

"How old are you?"

"Thanks to you and your friends, today I feel young."

She stares at me. "What's that on your sweater?"

"Do you mean my Christmas pin? I've been wearing it since I was about your age."

"No," she points, "that spot."

Oh dear, did I spill? There it is. On my collar and down the front of my sweater—oatmeal. I'm mortified. *How could I not have seen this before?* I reach for a napkin and blot at the dribble. I've never been a spiller.

"I had oatmeal this morning, too. Mother makes me wear a napkin under my chin."

"That's good motherly advice. I'm going to start doing that."

The elf comes over and taps her watch. "Now children, make sure all our residents get their cookies. We have to stay on schedule."

I turn to my little companion. "Now, what we're going to do is head over to the banquet table so I can pick out my Christmas cookies myself. You just grab the handles of the chair, back me up, then a little push."

I hang on for dear life as we veer towards one table then another, trying to stay on course through the sea of rolling chairs, steered by my little captain. This whole year has been one wild ride.

As we near the head table, the mayor with his loud voice turns towards the fireman and points at Nellie, who is pulling tinsel from a tree. "Look at that one. She's taking decorations *off* the trees. I don't know how *I* do it, Santelli." He slicks back his hair. "It's been Santa, Santa, Santa all morning. First, it was the little league pancakes with Santa, then the Girl Scouts at the community center with Santa, but I wouldn't worry about Santa showing up here in the land of the lost. Most of these folks probably don't even *remember* it's Christmas."

"Keep your voice down," the fireman says. "They're not all deaf."

Did I just hear that?

"Dear, did that man just say no one here remembers it's Christmas?"

"I think so."

My back stiffens. "Well, he's in for a surprise on our way back."

We reach the buffet table, which is covered with desserts: decorated gingerbread men, snowflake cookies, star-shaped cookies, chocolate chip cookies with red and green sprinkles, pieces of cake with chocolate and vanilla icing, and brownies with candy cane topping. Stella's napoleons have center stage, and there's even an enormous bowl of cut fruit. But I'm not hungry. The only thing that's going to satisfy me is giving the mayor a piece of my mind.

The little girl has assembled a plate of sweets so full she needs both hands to hold it. "For you and the other grandmas," she says.

"Put those down on my lap. I had a friend here, who actually couldn't remember what he said five minutes ago but knew a few things about driving a chair and taught me all his tricks. These chairs can be quite useful. He could ride while balancing everything. Now let's get moving. We need to stop at the mayor's table and you're going to learn something today."

We arrive to find the mayor and the fireman standing behind their chairs. The fireman towers over the mayor, who is struggling to button his suit coat. They are both sipping what Stella calls "River's Edge Champagne" from clear plastic cups.

The mayor spits his drink back into the cup and says to the fireman, "Even the ginger ale here tastes old."

I clear my throat for what seems like the fifteenth time today. "Excuse me, Mr. Mayor."

He turns his head slightly towards me. "I'm sorry, have we met?" He glances over at the fireman and whispers loudly into his ear. "These people, they're all confused. She probably doesn't even know her own name."

Well, I never. I feel the crisp edge of my shirt collar and straighten it under my sweater. "My name is Edith Sharp. I'm 99 years old, and I've lived in Poughkeepsie nearly all my life. I had a house, and now *this* is my home. I can't stand up to say this, but you," I wag my finger at the mayor, "can sit down to listen."

The mayor crosses his arms. The fireman places his large hand on the mayor's shoulder, and the mayor lowers himself into his seat.

"One day," I continue, "you'll be in my shoes, or maybe stuck in bed, or in a chair just like this one. And a holiday celebration, whether or not you know what holiday it is, will be one of the few things that brightens your day. And the last thing you'll need will be people saying about you what you just said about me and my friends here."

The mayor turns to the fireman. "Santelli, did I do it again? What did I say this time?"

I sit up straighter in my chair. "Oh, you don't *remember*? And I don't care to repeat it, especially at our *Christmas* party."

He shifts the angle of his chair, turning it away.

"I'm not finished. Angela, dear, wheel me closer." Facing the mayor, I continue. "This is a home, our home. And you are our honored guest. But you're not behaving with honor. You don't know anything about any of us. See that woman in the yellow raincoat?" I point to Nellie. "It's true that half the time, she doesn't remember who she is. But she's my friend. She shows up for me. She takes her seat at the party, not once a year like you, but every single time. And *you* don't know anything about her. You just see old people. You see our infirmities but not our... resilience." The mayor looks down, and I soften my tone. "You're uncomfortable and, dare I say, afraid of reaching this stage yourself, just like I was. But it can happen to all of us... you never know what's going to knock you off your feet." I let out a breath.

I hear coughing and realize Stella is behind me. "Ain't that the truth," she wheezes. "That man don't know what's comin' at him one day, *if* he's lucky enough to get old."

"And one more thing," I sigh, "you went on and on about planning for the future of this town. A future most of *us* won't get to see. But you should be talking about the future we all want to share—caring, celebrating, and valuing people at every age. So don't turn away from us. Get comfortable with us. Talk to us, and listen to us, so we can help you understand."

The mayor bows his head.

"Mr. Mayor," I keep on, "You have a responsibility by virtue of your honorable position. We need you to understand that we're no different just because we're old. We're still the same people we once were. So, find your compassion, find your respect, and for God's sake, find your Christmas spirit. It's not just because we need you to understand, but because," I point to the little girl, "you'll need *her* to understand."

A look of understanding crosses the mayor's face. "I'll try, Mrs. Sharp. I'll try."

The fireman looks at me, his eyes moist, his face soft with compassion. "Thank you, Mrs. Sharp. You're absolutely right. It's about finding the light. Thank you for that beautiful Christmas message reminding us that throughout life, there is so much to celebrate."

"Amen!" Stella shouts, before bursting into a worrisome fit of coughing.

"And don't forget, Mr. Mayor, we still vote."

The mayor stands up and puts both of his hands around mine.

I motion to my driver, "Mission accomplished. Let's go." Stella follows. The knot in my stomach is gone, and suddenly I'm eager to eat. Holding both plates on my lap, trying not to fall out of my chair, we make the hazardous ride back to my table, nearly bumping into three other drivers. After parking my chair, Angela offers treats to the others, and Stella, Roula, and Nellie dig in. It felt good to say my piece.

The choir director is back. "Our next song is everyone's favorite. Before we start, children, make sure everyone is settled in their seats with their holiday cookies, and we need everyone to have their bells. On the risers in five minutes!"

My little companion flits around the table, moving the jingle bells close to each one of us.

"How old are you, dear?" I ask.

"Eleven," she mumbles.

Raffee appears to refill our water glasses.

"Raffee," I say, tugging at my pin, "be a dear and help me take this off."

"You sure, Ms. Edith? That's your Christmas bling."

"I'm in no mood for debate."

Raffee carefully unhooks the sparkling pin from my sweater and hands it to me.

I turn to the little girl. "Give me your hand, dear. When I was around your age, my father gave me this pin. I've worn it every Christmas since. And now I want you to have it."

She shifts uncomfortably on her feet.

I take her hand in mine and place the clasped pin in it. Eyes wide, she looks at Raffee.

"Really, for me?"

"If Ms. Edith says it, she means it."

The little girl stares at me. "But I don't have anything for you."

"Silly girl, you and your friends being here, that's the gift. A room full of children will brighten the darkest winter. So, you'll need to come back to our home next Christmas."

"Is this your home? My grandma lives in a house. Are you going back home to your house after the party?"

"No, dear. Not tonight. But someday."

"I'll come back if I'm still in the choir next year."

"Well, old people forget things, so be sure to wear your pin. God willing, I'll be here waiting."

Suddenly Nellie stands up from the table, wobbling, hunched, and takes one step. I hold my breath as she hobbles. With one lurch after the other, she stumbles towards the piano.

The girl's face tenses. "That grandma—she's going to fall!"

"Oh, dear!" I look around for Raffee. "Raffee, Nellie needs you. Quick!"

Grabbing her hand, Raffee steadies Nellie, and tries walking her back towards her wheelchair, but she turns to go the other way.

"Errt piano—piano..." She shakes her bell wildly.

"Easy does it, Ms. Nellie. Let me help you." Raffee and Nellie walk in slow circles, hand in hand, towards the small electric piano. As she sways, he starts making disco motions.

"He's dancing with her!" the girl shouts.

"Oh, that's the River's Edge shuffle. It's what passes for dancing around here."

Nellie follows Raffee's lead as he guides her to the piano bench. She sits down with a thud. She has a distant look, but her fingers fly over the keys. I hear the notes of Jingle Bells, and Raffee begins to sing. "Jingle bells, jingle bells, jingle all the way..."

The boys and girls of the choir flood into a circle around her and join Raffee in song. Nellie doesn't miss a note. Everyone picks up their bells and starts jingling, even me. Raffee stands in front of the children, finding the beat as he always does, leading the choir. Will wonders never cease!

The song ends, and there is a round of applause for Nellie.

The elf scurries over and clasps her hands. "Thank you, Nellie, that was an amazing surprise! The Christmas spirit is alive and well in the young and the old. Let's ring our bells one more time!" Everyone jingles, and then the elf makes a hushing motion with her hands. The choir director calls the children back to the risers. The elf takes on a quiet tone. "New

Year's is right around the corner, and one of our River's Edge traditions is to take a moment to reflect, to be thankful for everyone who has joined us this year and become part of our family. You all have a cocktail glass of punch in front of you. Take a look around and toast your new friends."

Stella and Roula hold their plastic cups of pink punch up towards me. "Here's to you Edy."

I take a sip and raise my glass to my smiling companions. I wasn't so sure about any of them when I arrived, but now I can't imagine this place without them. "Here's to new friends."

The elf touches each earring, turning off the flashing lights, and says in a serious voice, "And now for our annual memorial tribute. Let's have a moment of silence," she bows her head, "a moment to celebrate the lives of those we've lost this year and remember the light they shared with us in our time together here at River's Edge. Each life is represented by a rose on our hallway walls."

Roses. There's one for Mr. Florida, one for dear Pearl, one for the good doctor, and so many others for those I never even knew. Rubbing my forehead, I wonder what Agnes would think about this place. She wouldn't have liked the food, but I wish she could see these decorations. She rolled her eyes at all my boxes, my taking them out only to put everything away three weeks later. For Christmas, all she needed was a small fake tree in the corner of her living room—with a trash bag over it eleven months of the year. But she did love coming over to my house just to see all of my displays.

The choir director strides back up and buttons her gold blazer. "Thank you all for inviting us to your holiday party. I've been on stages all over the world, and there's nothing sweeter than the joy of generations singing together. I hope you've enjoyed us as much as we have enjoyed you. We have one last song—one of my personal favorites. Please join us in singing 'Silent Night.'" She opens her arms wide. "And even if you have trouble hearing us," she taps her ears, "you can feel the vibrations and let the music enter your heart." She places her hand on her chest. "You all have beautiful voices. Let's hear everyone singing!"

"Mmmm hmmmm." Stella jiggles in her chair. "It's the celebration of the baby. Bring out the gold, the frankincense, the myrrh... and more cookies!" She breaks into a long cough and struggles to catch her breath.

The angels' voices swell, quiet at first then louder. "Silent night, silent night, all is calm, all is bright..." I'm so grateful my ears still work. Over at the head table there's the receptionist with that solid-steel bun, Grandma and her blonde-from-the-bottle-curls, my young hairdresser with the boyfriend who's not a boyfriend and her stegosaurus spikes, and Nurse Hurry, who is finally sitting down. The man with all those dreadful tattoos sits at the next table over, and he must not be able to hear himself, as he's nearly drowning out the children. Nellie is still playing the piano, tapping her fingers on her plate of cookies and scattering crumbs. Those ridiculous red glasses of Roula's finally seem right, set off against a string of green beads around her neck—a perfect Christmas pairing. Everyone is singing.

Amidst the children swaying on the risers, I spot my little strawberry blonde friend. My Christmas pin sparkles on her red plaid dress, just as it did on mine all those years ago.

The little angels, the residents, the staff—the harmony of voices makes my heart sing, yet my eyes fill with wet. My William could never fall asleep on Christmas Eve. He would keep waiting to hear Santa's sleigh, the reindeers' hooves on the roof. After we read "'Twas the Night Before Christmas," I would sing "Silent Night" over and over until his little eyes would finally close. He'll be coming to visit soon.

Am I singing? I hear words coming softly from my mouth. "Round yon Virgin, Mother and Child. Holy infant..."

Christmas finds me here, in this place, the trees twinkling, the fireplace warm. Through my tears the lights are brighter. The notes of the song fall like snow, and a peace comes over me. I know this feeling, but it's been so long. I'm relaxed—breathing in the tingle of delight.

So many Christmases, and yet the spirit of joy hasn't changed.

Who's coughing? And why don't I hear Stella singing with the angels? Oh dear, she's struggling, holding her tubing close to her nose. She can't be sick, not now. I'll have to keep checking on her.

Led by the children, all eyes are open. Heads and voices lifted as best they can, swaying to the rhythm surrounded by the winter wonderland. My voice tires, but my spirit is strong, and as the tune moves through my lips, the whole room sings in one voice, "Sleep in heavenly peace."

All these faces, vibrant with life.

The final note ends.

Eyes close. Heads droop. All is silent.

Epilogue

ow long have I been up here? I put down Mom's pages. Surrounded by boxes of stuff, my neck stiff, I see the mess in a different light. My childhood friends, all here: the bearded leprechaun, the chipped teacups, the painted pumpkin. But they're all older. Even the hair on the little blonde angel, the one with the plaid dress that always went on the Christmas tree, has turned grey. They're all coming with me.

Reading Mom's stories has brought me closer to her, but her passing leaves me searching and deepens the void. I wish she were here to talk. What I'd give to hear more about all her characters. Disagreeable O'Neill nagging the nurses for a drink; the antique girls gossiping at the tea party; Stella, a pumpkin weighed down in her wheelchair but floating through life in spirit and song; and Edith, dear Edith, God bless her at 98, the one Mom clearly intended to be a version of herself... if she'd lived that long. And her son, William, who is—no coincidence—much like me.

Mom always wanted to hear about where I was traveling, how the job was going, how the kids were doing, and most of all, when I would be visiting. When I asked about her, all I got was, "I'm fine. Tell me more about you and the family." After a while, I noticed I wasn't hearing the old stories, the ones she used to tell all the time... the stories from behind the doors. She'd stopped remembering them because she stopped remembering. Now those stories have come to life in these pages covered with her script, and in my mind her intentions are clear. Inside the crumbling stone building with the ivy-covered walls, down the long, cart-cluttered hallways, and behind the doors whose nameplates keep changing, there are rooms where the light is somehow brighter.

I've been chasing that light my whole life. I've sat in countless boardrooms, savored three-star meals, and been to the paradise of white sand beaches with cloudless blue skies and the soothing rhythm of the surf, but it turns out there's another kind of joy, one I haven't spent enough time getting to know, found in places I haven't visited as often. A joy that's not to be missed. It lives in a place where, when we can't get out anymore, we travel through the people who bring the world to us, a place where we sustain ourselves through the memories we share, an unlikely—yet perfect—place for celebration.

There's something I have to tell my family. They're looking forward to a vacation in the sun as much as I am. And Bora Bora is just around the corner. But there's a place I need to take them first.

Resources

While the characters, places, and situations in this book are fictional, the topics presented are relevant to real world issues.

For information on global aging:
World Health Organization - https://www.who.int/news-room/fact-sheets/detail/ageing-and-health

For information on Alzheimer's disease:
Alzheimer's Association - https://act.alz.org

For information on health and aging:
National Institute on Aging - https://www.nia.nih.gov